THE GUARDIAN

The Soul Summoner Series Book 8

ELICIA HYDER

Inkwell & Quill, LLC

Inkwell & Quill, LLC
Print ISBN: 978-1-945775-30-7

Edited by Nicole Ayers
Cover by Christian Bentulan

For More Information:
www.eliciahyder.com

GET A FREE BOOK
at www.eliciahyder.com

Robbery · Arson · Murder
And the one-night stand that just won't end.

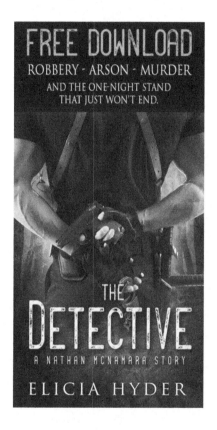

CHARACTER LIST

Warren Parish
the Archangel of Death. Father of Iliana. Son of Azrael and Nadine.

Nathan McNamara
Warren's best friend. Married to Sloan Jordan. Commander of SF-12.

Sloan Jordan
Mother of Iliana. Married to Nathan McNamara. Daughter of fallen Angel of Life Kasyade.

Azrael
Former Archangel of Death. Father of Warren and father of Adrianne's unborn child. Owner of Claymore Worldwide Security.

Reuel
Angel of Protection. Now in charge of the Angels of Protection (aka Guardians).

Adrianne Marx
Sloan's best friend. Girlfriend of Azrael.

Fury (Allison)
Member of SF - 12. Human daughter of Abaddon, the Destroyer. Twin sister of Anya. Former girlfriend of Warren.

Anya
(presumed deceased)
Seramorta Angel of Protection. Twin sister of Fury. Daughter of Abaddon, the Destroyer.

The Morning Star
Fallen Angel of Life and Angel of Knowledge.

Johnny McNamara
Uncle of Nathan McNamara. Father of Fury's unborn child.

Abaddon "The Destroyer"
(Deceased)
Father of Fury and Anya. Former guardian of Nulterra, and former Archangel of Protection.

Phenex
(Deceased)
Mother of Alice. Fallen Angel of Life.

Alice
(Deceased)
Childhood best friend of Warren.

Ysha
(Deceased)
Father of Taiya. Fallen Angel of Life.

Taiya
Seramorta Angel of Life. Daughter of Ysha and Melinda Harmon.

Shannon Green
Nathan's former girlfriend. Now possibly pregnant with an angel.

Kasyade
(Deceased)
Biological mother of Sloan. Fallen Angel of Life.

Nadine
(Deceased)
Mother of Warren.

Audrey Jordan
(Deceased)
Adoptive mother of Sloan.

Robert Jordan
Adoptive father of Sloan.

Enzo
Special Operations Director of SF-12

Samael
Angel of Death who guards the spirit line.

Ionis
Messenger Angel.

Sandalphon
Angel of Prophecy and Knowledge (Born on Earth)

Metatron
Angel of Life and Ministry (Born on Earth)

Theta
The Archangel of Prophecy

Huffman
Claymore operative. Works at the armory at Claymore Headquarters in New Hope, NC.

Chimera
Hacker, security specialist. Newest member of SF-12

Members of Sf-12 (*denotes ability to see angels):
1. Enzo*
2. Kane*
3. Cooper
4. NAG* (Mandi) - pilot
5. Lex
6. Doc*
7. Wings - pilot
8. Cruz
9. Pirez
10. Justice
11. Dalton
12. Chimera
Fury (Retired)*

THE SOUL SUMMONER SERIES ORDER

For Trysten, Adrianna, and Evan.
DNA is nothing but molecules. I couldn't love you any more even if ours matched.

I'm so thankful to be your "Guardian."
Love always, Mom.

CHAPTER ONE

*I*t was weird seeing myself floating in the sky.

Cassiel and I were suspended about ten stories above the salt mirror on la Isla del Fuego, the Island of Fire. The mirror, a "natural" phenomenon made of salt, was a perfect circle measuring over a hundred yards in diameter.

We knew, however, there was nothing *natural* about it.

I aimed my hands at the circle and used telekinesis to try to open it. The circle's perimeter glowed purple, and a diagonal line crossed its center.

From our vantage point, it was a clear "No" sign.

I took a deep breath, letting the sea and sweet jasmine fill my nose. "I have a bad feeling about this."

"It's the gate to Hell, Warren. I'd worry if you didn't." Cassiel's golden ponytail whipped on the island breeze.

"It's clearly telling us 'Do Not Enter.'" I traced the circle in the air with my finger.

"You know, the circle with a slash across it is also one of the alchemical signs for salt."

I smirked. "Of course I didn't know that."

As an Angel of Knowledge, Cassiel was full of all sorts of

information. She also thrived on sharing that information. A perfect example? She's the only reason I knew it was jasmine I was smelling.

Her never-ending thirst for learning had served me well. Without her, I wouldn't have found what we were looking at, and more importantly—I wouldn't have learned how to destroy it.

And the Nulterra Gate needed to be destroyed.

"What do you think it's like down there?" I asked.

"For you? I don't think it will be too bad. I mean, the Morning Star created it to be his home. I doubt it will be miserable for other angels."

"And for humans?"

"Well, we know little about Nulterra, except that its energy comes from the destruction of human souls. And souls must be made unstable before they can be broken. I doubt it will be a pleasant experience for Fury."

"What do you mean by broken?"

"Do you know anything about nuclear energy?"

I glared at her. "Are you making fun of me now?"

She laughed. "No. It fascinated your father, so I thought you might have learned something from his blood stone."

"I haven't worn his blood stone in a very long time. Refresh my memory."

"In nuclear power stations, or in atomic bombs, energy is released from uranium atoms by blowing them apart. However, uranium in its natural form is too stable to explode. It has to go through an enrichment process to increase the number of unstable uranium atoms that will make it explosive.

"Nulterra is similar. To harness the power of the souls, they first have to destabilize them. Then they're cast into the pit for destruction."

I thought of Fury. "Destabilized how?"

"Torture." She grimaced. "Which is why I think the deal

between the angels and the Morning Star was such an attractive option for your father."

Azrael, the original Archangel of Death, had seen Nulterra as an opportunity. A place to send the ultra-wicked as punishment for their deeds on Earth.

The deal worked well until three souls were sent back to Earth to unleash havoc on humanity once more. Cassiel and I were just coming off the heels of that shitshow. And the memory of it still turned my stomach sour.

I looked over the island. "Why do they call it la Isla del Fuego? Isn't that a Spanish name?"

"In 1521, Magellan discovered and claimed these islands for the Spanish Empire. The first explorers said this island gave off a glow at night. They thought it was from swarms of fireflies in the molave trees." She gestured toward the short, crooked, leafy trees that surrounded the circle.

"It's not fireflies though, is it?"

She shook her head.

"Do you really think it will work?" I asked.

"Sealing the gate or getting out alive?"

"Both."

She didn't answer, which stirred all the dread that had been rising in my stomach for the last few weeks.

My phone buzzed in my pocket. I pulled it out and looked at the screen.

Nathan McNamara: *You need to talk to your father. He's doing it again.*

I smiled and shook my head.

"What is it?" Cassiel asked.

"Azrael keeps experimenting with Iliana. He's trying to get her to give his powers back."

"What? How?"

"He started small by dry stunning himself with Nathan's Taser in front of her."

"He thought that would work?"

"I guess he figured it was worth a shot. Iliana just cracked up. She thought it was hilarious."

Eight weeks before, Sloan McNamara and I had been struck by lightning in front of our daughter, Iliana. Even as an infant, she'd been able to use her power as the Vitamorte to protect us. Somehow, by doing so, she'd restored some of Sloan's lost powers as an Angel of Life.

My father was now trying to get his powers back as well.

The phone buzzed again. "Listen to this," I said to Cassiel as I read the new message. *Went to their house for dinner last night. Adrianne walked into their bathroom and found Az in all his clothes standing in a bathtub full of water. He was holding a hair dryer while Iliana watched from a towel on the floor.*"

Cassiel's mouth fell open. "Are you serious? That's from Nathan?"

"Yeah."

Another message came through. *I'm going to kill him if he doesn't kill himself first.*

I tapped out a response. *I'll have a chat when I see him later today.*

"How does that work?" I asked Cassiel.

"Iliana restoring Sloan's power?"

I nodded, stuffing the phone back into my pocket.

"Everything with Iliana is new. We have no idea what to expect from her."

"What's it like?"

Her brow lifted. "What's *what* like?"

"You having no idea about something," I said with a grin.

She stuck her tongue out at me.

My keen ears heard a rustle of leaves behind us. I turned in the air and glimpsed a young boy duck behind a bush. "We have company." I slowly descended to the ground, landing in the center of the salt flat.

Cassiel came to rest beside me. "Who?"

"A local boy. Hello?" I called out.

Two small black eyes peered out from between the giant leaves of a Kris plant, more commonly known as the elephant ear (thank you, Cassiel).

I looked at Cassiel and pointed toward the boy.

She eased forward, as she was the less intimidating of us two. "Hello?" she said, her voice gentle and melodic. *"Maayong gabii."*

The kid jumped up and ran away.

She sighed and put her hands on her hips. "That went well."

"Have a way with kids, huh?" I walked over and stood beside her.

"Shut up, Warren."

I smiled. "Guess we can't expect much from a kid who's just seen us floating in the sky."

"Wonder where his parents are." She closed her eyes and turned her ear in the direction the boy had run.

I looked at my feet and picked up my left boot. Water dripped off it. "It's wet."

"This is the rainy season. The thin layer of water creates the mirror effect. When I was here before, the salt was powdery."

Crouching down, I touched the tip of my index finger to the glassy surface of the water. Then I touched it to my tongue. "Yep. Salt."

Cassiel's face soured. "You licked the ground."

She had a thing about germs on Earth.

"I licked my finger." My head tilted, looking up at her. "You know you can't get sick, right?"

"That's beside the point."

I shook my head and used my power on the gate again. This time, with my closer vantage point to the center line across the circle, I noticed the purple glow was more than an illusion. The sparkling color moved and twisted over the salt. I passed my hand through it and felt the familiar buzz of the supernatural.

"I believe it's powered by the Neverworld," Cassiel said.

I looked across the circle. "Powered by Nulterra."

"Are you sure you want to do this?"

I chuckled. "No."

"Why are you?"

The cartilage in my knees crackled as I stood. "Because it's clearer than ever an innocent woman is trapped down there."

Cassiel lifted an eyebrow. "Don't you mean it's clearer than ever that, even after all these years, there's nothing you wouldn't do for Fury?"

"I'm going to save her sister. That's all."

She grinned. "You're such a bad liar."

One of Cassiel's gifts was the ability to tell when people were lying. If she was seeing something in me now, then her powers extended to people even lying to *themselves*. I had zero intention of doing anything simply for Fury's sake—even rescuing her sister from the pit of Hell.

That ship sailed eons ago.

Still, I didn't argue.

"Did Fury know she has the key to Nulterra?" Cassiel asked.

"I don't think so."

"Why did she try to hide it from you?"

My eyes were fixed on the glassy ground. "Secrets are what Fury does best."

"Hmm," Cassiel said without further comment.

"I suspect she feared the symbol's appearance was a super-natural mark that her child was the Morning Star. She didn't want anyone to know the child wasn't human."

"More maternal than you thought, huh?"

"Absolutely." I jerked my head toward the bank. "You ready?"

"Yes." She walked close beside me. "While you're in Asheville, you should visit the second-born angel and prepare his parents for what is to come."

"Shannon's child?"

She nodded.

"Is this a suggestion, or an official request as a Council member?"

"Does it matter?"

"No." I looked at her. "I'll do it if you think I should."

She thought for a moment. "War is coming. That much is inevitable. They deserve the truth."

"I agree. Sometimes I wish I'd known everything back when everyone was trying to keep me in the dark," I said.

Her head tilted from side to side. "If he so desired, the Father could tell us everything before it happens."

"Why doesn't he?"

"Because maybe omniscience is a curse. Sometimes knowing too much can cause us to not act at all. Would you really wish for a life without Iliana in it?"

"No."

"So maybe you not knowing made everything fall into place as it should."

"I hope so, Cassiel. There are far better places to spend my time away from Eden than Nulterra."

"Venice?" she asked, smiling but not looking at me.

"Most definitely."

When we reached the grass where I'd left the backpack I'd brought along, Cassiel took off the brown bag strapped across her chest. "I want you to take this."

It was the satchel she'd used to smuggle items into Eden after our last trip. When I grabbed it, my arm sank with its weight. "Whoa. What's in here?"

"Something I hope you won't need. Don't open the bag unless it's a life-or-death situation."

"Why?" I shook the bag next to my ear.

She grabbed my arm to stop me. "I mean it, Warren. Life or death only. Don't even unzip the bag. It could mean my expulsion from Eden if it's found."

That was worrisome. "I don't want it." I tried handing it back to her, but she pulled her hands back, refusing to take it.

"Like I said, hopefully we won't ever have to risk it." She put her hands down when I lowered the bag. "But if you find yourself in a situation you can't get out of, the risk will be worth it."

My cell phone rang, but I was still staring at her.

"You gonna get that?"

With a sigh, I pulled out the phone and looked at the screen. "It's Azrael." I tapped the answer button and put it to my ear. "Are you playing with electricity again?" I asked my father without a greeting.

"I don't know what you're talking about."

"Mmm-hmm."

Cassiel took the bag from me, knelt, and put it inside my backpack.

"Where are you?" Azrael asked.

"La Isla del Fuego. You should see this place. It's incredible."

"I hope I never have to."

Fair enough. It was demon-made, after all.

"Fury has arrived at headquarters," he continued. "Are you leaving the island soon?"

"Momentarily."

"Is Cassiel coming with you?"

I looked at her. "No."

"Good."

For once, my father wasn't just being a jerk where Cassiel was concerned. He had good reason to not want her around this time. And thankfully, Cassiel not coming was *her* idea.

"What's the boat's ETA at the pickup spot?" I asked.

"About half an hour."

My tactical watch was set to Asheville's time zone on the

opposite side of the world. It was after 6 a.m. there, but the sun was fading on the Island of Fire. "I'll be ready. I'm leaving here soon. We need to talk when I get there."

"About?"

"About you trying to kill yourself to get your powers back."

He sighed over the line.

"Will you be at Claymore when I arrive?" I asked.

"We're passing through Williamston now, so if not when you arrive, soon after."

"We?"

"Adrianne's with me."

Static—*not* from the phone—crackled in my ear. "Az, I need to go. Someone from Eden is trying to contact me. I'll text you when I land."

"Roger that. Give my regards to Cassiel. Tell her I'll miss seeing her."

"Right," I said with a smirk. "Bye." I ended the call and put my finger to my ear, listening to the spirit world for a moment. Nothing. Then I turned toward Cassiel. "Az says hello."

"I heard him. Tell him I said—" She held up her middle finger.

I burst out laughing. "Who are you, and what have you done with my serious and proper friend Cassiel?"

The slightest hint of pink rose in her cheeks. "Hanging out with humans has had a bad effect on me."

"Or a great effect."

Cassiel certainly dressed more humanlike these days. She wore a pair of olive-green cargo pants and a loose gray tank that looked straight off the rack of a military base Exchange. The only thing telling that the clothes were Eden-made was the slight shimmer of the fabric.

I trailed my fingertips down her forearm. "You sure you don't want to come with me?" As soon as the words left my mouth, I regretted them. Not because I didn't want her to come, but because I wasn't sure how I'd backtrack out of it if she changed her mind.

"I'm sure."

I relaxed.

She took a small step closer to me. "Some time away from Eden...and from me would be good for you. Would be good for *us*, if there is ever to be such a thing."

It wasn't the first time we'd had this conversation. Cassiel and I still weren't *together* after the last shitstorm on Earth, but it was looking like a possibility.

Cassiel was convinced that Eden clouded my judgment. Made me forget there were things on Earth I still wanted. Made me forget there were still years I wanted to spend there with my daughter, Iliana.

And years on Earth translated to centuries in Eden. Too long for angels committed to each other to spend apart. At least, that's how Cassiel saw it. She'd shot down the idea of living with me on Earth when Iliana was older. Saying she "wouldn't belong," neither on Earth nor as a part of my old life, something she'd never fully understand.

As an angel who'd spent almost her entire existence in Eden, Cassiel wasn't just out of touch with her humanity—as I sometimes felt; she'd never had it to begin with.

Life on Earth would be hell for her.

She slipped her fingers between mine, and my breath caught in my throat. "I will miss you though."

I pulled her into a tight hug. "I'll miss you too. Look in on my family from time to time?"

She nodded against my chest.

I held her for a long time, inhaling the sweet scent of Eden still fresh in her hair, our intoxicating power radiating between us. There was so much I wanted to say...

My "ears" crackled with supernatural static again. I pressed my finger to my ear once more, straining to listen for voices. Still nothing.

"What's the matter?" Cassiel asked.

"I'm not sure. Sounds like one of my angels is trying to call out to me, but nothing is coming through."

More static. Then a tiny voice. Baby babble?

I listened harder. Realization exploded in me like a warhead. "Iliana?"

More static. More baby babble.

"Illy, can you hear me?"

"*Appa!*"

At the sound of my daughter's voice, my knees buckled. I dropped to the earth like I'd been punched in the stomach by a hurricane.

Appa was the word for "father" in *Katavukai,* the language of angels.

"Warren?" Cassiel asked, concerned.

I plugged both my ears with my fingers. "Iliana?"

"*Appa!*" she said again, followed by more words I couldn't understand.

I put my hand over my chest to make sure my heart was still inside me. Then I braced with it against the ground. "It's Iliana," I told Cassiel, tears rushing to my eyes. "She's figured out how to call into the spirit world."

Cassiel clasped her hands beneath her chin, her face soft with gladness.

I turned my face to the sky and whispered, "Thank you," to the Father, or whoever might be listening.

But before I could reach out to my daughter again, distant voices echoed through the jungle. Angry voices.

I stood, and Cassiel and I looked in their direction. "That doesn't sound good," she said quietly.

I pulled her behind me as a group of men, ten or so, ran

through the tree line. Most of them carried machetes or bats. A couple carried assault rifles.

Cassiel grabbed the scabbard across my back with one hand and my bicep with the other. "Why is it every time we come to Earth together, we wind up in front of a firing squad?"

One man shouted something in a language I didn't understand.

"What'd he say?" I asked her.

"He wants to know why we killed his daughter."

"What? Tell him we didn't."

"Thanks, Warren. I didn't think of that."

The man started shouting again.

"He wants us to repay him," she translated.

"With what? I've got sixty bucks in my pocket."

"I'm not sure what he's talking about."

The men with the guns inched forward.

"Warren." Cassiel's voice was laced with panic, and her nails were so deep in my skin that I worried she might draw blood.

"Looks like this will be a quick goodbye, Cassiel."

"How long will you be gone?"

"No clue, but I'll see you back in Eden when I'm finished."

"Be safe, Warren."

I put my hand on hers and squeezed.

Then as the first bullet exploded from its chamber, I grabbed my bag, and Cassiel and I blinked out of sight.

CHAPTER TWO

*O*n the other side of the spirit line, Cassiel was gone, whisked back to the Eden Gate. And in less than a second, I was transported halfway around the Earth to the United States, to an unnamed location somewhere in North Carolina. It was the only spot in the whole state which still had access to the spirit line.

Even I had no idea where I was. Looking around me, I saw nothing but trees, so I closed my eyes and focused on the sounds of the forest.

Seagulls cawing.

Water crashing against the shore.

The faint sound of a boat's engine and its bottom slamming against the waves.

I followed the sound through the tree line, up over a sand dune, and down onto the beach. A sign was staked in the ground.

KILL DEVIL HILLS, NC

Private Property
No Trespassing

I laughed really hard. God, the Father, had a wicked sense of humor. Who knew?

In a narrow stretch of the Outer Banks, Kill Devil Hills was directly across the Albemarle Sound from Claymore Worldwide Security, the private army built by my father.

I guess the Father figured any demon wishing harm on my daughter would have to cross Azrael to do it.

A ski boat zoomed across the sound. None of Claymore's boats were anywhere in sight. I pulled out my phone. Only one bar of service. I opened the map, and my GPS location dot hovered almost directly on top of the coordinates Azrael had sent me.

I tapped his name in my recent call list. The call dropped. I tried to send him a text message, but it wouldn't go through.

Behind me, the creak of a door caught my ear.

A gray two-story house on stilts was tucked into the tree line three hundred yards up the beach. It had a long dock leading up to a white double-deck porch overlooking the ocean.

A guy wearing khakis and a black polo walked out onto the lower deck and waved for me to join him. I checked the sound again. There was still no sign of the boat, so I started toward the house.

The man came down to the end of the dock to meet me. He was young. Maybe not even old enough to drink. CLAYMORE was embroidered in gold on the front of his shirt.

He stretched out his hand. "You must be Warren."

"I am."

"Excellent. We've been expecting you." Craning his neck, he

looked behind me. "Did someone escort you through the security gate?"

"No."

"Did you come through the gate?"

I shook my head.

For a beat, he looked unsure of what else to say.

"And you are?" I asked.

"Sorry. Nash Wright. I'm supposed to tell you that your ride is running late, but to sit tight and they'll be here soon."

"Sit?" I looked around the empty dock.

"Come on up to the house. I just made coffee."

As I followed him up the dock, I noticed a large black box mounted to a tall pole in the trees. It had black rods sticking out of the top. A cell signal jammer. This place was intentionally off the public grid.

He led me through the bottom door into a large kitchen and gestured toward the dining table in front of the bay window. "Make yourself comfortable."

I dropped my bag onto the floor and pulled out a chair. Then I removed my scabbard and sword before sitting down.

The kid's eyes doubled, looking at the sword on the table.

"Coffee?" I asked.

He blinked. "Right. One sec."

When he walked away, I checked my phone again. It auto connected to the Claymore network inside the house. A message popped up from Fury. *Running late. Be there soon.*

I started to tap out a response, then realized I could only see half the keyboard. "Shit."

I checked my watch. I'd been on the ground in North Carolina for nineteen minutes. The migraine would be in full force soon.

"Here you are." He handed me a warm paper cup. "We've got cream and sugar if you need it."

I popped the lid off the cup and let the steam roll out. "Black's fine. Thank you."

"You're welcome."

I took a long drink of the hot coffee, hoping the caffeine would take the edge off my coming headache. The kid still stared at me. "Yes?" I finally asked.

He awkwardly rocked on his feet. "Who are you?"

"The Angel of Death."

He laughed. "I could almost believe that."

Almost?

"You certainly look the part. How'd you get here?"

I pointed up.

"Parachute?"

"Something like that."

Nash pointed to the sword. "Is that thing real?"

"You ask a lot of questions."

He shrugged. "We're behind a locked gate. We don't get many visitors, and never ones called in by the big guy."

"Claymore called in my arrival?"

"Yup." His chest swelled. "Talked to him myself."

"Congratulations." I'd talked to Azrael, aka Damon Claymore, that day myself. But somehow I doubted my lecture on playing with electricity would impress the kid.

If anything, it would probably make him ask even more questions, and my head was starting to hurt. The pain began like a dull pinprick about three inches behind my left ear. It was going to be a bad one.

Maybe I should have brought Cassiel.

Nash was still mesmerized by the sword. "Can I see it?"

"No. What is this place?"

"I'm sorry, sir. That information's classified."

I laughed over the rim of my coffee. "OK."

A loud buzzer chimed down the hall, and Nash turned and walked out of the room. When he left, I went into the den, which was centered around more windows overlooking the ocean.

Throw pillows were on the sofa. Magazines were arranged on the coffee table. And a few framed photos were on the mantle.

This was someone's home.

I walked to the fireplace and picked up a photo. A group shot. Az and his pregnant girlfriend, Adrianne Marx, were in the center. Next to them were Sloan, Nathan, and Iliana. My heart twisted. I ran my thumb over her face.

I put my finger to my ear and called out to the spirit world again. "Iliana?"

No response.

Nash cleared his throat behind me. "You're not authorized to be in here, sir."

I put the photo back. "Who lives here, Nash?"

"I'm sorry, but that's—"

"Classified," I finished for him. A familiar sound drew me to the window. A faint black dot appeared in the sky with the *chk chk chk* of a helo's blades.

Nash stood beside me. "I thought they were sending a boat."

"So did I." I drained the last of my coffee and crushed the cup in my hand. Then I handed it to him and walked back to the kitchen.

"What are you doing?" he asked as I reached for my sword.

"My ride's here." I put the scabbard across my back.

The helicopter slowed as it neared the beach, turned sideways, and eased onto the ground. It was solid black except for the shiny gold letters down the tail: *Claymore*.

"But you can't leave. My boss just called and said I'll need to open the gate soon for the man himself."

I blinked. "Damon Claymore?"

"Yeah." He had a wild smile. "Don't you want to meet him?"

I chuckled. "Sure. I'd love to."

In a way, I couldn't blame the kid. Damon Claymore was the best-kept secret in the billion-dollar company. I'd worked for the man for years before I ever saw his face—and I was his son.

Nash let out a long, deep whistle. He stared over my shoulder out the window. I didn't need to ask why he sounded so impressed.

"Damn." He shook his head with awe. "Have you ever seen a woman like that?"

I turned.

"Yes. Yes, I have."

Fury's dark hair was braided over one shoulder, and she wore desert-cam fatigue pants, tan boots, and a black tank top cut low in the front. Motherhood had been good to her, softening and plumping all the right parts.

Too bad her curves were the only things soft about her. Allison Fury McGrath's heart and personality had lethal edges.

"You might wanna wipe the drool off your chin before she gets here, kid. She's killed men for less."

His wide eyes turned toward me. "Really?"

I gave a noncommittal shrug.

She walked through the door and took off her sunglasses, looking up at me with her stunning mismatched eyes. One iris was almost black. The other was bright emerald. "Hey. Sorry I'm late."

"What's with the bird?" I asked.

"Got to the docks and the boats were gone. Training mission or something." She slid the temple piece of her sunglasses down the deep crevice behind the scooped neck of her tank top.

The poor kid's eyes followed.

She held up both middle fingers in front of her breasts. "Eyes up top, Sparky. Or I'll gouge them out."

With a frightened jerk, Nash's head shot upright. "Sorry, ma'am."

"You ready to go?" she asked me.

"Damon Claymore *himself*"—I gave a small, excited squeak —"is on his way. Nash, here, thinks we should meet him." Fury waved her hands with all the enthusiasm of a kid getting socks for Christmas. "Yay."

"Is he living here?" I asked her.

"You tell me. I hear from everyone here and in Asheville that he's been MIA a lot lately." Fury's tone suggested I should comment.

But Azrael's official activities were exactly what I *didn't* want to discuss, not with her or anyone else, so I just shrugged.

Fury stared at me.

The buzzer sounded in the kitchen again, this time making me wince.

"You all right?" Fury asked as Nash went to see about the noise as he'd done before.

I touched my temple. "Getting a migraine."

"Oh." Then she turned toward me. "*Oh*." The second one was full of understanding.

"Yeah. I didn't really think this through."

Migraines for angels—and I suspected for humans too— were withdrawal symptoms from the supernatural. The last few times I'd been to Earth, I had traveled either with Reuel or Cassiel. Sometimes others. Their presence was enough to keep the symptoms at bay.

This time, I wouldn't be so lucky.

"Where's your lady friend?" Fury asked as if reading my mind.

"Back in Eden. She'll come if we need her, but she thought it best to sit this one out."

"Why?" Fury crossed one arm over the other to deepen her

cleavage. The move told me she knew *exactly* why Cassiel hadn't come.

I didn't bother with an answer. Instead, I breathed through the pain and focused on anything but the throbbing veins in my skull or the perfect breasts beside me.

After a few minutes, the pain began to subside.

Two car doors slammed outside.

Nash ran back to the living room. "He's here!" He was trying to contain his excitement but not doing a very good job of it. I grinned, never in my life more thankful for a change in conversation.

But before either of us could speak again, a door past the kitchen swung open, and a force almost as strong as any I'd ever felt on Earth pulled at my attention.

Adrianne lugged a small pink suitcase up the last step. "Oh my god!"

Nash rushed forward. "Let me help you with that, ma'am."

"Thanks, you're a doll. First bedroom on the right, down the hall." She wore dark skinny jeans with a fitted black shirt under some kind of floral smock.

My eyes fell to her swollen belly as Nash took off as directed.

Adrianne turned back toward the stairs behind her. "Damon, don't forget my body pillow in the trunk!"

He shouted something back that spawned an argument, but I'd stopped listening.

Fury touched my arm. "My god, do you feel that?"

I nodded. "The fetus is viable."

"How far along is she?"

"Far enough."

"Still have a migraine?"

I shook my head slowly, realizing the pain was gone.

Fury's fingernails dug into my skin. "What is that thing?"

"Warren! I didn't even see you!" Adrianne turned, her tone

flipping from annoyed to elated with dizzying speed. "Come here and give me a hug!"

"Hi, Adrianne." As we embraced, supernatural energy from inside her made my head spin. But I had to ignore it. "How are you feeling?"

"Like I might pop." She took a step back and put both hands on the sides of her belly. "Your little brother likes doing somersaults."

He wasn't my little brother.

"I'm happy for you," I lied.

"Thank you." Her eyes dimmed when they fell on Fury beside me. "Hello."

Had I not been so worried, I might have found her reaction amusing. Sloan and I hadn't been together in ages, and she was happily married to someone else. Still, as Sloan's loyal best friend, Adrianne hated Fury.

Fury said nothing snarky back, meaning she was just as concerned as I was.

Azrael appeared in the doorway behind Adrianne. Our eyes locked, and I widened mine to let him know Adrianne's condition was glaringly obvious.

He had a small duffel bag in one hand and a pillow larger than his whole six-two frame under the other arm. "Hello, son."

I looked around for Nash as he came through the den. I cleared my throat and jerked my head in his direction as if to say, "Human inbound."

Nash nearly tripped over his feet as he entered the room. "D-Damon Claymore?" Nash's eyes whipped from Azrael's face to mine and back again.

"He's my brother," I lied again. "Surprise." Azrael and I looked almost identical.

Except, at the moment, Azrael looked borderline hostile. "Who are you?"

"I'm...I'm Nash, sir."

"That tells me nothing. Why are you here?"

"Um...I'm an intern."

Azrael's eyes narrowed. "I don't hire interns."

"I work for Flint, sir."

"Oh shit," Fury said.

"Who?" I asked.

Azrael's glare shifted to Fury. "Where is he? Is that him in the helicopter? Tell him to get his ass in here."

Fury tapped her wrist. "You can chew him out later. We've got a schedule. Huffman is expecting us at the armory by eight."

"Can I take your things, Mr. Claymore?" Nash asked, extending two very shaky hands.

I put my hand on his shoulder. "Cut the kid some slack, *brother.* He's one of your biggest fans."

Azrael pushed the pillow against Nash's chest then offered him the duffel bag. When Nash took hold of the handle, Az jerked him close. "You ever speak of me to anyone, and I'll kill you. Understand?"

All the blood drained from Nash's face. "Y-yes, sir."

"Go." Azrael released the bag, and Nash hurried away. Az turned back and pointed at Fury. "I'm going to murder your father."

I flinched as Abaddon, the Destroyer, flashed through my mind. Fury's biological father was the fallen—and now permanently deceased—Archangel of Protection and Guardian of Nulterra.

"Your father?" I asked.

Fury shook her head. "Not Abaddon, if that's what you're thinking."

"I'm not." Boy, I was on a roll for dishonesty.

"Flint McGrath is the man who raised Fury," Adrianne clarified. "He's been keeping an eye on this place for your dad."

I should have known all this. If not from Fury, then at least from the memories in Azrael's blood stone. But to be fair, I hadn't worn Azrael's blood stone in well over a decade in Eden's time. And Fury...hell, in all the time we were together, she'd never told me anything about anything.

Nash returned. "Can I do anything else for you, Mr. Claymore, sir?"

Azrael's jaw shifted. "Yes. Go outside to the helicopter and tell your *boss* to get in here."

"Yes, sir," Nash said with a nod before darting past me toward the back door.

"Where'd your dad find him?" Azrael asked Fury, clearly worried about how much he could trust the kid.

Fury shrugged her sculpted shoulders. "Flint and I haven't exactly been on speaking terms."

Azrael lifted an eyebrow but didn't comment.

"What is this place?" I asked to break the tension.

"One of our new summer homes," Adrianne said, with much more disdain than would typically accompany such a declaration. "Your father's been dragging me all over the world lately. Isn't that lovely?"

It didn't sound lovely.

"Really?" I asked. "Where have you gone?"

"Mostly New Hope." Adrianne started to count on her fingers. "But we've been to Chicago, New Mexico, California. He's even taken me halfway around the world to Vietnam and then Germany."

Azrael was taking her to different Claymore installations. Perhaps to find the perfect place to hide her when the time came for the birth.

She touched both sides of her belly. "Do you know how hard it is to spend twenty-four hours on a plane when you're pregnant?" She rolled her eyes toward him. "Or twelve hours in a car?"

"You drove in this morning?" I asked.

"All night," Adrianne answered.

Azrael walked around to face her. Then he cupped her face in his hands. "For the millionth time, I'm sorry." He kissed the tip of her nose. "Go rest. I'll be back in time for dinner."

"Can we eat Italian?" Her bottom lip poked out.

He kissed it. "We'll eat whatever you want."

"OK." She turned toward me again, opening her arms. "It's so good to see you, Warren. We'll catch up later, yeah?"

My head swam again as she hugged me. "You bet."

"Bye, Fury."

Fury didn't even wave.

When Adrianne left, Nash returned alone. He looked even more nervous, if that was possible. "Mr. McGrath said, with all due respect, that if you want to talk to him, you can get your happy ass on that chopper." Nash cringed and put his hands up in defense. "Those were his words, not mine, sir."

A growl rolled deep in Azrael's throat.

"Come on. You can talk in the air," I said. "Fury's right. We've got shit to do."

Azrael took a step back. "I'm not flying. I'll drive and meet you there."

"Good god," Fury grumbled.

I smirked. "Az, it's like a mile across the water. It will take you an hour to drive around the inlet and get there by car."

The angry lines in Azrael's forehead were severe.

Fury started toward the back door. "You'll be fine, you big chicken."

"Allison, I have absolutely no—"

"*Bwooock, bwock, bwock, bwooock,*" she teased, holding the door open.

I smiled at him. "You're not gonna prove her right, are you?"

"I hate you both." Azrael shook his head and walked past me, then stormed by Fury and out the door.

Nash's gaze followed him. "Is Damon Claymore afraid of flying?"

"It's a long story, kid. Take care of yourself, and by that, I mean never breathe a word of this to anyone."

"Oh, I won't," he said, violently shaking his head.

I gave him a halfhearted salute, grabbed my backpack, then caught up with Azrael halfway down the dock. I pulled on his arm. "I need to talk to you! Alone!" I shouted over the roar of the helicopter.

He shook his head, squinting against the sun. "I already know what you're going to say! We can't talk here!" His eyes shifted toward the house. "Come on, before I change my mind!"

My eyes drifted back to the house again, and though I knew it was my imagination, the power within it seemed to make the whole building breathe.

With a shudder, I turned back toward the helicopter. Fury was watching me. She mouthed the words, "You know something."

I darted my eyes away...because I did.

I knew *why* my father was acting weird. I knew why he was on high alert. And I knew why he was keeping Adrianne away as much as possible.

The child she carried wasn't my brother. It wasn't Azrael's son. And aside from some shared DNA, the baby wasn't even Adrianne's.

The vilest angel of all time was about to be reborn.

The prince of demons.

The Morning Star.

CHAPTER THREE

*W*hen we reached the helicopter, Az got up front with the pilot, and I got in the back seat beside Fury. I put my sword and bag on the seat between us.

Fury dangled a headset on the end of her finger. I put it on and fastened my seat belt. She lifted an eyebrow behind her low-profile sunglasses.

"What?" I asked into the microphone. "I'm immortal, not indestructible."

The white-haired man in the cockpit turned all the way around. Only then did I remember it wasn't Wings or NAG, our usual pilots. This guy, Flint McGrath, was a complete stranger to me. He was older and not a member of SF-12, Azrael's special division of Claymore operators who knew exactly who—and what—I was.

Crap.

The old man must have sensed my inner panic attack. "It's OK, son, I know who you are."

Flint's voice had the rasp of a lifelong smoker, and the skin sagged heavily around his deeply lined face. He wore a blue-gray ball cap and a khaki Members Only jacket about as old as me.

"Flint is a former SF-12 pilot. You can speak freely," Azrael said, buckling into his seat. "But you'd better speak fast because I might throw him out of this helicopter once we're airborne."

"The hell you will. You're sure as shit not gonna fly this thing," Flint said, flipping some switches over his head.

"You were part of SF-12?" I asked.

He glanced back and lowered his aviators, displaying a pair of mismatched eyes. One brown. One blue. "The original member."

"Flint was around when it was SF-3," Fury said with a smile.

Flint shook his head. "Not even, my dear. I was around before the team had a title."

"Too bad he didn't learn a damn thing," Azrael muttered into the microphone. "I can't believe you—"

Flint reached up and unplugged Azrael's headset from the communication system. Azrael glared. Flint just chuckled. So did I. "This is the guy who raised you?" I asked Fury.

"Tried to," Flint answered instead. "It's a constant debate on how well I did at the job."

Shaking her head, Fury sat back in her seat.

"It's a pleasure to make your acquaintance finally, Warren." Flint reached one hand over the seatback, and I shook it. "I've heard about you your entire life."

A familiar twinge of anger prickled my spine, and I lifted an eyebrow in Fury's direction. "Interesting. I can't say the same thing about you."

Fury looked out the side window. "He raised me and my sister. What else do you need to know?"

Nope. Motherhood definitely hadn't softened *everything*. I didn't bother pointing out she'd never even told me that much before.

Sloan had once accused my past relationship with Fury of being nothing more than a lot of sex and blowing shit up. She hadn't been wrong. Azrael had used her to keep me busy. To keep me away from Sloan. To keep me and Sloan from breeding the most powerful angel in all of history.

Needless to say, that hadn't worked out as Azrael had hoped.

And the woman beside me was as much of an enigma as ever. She kept her secrets closer than the sidearm strapped to her thigh.

Azrael plugged his headset back in. "What were you thinking hiring some kid off the street without my permission? And inviting him into my home, no less."

The helicopter rocked forward as we lifted off the ground. Flint was checking out all the windows. "Oh, he's not some kid off the street. That's Bobby Wright's boy."

"Bobby Wright," I repeated, searching my memory—or Azrael's memory, rather. "Why does that sound familiar?"

Then one of *my* memories hit me.

In the middle of hell week, my first week of training as a Claymore recruit, Fury had shown up at my barracks, reeking of Tennessee whiskey. It was the one and only time I'd ever seen her drunk.

She'd literally dragged me out of my rack and down the hall to the laundry room. On the metal table where I'd folded ninety-degree angles into my T-shirts, we popped the cherry on our "relationship," or whatever the hell it was.

When her phone rang that night, she was still on top of me. "Yeah, Bobby Wright," she'd said, out of breath. "Ambushed by two AOPs outside Durham."

I wondered now if one of those AOPs had been Fury's biological father, the Destroyer.

"No shit," Azrael said, bringing me back to the conversation inside the helicopter. "Man, how old was that kid when that happened?"

"His name's Nash," Flint said. "And he was fourteen when his daddy got killed working for you. The least you could do is give him a job and *not* be an asshole about it."

Azrael didn't respond.

"What's this?" Fury asked, obviously trying to steer the conversation somewhere else. I wondered if her mind had gone back to the laundry room as well.

She pulled my sword partway from its scabbard.

"What does it look like?" I asked.

"Don't be a dick. It's a weird thing for a sniper to be carrying around."

"*Former* sniper."

"Obviously. Where'd you get it?"

"Lifted it off the demon Uko when we fought Moloch and his minions at Wolf Gap a couple of months ago."

"This is the sword they're saying can kill angels?"

I nodded. "Forged in Nulterra apparently."

She slid the sword back into its sheath.

"Wonder what else is down there that'll try to kill you," Flint said.

Fury groaned. "You're not still harping on that, are you?"

"You still planning on going?" Flint asked.

"Yes."

"Then I'm still harping on it." Flint looked across the cockpit at Azrael. "And what happened to you going soft on me? You've thought all along this mission was nuts just as much as I have."

Azrael shrugged. "That was before we were certain Anya survived."

"But how is that even possible? You always told me she'd never survive being taken into Nulterra. Then you told me she'd never survive if Abaddon was killed. Now both things have happened, but suddenly you're sure she's alive."

Anya and Fury were twins, and when the zygote split, Fury received the human spirit and Anya was born angelic. Anya should have died with Abaddon, as she had no human spirit to carry on. But she didn't.

"An Angel of Knowledge told us Anya opened the Nulterra Gate," Azrael said.

Fury jerked. "Excuse me?"

I groaned with dread.

The last time I had visited Earth, I had been hunting down three damned human souls who'd been unleashed from the pit of Nulterra. Someone had let them out, and only two keys to the gate existed. Fury had one. And I hadn't told her what I'd learned about the other.

I took a deep breath, bracing for her wrath. "The Angels of Knowledge know Anya opened the Nulterra Gate."

"Bullshit!" Fury was almost shouting through our headsets.

"Cassiel forced the angel to tell the truth. He couldn't lie about her having the other key," I said.

"Anya would never do such a thing. She'd die first!"

Azrael turned all the way around. "Fury, we agree with you. I'm sure she was being coerced." He looked at Flint. "Which makes it even more dire that we get her out of there."

Flint was staring straight ahead.

"Don't you want us to bring her back alive?" Fury asked him.

"Of course I do, but I don't want to sacrifice another daughter to do it. Warren's fully capable of going all by himself."

She crossed her arms. "Is the only reason you came to spend every second until I leave trying to talk me out of going?"

"Bet your ass it is," he said.

I grinned. "I'm seeing where Fury gets her stubbornness."

Azrael shook his head. "Son, you have no idea."

"Flint's not the only who doesn't want you to go," I said to Fury.

"Reuel?" she asked.

"He's worried, with good reason. He's pissed that you don't want to listen."

"I always liked Reuel," Flint said.

Fury leaned toward Flint's ear, as if that might help her case on the deafening helicopter. "Neither you nor Reuel should doubt I'd go after my sister."

Flint tossed up a hand. "I thought you might change your mind after Jett was born."

"Hell, we *all* thought that," I agreed.

She sat back hard in her seat. "Then none of you know me very well at all."

"That's for damn sure," I muttered.

"What was that?" she snapped.

"I said, your hair looks nice."

Flint grinned over his shoulder.

"Where is Reuel? The *auranos?*" Azrael asked.

"Not sure. Last we spoke, he was searching to find out who Jett is."

"Excuse me?" Fury asked, alarmed.

"We know Jett is an Angel of Protection reborn here on Earth into human form. Reuel's trying to find out who he is."

Her eyes were puzzled. An expression I wasn't used to seeing on her. Fury knew what we were. She knew what her son was. But it was clear in that split second, as Jett's mother, she was having a hard time reconciling facts.

I decided more explanation was necessary. "Reuel's spent the last few months investigating which guardians may have recently chosen incarnation on Earth. If the angel is one of ours, he believes he'll be able to find out who. If Jett is one of the fallen—"

"One of the *what?*" The swift change in her expression from confused to dangerous made me lean cautiously away from her.

"Fury, it's always been a possibility," Azrael reminded her.

"My son is *not* one of the fallen." The quiver in her voice betrayed her. "Just let it go."

"OK. We'll let it go," I said.

Her tensed shoulders relaxed, and she gulped so hard I could see the muscles working in her neck. Fear, it seemed—at least where her son was concerned—had become a tough pill for her to swallow.

"How is Jett?" I asked when I dared to speak again.

As if I'd flipped a switch, Fury's countenance brightened. "He's good."

"He's adorable," Flint added. "Real cute kid."

"What's he like?" I asked.

"Jett is absolutely unremarkable," she said.

From any other mother, it would have been sad to hear. But from Fury, it was almost a relief. Her son, Jett, wasn't human. He was an Angel of Protection—a guardian—born into human flesh. Unlike me, he'd existed since the beginning of time.

As one of the most powerful beings on Earth, Jett being unremarkable *was* remarkable.

"He's finally sleeping through most of the night, which feels like a miracle after being a forced insomniac for the past two months," she said.

"I bet. Is he big?"

She shook her head. "The doctor says he's average size."

"They're not all big," Azrael said with a smirk.

"I know." And I did. Forfax—the girlfriend of my pseudo-sister, Alice—was downright dainty, and she was a guardian. I spent most of my time with Reuel though, and he could put most WWE wrestlers to shame.

"Are the doctor's suspicious of him?" I asked.

"We avoid going if we can. Thankfully, he's a healthy kid, and the only tell-tale sign he's different would be his blood type. So far, they haven't tested it."

Angels born on Earth had Rh-null blood, the "golden" blood type. It made them medical marvels—and targets.

"Have you told John the truth?" Azrael asked.

She frowned.

"No, she hasn't," Flint said, his disdain clear in his answer.

"I'm hoping Warren can talk some sense into her. About telling him, and about this suicide mission she's hell-bent on going on."

I laughed. "It's funny you think she'll listen to me."

"You've got a better shot than anybody," Flint said.

I doubted that.

"Warren, do you come to Earth often?" he asked.

"I popped in once recently to check on some things, but the last time I spent any real time here was about eight weeks ago on this planet's time. It was over fifteen years in Eden."

Fury shook her head. "How do you keep track?"

"I do a shitty job of it."

"I always did too," Azrael agreed.

Flint let out a slow whistle. "Fifteen years? Long time."

"Yeah, a long time to plan a successful mission," she said, elevating her volume.

"I have had a lot of time to think about it and plan," I said.

"What have you figured out?" she asked.

"Cassiel did most of the figuring stuff out. It's what she's good at. She learned how to seal the Nulterra Gate."

Fury seemed impressed, if that was possible. "Do tell."

"The gate is made of salt. If we mix sanguinite with it and heat both until they liquefy, the substance will harden into a solid, creating a supernaturally armored plate. No more in and out at all."

"Where would we get enough blood stone to do it?" she asked.

"Abaddon's pillory."

Fury's hand went to her throat, where she'd once been burned by the sanguinite punishment device. Now, only a faint band of scar tissue remained.

"Cassiel said the pillory would be more than enough, and we won't need it anymore after you are back on Earth."

"That's genius, Warren," Fury said.

"Cassiel's a genius."

Sanguinite was like angelic spirit in solid form. It kept a few of its original supernatural properties: an eternal memory, like with Azrael's necklace; and most important to us right now— the ability to cross the spirit line.

Also known as blood stone, it was created when pure angel blood was spilled and boiled, purifying it of any lingering contaminants from Earth. When worn, its supernatural energy could flow through the wearer's bloodstream. And if worn by a mortal, it would allow passage into an immortal world.

In its heated liquid state, sanguinite could be poured and molded into almost anything. A pendant. Handcuffs. A pillory.

Abaddon, the Destroyer—Fury's deceased biological Father and former Archangel of Protection—had once tried to use a sanguinite pillory on Sloan. Their plan had been to drag her into the breach and force her to give birth to Iliana there. Iliana's unbridled power would destroy the spirit line completely, forever separating this world from the next, and freeing the demons from the watchful eye of the Father.

It was that same pillory we would use to sneak Fury into Nulterra.

If Flint didn't stop her first.

"I still think Warren's fully capable of handling this mission on his own," Flint said, as if on cue. "Your dad told me about the last one."

Azrael smiled back at me with pride. "He saved the entire nation of Malab and tracked down the most notorious serial killer in Venice."

My eyes drifted away. "Not before Saez killed six more innocent people."

Azrael stretched his arm across Flint's seatback to turn all the way toward me. "And it would have been a lot more had it not been for you."

I appreciated his praise, but it was hard not to feel like a failure. Sure, I may have stopped Vito Saez and the others, but it was because of me they'd been let out of Nulterra in the first place. I couldn't let that happen again.

"I think we should go over our game plan," Fury said, nudging my arm.

I cleared my throat and straightened in my seat. "That's a great idea."

"Our first meeting is with Huffman at eight. He said he'd need us for a couple of hours. After that, we should have plenty of time to pack all the gear we need to take with us."

Azrael raised a hand. "Save some time for me. There are things I want to show you both, and I want you to meet Chimera."

Fury sat forward. "She's here?"

"She'll be back in town later today."

During my last extended visit to Earth, while I was chasing down an undead serial killer in Italy, the fallen Archangel of Knowledge, Moloch, had discovered a way into my daughter's supernaturally secure home via its online network. He'd literally tried to upload himself into the building.

Fortunately, one of the most intelligent beings in existence had been outsmarted by a human. Azrael's new elusive tech guru, Chimera, had used a computer chip buried inside a stone gargoyle to trap him.

So far, I'd never met said human, but I'd been hoping to since the battle at Wolf Gap.

Chimera must have been as impressive in person as her legend implied because Azrael had hired her as soon as they'd met.

"How well do you know Chimera?" I asked Fury. She was the one who'd brought Chimera into the picture, as she'd been doing investigative work about Anya's disappearance.

"I don't. I've never even met her in person."

"Really?"

Fury shrugged. "She's a hacker. It's not like she keeps office hours."

"How did you find her?"

"I didn't. She found me." Fury's eyes snapped up with alarm.

"What?" I asked.

"Nothing."

Fury looked caught. Like a kid sneaking candy.

I pointed at her. "Not nothing. How'd she find you?" Something else occurred to me. "Or *why* did she find you?"

She turned toward the window.

"Fury?"

"She actually found you. And Sloan," Azrael answered.

My brain was having a hard time processing what he might be saying. "What do you mean?"

"Fury, I feel you'd better take that one, or you'll regret it," Flint said.

Great. So everyone knew about Fury and Chimera's relationship but me.

With a deep breath, Fury finally turned toward me. "It was Chimera who found the video clip of Sloan."

Almost two years before, Fury had posted a video clip of Sloan on the news in an online Claymore forum. Because Fury was an expert at manipulating me, she'd known I would pay attention if she posted.

It wasn't only the first time I'd seen Sloan; it was the first time I'd seen anyone else like me—a Seramorta. Part-human. Part-angel. I'd sought Sloan out, like Fury knew I would.

"Why would Chimera want me to find Sloan?"

"She's never told me. Said she had a personal interest."

"A personal interest?"

"She didn't elaborate."

"Why didn't you tell me?"

I'd heard *reasons* from half of Claymore over the past year since Fury resurfaced in my life.

The most repeated reason was that it was one last "F-you" to Azrael after she quit the company. He'd worked really hard to keep me and Sloan apart, including employing Fury to *distract* me. Defying her orders and telling me had been the final middle finger to my father.

Another popular opinion—and Azrael's opinion—was if Sloan and I had a child together, that baby would have the power to destroy Abaddon, Fury's biological father. And nobody wanted Abaddon dead more than Fury.

There were also a few more whispers...hints that she thought I deserved the truth.

Right.

Whatever the real reason, Fury and I had never had an honest conversation about it. Or hell, an honest conversation about anything.

Now, she was doing a spectacular job of not making eye contact, studying the water below us like she was counting fish in the sea.

"Allison, I want an answer."

Her eyes cut toward me. "Don't call me that."

"Why not? After everything, I still don't merit using your first name?"

"No."

Well, then.

"Oh boy," Flint said over the radio. "You two are gonna have a fun time together."

Fury turned toward the window, and I sat back hard in my seat.

Azrael glanced over his shoulder. "On a much brighter note, Chimera has some very interesting theories about that sword of yours."

"What theories?" I asked.

"I'll let her explain, but you will like it."

At least I'd like something on this trip.

"What's the plan for tomorrow, Fury?" Azrael asked.

"Tomorrow, we'll fly to Oregon—"

I held up a hand. "I need to fly to Asheville first. The Council wants me to see McNamara's ex-girlfriend, Shannon."

"Ugh. Why?" Fury couldn't have sounded more annoyed if she tried. Never mind the detour, Shannon drove us all crazy.

"She's given birth to an angel too. They want me to tell them," I said.

Fury pulled out her phone and began tapping the screen.

"Did they give you a reason?" Azrael asked me.

"Cassiel thinks they should know."

"There's a nonstop flight from Asheville to Portland on Sunday at eight a.m.," Fury said.

"Commercial?" Azrael asked.

Fury looked up. "Is that a problem?"

"It's dangerous," he said.

"Do you have a better solution?"

"We could take the Eagle," I suggested. "It would be easier if Fury's traveling with firepower."

"For two people?" Azrael smirked. "Fury can fly alone and check her guns."

"That reminds me." I turned toward Fury in my seat. "We might need some backup when we reach the island."

"Why?" she asked.

"Cassiel and I were just there. We encountered some very unfriendly natives. A full-blown militia. A few were carrying assault rifles."

"Excellent news. A firing squad before you descend through the gates of Hell," Flint muttered over the microphone.

Fury ignored him, lost in thought.

"Some guy was demanding payment because his daughter was killed."

"Who killed her?" Azrael asked.

"Not sure. I couldn't understand the guy. Cassiel had to

translate, and she was having trouble concentrating because of the ARs trained on her face."

"I guess we'll be tapping into the armory before we leave New Hope."

"No," I said. "Using lethal force on humans is out of the scope of this mission. We have to find a peaceful way to get in there."

She turned her palms up. "How?"

"I don't know."

"When do you leave Oregon?" Azrael asked.

"Monday. We'll be on a flight with an outgoing crew to South Korea. From there we'll fly to Manila, commercial again, and Flint will take us by helicopter from Manila to la Isla del Fuego."

"I'm not taking you anywhere except back to New Hope or Raleigh, where you belong," he said, checking out his side window.

Fury crossed her arms again. "Then I guess we'll charter a ride when we get there."

"You'll do no such thing. No daughter of mine is going up in the air with some unknown pilot."

"So you'll be getting over yourself then?"

"I'll be working twice as hard to keep you from going."

I smiled. "This is fun, watching you two."

"Shut up, Warren," Fury said, shaking her head.

Flint glanced over his shoulder at me. "I hear you have a daughter of your own. I'm sorry."

I chuckled. "And she's the most powerful being in existence next to the Father himself."

Flint let out a low whistle. "You're in trouble, son."

"Don't I know it."

The helicopter started its descent across the water. "How's Adrianne and the baby? Did she come with you this time?" Flint asked.

"Yeah, she's back at the house," Azrael said. "She's fine."

"Just *fine?*" Fury asked, crossing her arms.

"Oh, you know. Hormonal and achy. All the stuff that goes with the last trimester of pregnancy."

Flint turned the helicopter toward the airfield. "I'd like to see her. It's been a while."

"You're in for a surprise," Fury said.

Azrael whirled around.

Fury turned up her palms, pretending to be stupid. Azrael's glare heated, and Fury sat back in her seat, letting her attitude fizzle.

I needed to learn how to get her to do that.

"While you're in Asheville, I think you should see Sloan," Azrael told me.

My spine went rigid.

Nothing in me wanted to see, or even talk about, Sloan. I'd just spent another fifteen (Eden) years licking my wounds from the last time I saw her and our daughter.

This trip wasn't about Sloan. Or even Iliana. For now, they were safe. My purpose was simple: rescue Fury's sister, Anya, and seal the Nulterra Gate once and for all.

Flint lowered the helicopter toward the ground.

"Why?" My voice cracked with the question.

"She's struggled since the electrical storm."

"Is it true what they say about her?" Fury's voice snapped me out of my thoughts. "Sloan really got her powers back?"

"Some of them, but it hasn't been easy for her." Azrael watched the ground beneath us nervously as Flint eased the helicopter down.

"How is that even possible?" Fury asked.

Azrael shook his head. "I have no clue, but I'm determined to figure out how."

CHAPTER FOUR

*A*s an orphan and then a Marine, my entire human life had been spent bouncing from bed to bed, and then rack to rack. Claymore headquarters was the first place on Earth I'd ever lived for more than a year. The first place I'd ever called home. And the first place I'd ever fallen in love.

Fury walked beside me as the four of us crossed the airfield toward the main grounds. We passed the chow hall and then the PT field.

A platoon of new recruits was climbing the fifty-foot rock wall tower and rappelling down the other side. It was eighty-four degrees, and they all looked like they were about to die.

"I don't miss those days," I said, shaking my head as we passed.

"Me either," Fury agreed.

Across from the PT field was Echo-10, a six-story concrete building with zero windows and only one door in and out. Even when it wasn't locked down, only a handful of Claymore staff could access it. So it had become something of legend throughout the company.

When I worked for Claymore as a civilian, before I knew I

was part-angel or that Azrael was my father, Echo-10 perplexed me as much as all my colleagues. The rumor was it got its name because it had ten torture chambers, and all you could hear inside it were the echoes of your own screams.

Ironically, the truth was even more impressive.

Echo-10 was a supernatural fortress constructed from steel, concrete, lead, and a composite metal foam called high-Z. It had originally been made by a group of scientists at NC State to block radiation, but Azrael had found another use for it: blocking the supernatural.

My daughter's home in Asheville, a smaller version called Echo-5, was made of the same materials.

Azrael stopped walking. I wondered if he would turn toward Echo-10. He didn't. "Fury and Flint, you two head on to the armory. I need to talk to Warren for a minute."

Fury hesitated. She hated being left out of the loop.

"We'll fill you in soon," Azrael said. "I promise."

Flint took her arm. "Come on. Gives us a chance for a little father-daughter time."

Fury groaned as he pulled her forward.

Azrael put his hands on his hips and watched them until they were out of earshot. "Does she know?"

"About Adrianne?"

"No, Warren, that it's physically impossible for an average human to lick their elbow." He gripped his forehead like *he* was getting a migraine. "Of course about Adrianne."

"I haven't confirmed anything, but she highly suspects something." I lowered my voice. "You won't be able to keep this secret for long."

He sighed, looking at the ground. "I want you to tell her."

"Are you sure?"

"Yes. Fury will be an asset."

"What are you planning? She said you've been MIA a lot," I said.

"I'm making arrangements for when the baby's born. I'll show you when we have more time—"

"Show me?"

He nodded. "But get Fury alone and tell her. She's the only one I trust to keep her mouth shut."

My jaw tightened. "She *is* an expert at it."

"You need to let it go, Warren." He put a hand on my shoulder. "The two of you need to trust each other more than ever right now, and I'll need her help when the time comes. We need to bring her back on board with SF-12."

"You have Chimera now. Chimera took Fury's spot on the team."

"We'll rename the team SF-13 if we have to. I need Fury."

"Why?"

"I'll explain everything once you're back from Nulterra." He started walking again. "Hopefully, your mission will be successful. We could use Anya as well."

"But you do have a plan?"

"Of course I have a plan. I'll tell you everything soon."

I looked around to make sure no one else was close enough to hear us. "Well, I hope whatever plan you've concocted is more solid than your plan for getting your powers back."

Az dropped his head.

"A hair dryer in the bathtub? What were you thinking?"

"I thought perhaps Illy could reinstate my powers the way she did when Sloan was struck by lightning," he admitted.

"You have to knock it off." I nudged him with my elbow. "You're no longer immortal."

"You think I don't know that?" His face fell, and there was an unmistakable hitch in his throat.

For the first time ever, my father was vulnerable.

I swallowed. "I've asked all over Eden. No one knows how Iliana restored Sloan's powers."

"They aren't *restored*, exactly." Azrael shook his head. "They aren't as strong as they used to be."

"Has she tried summoning anyone?"

"Yeah. It might have worked one time on Adrianne, but it's hard to say because Adrianne calls a lot and shows up unannounced all the time anyway."

"What about healing?"

His head tilted from side to side. "Again, maybe it works, maybe it doesn't."

"Can she bring anyone back to life?"

"Of course not."

I pointed at him. "So cut it out."

Azrael put his hands up. "I'll stop."

"Good." We walked several feet in silence. "Guess what happened today?"

Azrael's brow rose in question.

I tapped my temple. "Iliana figured out how to talk to me."

"Really?"

"Yeah. It only happened once, when Cassiel and I were still on the island, but she said Appa as clearly as I'm talking right now."

"That's excellent, son." He looked truly happy for me.

Voices drew our attention up ahead. Flint and Fury were arguing outside the armory. "I couldn't tell if they were joking or serious on the helicopter. Is he really trying to stop her from going?" I asked.

"You're a father. Wouldn't you?"

Valid point.

"Do I need to separate the two of you?" Azrael asked as we approached.

Fury's face was red, and her fists were clenched at her sides. "No."

Azrael opened the door to the armory. "Well, come on. We're already late."

"Holy hell," Huffman said when the four of us entered the armory. My former colleague walked around from behind the front desk with his hand extended. "I heard your ass might stop by today, but I didn't believe it."

I pumped his fist. "Good to see you, man."

"Good to see you too, Parish." When he released me, he grabbed Fury and pulled her into a tight hug. "Hey, heartbreaker. Long time no see."

She pushed him back and scowled, but I was fairly certain she liked the attention.

Huffman looked at Flint. "Hello, Mr. McGrath."

Damn. Even Huffman knew who Fury's father was.

"Mr. Claymore, good to see you again," Huffman said so politely I knew it was bullshit.

"I can't believe I'm still paying you to sit on your ass here all day," Azrael said, shaking his head.

Fury was looking around at the enclosed racks of weapons. "Right? Do you really expect Huffy to save the day if shit goes sideways?"

"I've saved your ass a few times, haven't I?" he asked.

She smiled. "Fair enough. Do you have what I asked for?"

"Yes, ma'am."

"Really?" Fury rubbed her palms together. "Lemme see."

"One sec." Huffman walked back to his desk, leaned over it, and pressed a button hidden behind a file rack. Behind us, the front door buzzed and bolted shut. Then metal bars slid down over it.

"OK. That's pretty cool," I said, impressed.

"Have you not been to the vault before?" Azrael asked.

I shook my head. "Not in all the time I worked for Claymore. And definitely not since."

"It's been over a year since I've seen you in here at all," Huffman said, leading us to a door in the center of the room's back wall.

"Longer than that," I told him. The last time I'd been in the armory was the day Sloan first met Fury. That was an ugly day.

Azrael looked at his watch. "There's something else I need to attend to while I'm here. I think I'll catch up with you at the clinic. You still planning to be there at nine?"

"Yes, sir," Huffman said.

"The clinic?" I asked.

Azrael nodded. "I want medical supervision when Fury tests out her new gear. Huffman's got something pretty cool to show you. Flint, you wanna come with me?"

"Nah, I think I'll stay here and supervise. Keep her out of trouble," Flint said.

Fury shook her head and rolled her eyes. It cracked me up. This day had shown me the most genuine interaction I'd ever seen her have with anyone. Simply a daughter bickering with her dad.

"I'll see you guys in about an hour," Azrael said, backing toward the exit. "I'll let myself out and lock everything back up."

When Az was gone, Huffman used a numeric keypad to open the metal door. There was another buzz, and the heavy door slid back into the wall with a *thud*. "Welcome to my real office." His voice echoed off the walls of the concrete hall.

"Lovely," I said as we followed him.

"I hear you've got a kid now, Warren."

"That's right. A little girl."

"You, Fury, now Damon. It's like a baby factory around here."

"You next?" I asked.

"Ha! Man, I'm done. One is enough."

I stopped. "You have a kid?"

"My wife and I have a daughter. Same as you. She's three."

"You have a wife too?"

He chuckled. "Her name's Brittany." He opened another door to a stairwell.

"I had no idea."

"You would if you came around more."

We started down the stairs. "I don't really live in the area anymore."

Fury flashed a knowing smile over her shoulder, and behind me, Flint snickered.

Huffman had been with Claymore a long time, but he wasn't part of SF-12, so I wasn't sure how much he'd been told.

"The rumor is you're dead," he said as he turned at the midway landing.

I froze.

He grinned back at me. "I've even stood on your grave."

"I have a grave?" I asked Fury.

"So I hear."

At the bottom of the stairs, Huffman took a hard right. "Got a headstone with your name and everything."

"Sure do. I can take you to see it if you'd like," Flint offered.

"Isn't that something?" Huffman asked. "Good thing we've all got that confidentiality clause in our contracts."

"Yeah. Good thing."

"You missing Eden?"

"Like crazy," I said.

Huffman turned on his heel, his jaw dropped. Fury started laughing, and Flint just shook his head.

"I didn't think you'd actually fess up," Huffman said through a laugh.

I looked at Fury. "He knows?"

She was laughing too. "Yes. He knows."

"You're all a bunch of assholes." I shook my head as we walked on toward another door. This one was round, massive, and shiny.

The vault.

It looked a lot like vaults in the movies, except it had a combination lock *and* a retina scanner. After successfully turning the dial and letting the machine scan his eyeball, he was able to turn the wheel on the door until the bolt finally slid away. He pulled the heavy door open. It must have been ten inches thick.

When he and Fury walked inside, the lights flipped on. I froze halfway through the doorway. *"Day-um,"* I said, drawing the word out slowly.

The vault was a huge octagon. Easily as big as the armory above us and part of the indoor range attached to it.

The half of the octagon to our left was a series of lockers, or safe-deposit boxes, that got bigger as they went around the room. But the right side was nothing but weapons in mass quantity. RPGs, grenades, Claymore mines—no affiliation, I'd learned—and guns. Cases and cases of guns.

"They're back here," Huffman said, crossing the room to the far wall. He opened another combination lock on a smaller vault door. It led to another room lined with thick glass cases.

The center one in front of us housed the gargoyle. It was dark and stone except for the eyes. The eyes glowed with an eerie green light. I had never seen it up close before, but it radiated supernatural energy.

And it was kind of hilarious that an Archangel was trapped inside it. Moloch seemed to be glaring at me.

"It's creepy isn't it?" Fury asked, leaning toward the statue.

"Yeah. It's like he's watching me all the time. Freaks me the hell out. But that's not what I wanted to show you." Huffman turned to the case beside Moloch.

Inside was a full-length mannequin wearing bloodred cuffs around the wrists, a collar around the neck, wide bands just above the elbows, and what looked like shin guards fastened backward over the calves.

"You did it," Fury said, a little mystified.

Huffman unfastened the latches on the glass, letting it swing open. "To your specifications, my dear." He pulled the mannequin forward, and it rolled on the platform underneath it. "The blood stone will cover most of the major superficial arteries." He pointed to the neck first. "Carotid, brachial, radial, popliteal, and posterior tibial."

"Been studying anatomy?" I asked.

"Dana helped with the design."

"Who is Dana?" I asked again.

"Head nurse at Echo-10," Flint answered. "Nice gal."

I looked over all the magical pieces. "It's a little overkill, isn't it? Azrael lived in Eden for years with only wrist cuffs."

When Azrael had sacrificed himself to save Sloan, the Father had used blood stone to allow him passage into Eden. He'd lived there with my mother for many years before returning to Earth to help with Iliana.

Fury shrugged. "We had a lot of blood stone to work with. Figured we'd use it."

I leaned in for a closer look at the reddish-black stone pieces. "How'd you make them?"

"Melted down that pillory Enzo and Cooper brought back last year," Huffman answered. "Had to heat it to over six thousand degrees to get it to melt."

"What about the burns?" Flint asked. "Is what happened to her neck before going to happen again?"

"I hope not." Smiling, Huffman carefully slid off one of the wrist cuffs. "I added the quick release latch you asked for." He showed Fury, then pressed a button on the side. The cuff sprang open on a hinge.

"Nifty, son, but how will that keep her skin from getting scorched again?" Flint asked.

"It won't, but after Azrael told me all he could about blood stone, it sounds like it transmits supernatural energy much like we can transmit electricity. That energy creates heat, and like I said, this stuff has a crazy-high melting point. It can hold a *lot* of heat before it begins to break down." He pointed at Fury's throat. "Hence the burns.

"So I started wondering if there might be something we could coat it with that conducts energy without conducting heat. Now there's nothing at the hardware store that can do that, but I called our buddies at the NC State lab."

"The ones who created high-Z?" I asked.

He nodded. "They directed us to a team at the Department of Energy that's working with a substance called vanadium dioxide. Az has some very powerful friends at the DOE, and he was able to get them to help us come up with a coating that will hopefully protect Fury's skin from the blood stone."

"Shut up." Fury shoved Huffman's shoulder. "Since when are you so smart?"

He laughed. "Right?"

I took the cuff from his hand for a closer look. "I don't see any coating."

"It's clear when it's below thirty degrees Celsius. You can see it when it heats up."

"Does it work?" Flint asked.

Huffman's smile faltered. "No one's tried it yet."

"Give it here. I'll try right now," Fury said, sliding the elastic band off the end of her braid. She ran her fingers through her long dark hair, then *Houdinied* it up into a knot on the top of her head.

My eyes fell to the silvery scar encircling her neck already. Flint's did too.

When she reached for the blood stone, I held it out of her reach.

She scowled. "Don't start, Warren. My body. My choice."

Still, I didn't lower the cuff enough for her to grab it.

"Nobody's trying it on down here in the vault. Az wants to do a test run with it in the clinic so they can monitor Fury's vitals." Huffman held out his hand, and I gave the cuff back to him. "We should make sure it isn't lethal before you guys go to the jungle."

Flint raked his hands through his hair.

Fury looked at her watch. "No time like the present."

Flint began to argue, so I moved out of his way and paced the room behind them.

Huffman joined me. "We've all tried to talk her out of it. But she's determined. I honestly think she'd rather die trying than not do it at all."

"That doesn't make me feel any better," I said.

"She's tough. If anyone can stand it, it's her."

Fury's and Flint's argument ended with Flint stalking past us, out of the vault.

"Can we go to the clinic now?" Fury asked.

"Yeah. Everyone should be there soon." Huffman knelt down to open an armored case on the floor.

"Shouldn't we take it to Echo-10?" I asked.

"Echo-10's on lockdown."

"Why?" Fury asked.

Huffman shrugged. "Beats me."

"Before we leave..." I lifted the strap of my sword's scabbard over my head. "Can I lock this up in here until we come back from the clinic? It feels a bit like World of Warcraft carrying it around in public."

"Traded in your Remington for steel, huh?" Huffman asked, reaching for it.

I handed it to him along with my backpack. "Something like that."

Flint was sitting on the steps outside the vault when the three of us walked out with Huffman carrying the shiny aluminum case. Fury stopped in front of him and held out her hand. He looked at it for a moment before taking it. She pulled him up and hugged him.

Outside, Huffman loaded the case into a camouflaged HOK —a golf cart infused with steroids and testosterone. Flint got in the front seat with him.

I grabbed Fury's arm. "Will you walk with me? We need to talk."

"Are you breaking up with me, Warren?" She grinned, shielding her face from the sun with her hand.

"This is serious."

"Isn't everything we do together serious?"

The thought of her skin on mine flashed through my brain, and I stopped myself from answering "apparently not."

She put her hands on her hips. "Are you going to try to talk me out of doing this?"

"No, I promise." I leaned toward her and lowered my voice. "Azrael wants me to fill you in on our *other* situation."

"Oh." She turned back to the HOK. "Flint, Huffman, we'll meet you guys at the clinic. We'll walk."

"Suit yourself." Huffman started the engine.

"Everything all right?" Flint asked.

I gave him a thumbs-up.

As they pulled away from the armory, Fury and I started walking. I looked all the way around us before speaking. "Azrael wanted me to tell you that Adrianne's child—"

"Is the Morning Star," she said as calmly as if she were telling me it was a boy.

My head snapped back. "Yes. How did you know?"

"I've known Azrael almost my entire life. He's never been the most subtle creature on the planet. And now that he's human, he's getting sloppy."

"How so?"

"He has emotions now. He's super defensive whenever Adrianne is mentioned."

"Do you think anyone else knows?" I asked.

"I'm sure all of SF-12 has at least considered it. Enzo and Kane have both mentioned it."

"What about Nathan and Sloan?"

"I don't talk to them, but they don't know him like we do. So I doubt it, unless Iliana is starting to act strange around Adrianne." She looked at me. "Which she totally might be."

"It's really obvious, isn't it?"

"I felt the power of that kid when the helicopter landed in the yard."

Because she was Abaddon's human daughter, Fury's ability to sense the supernatural was much stronger than just her ability to see angels. Our power was almost a tangible thing to her. She could see it, feel it, and, most importantly, avoid it. It was more than even I could do.

"So what's his plan? Is that why he's been gone so much?"

"You know as much as I do about that, but whatever it is, I'll bet it has something to do with Echo-10 being on lockdown."

"I wonder if he's transforming it into a supernatural prison," she said.

"I thought the same thing, but how will he explain to Adrianne that he's locking up their kid?"

"Maybe he'll lock her up too."

I laughed. "That will go over well."

Her head tilted. "Wouldn't be the first time he's tried."

"To lock up Adrianne?"

"No."

A distant memory, one of Azrael's memories from the blood stone, rose in my mind. "Oh. He was going to lock up my mother."

"And you. I was told the whole reason he built the bunker beneath the house in Chicago was to keep you and Nadine there."

I'd forgotten that. "Maybe you're right, but hopefully now

that he's had a little more experience with human relationships, he'll realize it won't work."

"Perhaps, but Adrianne might stay willingly so she's not separated from her child."

"Would you?"

She looked up the road ahead. "Without question."

We walked in silence around the barracks and the commissary.

"Fury, why don't you stay home?" I finally asked.

She groaned. "Warren, you promised."

"Just listen. I can force my way into Nulterra from the spirit world. There are channels through which souls are cast out of Eden and into—"

"And get yourself, and most likely my sister, killed?" She stopped walking and faced me. "Why do you think they've developed weapons like that sword you've been carrying around?"

I had actually considered that. Even before we knew about the sword, the Council had forbidden me from attempting to enter Nulterra through the spirit line. They—the wisest of all angels—had agreed the risk was too great. I was only cleared to attempt entering through the gate on Earth.

"So why don't you open the gate and let me go alone," I said. "You can return home to Jett and John."

She held up her wrist, the one marked with the same "No" sign as the gate itself. "When I found out this was the key, I could have gone anytime into Nulterra by myself. But I'm not stupid. My best chance of getting in and getting out alive is with you."

"But that doesn't mean you have to—"

"And if you don't know by now that I'm an asset on a dangerous mission, I'm going to punch you in the throat."

I cracked a smile.

"I'm going. Don't bring it up again. Arguing with Flint

about it is all I can stand." Shaking her head, she started walking again.

"Why'd you never tell me about him?"

"Never had a reason to."

Sure. No reason at all. We'd only known each other the better part of a decade. Had slept together, had fought in a few wars together, and had almost died together more than once.

Her eyes fell to the pavement. "I keep my work and personal lives separate."

"Which was I?"

She didn't answer because she didn't have to. We both knew I was a job. At least, we both knew it *now*. And she had quit me without any notice whatsoever.

Neither of us spoke as we started down the main road through the base.

Finally, Fury quickened her pace. "Come on, Warren. Those cuffs can't be any more painful than this silence."

CHAPTER FIVE

$\mathcal{T}$he Claymore medical clinic was the equivalent of a civilian urgent care with an X-ray machine. They could diagnose the flu, broken bones, and jock itch. For anything more serious, Claymore employees were sent to the local hospital in New Hope or flown to Duke in Durham.

There likely weren't any patients I might send into the afterlife with my presence, so I followed Fury inside.

Huffman and Flint stood when we entered. "Nice stroll?" Huffman asked.

"Peachy," Fury said. "We ready to do this?"

"Just waiting for Nurse Dana to get here."

Flint got up and touched Fury's elbow. "Can we talk for a second outside?"

"Are we going to argue again?"

He didn't answer.

"Then no," she said.

The front door to the clinic opened behind us, and Azrael walked through it. A woman in black scrubs was behind him.

"Good, you're already here," Az said when he saw us. He

walked over next to me. "Warren, this is Nurse Dana Mohn. Dana, this is my son, Warren."

"Hello, Warren." Dana's eyes were mismatched. One was blue, the other hazel.

As I shook her hand, my eyes narrowed. I'd seen this woman before. I was sure of it. Same height. Same curves. Same ginger hair. "Hi. Have we met?"

Azrael slapped my shoulder. "Dana's been with us for a long time. She cared for Taiya when she was here."

The memory of our friend Taiya's time at Echo-10 stirred all the doubt and mistrust I feared would surface on this trip. That was the first time we realized how cunning Azrael could be. And how far he would go to keep us in the dark.

But that wasn't it. I'd seen Dana much more recently...

My mind flashed back to the day Fury gave birth to Jett. I had thought the woman working in the nursery had heard me through the glass window.

I turned toward Azrael, my jaw slack. "Was she there the day Jett was born?"

Fury's head jerked. "What?"

"Yes," Azrael said.

"Why?" Fury asked. "Jett wasn't born anywhere near here."

Something caught Azrael's eye behind me. I turned to see a man emerge from the hallway beyond the welcome desk. "Huffman, Dr. Rothwell is ready for you."

"Rothwell?" I asked. "He's still here?"

Azrael nodded. "He left a couple of years ago, but I recently called and asked if he'd be interested in coming out of retirement."

"You mean, you paid him to come out of retirement," I said.

Azrael shrugged. "Same thing."

"And he knows about us?" I asked.

"More or less. Back before we added Doc to SF-12, there may have been an incident involving me and an RPG. Let's just say Dr. Rothwell was introduced to the supernatural world and my ability to heal very quickly."

Huffman chuckled. "I, however, still wasn't finding any of this humorous. Neither was Flint.

Azrael looked at Fury. "Are you sure you want to do this? You don't have to."

"He's right," Flint said. "You don't have—"

"I'm positive." Fury nodded without breaking eye contact with Az.

"Great." Dana gestured toward the hallway.

"I'll wait out here with Flint," Azrael said.

Flint started forward. "The hell you—"

Azrael flattened his hand against Flint's chest. "Stay with me. You'll give yourself a heart attack."

Fury touched her father's cheek. "I'll be fine."

It was clear Flint was having a hard time controlling his emotions. His jaw was set, and his eyes blinked with the speed of hummingbird wings. He put his hands on his hips and nodded.

Huffman offered me the case. "You should probably go back with her, so you know how to get them on and off."

I reluctantly accepted it. "If this goes bad, I'm holding you responsible."

"Man, I'm just the craftsman. I don't want her to do this any more than you do."

I looked at the nurse. "Do you think it's safe for me to be with her?"

Dana already knew I was an angel, and if she was really the head nurse of Echo-10, she should know exactly what kind. As the Archangel of Death, people often died in my presence. The sick got sicker. Injuries worsened.

Death was literally in my job title.

Dana looked around the waiting room, probably to be sure it was safe to speak. "No matter how severe the reaction, it shouldn't be fatal. As long as you're willing to leave if I give the order, it's not a problem."

In other words, she would only give the order if the blood stone took a lethal turn.

"OK."

"Fury, you ready?" Dana asked.

Fury nodded, then crossed the room and hugged her father one more time. "I'll be fine," she whispered only loud enough for him and my supernatural hearing to hear. "Don't worry."

Not worrying was a lost cause for all of us.

The exam room was spacious with an adjustable exam table, two straight-back blue chairs, a rolling stool, and a counter with cabinets and a sink.

I laid the case on the counter and moved out of the way.

Dana rolled a vital-signs monitor over beside the exam table. She slipped a small monitor onto Fury's index finger, then slipped Fury's other arm into a blood pressure cuff.

Dr. Ben Rothwell walked into the room. He looked mostly the same as I remembered, except now there was a little more salt than pepper in the rim of hair around his ebony head.

He smiled when he saw me. "Warren Parish."

I was surprised, but I took a step forward and extended my hand. "Hello, Dr. Rothwell. I'm impressed you remember me."

"How could I forget? Biggest scaredy-cat of needles I've ever seen in my forty years of practicing medicine."

Fury laughed and shook her head. "Needles? Really?"

My mouth was gaping. "Aren't there HIPAA laws preventing you from saying things like that?"

"Probably." He laughed. "Can I tell the story?"

I rolled my eyes but nodded.

He sat down on the rolling stool and scooted toward Fury. "This guy cut his hand open on the rappel tower, but he's afraid of needles so he didn't come in for stitches. Instead, he poured the cut full of wood glue."

"Hey, it worked," I defended.

Dr. Rothwell chuckled. "Sure. Until it got infected, and you had to come in for a penicillin shot." He leaned toward Fury. "I thought he might cry."

She laughed.

"I didn't," I said.

"How have you been, Warren?" he asked.

I crossed my arms. "I enjoy not working here anymore."

"Yeah, I understand that. Can't believe Damon dragged me back. But hopefully, it won't be for too long. Those fish in the canal won't catch themselves." He looked down at Fury. "Are we ready to do this, young lady?"

"Yes, sir."

"You understand there's no precedent for what we're about to do, correct?"

She nodded.

"And that this is well outside my sphere of practice, yes?"

"Yes. I understand. Off the books."

"And even with the protective coating, you know it will probably be painful."

"I've done this before." She touched her throat. "Without the protective coating."

"All right." He looked around the room. "Dana, let's get a crash cart in here just to be safe."

My body temp jumped about a thousand degrees. As Dana left the room, I pumped the front of my shirt's collar to force air down it.

"It's just a precaution," Dr. Rothwell said, probably noting my pending hysteria.

A moment later, Dana returned with a rolling blue-and-white cart. She pushed it against the wall, then returned to the counter where she'd left the metal case from the vault. "Ready?" she asked.

Dr. Rothwell looked at Fury, and she nodded. Dana opened the case.

"No!" My sudden outburst shocked even me.

Everyone looked at me.

"Put it on me first."

Dr. Rothwell's head fell to the side. "It likely won't have the same effect because you're an—"

"We'll at least be able to tell if it's generating heat." I unfastened my tactical watch, then held out my arm. "Me first."

Dr. Rothwell looked at Fury, then back at me. "All right. Dana, give me the brachial cuff. It will probably fit Warren's wrist."

Dana removed a cuff from the box. She slowly pressed the button on the side, and it sprang open. Cradling it carefully with both hands, she offered it to the doctor.

I lowered my arm toward him and took a breath as he fastened it around my wrist.

Energy hit me like a tidal wave. My head swam, and I rocked back a step before catching myself on the wall. "Whoa." I blinked to clear my head.

Fury touched my side. "Are you OK?"

I nodded and grabbed her backrest to steady myself. "It's a rush."

"May I?" Dr. Rothwell pushed his bifocals up onto the bridge of his nose. I lowered my arm for him to inspect it. "Dana, hand me the thermometer." When he had it, he slid the tip under the cuff and looked at the screen by Fury.

We all watched the number climb.

99.7

101.1

101.4

101.6...

"Looks like it's holding at 101.6," he said after a moment.

"That's the temperature of bathwater. I can do this," Fury said confidently.

"How do you feel, Warren?" Dr. Rothwell asked.

"I feel the energy but very little heat." I also knew I was an angel and spiritual things would affect me *very* differently than Fury.

I looked at her. So hopeful. So excited. And fear soared in my heart again. Even after everything she'd put me through, I'd die if anything happened to her.

With a sigh, I pressed the button on the side of the cuff. It popped open, and I handed it back to Dana. Then Dr. Rothwell examined my unmarked wrist.

"Trial run's over." Fury's arm shot forward. "My turn!"

We both looked down at her hand. It was the wrist with the key to the Nulterra Gate etched into it. The "No" sign seemed even more ominous than it had before.

"Maybe we shouldn't cover this up," she said, rubbing her palm over it.

I shrugged. "Or we could cut off your hand, and I could take it to the Nulterra Gate and leave you safe at home."

"Nice try." She wrapped her fingers around her forearm. "Doc, think we can put it a little higher?"

"Should be fine." He used his index finger to draw a line up the inside of her arm. "The radial artery runs throughout here."

That made me feel even worse.

"Ready?" Dr. Rothwell asked.

"Ready," she said.

I offered her my hand. She hesitated for a half second. Then her face softened, and she laced her fingers with mine. I was pretty sure the move was more for my benefit than hers, but I appreciated it.

I squeezed. She squeezed back.

Dana carefully handed the doctor the smaller cuff. He took it and swiveled around on his stool toward Fury's free arm.

"Here we go." He looked up above his glasses for any last-minute change of heart.

There wasn't one, but her hand tensed in mine.

He carefully folded the cuff around her wrist until...

Click!

Fury's blood-chilling scream echoed through eternity.

Her instincts took over.

Red-faced and screaming, Fury's arm flailed wildly as she tried to shake the cuff from her wrist. She kicked the front of the exam table, narrowly missing Dr. Rothwell's face by inches. My knuckles cracked under the pressure of her fingertips.

But we had to get it off her.

Nurse Dana jumped for her arm and caught it, trapping it against her chest. I reached over her and grabbed the cuff, somehow managing to hit the button on the side. The cuff fell open and clanged to the floor.

Her bright-red skin sizzled and smoked and immediately bubbled with blisters. The sides of her wrist were black, nearly melted through to the bone.

She was still screaming and fighting against Dana.

"Fury," I said sternly, leaning into her face. "Fury, look at me."

My god, her eyes were horrified, stretched to the max, and weeping giant tears.

"Breathe with me." I inhaled deep, my own breath shaky. She attempted a steady breath but cried out in pain again. "Breathe," I said and exhaled slowly.

"It didn't burn through to the artery," Dr. Rothwell said, standing now to examine her wrist.

Fury tried to look, but I stayed in her face. "You focus on

me." I cupped her jaw in my free hand, forcing her head to stay level with mine. "Breathe."

Her whole body trembled, and tears poured down her cheeks. But she inhaled and exhaled in time with me.

The door flew open. I looked back to see Flint with Azrael on his heels. Flint rushed the bed. "Allison?"

I moved out of his way.

"What happened?" Azrael asked.

"It didn't work." Dr. Rothwell sadly shook his head. "The vanadium didn't protect her the way we hoped it would."

"Damn it!" Huffman yelled out in the hall.

Dana was examining the burn. "Definitely a second-degree, maybe a third-degree burn."

Dr. Rothwell scooted closer for a better look. "We need to take you to the burn center. This needs a skin graft."

"No," Fury said through clenched teeth. "It's a supernatural thing. It will heal better than it looks. No burn center."

The doctor looked frustrated, but we all knew there would be no arguing with Fury.

"Just wrap it and let me out of here," she insisted. The tendons were still strained in her neck, but she finally seemed to have gotten control of herself.

Dr. Rothwell huffed. "Dana, debride the burn. Then wrap it in a silver-infused dressing."

"Yes, sir." She looked at Fury. "I'm letting go now, but keep it elevated."

Fury nodded, holding her arm in the air. "It doesn't even hurt that bad," she said through clenched teeth.

"Right." Dana had a knowing smile. "If there's any decrease in pain, I'm sure it's your nerve endings realizing they're dead. That's going to leave a major scar."

Fury tilted her chin up, displaying the shiny band of scar tissue around her throat. "A scar that will look a lot like this."

"It's a wonder that one didn't kill you," Azrael said, behind the doctor.

Flint was shaking beside her. "Screw this." He released Fury's hand and started toward the door.

"Where are you going?" Fury asked, her chin still quivering from the shock of the adrenaline.

He turned and pointed at her. "I'm putting a stop to this shit right now."

"What are you going to do?"

But Flint didn't answer. He stormed out of the room. My eyes followed him. "Think we should go after him?"

Azrael shook his head. "No. Give him some space."

"Arm up, Fury," Dana instructed. She looked over at me. "Can you help her?"

With a nod, I retook my place at Fury's side, holding her arm in the air. The smell of charred flesh turned my stomach, and I instinctively curled my arm around Fury's shoulder. Surprisingly, she didn't fight it as I pulled her against me.

Instead, she leaned her head against my chest. I pressed a kiss to the top of her head.

The next twenty minutes were brutal. Dana peeled the bubbled and charred skin away, rupturing watery blisters and exposing the tender pink dermis underneath. At one point, Fury buried her face in my shirt and cried again.

Even Azrael had to leave the room twice. When he came back in the last time, his face was as pale as the paper sheet on Fury's bed. "I think I'm officially in agreement with your father. Warren should go alone."

Fury looked up and sniffed. "This won't make me quit."

"You're kidding, right?" Dana asked, still holding a strip of Fury's skin with a pair of tweezers.

"Azrael, you wore them in Eden without a problem, correct?" Fury asked.

"That's different. I'm—"

"Mortal, just like me."

He opened his mouth, but no words came out.

"You said it yourself. Blood stone only burns on this side of the spirit line." She looked up at me. "So I put it on right before we walk through the gate."

Dr. Rothwell looked as stunned as we all were. "You were lucky this time, and the last time. These devices are designed to fit as close to your major arteries as possible." He nodded to her arm. "This cuff was on you for less than thirty seconds. Any longer and it could have severed the radial artery." He pointed to her neck. "Or your carotid artery."

A chill rippled my spine.

"And do you see these blisters?" Dr. Rothwell turned her hand over. "This is your body losing water, making dehydration a very serious complication of burns." He gestured toward the case. "If you wear all these pieces, you're talking about third-degree burns on fifteen to twenty percent of your body. That could be as much as three liters of water lost in a day."

"So I won't wear all the pieces. Just the wrists, and maybe the neck," she said.

Dr. Rothwell took both her hands. "Fury, this could kill you, and we haven't even talked about infection."

She looked around at all our worried faces. "I don't want anyone to think I'm deluding myself as to what's at stake here. I want everyone in here to know that I understand the risk, and I accept it."

Azrael held up his hands. "It's your life."

"Thank you, Az."

"Warren, can I talk to you outside a moment?" Azrael asked, backing toward the door.

Dana was applying a silver-tinted wrap around Fury's wrist. I looked down at her. "You all right for a minute?"

She finally released my hand with an embarrassed smile. "Yes. Sorry. Kinda forgot I was clinging to you."

I stretched my fingers then made a fist. "I'm worried I might need an X-ray."

She laughed, and after what we'd just been through, it was one of the best sounds in the world.

"I'll be right back." I walked out into the hallway and spotted Az near the lobby. "What's up?"

"Leave her here."

I was stunned. "What?"

"You heard me. Leave her here."

I threw my hand toward the room. "You just said—"

"I know what I said, but if she goes, she dies." He took a step toward me. "Wait until tonight. Then I'll drive you up to Virginia, and you can warp back to Eden and enter Nulterra through the spirit line."

"The Council has forbidden it. Everyone agrees the risk is too great that way. Trust me, that was my first thought."

"Then forget about Anya. Chances are good she's already dead anyway. We can't lose them both."

I knew Azrael no longer believed Anya was dead. And now that I was sure of it, there was no way I could ignore her.

Besides, the Council had basically mandated that I go. None of us wanted to risk the damned being unleashed on Earth again, and that would always be a risk if Anya and the second key she held were left in the hands of demons.

"Maybe I can somehow force Fury to stay on the island once she's opened the gate."

Azrael laughed. "OK."

"I don't see another way. You know I have to go."

He stared at the floor. "I'm worried."

"You and me both."

CHAPTER SIX

"Finally done," Fury announced, walking outside to where Huffman and I waited.

His elbow was bent at an odd angle toward his mouth.

She stopped. "What the hell are you doing?"

Huffman dropped his arm. "Did you know it's impossible for the average human to lick their elbow?"

She slipped on her sunglasses. "You're so weird."

"You can leave?" I asked. We'd been there for over two hours, hence the boredom and consequent attempts at elbow-licking. Huffman had stayed with us the whole time.

"Yeah. I think he was trying to keep me there to change my mind about the burn center." She held up a white paper bag. "He finally released me with a bottle of preemptive antibiotics."

"That's good."

Az walked out the door behind her. "You guys ready?"

"Yeah," Fury said. "Where's Flint?"

"Hopefully calming down at the bar." Azrael looked around us. "But we should take advantage of his absence. Huffman, is this your HOK?"

"Yes, sir," Huffman said, loading the blood-stone case into the passenger-side floorboard.

"Mind dropping us at Echo-10 before you head back to the armory?"

"Sure thing. Hop in."

My ears heard a buzz, and Fury pulled out her phone. "I'd better take it."

"We'll wait," Huffman said.

"Hello," Fury said with the phone to her ear. She walked to the other side of the building.

Az, Huffman, and I got in the HOK to wait. After about thirty seconds, Fury's voice was raised, and she'd started pacing the grass strip along the side of the clinic.

"Looks like she's giving somebody an ass-chewing," Huffman said.

"Glad it isn't me," Azrael said with a grin.

Huffman laughed. "Preach."

If I tried, I could probably hear who was on the receiving end of that call, as she was pretty loud and I had ultrasonic hearing. But I refrained. Partly out of respect, but mostly out of fear that she'd kick my ass.

The call seemed to end quickly, as she ripped the phone away from her ear and gawked at it. Then she stalked toward us.

When she was close, she threw her bag into the back seat beside me. I flinched.

"You all right?" I asked, leaning away from her.

"No." She ripped off her sunglasses. "John wants a paternity test. *Someone* told him he might not be Jett's father."

I put my hands up. "It wasn't me."

"I know it wasn't you."

"You think it was Flint?" Azrael asked.

"Who else?" With a huff, she pushed her stuff onto the floorboard and sat down. "He'd obviously stop at nothing to try to keep me home. Now the whole world is about to know that Jett has the golden blood type."

"What are you going to do?" I asked.

"I have no idea."

"Are you still going?" Azrael asked, turning around in his seat.

Her face went slack. "Of course I am."

His brow rose. "You think John will be your nanny once he finds out he's not the father, and that you've been lying to him for the better part of a year?"

"Shit." She obviously hadn't thought that far ahead. "Could you and Adrianne keep him?"

"Oh no. We've got enough baby drama all on our own without taking on yours."

"What about Sloan?" She looked at me.

The thought of Sloan babysitting for Fury nearly short-circuited my brain. But besides the messed-up-ness of the idea, it wouldn't be healthy for either kid. "Iliana and Jett can't be around each other."

Fury's shoulders dropped.

"Maybe you'll have to stay home then," Huffman said, turning his palms up on the steering wheel.

Ignoring him, she sat back so hard in her seat that it shook the whole HOK.

"What'd he say?" I asked her quietly as Huffman backed out of the parking space.

It took a second for her to acknowledge me, which indicated she was fighting hard to keep her emotions in check. "He said he heard from a reliable source that he might want to test Jett's paternity."

"Did you tell him the truth?"

"I told him we needed to talk in person, and he said, 'Oh, we will.'"

"At least you'll have a chance to explain."

"He said he would take Jett to the doctor, either way, to have the test done. Then he hung up on me." She slumped forward and buried her face in her hands. "Damn it."

"Want me to talk to him?" I asked.

She spoke through her fingers. "No offense, but I'm pretty sure you're the last person he'd like to talk to."

I wondered what she'd told him about me.

"Have Nathan talk to him," Azrael said.

Fury straightened, obviously surprised that she hadn't already thought of that. "That's a great idea. Thanks, Az."

When we stopped at Echo-10, Fury nudged my ribs as we got out of the HOK. Then she pointed behind me.

A massive man, like Reuel-massive, was walking straight toward us. He wore MultiCam fatigues and a full weapons belt. I recognized him immediately.

He worked Claymore's main entrance gate. I'd once blasted it off its hinges. I followed Fury toward him.

"You have a visitor!" he shouted, his deep voice booming over the distance.

It took a second to realize he was talking to Fury, not me or Az. He wouldn't even look at me as I walked up beside her. Perhaps I still wasn't forgiven.

"Who is it?" she asked.

"A civilian. Says his name is John McNamara."

Oh hell.

"Did you know he was coming?" Azrael asked Fury.

She shook her head. "No. He hung up on me." She looked at guard again. "Did he say what he wants?"

"No, ma'am. But he's furious, and he said if you're not at the gate in five minutes, he's going to drive through it." The guard scowled at me.

Nope. Definitely not forgiven.

She took a deep breath. "I'll go talk to him."

"I'm coming with you," I said.

I expected her to argue. She didn't.

"No. Bring him back here to the lobby of Echo-10," Azrael said to the guard. "I don't want anybody making a scene at my gate."

"Roger that, sir," the guard said, turning on his heel.

I looked down at Fury as we followed Az to the building. "It's going to be ugly."

She sighed. "You think?"

After my earlier conversation with Fury, I half expected the inside of Echo-10 to be transformed to something resembling the inside of Alcatraz, but when Az used the retina scanner to let us in, everything was exactly the same. Visually, anyway.

The way the building felt, however?

My heart began to palpitate.

"What's going on here?" I looked around the L-shaped lobby. To our left was an elevator to the apartments upstairs. To the right, two glass sliding doors led into the common living room and kitchen. And down the hallway ahead of us...

Fresh death pulled at me like a magnet.

"Azrael?" I asked.

"Follow me," he said, walking past.

Fury stopped next to me. "What is it?"

"There's a body here."

Fury looked around like the body might be somewhere around our feet. Grabbing her shoulder, I turned her body toward the hallway, just as Nurse Dana stepped out of a door on the right side.

It was the Echo-10 infirmary. Sloan and I had spent a lot of time there with our friend Taiya. A memory that haunted me now.

Fury and I reluctantly joined Azrael.

"Dana, the door," he said.

The nurse hesitated. Her mismatched eyes were set on me. She knew what I was, and while it hadn't seemed to bother her much before, now, she was frightened. "Azrael, I don't feel the patient is stable enough to—"

"Dana." My father's tone was scolding.

Without further objection, Dana pushed open the door marked with a medical cross, and my ears immediately heard the sound of life support. The rise and fall of the hissing respirator. The slow and steady *beep beep beep* of the heart monitor.

Inside, a nurse's station faced two square cubicles with wide glass doors. Through the door on the right, I saw a woman lying on the bed. I'd seen her before in a similar state:

Tied to a bed in Venice, Italy.

Only now, her midsection was swollen.

I stumbled back a step, Azrael's "plan" suddenly crystal clear. I raked my hand through my hair. "What have you done?"

"She was already dead, Warren." Azrael walked around to the woman's bedside. "But her child was not."

Suddenly sick, I turned my back to them. Fury was in front of me, concern clear on her face. "What's happening?"

I looked past her, unable to focus on anything. "This is the woman Cassiel and I failed to save in Venice. The last victim of Vito Saez. She was pregnant when he killed her."

"My god." Fury covered her mouth and looked toward Azrael. "And you're keeping her alive to what? Swap out the Morning Star and hope Adrianne won't notice?"

"That's the idea," Azrael said.

When I turned back toward the bed, Azrael was leaning over the woman's body. Part of me wanted to drag him away from her. "This is twisted, Az. Even for you."

"I thought it was pretty genius," he argued. "They're close to the same gestation. Both boys. Both part of our world."

"Part of our world?" Fury asked.

"The child's mother had the sight," I said. "It's what made her Saez's target."

"And if this boy inherits the gift, he'll be an asset to Iliana. And to Jett," Azrael said to Fury.

I took a step forward, but Dana grabbed onto the back of my shirt. "That's close enough, Archangel. We've worked really hard to keep her alive. We don't need you screwing up the plan."

"You're both insane," Fury said, shaking her head.

Azrael's head tilted. "Why? Save the child. Neutralize the situation."

"How do you even plan on making the swap?" she asked.

"Nurse Dana." I looked back at her standing in the doorway. "You were there to take Jett the day he was born if he was the Morning Star, weren't you?"

"What?" Fury's face whipped toward my father. "Are you kidding me?"

With an exasperated sigh, Azrael walked over and put his hands on Fury's shoulders. "I've never made it a secret that I'll go to any lengths to do what's necessary. Now, this is in the past, Allison. Jett is safe. It's over."

There was hard pounding on the door outside.

"That will be John." Azrael's eyes flicked toward the door. "Go deal with him."

Fury was angry. Dangerously angry. But she took a few steps backward, then walked out.

When she was gone, I leaned against the glass wall. "So how's this supposed to work? You'll bring Adrianne here when she goes into labor?"

Azrael's head bent, and his eyes locked with mine. "Don't worry about the details, son. The less you know the better."

"And the Morning Star? Where will you keep him?" I asked.

"We have facilities in place to take care of him until permanent arrangements can be made." He looked me up and down. "Where's your sword?"

That's right. *I* was the catalyst for the permanent arrangements.

"It's locked up in the armory." Nausea churned in my stomach again. I touched my temples. "Who knows about this?"

"No one else outside this building except for the medical flight crew who helped me bring her here from Italy. Though they don't know the details. Also, Chimera."

"The new girl?" I was surprised. "You trust her that much?"

"Yes, and you will too."

"The doctor also knows," Dana said.

I looked up at the ceiling. "That's why you brought Rothwell back."

"Yes," Azrael said.

There was shouting down the hall, and something slammed against the floor. I was out of the room first with Azrael right behind me. When we stopped in front of the glass doors, John was lunging toward Fury on the other side.

Before the doors could open and Azrael or I could step in, Fury's hand shot forward, and she caught John's Adam's apple in the webbing between her thumb and index fingers.

He gagged and fell back coughing.

Fury snarled. "Don't come at me, John McNamara. You won't live to regret it."

Azrael and I just looked at each other. Azrael smiled.

Looking around the room, I saw they had turned over a small bookcase, and a baby's car seat sat on the conference table. Baby Jett was inside it, kicking his tiny feet and screaming.

"What the hell's going on in here?" I asked.

Panting and holding his throat, John looked at me. "Just who I wanted to see." John coughed again. "Hello, Warren."

John was older than me with a shock of gray in his hair and

scruffy beard. He was smaller, too, by at least twenty pounds. And shorter. Five-eleven, tops. But none of that was to say I wouldn't have to use my super-powers if he got physical. John was a retired Navy Seal commander and (I'd heard) still fighting in the local MMA circuit around Raleigh.

"Hi, John. Fury, are you all right?"

Fury was unbuckling the baby. "I'm fine. We were just arguing."

"Looked like more than that to me," I said.

She lifted the baby out and held him against her chest. "John kicked over the bookcase. He didn't touch me."

"Can't say as much for her." John was still holding his throat.

Fury straightened Jett's black T-shirt. "You shouldn't have tried to get in my face."

"No. You shouldn't have," I said.

John took a step toward me. "Think you need to protect her from me, Warren?"

I shook my head. "She can do a good job of that all by herself. But she probably won't kill you. I will."

John smirked. "OK." He looked at Fury. "So is it him then? Is he Jett's father?"

"You're ridiculous," Fury said with a hard eyeroll.

"You didn't answer my question."

"No. He's not the father!"

"Then who is?"

Fury bounced the crying baby and rubbed his back. "He doesn't have a father, John!"

Whatever John was expecting to hear, that clearly wasn't it. "Come again?"

"Jett doesn't have a father." She took a deep breath. "He's an angel, not a human."

John looked a bit like a cartoon character who'd been

smacked in the face with a frying pan. All that was missing were tiny birds circling his head.

"She's telling you the truth," I said.

His dangerous eyes darted toward me. "Stay out of it, Warren."

"How about if I get involved?" Azrael walked around me. "You're a guest in the middle of *my* army. I suggest you not forget that."

John spat on the floor at Azrael's feet.

I lurched toward him.

"Enough!" Fury yelled.

Azrael threw his arm across my chest to hold me back.

Fury walked over. "Can you take Jett and give us a minute?" She turned the baby around in her arms. His black T-shirt said SECURITY across the front in all white caps.

"Please?" she said, holding him toward me.

I didn't want to move. My eyes flashed toward John again.

Azrael pulled me back a step. "Take the baby and give them the room. You can watch from the lobby." I didn't budge. "Come on, Warren. She'll kill him faster than either of us if she has to."

With a deep breath, I carefully took Jett from Fury's hands, dangling him like a rag doll.

"Good grief, Warren. Hold him like a football," she said.

I'd never really played football, but I tucked Jett into the crook of my arm and cradled him against my ribs. "You know me being this close isn't healthy for him."

Too much exposure to me or any other angel would cause Jett—or any other baby—irreparable damage. Even with limited contact, he'd suffer from a migraine when taken from me. It was the primary reason I'd had to leave my family when Iliana was born.

"It's better than him listening to us fight," she said. "It will only be a minute."

I took a step backward toward the lobby, keeping my eyes on John. "I'll be out there listening to every word."

"I expect no less," Fury said.

Azrael followed me into the lobby. Through the walls, we listened intently to the conversation in the living room.

It didn't take long for John to swallow the idea that Jett was supernatural. He'd seen enough unexplainable things in his time with Fury to not be completely thrown off the dock by the revelation. Sloan had brought John back from the edge of death once, after all.

But it was Fury lying to him he couldn't seem to get past. And honestly, I couldn't blame him. He'd gone through her whole pregnancy and the first two months of Jett's life believing he was a dad. And he wasn't. That'd be hard for anyone to forgive. Including me.

Finally, he shook his head, staring at the floor between them. "I can't do this anymore. You don't love me. You don't respect me—"

Fury started to object, but John held up a hand to stop her. "Allison, if you had a shred of respect for me, you'd have told me all this in the beginning."

Her face fell, but she didn't argue.

"I'll keep Jett until you get back, but after that, you're both on your own."

"John, I'm so—"

"Don't. Don't you dare."

Az and I both cringed.

John pointed at Fury. "You've got two weeks to get back, or I'm dumping Jett outside that gate."

I looked down at the baby in my arms. Black hair. Dark skin. One eye green and the other dark-chocolate, just like his mother's.

He reached toward my face, seemingly mesmerized. I was probably the only angel he'd seen since the day he was born. I bent to meet his fingers. "Don't worry, little one. I'll bring your mom back in no time."

The sliding doors opened, and John walked out carrying the car seat. He put it down on the table against the wall, then walked toward me with his arms outstretched.

I wanted to say something, but what? I opted for silence instead as I handed him the baby.

As John wrestled with the seat's straps, Fury carried the diaper bag through the doors. "He'll have a migraine soon after you leave. There's baby Tylenol in the inside pocket."

"We'll be fine," John said, pushing her aside.

She forced her way in front of him again and bent over the car seat. She kissed the top of the baby's head. "I love you, Jett."

John moved her out of the way again and hooked the car seat's handle over his arm. "Two weeks, Allison," he said, grabbing the diaper bag. "You've got two weeks."

When John threw the door open, Fury walked over beside me. "You OK?" I asked.

"Yes."

"Are you lying?"

"Yes."

I put my arm around her shoulders, and she let me. She leaned into me and shook her head against my chest. "I'm going to kill Flint when I get my hands on him."

Before the heavy front door closed, a hand pulled it back open. A figure darkened the doorway. I half expected it to be Flint.

It wasn't.

This person was short with dark skin and wild hair... and an unearthly power that radiated off her.

"Who is that?" Fury whispered.

The door closed behind the woman.

"Oh my god." I took a step back. "She's a Seramorta."

CHAPTER SEVEN

Seramorta—half-angel and half-human beings—were rare. Nonexistent, I had mistakenly thought.

I was one before I died and Azrael brought me back as an angel. Sloan and our friend Taiya had been too before their angelic parents had been destroyed. Now, all three of us were either one thing or the other. Angel *or* human. No longer both.

As far as I knew, this woman was the only Seramorta left on Earth.

She was young, at least younger than I was. With olive skin and wavy red-and-black hair—the right half of which was shaved. Her nose had a shiny diamond stud, and her chest was covered with a colorful tattoo. She was dressed all in black. Torn jean shorts and a shredded leather top.

She waved, and the bangles around her wrist jingled. "Hi, I'm Chimera."

"Holy shit." I fell back a step. "You're an Angel of Knowledge."

Chimera cupped her hand around her mouth. "And I'm a human, but don't tell anybody."

"Wow." I looked at Fury. "Wow."

"I thought you'd be surprised," Azrael said behind me.

I turned, nodding my head emphatically. "You were right. I didn't know there were any of us left."

Chimera laughed. "I've known about you for years."

"So I just found out." I cut my eyes toward Fury.

Perhaps sensing the potential of tension, Azrael gestured toward the living room. "This is a conversation that requires a chair." He gestured toward the living area. "Shall we sit? There's much to discuss."

Azrael and Chimera went first. Fury and I hung back in the lobby. "Did you know?" I asked her.

"I'm just as surprised as you."

"Any idea who her parent is?"

She shook her head. "I wish it were that easy."

"What do you think? Azrael wouldn't bring her on if he didn't trust her. And she has helped you a lot, right?"

"She has, but don't forget, Azrael's getting sloppy."

The excitement I felt waned a bit.

Azrael stuck his head out the door. "You coming?"

We joined them in the living area. Azrael sat at the head of the conference table, and Fury and I sat across from Chimera.

Fury leaned back in her chair, crossing her legs at the knee. "Where did you come from, and who is your angel sire?"

I blinked. Fury's bluntness might just come in handy. I looked at Chimera for her answer. She looked just as surprised as the rest of us. Nervously, she put her hands on the table. "Well, I'm originally from San Francisco, and my father is a demon named Torman."

"A demon," Fury repeated.

"Yes."

"And we can trust you?"

"Well..." Chimera drummed her short black fingers on the tabletop. "Fury, your father was a demon. Sloan's mother was a demon. And, technically, Azrael was a demon. So...can I trust *you?*"

Point for Chimera.

I looked over at my father. "You're right. I like her."

He chuckled.

Fury wasn't laughing. "You've done work for me online for years. Why didn't you tell me who you were?"

Chimera started counting on her fingers. "First, you never asked. Second, you wouldn't have trusted me if I had, and third, you didn't tell me who you were either. It's not like it was part of the job description."

"But, as I understand it, you sought her out and volunteered the information about Sloan, right?" I asked.

"Thank you, Warren."

I was pretty sure that was the first time Fury had ever uttered those words to me.

"You're right, I did," Chimera said. "But I didn't set out to find Fury. I was looking for Azrael."

"Why?" I asked.

"At six years old, I became a ward of the state of California when my grandmother died. My mom was a total piece of shit, barely better than my demon father, so I didn't have anybody else. Right away, my caseworker knew I was smart. Like, crazy-smart."

"She has a photographic memory, and they can't even measure her IQ," Azrael said.

"Yeah, I basically became a human lab rat at SanTech University until I was a teenager."

That was one of my greatest fears for Iliana.

"My only link to the outside world was the web, and as Azrael already said, I'm smart, so it didn't take long to figure out I could do things I shouldn't.

"I started small, getting into the university's databases, changing people's schedules around and screwing up their payroll. By the time I was fifteen, I'd cracked California's system. I created myself a whole new identity, changed my age to eighteen, and erased every bit of information that anyone had ever stored on me. Once my fake credit cards showed up in the mail, I was gone."

"You were on your own when you were fifteen?" I asked, impressed.

"Yep. And I moved abroad when I turned eighteen because getting a passport was a little bit harder."

"How old are you now?" Fury asked.

"Twenty-eight."

I leaned on my elbow. "Is it true you hacked the Pentagon in 2009?"

"Yes." She pointed at me. "But on that one, I got caught."

I straightened. "They said they never found out who did it."

"That was the official statement, but they found me shockingly fast. I learned then the importance of living in a country that doesn't extradite to the States."

We all laughed.

"But instead of jail time, they hired me to fix their system, and I did." She sat back and steepled her fingers. "But not before I did a little poking around, of course. That's how I found Alfie Davies, Assistant Director of Intelligence to General Michael Barker."

"The Commandant of the Marine Corps?" I asked.

She nodded. "Davies, the guy who worked for him, isn't from around here. Wink, wink."

"He's an angel?" I asked.

"Yes, but I didn't know it then. I had never met an angel before, but I'd also never seen a living person who didn't have a soul before either. And I wanted to know more."

I knew exactly what that was like. It was what had made me seek out Sloan after seeing the video footage of her.

"So I started digging to find out everything about Alfie

Davies, and that's how I found a guy named 'Damon Claymore.'" Chimera actually used air quotes. "The digital paper trail between Davies and Claymore Worldwide Security was as long as the state of California."

"Alfie Davies was an Angel of Protection named Rogan," Azrael explained. "He and his brother Malak both worked for the Pentagon for years. They were my contacts that got all of Claymore's security contracts."

"Angel brothers?" I asked.

"Not biologically, of course, but Malak and Rogan have been together for eons. Longer, maybe. You never see one without the other. They returned to the auranos last year," Azrael said.

"Never heard of them," I admitted.

"Well, you are pretty new on the job." My father had a teasing grin.

"How did they work at the Pentagon if angels weren't allowed to speak English?" Fury asked.

"The Father worried about nuclear war, so he placed them inside the American government himself. The Council's rules didn't apply for that assignment."

"As much information was out there, I never found any photos of this mysterious Damon Claymore." Chimera pointed at Azrael. "But once I found SF-12 in the company records, it all snowballed from there."

My mouth fell open. "You hacked the Claymore server?"

"Many times. It's how I found SF-12 and Fury. Even Sloan and yourself, eventually. It was Abaddon's name, which I'd read in some cryptic emails, that led me to research the supernatural. The more I learned, the more my life made sense."

"But why send Fury the information on Sloan?" I asked.

"Through the web of communication between Damon Claymore and SF-12, it was obvious objective number one was to keep the two of you apart. It was also obvious from her search history that Fury wanted to find Sloan. I thought if I helped her, it might get me into the company."

I swiveled my chair toward Fury. "*You* were searching for Sloan?"

"Sure." She didn't look at me. "I'd heard about her for years. I was curious."

Chimera's brow scrunched with doubt across the table.

"You were curious," I repeated.

"Yes. I wanted to know more." Fury shrugged. "Not a punishable offense."

It was clear from Azrael's narrowed eyes, he wasn't buying it either.

"Why did you want in at Claymore?" Fury asked, conveniently moving the conversation along.

Chimera sat back in her chair. "I thought I might find out where I came from. Why I was the way I was. Hell, I even wondered if the mythical Damon Claymore might be my father."

Azrael laughed. "Got that wrong. I'm not nearly smart enough for that job."

"How did you find out your father was what's his name?" I asked.

"He found me, actually. Not long after I sent that video to Fury. Now that I know my father is a demon, I'm sure he was probably watching Fury's communications as well because they had taken her sister, Anya."

"Damn." I looked at Azrael. "You should have had an Angel of Knowledge on staff a lot sooner."

"Tell me about it."

"Well, he's got me now," Chimera said proudly.

"Why didn't you want to work with your father?" Fury asked her.

Chimera frowned. "Screw that guy. I've been kept from the human world, the angelic world, and even the fallen my whole life. I wouldn't wish that kind of isolation on anyone. Now they're trying to mess up another kid's life? Hell no."

"Tell him about your necklace," Azrael said.

"Oh." She straightened. "Did you bring the sword?"

"No. It's locked up in the armory right now. Why? Azrael said you knew something about it."

"Maybe." She pulled a simple chain from under her collar. On it was a tiny bright-purple stone. It looked like an amethyst from across the table. "When Torman was trying to recruit me to the dark side, he told me the demons had this all-powerful stone. Said it had all sorts of powers, like the power to kill angels. That's how we got to talking about it when Az told me about your sword."

She gripped the purple stone with her fingers. "He said this was made from the same stone, and that it would keep me well when he left.

"I didn't know what that meant at the time, nor did I trust the bastard, but once he left and the migraine started, I became a quick believer." She blew out a sigh that puffed out her cheeks. "I put on the necklace, and the migraine went away."

I felt like someone had sucked all the air out of my lungs. Could she be saying what I think she was saying?

I caught Azrael watching me, like he was waiting for a reaction. That was all the confirmation I needed. I stood and leaned both hands on the table. "Are you telling me that stone keeps your migraines away?"

Chimera looked at Azrael. "You said he'd be excited."

"It can protect you from the effects of angels?" My volume jumped up a notch.

She nodded. "I haven't been sick once since I started hanging around you weirdos."

A squeal escaped my throat as my eyes flooded with tears. "I'll pay you a million dollars for that necklace, Chimera."

"You don't have a million dollars, Warren," Azrael said.

"No, but you do, and I'll give her your whole damn company."

Azrael, and even Fury, laughed.

"Do tell, Mr. Archangel. Why would you want my necklace?" Chimera's playfulness already told me she knew, but I wanted to say it out loud anyway.

The tears spilled down my cheeks. "Because I want to go home to my daughter."

"So here's the bad news."

At least Azrael gave me a few minutes to get my shit under control before ripping the world out from under me again.

"That necklace is priceless," he said. "Trust me, I've already offered her everything I've got."

With the weight of the world back on me, I sank into my seat, drying my eyes on the back of my hand.

"He did, but I refused. I'm a nice person, but I've only gotten this far because I take care of myself first." Chimera tucked the necklace beneath her shirt again. "However..."

Fury shifted on her chair. "Oh, thank God you said however. I was about to pull out my nine mil and shoot you."

I smiled, appreciating the odd solidarity.

Chimera scooted toward the table. "I know there's more of it down in Nulterra. From what Torman said, it powers the whole damn place."

"What exactly is it?" Fury asked.

"I don't know. I've had several geologists and jewelers check it out over the years, but no one has ever seen it."

Azrael got up from the end of the table. "One of our friends at the NC State lab even said it may not be from this planet."

"You think it might be Nulterra-borne?" Fury asked.

Chimera's head tilted. "Maybe. Maybe not. There is someone who could tell us for sure, but I can't get him to talk."

I gripped the table. "Point me that direction. I'll get him to talk."

She smiled. "I thought you might say that."

"Who is it?" I asked.

"Moloch."

"You want him to work with a gargoyle statue?" Fury crossed her arms. "That's hysterical."

"Don't discount what's locked inside that statue," Azrael warned.

"What makes you think Moloch will tell him the truth? Isn't lying the MO of the fallen?" Fury asked.

"The sword." I looked at Fury. "I've considered using it on Moloch anyway. Maybe we could make a deal."

"And leave the demon alive?" she asked. "That's insane."

"Don't worry," Azrael said. "We're working on security measures for our supernatural prisoners."

I'll bet he was.

"But it's a statue. How will you get it to talk?" Fury asked.

"It's not just a statue. It's a computer. Communication is easy," Chimera said.

I stood. "What are we waiting for? Let's go have a chat with a demon."

———

Back in the vault, Chimera attached what looked like a cell phone to the back of the statue via a USB cable.

"You can really communicate with him like that?" I asked.

She nodded. "You bet."

Fury waved her hand in front of the gargoyle's face. "How does it work?"

"It's actually pretty simple. The spirit form of an angel is little more than a consciousness, and on this side of the spirit line, that consciousness is very similar to our radio waves. All you need to transmit those waves are a transmitter"—she tapped the gargoyle's head—"and a receiver." She held up the phone. "The receiver intercepts the waves and turns the electrical signals back into sound."

"That's genius," I said.

"It'll take just a second to pull up and decode the program," she said.

I tugged on the hem of Fury's shirt and stepped a few feet away. "How are you feeling?"

"Better." She held it up to show off the white bandage. "But I look like a suicide failure."

"I'm starting to think you are."

She shook her head. "Don't start."

"I'm not. I give up."

"Good."

"Have you heard from Flint?"

"No."

"What will you do when you find him?"

She let out a breath. "I'm not sure."

"Well, speaking as a father who's about to go to Hell and back for his daughter, don't be too hard on him for wanting to protect you. It's clear how much he loves you."

"I know he does. I just can't believe he'd pull Jett and John into this."

After seeing Fury and John fight that day, I could think of one reason a dad might.

"Does John hit you?" I asked gently.

She didn't look at me. "No. I'd kill him if he did."

Of that, I had no doubt. Still, even if she deserved his anger, I could have snapped his neck for coming at her like he had.

Azrael walked into the vault after taking a call outside with Adrianne. "Did I miss anything?"

"Not yet. Chimera's getting set up now. How's Adrianne?" I asked.

"Better now that she's had some sleep. She wants to know if the two of you will be staying with us tonight. Echo-10 is also an option if you'd rather not, but do keep in mind the pregnant woman's wrath. It's brutal."

"I don't care where I sleep," I said.

"Me either," Fury agreed. "What's with the beach house, anyway?"

"It took some convincing, but I got her to agree to have the baby here with our own private medical staff rather than in Asheville."

"How'd you do it?" I asked.

"I bought her a beach house."

Fury put her hands on her hips. "Sometimes I wonder what it must be like to be you. Even without your powers, you can still wiggle your nose and get your way, every time."

"Not every time," he said. "But close."

"You guys ready?" Chimera asked.

She flipped a switch on the front of the gargoyle as we walked back over. The crackle of static flooded the vault, just like when the Angels of Death tried to contact me. "Radio waves," I said to no one in particular.

"Huh?" Fury asked.

I pointed to my ear. "Same sound when angels communicate with each other."

Chimera turned the volume down. "It's probably similar to radio waves. I've heard this world is like a knockoff of Eden."

"A bad knockoff," Azrael said.

More static echoed around the vault.

"Oh great. Azrael is here." The voice coming through the phone sounded like a Speak & Spell. "Is that Moloch?" Fury asked, wide-eyed.

"Were you expecting someone else?" the voice replied.

Azrael walked up beside me. "He sounds like Stephen Hawking."

"It's a similar system," Chimera said. "Hawking's system translates data he inputs. Here, Moloch *is* the data."

"So is he ready to talk?" I asked.

"I'm right here," the robotic voice answered. "What would you like to talk about, Warren?"

I took a step closer, so I was almost nose-to-snout with the winged stone beast. I could swear the thing was staring at me. "This is weird."

"You think it's weird for you," Moloch replied. "What do you want?"

"I want you to tell me about Nulterra."

"Ha," the statue said. "No."

"You don't want to talk?" I reached for the sword leaning inside the open cabinet. When I pulled it from its scabbard, the demon's green eyes flared.

"No need to get violent," Moloch said.

"Then maybe you should start talking."

"What do you want to know?"

"Is my sister alive and in Nulterra?" Fury asked, wasting no time.

"She is."

Peace washed over Fury's face. "Was she taken across the spirit line in blood stone?"

"She was."

"Did it stop burning her once she was through the gate?"

"It did."

Fury looked at me as if to say, "See?"

"I think he's telling the truth," Chimera said.

My head pulled back. "Oh, you're an Angel of Knowledge. I forgot you can do that." I lowered the sword an inch. "Moloch, do you know where Anya is now?"

The green eyes turned from Fury to me. "The last I knew, she was being held in the tower beyond *Ket Nhila*."

"The Bad Lands," Azrael translated with a smirk. "How original."

"I imagine they were named with good reason," Chimera said.

"How do we find Ket Nhila?" I asked.

There was a pause. Finally, the robot spoke again. "I honestly can't tell you. The experience for everyone is different. What might be the Bad Lands to one might not be the Bad Lands for another. Ket Nhila will depend on your human."

"On me? That makes no sense," Fury said.

Azrael's head tilted back and forth. "Perhaps it does. I'd imagine the Morning Star created Nulterra in the image of what he already knew...Eden. And Eden can be quite subjective."

"That's true," I agreed. "Sloan's mom lives in a place exactly like her home in Asheville. I'm sure that never existed before she came to Eden."

"So things in Heaven are created to suit humans?" Chimera asked.

I shook my head. "I think things in Heaven exist because humans bring the best of their existence back with them."

"He's smarter than he looks," Moloch said.

"I'm right?"

"Yes," the robot voice replied. "Eden is an illusion. What exists is a projection of the spirit."

"We create our own heaven," Chimera said.

I nodded. "Kind of."

"But that also means..." Fury was staring straight ahead at the wall. "We also create our own hell."

I gave the back of her neck a reassuring squeeze, but when her eyes met mine, they were filled with worry. Understandable since she'd probably seen enough horrors in her life to level even an angel.

"What's down in that pit that's going to try to kill them?" Azrael asked.

I swear the demon smiled. "Everything."

"Can you be more specific?" I asked, annoyed.

"Why should I?"

I raised the sword again. "Because the only chance you have to continue to exist, even locked up inside that statue, lies with me. Perhaps, if you answer all my questions, I'll let you live when I get back."

"When you get back," he repeated. "That is the question, isn't it?"

"Well, it's not a question of *if*, if that's what you're insinuating."

"I wouldn't dream of it."

"Do we have a deal, Moloch? You keep your life if you help us get back from Nulterra alive."

He didn't answer.

I tapped the statue between the eyes with the tip of the sword. "I could end you right now."

"Nulterra was built on a bedrock of osmium," Moloch said.

I looked over my shoulder at Fury. "Osmium. Write that down somewhere."

"No need." Chimera raised the phone. "Everything's recorded. I'll send it to you."

"When the gate is opened and oxygen fills the entrance chamber, osmium tetroxide will begin to crystallize on the rocks. The crystals will immediately begin to vaporize. It won't affect you, Warren, but the human will need protective eye covering and an air-purifying respirator until you get away from the gate."

"Goggles and a gas mask?" Fury asked.

"That should be sufficient, but you've been warned. The gas

will blind you, and if you breathe it in long enough, it will cause your lungs to fill with fluid and cause respiratory failure."

"That's all true of osmium," Chimera said. "Osmium tetroxide is highly toxic to humans."

"What else do you know about it?" I asked her.

"It's the densest of all known metals on Earth. The rarest, too, in the Earth's crust."

"It didn't exist in the Earth's crust at all before Nulterra," Moloch added. "And you'll only see it just beyond the gate. Once you're inside, the osmium is so far beneath the surface, it won't be dangerous."

"How will we know when it's no longer dangerous?" I asked.

"You will know," he replied. I could almost see his smartass face smirking through that damn statue.

I looked at Chimera. "When you no longer see the crystals, it should be safe."

"Thank you," I said.

"So how would a bedrock made of osmium differ from what we have here on Earth?" Fury asked.

"Besides its toxicity?" Chimera teased.

Fury wasn't amused. "Of course."

"Well, it's about four times as dense as the Earth's crust, so depending on Nulterra's overall mass, gravity might be more intense."

"It is," the robot said. "It should not alter your ability to walk, but you won't be able to fly. Other than that, much of what you will experience there, you're already familiar with."

I looked at Chimera for confirmation. She nodded. "I think the takeaway here is if the foundation is made from osmium, then it's safe to say the demon is right. Everything there will try to kill you."

For me, that wouldn't be a problem. But for Fury...

"Will the demons know we're there?" Fury asked.

"They will know the gate was open, and they will send a

sentinel to investigate, but Nulterra wasn't built under the fear of intruders. There aren't very many defensive mechanisms in place to trap you."

"Not *many*, but there are some?"

"Yes. However, those are mostly centered around the bridge to the spirit line. The Morning Star's biggest concern was keeping Eden out."

"More weapons like the sword?" I asked.

"Yes, but unless you plan to abandon your human, you should have no reason to go near Eden's spirit line."

"Tell us about the sword," Azrael said. "What's it made of."

"Helkrymite. It is a metal foreign to Earth. I'm not sure it has an equal for comparison," he said.

Chimera pulled out her necklace. "Is this helkrymite?"

I turned my ear to be sure to not miss the answer.

"No. That is blood stone."

We all shared a look of confusion. Azrael pulled out his own blood-stone necklace. It was so red it was almost black. "*This* is blood stone."

"They both are, but all blood stone is not created equal, as all beings are not created equal," Moloch said. "What you have is sanguinite. What we have is sanctonite. Our blood stone gives the helkrymite its power. Gives Nulterra its power."

Fury looked at Azrael. "Sanguinite is made of angel blood, right?"

He nodded.

"So which angels can kill other angels?"

"Only Iliana," I said. And I'd worked damn hard to make sure none of her blood had been spilled.

"No." Azrael looked lost in thought. "The Father can as well." He looked at Chimera's necklace. "Moloch, are you saying that's the blood of the Father?"

"Precisely."

"How the hell did the demons get the Father's blood?" I asked.

"Antioch."

"What's Antioch?" Fury asked.

"A city," Chimera said. "Well, at least it *was* a city in modern-day Turkey until it collapsed about nine hundred years ago."

"It literally collapsed about seven hundred years before that," Azrael said.

I looked down at Fury. "The Morning Star tried to start a second war with the angels by sending the demons to attack the city. It became a full-on war that triggered an earthquake, killing hundreds of thousands of people."

"But the Father wasn't there." Azrael pointed to his chest. "I was there."

"In all your splendor, I know." It was almost impressive how Moloch could be so smug even with a robot voice. "You know who else wasn't there? The Morning Star. Do you really think you won that day, Azrael?"

"Yes," my father said with his signature cockiness.

"Would you like all of the facts?" Moloch asked.

Azrael crossed his arms. "Oh great and powerful castle ornament, please enlighten me."

"While you were busy helping fulfill the Morning Star's threat, the two of them were in *Siri*."

"What's Siri?" Fury asked.

"It was a place between worlds where angels and demons could meet in secrecy. The Father destroyed it after the destruction of Antioch," I explained.

"The Morning Star wanted to create a home for us, something separate from the humans the Father loved so dearly. But in order to create a new Eden, the Morning Star needed the power of the Father at Nulterra's core.

"When the Father refused, the Morning Star vowed to level the city to prove the humans would be safer without us here.

When the Father refused again, the Morning Star kept his word. He ignited the war in Antioch."

"And we won," Azrael said.

"You won because the Morning Star called off the demons. The Father agreed to trade his blood to save the people."

Azrael's face tightened. "Bullshit."

"He's telling the truth," Chimera whispered nervously.

"Why wouldn't the Father just destroy the Morning Star?" Fury asked. "He could wipe him out and the demons."

"As easily as you could wipe out your son?" Moloch asked. "Don't forget, the Morning Star was the Father's first creation."

"The Father wouldn't do that," Azrael insisted.

"Are you sure?" Moloch asked.

Azrael didn't answer. He walked to the other side of the room.

"After Antioch, the Father no longer allowed himself to come to this realm with the power to undo it. That's the real reason he parades the Earth as an old man."

"Lies." Azrael spun around. "The Father gives up his power to come to Earth so that he's not tempted to rule by force."

"Of course," Moloch said. "Otherwise, it would be a very dangerous precedent for the angels and humans alike to know the Almighty Creator of the Universe could be so easily manipulated."

In a few quick strides, Azrael crossed the room and ripped the sword from my unsuspecting hand. With a mighty swing, the gargoyle shattered in a million shards of stone and light.

Moloch, the Archangel of Knowledge, was gone.

CHAPTER EIGHT

"*C*assiel is an Archangel now." I tilted my beer bottle up to my lips as I stared out at the moonlit bay from Azrael's lower deck. I'd gotten word earlier from Samael, almost as soon as we'd left the armory.

It had taken me all day to process it. Now, not only was she infinitely smarter than me—she was just as powerful.

Azrael was peeling the label on his beer. "She'll be good at it, and it's time for Eden to have a sitting Archangel on the Council again."

"She's already lifted the language ban."

Since the First Angel War, it had been forbidden for the angels of Eden to speak anything other than Katavukai. The language was a mark of their loyalty and a tell-tale sign for the fallen. The rule didn't apply to me only because I was born human.

"Really?" Azrael asked surprised. "I guess we know who influenced that."

I took a long swig of my beer. A sailboat was passing by on the water.

"As crazy as she makes me, and as much as I don't trust her

after what she did, you and Cassiel could make a powerful alliance." He raised his bottle to his mouth. "Two archangels working directly together? That's never happened before." His beer sloshed against the glass as he drank.

"Cassiel never wants to live on Earth," I said, crossing my boot over my knee.

His head tilted. "She is a habitual tourist. She comes, collects her shells, and leaves."

"Magnets," I said.

"What?"

"Cassiel collects refrigerator magnets."

"Ah, but she didn't always. Before refrigerators were a thing, she collected rocks and seashells."

I smiled.

"Earth, huh? You planning to come back for good?"

"I've always planned to come back when Iliana was old enough. Looks like that might happen even sooner."

"I knew you'd be happy about that necklace." He reached over and squeezed my forearm. "It'll be so good to have you back."

"Think it really works?"

"Chimera says it does."

"But you've never *seen* it work."

"How could I? You're the only angel around anymore."

"She's been around Adrianne, and she worked inside Echo-5 that one time when Iliana was there. And I assume she's at least been down in the vault to check on Moloch."

"Yeah, I guess that's true. I've never seen her sick."

I took another drink. "I can't believe you destroyed him today."

"Really?" He lifted an eyebrow. "You can't believe it?"

"Well, I can..." I sighed. "We could've gotten more information out of him though."

"Nah. He was done talking. He got that indignant snarl—"

"His face was *literally* frozen in stone."

"You know what I mean. Did you pack up the stuff you need for the trip?"

"Yeah. We raided the supply room while you were back at Echo-10." Fury and I had packed rucksacks full of MREs, gas masks, and first-aid supplies.

Sitting my beer on the arm of the wooden deck chair, I laid my head back against the backrest and closed my eyes.

Laughter in the house caught my ear. A welcome sound after the day we'd had. I lifted my head and glanced over my shoulder to see Adrianne and Chimera in the kitchen. They were eating brownies straight out of the pan. "I see why you like her."

"Yeah, she's *hot*," Azrael said, tilting his face toward the sky.

"Chimera," I clarified.

"She's been a huge asset."

"You trust her?"

"I do. She's a good kid. There have been *plenty* of times she could have screwed us over and didn't."

The *chk chk chk* of a helicopter came in on the cool night breeze. "Sounds like your buddy's coming back," I said, sitting up and searching the horizon.

"Flint?"

"I think so." I spotted flashing lights over the water. "There."

"He's either a very brave man or a very stupid one," Azrael said.

"He raised Fury. I'm sure he has balls of steel."

Azrael chuckled. "Yeah."

When the helicopter was right over the yard, Adrianne and Chimera came outside. "Is that Flint?" Adrianne asked with one hand on her supernatural belly.

The helicopter turned, displaying the word CLAYMORE down the tail. "Yep." Azrael stood. "Here, babe. You want my seat?"

"No." Adrianne walked over and stood behind him. "No, I was just coming to say goodnight, but now, I want to watch."

He sat down and reached back for her hand. "You should go pop some popcorn. This is gonna be good."

"Where's Fury?" she asked.

"She went out for a walk," I said.

Chimera walked to the railing. "Why? What happened?"

I finished the last of my beer. "I'm sure you're about to get an earful."

The helicopter powered all the way down before Flint got out and started making his way up the dock. There was a slight hunch to his gait I hadn't noticed early in the day. His eyes were searching our faces, looking for Fury, I was sure.

"I hope you're wearing a cup," Azrael said when he was close enough.

Flint walked up onto the deck. "Man, what choice did I have?"

"No need to explain yourself to me. I get it." Azrael released Adrianne and dunked his hand into the cooler beside his chair. "Here. Liquid courage."

"Thanks." Flint twisted off the cap. "Where is she?"

"Jogging. So maybe she'll be too tired to kick your ass when she gets back," Azrael said.

"God willing." Flint drained a quarter of the bottle.

"Have you talked to her at all?" I asked.

"No, but I talked to John. So a lot of good it did. He's still keeping the baby while she goes."

"He got pretty rough with her," Azrael said.

"Oh, they fight like two gamecocks. He might be even more bullheaded than she is." He pointed his beer at Azrael. "I tell you what. I won't miss the son of a bitch when he's gone."

I shook my head. "That's crazy. His nephew married Sloan, and Nate's one of the best guys I know."

"You can't judge anyone by their family," Flint said.

"Amen to that," Adrianne agreed.

"And people keep a lot hidden behind closed doors," Chimera added.

"True story," Azrael said.

Movement down the deck caught my eye. Fury stopped when she saw all of us.

"Uh oh. Here we go," I said.

She plucked her earbuds out as she came up onto the deck in her T-shirt and shorts. Anger burned in her eyes. "I'm shocked you came back."

He rested his beer on the deck railing. "You're my daughter. Of course I came back."

She pointed toward the house. "Can I talk to you inside?"

With a heavy sigh, he followed her in. When the door closed behind them, every one of us exhaled.

Azrael shook his head. "Damn."

"I don't envy him," Chimera said.

I got up and carried my empty bottle to the recycling bag Az had brought onto the porch. "I hope they make up before morning. I don't have time to drive back to Asheville tomorrow."

"You can leave with us at about four a.m.," Azrael said.

"Excuse me?" Adrianne's high pitch hurt even my ears.

Azrael laughed. "I'm kidding."

"Thank God."

"We're leaving at three," he said.

Adrianne's whole body slumped. "Forget being an angel. Someone needs to turn my ass into a vampire." She leaned over Azrael's shoulder. "I'm going to bed. Will you be up long?"

"Nah. I'll be in there soon." He kissed her. "I love you."

"I love you too." Adrianne stood and reached for my hand. "Will I see you tomorrow?"

"I'm probably staying at your house tomorrow night, if that's OK."

"Of course it is. Maybe we'll throw a barbecue. We'll have a little downtime before you go trekking off to Hell."

"That sounds great," I said.

"I'll even invite Sloan and Nathan."

For the first time, I didn't tense at the thought. "Maybe next time you can invite Iliana too."

Adrianne clapped her hands together. "I know!"

"What if you invite Iliana tomorrow?" Chimera said.

All our faces turned toward her.

She leaned against the rail. "I mean, it's not really fair to know the power exists to see her and not be able to try it out, right?"

I lost feeling in my whole body. "Are you serious?"

"Yeah, why not? Our big prisoner here is gone, so my boss might give me the time off. And I've never been to Ash—"

I jumped out of my seat and hugged her before she finished whatever the hell she was saying. "Thank you, Chimera."

She patted me on the back. "You're welcome." She wiggled away from me. "Just don't get all weepy again. Seeing hot men cry weirds my shit out."

"No more crying." I put my hands in the prayer position. "Thank you," I repeated. "You wanna fly out with us in the morning?"

"After the horror stories from your dad about aviation and angels? Hell no."

"See?" Azrael said.

"Seriously, I'll drive myself. I'll need a car to get back anyway, but thanks for the offer."

"Here." I angled to the side and pulled my wallet out of my back pocket. I handed her all the cash I had, a whopping fifty-two dollars. "Let me buy your gas. That's the very least I can do."

She pulled the money from my fingers. "Fair trade. Good-night, everyone."

Azrael waved. "See you tomorrow."

"I like her," Adrianne said when Chimera was gone.

Azrael got up and stretched. "I like her too," he said through a yawn. He slapped my shoulder. "I'm going to bed. Early morning."

"Be safe driving tomorrow."

"I will."

I followed them inside, expecting to hear raised voices. There weren't any, but Fury and Flint were talking in the dining room.

I took a shower and got ready for bed. When I walked back down the hall, the rest of the house was silent, and the light was on in Fury's room. I tapped the door with my knuckles.

"Come in."

She was sitting on the floor by her bed, looking at her phone when I walked in. A picture of Jett was on the screen. "Why are you on the floor?" I asked quietly.

"I'm sandy. I was waiting for you to finish in the shower."

"All done." I put my stuff on the foot of her mattress and sat on the floor across from her. "How'd it go?"

"He's not sorry he did it."

"I'm sure he didn't do it lightly."

"No. He said he talked to John, and John isn't going to do the test."

"That's gotta make you feel better."

She looked up at the ceiling. "I don't feel good about any of this."

It was a rare glimpse past her icy exterior.

"Did you and Flint smooth things over?"

"As well as they can be for now. We're leaving at six in the morning."

"Good. Did you hear Chimera is coming?"

"So you can see Iliana?"

I nodded.

"I'm really happy for you, Warren."

For the first time, I was sure she meant it. "Thanks. Do you need anything? Help with your bandage or something?"

"Actually, yeah. Could you help me wrap this around it?" She handed me a box of plastic wrap. "I'm supposed to leave the bandage on and not get it wet."

"Sure. Got any tape?"

She held up a roll.

I tore off a long piece of plastic. "How's the pain?"

"It sucks so hard," she said.

"I'm sorry." I grimaced as I gently wound the clingy plastic around her arm. By the time I finished wrapping her arm up like Thanksgiving leftovers, I realized it was the longest she and I had ever talked.

I offered her a hand up. Surprisingly, she took it. "Thanks, Warren," she said for the second time that day.

"You're welcome. I'll be next door if you need me. Goodnight."

"Goodnight."

Razor blades slicing through my brain woke me from a rare sleep before dawn. Pulling the pillow over my head, I rolled onto my side and into the fetal position. For a moment, I considered stabbing myself through the heart with the sword.

The sword.

My hand blindly fumbled across the hardwood floor until my fingers found it. Then I pulled it onto the bed and hugged it against my chest.

The pain weakened, but only slightly. I felt like I might puke. There was a light knock on the door that was gunshot-loud in my head, and I hurt so much I couldn't even answer.

"Warren?" Fury asked, coming into my room. "OK, I know

you like the sword, but this is stepping into some seriously codependent territory."

"Shh."

"What's the matter?" she asked quieter, but not nearly quiet enough. "Oh shit. It's a migraine. Adrianne and Chimera are gone."

I tried to nod, but I had no idea if I was successful or not. The side of the bed dipped, and I felt her—I assumed it was her ass—press against my shoulder. "What can I do?" Her quiet voice was gentle. Concerned, even.

I shook my head.

"Let me try something." Both her hands pressed against the sides of my skull. She squeezed.

The pressure inside my brain eased, even if only a little. "What are you doing to me?"

"I'm not sure. It never made them fully go away, but it helped Anya when she would get the migraines. Try to relax."

Yeah right.

I lost track of how long she held my head, but after some time, I could crack open my eyes. "You're more powerful than you think."

"Hmm. Maybe." She had the slightest hint of a smile as she moved off the bed. "Better?"

I was able to sit up. "Definitely took a bite out of the pain. Thank you."

"I'm afraid it won't last, and we have a helicopter to load. Flint's ready. Can you make the trip?"

"Yeah." I stood, then wobbled. Fury caught me around the waist. "I'm OK."

She laughed softly against me. "No, you're really not."

"No, I'm not."

Her hands grasped my sides and pulled my shirt up. I flinched. "Whoa. What are you doing?"

"You have to get dressed."

"I can dress myself."

"You can't even hold your eyes open."

My eyes are closed? I hadn't even realized I'd closed them again. I forced them open, and the dim sunlight through the window burned all the way through to the back of my skull.

She pulled my shirt up again. This time, I didn't stop her. "Do you care what you wear?" I heard her moving stuff around in my bag.

"Got any of the Father's blood stone?"

"Unfortunately not." Eden-fabric came over my head. Too bad it didn't contain enough of home to dull the throbbing in my head. "Arms up."

I stuffed my arms into the T-shirt, then she helped me put on a button-up over it.

When she finished with the buttons, her cool fingers slide under the waistband of my shorts. Tingles rippled through me, and I scooted back until I bumped into the bed. "Oh no."

"It's not like there's anything down there I haven't seen bef —oh wait. Is there anything new postmortem?"

I pried my eyes open to see her smiling as she stared at (hopefully) the front bulge of my shorts. "I'm telling your dad you said that."

"He'd probably be thrilled. Seriously, are you capable of doing this yourself?"

"Of course." *Most likely not.* "Can you put some jeans on the bed?"

"Just jeans? Are you going commando? I know you don't wear anything under those gym shorts."

"Underwear too. And then leave. Please."

"Here." She put my underwear in my hand. "When did you become so modest?"

"I'm not modest. I'm just a little vulnerable right now."

She took a step so close her breasts brushed against my chest. "Because I'm in control?"

I pointed toward the door—I think. "Fury, out."

"I'll be right outside if you need me."

It only took a few tries to get my pants on. I put my underwear on backward the first time, then tried to stick two feet through the same leg of my jeans.

"You OK in there?" Fury asked from the hallway.

"Yeah. You can come in."

I stood, and the blood surged to my head again. Pain spread like wildfire through the left side of my brain. Lights exploded behind my eyelids.

Then everything went black.

When I came to, I was on the floor. Flint was on his knees, leaning toward my face. "Hi, Warren."

"Hi, Flint. What's going—"

He compressed my chest. *Crack!*

I screamed out in pain.

He stood.

"What the hell?" I curled up on my side again, this time holding my chest as well as my head.

Fury crouched beside me. "You passed out and hit the nightstand. Broke it and your collarbone."

I swore.

"Sorry about that. We had to set the bone. It wasn't healing right," Flint said. "I'm going to start the bird. You kids about ready to go?"

No. I was too busy writhing on the floor.

"We'll be there in a few."

"You need some help getting him outside?"

"I got it." Fury's short nails raked through the side of my hair. "I knew I should've helped you."

"Just let me die."

It hurt to think, but I was pretty sure this was the first time anyone had ever seen me agonize through one of these things. In all my time on Earth, I'd gotten used to suffering alone.

"How long will it last?" Fury asked quietly.

I lifted my shoulders. "Been a long time since I've had one."

A long time was an understatement. It had been about a century, counting in Eden time. On Earth, my last full-blown migraine had been when Sloan and I were still together. When I was still part human. When I was still a resident of this realm.

"Be right back," she whispered.

I held up my thumb.

After a few minutes? hours?—I'd lost all track of time—Fury returned. I felt the vibrations of the floor as she crossed the room. Then her hand was on my shoulder rolling me onto my back.

My eyes opened to slits. She was rolling something in her fingers. Then she pushed something into my right ear canal. An earplug. I could've cried with appreciation. She did the left, and then put her hands on my chest.

I covered her hand with mine and squeezed.

She squeezed back. "Let's get you into the helicopter before it gets any worse." Her voice was muffled, but the sound was so much more tolerable. I could've kissed her.

She hooked her arms under mine and helped me to my feet. "My stuff," I croaked out.

"Already in the helicopter."

She put my sunglasses on my face and led me through the house. As soon as we stepped outside, the *whomp whomp whomp* of the helicopter's blades ricocheted around my skull. When I finally settled in the back, she fastened my seat belt around me and put a headset over my ears.

With a moan, I slouched deep in my seat and closed my eyes.

"Here." Fury's voice was muffled through the headset and earplugs.

Before I could look, something covered my head. Something soft and light. Breathable material that blocked out most of the sun. A jacket, maybe. Or an extra shirt. Whatever it was, it smelled like her. Sweet and spicy, half the things she was *not*.

"Thank you."

She didn't respond, or if she did, I didn't hear her. I laid my head back and took a few deep breaths. The helicopter rocked forward as we lifted off the ground, and when it pitched my head forward, I winced from the pain.

Laying my head against the window, I prayed for death. Ironic, I know. God, migraines are no joke. I felt like I could see my brain bleeding on the backs of my eyelids. Even my scalp burned.

After a few minutes, it was painfully clear that nothing would help the headache. And the vibration of my skull against the glass only made it worse. I straightened and pulled Fury's...*jacket* off my head. It was black and embroidered with the Claymore logo.

I draped it over her thigh.

"Not helping?" she asked.

I leaned toward her. "No. Will you squeeze my head again?"

She gripped my forehead and the back of my skull this time. As the pain began to assuage, I realized the paradox. This woman, who had once caused me so much pain was now the only thing that helped.

"How long until Asheville?" I asked, my head still in her magical hands.

"We've got a two-hour-and-forty-three-minute flight time until we reach Asheville," Flint said.

"Fury, what's the plan when we get there?" If I wasn't dead by then.

"We'll land at Wolf Gap, and Nathan will drive us to his ex-girlfriend's house."

"Should be interesting."

"I know, right? Do you really think she gave birth to an angel too?"

"So I've been told."

"Geez."

"My sentiments exactly," I said, pulling away from her hands. "Thank you."

"Is it better?"

"It's more tolerable. What's after our visit with Shannon?"

"Completely up to you. I have zero business in Asheville except getting on the plane to Oregon. Try to rest while you can. We've got a long way to go."

"Flint, thanks for the ride," I said, settling back in my seat.

"Anytime, son. Anytime."

Miraculously, I fell asleep. Or maybe I passed out again. Who knows? Either way, I was lost in blessed darkness until the helicopter pitched slightly forward.

I opened my eyes.

"Flint?" Fury asked.

Flint groaned over the headset. His hand was on his chest.

Shit.

Fury leaned forward. "Are you OK? What's the matter?"

"I...I don't know. I don't feel right." He gasped and pulled at his shirt with one hand while keeping the other on the helicopter's control stick.

Fury unbuckled and climbed across me and into the front seat beside him. She settled in front of the copilot's gears and turned to him. "Tell me what's wrong."

"Pain...pain here." Flint pounded his fist below his breastbone. His voice was strained, like his vocal cords were tied in knots, and his skin was turning pale gray. "I can't...can't feel my legs."

Death, a tangible force, had its grip on Fury's father. I felt it in my bones...because part of me was killing him.

The helicopter was beginning to sway and tilt out of control.

"Flint, can you land?" Panic was clear in Fury's voice for the first time ever.

He didn't answer.

"I'm taking the controls!" she shouted. "Hang on. We'll get you help."

All I could see below us was trees. The helicopter's alarm bells sounded. *Ernng! Ernng! Ernng!* Fury had grabbed the copilot's stick.

Flint slumped forward, but I grabbed his collar and held him back from leaning on the controls.

"Fury, can you fly this thing?" I asked.

She steadied the helicopter. "I've had a few lessons, but no. Check his pulse!"

I didn't need to. The spirit of death inside me could sense it. Hear it, almost. His pulse was rapid and weakening. Fast. "I think he's bleeding internally." I unbuckled my seat belt. "He's dying. Can you land us?"

"Dying?"

"Yes. Fury, can you land?"

She swore. "Sure. If you don't mind landing in a fireball!"

The helicopter lurched sideways, then nosedived for the trees.

I hooked my arm around Fury from behind, jerking her backward over the seat.

"No!" she screamed, fighting against me. "Dad!"

My hand shot toward the door, and my power blasted it off its hinges. The aircraft spun.

Pulling her against me, I dove out the door.

CHAPTER NINE

rees.

  Dirt.

Pine needles.

Rocks.

We'd been too close to the ground for me to execute a proper landing, so I'd held Fury tight against my chest and curled my wings around us. We landed hard on my shoulder and tumbled down a steep incline until...

Whump!

My back and ribs connected with a tree trunk.

Tears sprang to my eyes as the air was knocked from my lungs. My hand was on the back of Fury's head, holding it under my chin. I released the pressure enough so she could look at me.

Her sunglasses were gone, and her mismatched eyes were wide with terror.

"Are you OK?" I choked out with a cough that sprayed her forehead with a bloody mist.

She nodded, panting against me.

My wings relaxed and dimmed. They would be invisible to most humans—Fury was not most humans. And luckily, there was no one else around to witness two people fall from the sky and survive.

We were in the woods, halfway down a mountainside.

In my arms, Fury went limp. Her face buried into my shoulder, and her whole body convulsed. There was no sound, but she was crying.

My fingers tangled in her hair as I held her. "I'm sorry, Fury." I wheezed, and something gurgled in my chest.

"He's gone," she sobbed.

"He obviously loved you very—" I coughed and spewed more blood. Blinding pain ripped through my side.

Fury pulled back, sniffed, and blinked a few times. "Let me look at you," she said, rolling out of my grasp before sitting up beside me.

"I'm OK." I coughed again.

"Stop talking."

I nodded and slid away from the tree enough to lie on my back. Fury put her hands on my sides. "Breathe in."

I wheezed again, and we both heard an audible crackle coming from my ribcage. Her face soured. "Broken ribs."

"No shit." Groaning, I draped my arm over my eyes.

Fury pulled my shirt up. "Nothing came through the skin. That's good."

"I'm OK. Just give me a minute." My ribs were already starting to shift and click and pop back into place. I writhed on the dirt and pine needles, and she grabbed my hand and held it.

"Breathe, Warren."

"I don't need to breathe, remember?" It was a good thing too. It hurt too much to inhale.

The splintered bones ground against each other as they healed. Still, I wasn't sure what hurt more: them or my splitting head.

"What can I do?" she asked.

"Be quiet." My earplugs had been knocked out of my ears in the fall.

All I wanted in the world was darkness and silence. Out here in the woods, in broad daylight except for the canopy of trees, darkness wouldn't be possible. Besides, there was a helicopter nearby we needed to find.

Soon.

My sword was still in it.

With a painful wince, I forced myself to sit up.

Fury stared through the woods. Her face was covered in dirt, streaked mascara, and dry speckles of my blood. Her eyes were glassy...and lost.

"You OK?" I asked.

"Flint was...he was..." She took a deep, shaky breath. "I've done nothing but fight with him for weeks."

I covered her hand with my mine, but she immediately withdrew from it. She sniffed again and wiped her nose on the back of her knuckles.

"If it's any consolation, I'm sure he was gone before the helicopter hit the ground. I think it was his heart."

Her thick lashes blinked a few times before her eyes finally met mine. "A heart attack?"

"Worse. He was losing blood. A lot of it. Must've been internally."

She sighed. "An aneurysm, probably."

"Made weaker by my presence." My shoulders slumped. *Why the hell did I think I could rescue Anya? I couldn't even get us there without killing someone, much less actually—*

"Don't do that. You couldn't have known."

"Yeah. But this is the exact reason Azrael refuses to fly. I should've known better."

I started to get up, but Fury pressed her hand down on my leg. "You need to rest."

I shook my head. "We've got to find the helicopter. My stuff's in it."

"It can wait a minute. I still hear your ribs grinding back together. How's the head?"

"Excruciating."

She got on her knees and moved behind me. Then she squeezed my head again. My eyes nearly rolled back in my head. Whatever she was doing really did help. The tension in my neck released, and the searing blade that seemed to slice through my brain dulled.

"Thank you," I whispered, slowly opening my eyes.

"No. Thank you." She stood and walked around to face me. "You saved my life."

I arched my spine to make more room for my fusing ribs. "Happy to finally return the favor."

At that, she smiled and nodded her head.

Once upon a time, Fury had saved my ass in Iraq when my Marine Corps unit was ambushed. I had thought I was in a secure, hidden position with my sniper rifle. I'd been wrong. Dead wrong.

Luckily, Fury had been watching my six.

That was the day we first met. A long time ago—even longer for me than for her.

I took a deep breath, and it didn't hurt as much, thank the Father.

She stood, then turned back to offer a hand up. I took it and let her pull me to my feet. My head swirled, and I must have swayed because she grabbed my arm to steady me.

"You all right?"

I nodded and dusted off my clothes. "I think so." Squinting against all the freaking sunshine, I took in our surroundings. We were deep in the woods. No roads. No trails. No nothing except trees and foliage as far as I could see in any direction.

I listened carefully and heard a stream nearby and the crackle of a fire. Our fire most likely. I could smell burning fuel.

Fury patted her pockets. "My phone's gone."

I did the same. "Mine too." I put a finger to my ear and tapped into my *other* communication system. I called out to the Angels of Death. "Hey, does anyone know where the hell I am?"

Static popped in my ear. "I can't detect you anywhere, Warren." The voice was Samael's, the angel who guarded the spirit line.

I swore.

"What's the matter?" Fury asked.

"We're in North Carolina. The Father closed the spirit line, so Samael can't see us." I called out to the spirit world again. "Samael, I need you to get someone on the ground to call Azrael and tell him our helicopter went down somewhere over the border in North Carolina. We were in the air for about ten minutes, and we're in the woods now. That's all I know."

"I'll take care of it."

"And tell them Fury's safe. The pilot is dead. Natural causes."

"I'll tell them. Who was the pilot?"

"Flint McGrath."

"I'll keep an eye out for him."

"Roger that." I dropped my hand to my side. "Samael is letting them know we went down. Azrael will send help. If they don't find us by sundown, I'll fly us back to civilization. Don't worry."

"Warren Parish, have you ever known me to worry about anything?"

I shook my head. "I can honestly say I've never known you that well."

"Touché." She pointed uphill. "We need to climb to find the wreckage. Unless you want to fly around and scout the place out."

"Too risky. I can walk."

She started up the mountainside. I followed, but after a few steps, my head swirled with dizziness again. I stopped. So did she.

"You OK?"

"The migraine makes me dizzy." I pinched the bridge of my nose. "And I think I lost some blood internally myself."

Not surprising with broken ribs and a punctured lung. I coughed and spat more blood on the ground. Then I started up the mountain again.

Fury was ten steps ahead of me, and for a second, I was thankful for the migraine starbursts distorting my vision. Because of them, I wasn't tempted to stare at her ass.

We walked for a while in silence, until I noticed Fury shaking her head.

"What is it?"

"All he wanted to do was protect me, and I've been such a bitch about it."

It was clear the silence wasn't good for her psyche. No demon in the world was more powerful than a head full of regret with time and silence to dwell on it.

As much as my head and body hurt, I needed to fix this. Fast.

"How did Azrael and Flint meet?" I asked.

The swift U-turn in conversation made her stop. "What?"

"Azrael and Flint. How did they meet?"

"You don't know?"

"How would I?" It's not like she'd ever told me.

"I figured you'd know it from the memories in Azrael's blood stone."

"I remember a little about him, but I haven't worn the blood stone in a long time. It's kinda like trying to remember details from a book you read in high school."

She started up the mountainside again. "They met in eighty-three when the US invaded Grenada. Operation Urgent Fury, which is kinda where I got my nickname."

"Really?"

"Yeah. I was five. There were Nerf guns and old war stories involved. The name stuck."

"That's funny."

"Flint was a pilot for the Navy. When he got out, Azrael asked him to move to Chicago where he and your mom were living. Not long after, Nadine found out she was pregnant with you."

"How did you and Anya wind up with them?" I'd learned a few of the basics from Reuel, but Fury and I were on a roll of getting to know each other—or at least of me getting to know her—and I wanted to keep the momentum going.

"A few years after everything happened with you and your mom, Flint and his wife, Sheryl, got pregnant. There were complications, and the baby died at birth. Six months later, Reuel rescued me and Anya from a hunting cabin in Wyoming, and Azrael asked Flint and Sheryl to take us in. They did, and Azrael moved them to the property he'd bought in New Hope, North Carolina."

"Claymore."

"Yep. Flint helped get it off the ground."

"So your mom is Sheryl?"

"No. Sheryl was awful to me and my sister. She left when we were still really little. Flint raised us by himself."

"Makes sense."

"What makes sense?"

"Why you're such a hardass."

She spun around so fast I instinctively ducked out of the reach of her fist. Her mouth opened to probably object, but her eyes snagged on something in the distance. "There it is."

I turned and squinted against the painful sunlight to see black smoke rising through the trees about a half a mile away.

She walked past me back down the mountain we'd partially climbed. Neither of us spoke again until we reached the crash site. The only thing recognizable from the helicopter was its tail. *Claymore* was still legible in its shiny gold print. The thick trees had shredded the cabin and snapped off the tail. What was left lay in a smoking heap between two tall, gangly spruces. A few feet beyond the wreckage was a silvery figure.

Flint.

I put my arm out to stop Fury. "Maybe you should wait here."

"You see him, don't you?"

I gave a slight nod.

Fury could see angels and their power, but she was blind to human souls. I started forward, but she grabbed my sleeve. "I'm coming with you."

I didn't argue because me and my aching head would need her help to safely pick the way through the debris field.

"Warren." Fury stopped, looking down at one of the black doors.

The silver hilt of my sword gleamed through the busted window. I pulled it out, then drove the blade into the ground until I could find its scabbard.

Flint was watching us. Smiling.

The more violent the death, the more effect it had on the soul. So I was right; Flint had died before the aircraft hit the ground. "He didn't suffer," I whispered to Fury.

"Tell him—" Emotion choked her. "Tell him I'll miss him."

It was hard for me to believe that Fury could miss anyone. Her heart was battle-hardened and off-limits. God knows, I'd tried my damnedest to sway it. But in that moment, tears sparkled in her eyes. Maybe she was softer than I gave her credit for.

Flint was standing near his body, now charred from the

engine fire. As I walked over, I unbuttoned my black shirt and peeled it off, leaving my white undershirt. I carefully stepped through the wreckage, and when I was close enough, I draped the shirt over Flint's head and torso.

He didn't notice.

"Flint?" I approached his spirit cautiously. "Remember me?"

"I could never forget you, Warren. I'm glad we finally were able to meet."

"So am I. I'm sorry we didn't meet sooner, but we'll have plenty of time together in Eden."

"Eden." He smiled.

"You'll love it there."

"I know I will." His eyes drifted past me. "I'll miss her though."

"She said to tell you that she'll miss you too."

"Promise me you'll take care of her."

I glanced back at Fury. "I don't know, Flint. She has a habit of being the one taking care of me."

When I looked back at him, his face was serious. "Let her."

I blinked.

"And bring her back from Nulterra alive, Warren. I know she's too stubborn to stay home, but she has a long life ahead of her."

I nodded. "I will."

"I know you will. Ask her to come here."

I turned and motioned Fury forward. She carefully walked up on my left side. His eyes followed her. He reached toward her face, and she shuddered when his fingertips graced her cheek.

"I love her so much."

"He says he loves you," I repeated quietly.

That time, she couldn't fight the tears. She also couldn't—or wouldn't—respond, which (dickishly) made me feel a little better about the time I'd said those words and she'd walked out.

Now, she forced a smile and nodded her head.

I let my power build in my right hand. It sparkled and sizzled. "You ready to go home, Flint?"

"Will it hurt?"

I shook my head. "Quite the opposite, actually."

"Give my love to Anya. I know you'll find her," Flint said.

"I'll tell her." I took a deep breath. "You ready?"

He bowed his head.

Then I sent Flint's soul into the spirit world.

Fury took a walk through the woods while I sifted through the scorched rubble. Using my power, I moved a piece of a propeller off my scabbard. Then I bent and picked it up.

When Fury finally returned, her face was clean, and she'd obviously stripped down somewhere in the woods and washed off the dirt and pine needles.

"Feel better?" I asked.

"I'll be fine," she said, void of all emotion. Her eyes told a different story. They were red and puffy from crying.

But I knew better than to draw attention to them. "I have some bad news," I said instead.

She stepped over a log. "What is it?"

I lifted what was left of my rucksack's strap. "My passport was in the front pocket."

"What's in the man purse then?" She nodded toward Cassiel's bag across my chest, the only thing that had survived from the rucksack.

I glared at her.

She put her hands up. "I'm sorry. What's in your *satchel?*"

"I really have no idea. An angel gave it to me in case of emergency."

"Was that angel Cassiel?"

I wondered how much Fury knew about Cassiel. "Yeah, but that's not the point. The point is, my passport was in the backpack. Flying commercial will be a problem."

She shrugged. "Chimera can get you a new one pretty fast."

"You know, I can leave North Carolina and warp there."

She lifted an eyebrow. "So is this the moment you become afraid of flying, like your dad?"

"Seriously?" I gestured around at the wreckage. "Do you see where we're standing? This is what happens when we get on aircraft. Besides, I don't need a plane to fly."

"So why warp? Why don't you flap your arms all the way to the Philippines?"

"I'd get tired."

She grinned, a welcome sight after the trauma she'd just been through. "We'll figure it out tonight."

We picked through more smoldering remains from the wreckage.

"Got the blood-stone case," she announced, kicking one of the windows off of it. She opened it, and the cuffs glistened against the sunlight. "They're OK."

"Excellent," I said, sarcastically. I crouched down and moved a large scrap of metal off what used to be her rifle case. "Can't say as much for your case." I opened what remained of its lid. "Or the Remington. The barrel is melted." I tried to pick it up, but it was still too hot to touch. "Hey, is it true you gave up shooting when you were pregnant with Jett?"

She didn't answer. When I looked over, she was hugging a vintage thermos to her chest. It must have belonged to Flint.

I stood and carried the rifle over to our pile of stuff to keep.

"What'd you say?" she finally asked.

"Not important. Have you found your passport?"

"Yeah. It was in a separate bag from my clothes, which didn't survive."

"Clothes are replaceable."

"Yeah. How's your head?"

"Still hurts, but it's better since I used my power to—" I stopped.

"To send Flint into the spirit world?"

I nodded. "I'm sorry."

"Don't be. It's kinda nice that his last act on Earth was to make someone feel better."

"Aw, look at you being sentimental and shit."

She cracked a smile and held up her middle finger.

When we'd recovered anything salvageable, Fury carried her things up the hill behind me, plopped down near a tree, and leaned back against it.

I lay down across the tree trunk, bending my arm around Cassiel's satchel behind my head. I laid my sword beside me and rested one boot on the ground.

Staring up, pine peaks framed the clearing made by the crash. Smoke wafted up into the blue sky. Unfortunately, the migraine was strengthening again. I closed my eyes and focused on the sounds of the forest.

The rippling of the stream.

The song of a mockingbird.

The sizzle of dying embers.

Sleep crept over me like a breeze. Welcome relief from the swelling pain in my head and the chaos of the day. For a moment, I dipped into the welcome abyss of unconsciousness.

Then I was falling.

Falling.

My hip smacked the ground beside the log, jolting me awake.

Somewhere behind me, Fury was snickering. I pushed myself up in the dirt and pine needles. Pain splintered through my skull again. With a groan, I slumped against the log and curled my arm around my throbbing head.

"That was hilarious," I heard Fury say.

"The reason I ever cared for you eludes me more and more," I grumbled, which only made her laugh more.

Far away, the pulse of helicopter blades echoed against the Appalachians.

Pulling my head up, I looked at my tactical watch. The face had cracked. If the time was still correct, we'd been in the woods for over three hours. "Someone's coming," I said.

"Who?"

I raised both my hands in question, then covered my eyes again.

A few minutes later, the roar of a helicopter overhead made me look up. I shielded my eyes with my hand and could make out a man sitting on the helicopter's outboard.

He waved. I waved back. Then he dropped something. It was a radio on a parachute.

The radio landed close to Fury. She stood and went over to pick it up. I strapped my sword on my back and joined her as the helicopter hovered above.

She held the radio to her mouth. "That was fast. Couldn't resist bringing the new toy, huh?"

New toy? It hurt my head too much to try to look at the helicopter against the sunlight.

"We were actually testing it out when we got the call that you jokers were stuck out here. Is everybody whole?"

"Warren and I are both fine. We bailed out before it crashed. Our pilot is dead."

Her words were shockingly matter-of-fact, but I didn't miss the way her shoulders slumped.

"There's nowhere for us to safely land for miles, so how do you want to do this? Good old-fashioned extraction? I'd love to get nut-to-nut with Warren."

"Is that Nathan?" I asked with a laugh.

"Yeah."

I held my middle finger toward the sky.

"What do you want to do?" she asked.

"Depends. How much do you trust me?"

She smiled and pressed the button on the side of the radio. "Open the door. We're coming up." Then she hooked the radio onto her belt.

We gathered as much stuff as we could carry, and I looked over the wreckage once more. "You got everything you need?"

"We're supposed to leave him here?" Her eyes misted as she stared past me.

I put my hand on her arm. "I'll make sure they send a team right away to take care of him. Does he have other family?"

"Only some extended relatives, but no one I even know how to get in touch with."

"I'm really sorry," I said gently.

She nodded. Then she shook off all semblance of emotion. "Where do you want me?"

Tricky question. "On top," I finally said with a loaded grin.

Rolling her eyes, Fury stood in front of me and wrapped her arms around my neck, holding the blood-stone case against my back. She lifted an eyebrow. "Don't get any ideas."

"Can't promise that."

With a little jump, she locked her legs around my waist. It was all I could do not to shudder with unintentional delight. I tightened my right arm around her hips and curled my left around her back.

"Hang on," I said in her ear.

My wings carried us into the air.

The "new toy" was the assault version of the Little Bird helicopter. There were no back seats, only an outboard mounted above the skids. Fury and I strapped ourselves to it. Someone wearing a helmet was seated on the other side.

NAG, real name, Mandi, was in the pilot's seat.

Nathan McNamara was in the copilot's seat. He handed us headsets. "Welcome back, brother," he said when I had mine on. He smiled over his shoulder. The patch on the front of his olive-drab ball cap said "TOO OLD FOR THIS SHIT" in all caps.

"Good to see you, Nate." I jerked my thumb behind me. "Who's on the other side?"

"Wings," SF-12's second pilot answered for himself. "You didn't really think we'd let McNamara dangle out of this thing, did you?"

"I'd hate for my life to depend on it," Fury said, looking down at the treetops as we rose higher into the sky.

"Screw you all." Nathan held his middle finger over his head. "Hey, Warren, how do you like the new ride? We call it the Angry Bird."

"It's badass. Why'd you buy it?"

"Az insisted. He bought a few of them."

Worrisome. These types of helicopters were used for combat, and he hadn't said anything to me about it. "What's he planning for?"

"Everything," Nate and NAG said at the same time.

NAG looked out the side window as she turned the helicopter around. "He's preparing for almost every scenario."

"Anybody else concerned about that?" Fury asked.

No one answered.

"Is he back in Asheville?" I asked.

"He is now," Nathan said over the comms. "He was in Black Mountain when the call came in about you. What made your ride go down?"

Fury answered before I could. "Our pilot suffered a medical emergency. He died before the crash."

"Who was it?" Wings asked.

"New guy. Don't remember his name," she lied.

It was clear she didn't want to talk about it, so I moved the conversation along. "Nate, how's my baby girl?"

"She's awesome. Such a funny kid."

"I think she called out to me through the spirit world yesterday."

He turned his face toward me. "Really?"

"Yeah. Heard her while I was on the island yesterday. She said my name."

"I wouldn't put it past her. She's so smart."

"How was her birthday?"

"It was a blast. That kid loves cake almost as much as I do."

"I find that hard to believe," Fury said.

"It's true," Nathan insisted. "I'll show you some pictures once we get on the ground."

"No more issues from my world?" I asked.

"Nope. Aside from Az acting like the apocalypse is nigh, shit has been really peaceful lately." Nathan looked back at us. "Sloan and Adrianne even took Iliana to the park this morning."

My face whipped toward him. "Do they know we're coming?"

"Yeah. They're on their way back to Echo-5 now."

"Has Chimera showed up in town yet?" I asked.

"Don't think so, but we've been out and about for a while. She's coming?"

"So I hear." I decided to wait to tell him about the necklace until we were on the ground. He'd be understandably cautious, so I wanted a chance to fully explain.

Beside me, Fury's shoulders were hunched, and her eyes were misty as she stared at the mountains passing beneath us. I reached for her hand, and she didn't immediately pull away. For a moment, we took in the scenery together.

I'd once done a Google search of the most beautiful places in the world. The Blue Ridge Mountains were third on the list for good reason. The view from the helicopter was breathtaking.

After a few minutes, we seemed to be descending. We

passed over the roof of a house. And then over a cow pasture. We were not heading to the airport. Or even to Echo-5.

"Where are we going?" I asked over the radio.

"Az and Adrianne's," NAG replied.

"Nathan, is that legal?"

"Surrre." The way he dragged out the answer made me doubt him.

"NAG?" I asked.

"He's right. The FAA doesn't care as long as you don't plow into anything. And the county doesn't care as long as you don't piss off the neighbors."

I looked around the mountain and saw nothing but treetops, Azrael's looped driveway, and the roofs of his house and detached garage. "Does he have neighbors?"

"Never seen any," Nathan answered.

"He's got about forty acres," Wings said.

The most property I'd ever owned on Earth was the *only* property I'd ever owned. It was the house and half acre Sloan and I shared for about nineteen seconds right before Iliana was born. Before she married Nathan. And before I left the stratosphere to become the Archangel of Death.

That felt like a lifetime ago. I guess because, in Eden years, it was—a few lifetimes even.

The helicopter rocked to the side as NAG turned to land, and I flashed back to earlier in the day. Fury must have too because she grabbed the frame of the door.

"You all right?" I asked.

She nodded, staring at the ground below us. I wondered if she was thinking about Flint. "How's the migraine?" she asked as we descended.

"Gone." I was surprised. The pain had eased off so gradually I hadn't even noticed until she mentioned it.

"That's weird, isn't it?"

"Means another angel is close by." I looked at the ground again, like an angel might be wandering up Azrael's driveway.

"Chimera?"

"Probably. Or maybe Shannon's kid." I looked over my shoulder to where Nathan sat up front. "Nate, how close does Shannon live from here?"

"They moved to Flat Rock. So thirty miles maybe."

"Too far," I said to Fury. "Let's hope it's Chimera."

No other angels should be in the area. Since the Father had indefinitely closed the spirit line in North Carolina, limiting the access of all spirits to Asheville, even the guardians kept watch from above.

The auranos, the place in Eden where the veil between worlds was at its thinnest, had the best vantage point of Earth. Which—come to think of it—was probably why so many humans had the notion that Heaven was *up*.

Should there be trouble, the guardians sworn to protect Iliana, like Reuel, could breach through the spirit line outside the atmosphere and fall to the Earth like Incredible Hulk meteorites.

Technically, so could I, but my fingers were crossed that I'd never have to. I'd only recently mastered flying.

If anything sinister lurked in the area, the guardians would most likely see it and address it before we were the wiser. We'd yet to have to test the theory, however, so I wasn't 100 percent sure.

Another thought occurred to me too. One I couldn't say out loud over the comms. *Maybe it was Adrianne.* I wasn't exactly sure how migraines were affected by angels in utero, but it seemed her presence had killed my migraine before it really got started at the beach house.

NAG eased the bird onto the ground in the dead center of Azrael's lush green backyard. He was waiting on the porch as we descended.

"Thanks for the rescue, guys," I said as Fury and I unfastened our harnesses.

NAG flipped some switches on the controls. "Don't mention it. Glad we could come."

"And we're glad you guys are safe," Wings added.

"Thank you," Fury said before sliding onto the ground.

"Hold up. I'm coming with you," Nathan said, taking off his headset.

I passed my headset and Fury's to Wings, then grabbed my sword, which I'd been sitting on during the flight. "You ready?" I shouted to Fury over the noise.

She nodded and started toward the house. Nate and I ducked and followed her. When we were out of the brunt of the helicopter's windstorm, I realized Nathan was looking at me weird as we walked.

"What?" I shouted.

"When did you start carrying a purse?"

I pushed Cassiel's bag around my side, behind my back. "It's not a purse!"

"It's definitely a purse."

I shoved him sideways, and he laughed.

When I looked toward the house, I saw immediately why my migraine had dissipated.

Sloan was standing on the porch.

With Iliana in her arms.

CHAPTER TEN

*E*very eye in the yard was on me. In the auranos as well, I was sure.

And if they were waiting for a reaction, I'm sure my stunned face delivered. Jaw dropped. Eyes wide. Sudden onset of tears.

I covered my gaping mouth.

Nathan was smiling beside me. "Surprise." He hooked his arm around my neck and dragged me toward the house.

Iliana excitedly flailed her tiny hands as we neared them. Her mouth was moving, but I couldn't hear her words over the roar of the helicopter. It looked like she was chanting my name. "Appa! Appa! Appa!"

Black hair finally covered her head, and she wore a bright teal headband that matched her white-and-teal dress. Around her tiny neck, a purple stone sparkled in the sunlight.

She stretched her arms toward me, opening and closing her fists. Then she lunged for me when I was near enough. I thought my insides might turn to mush as I grabbed her, lifting her high above my head. She squealed with delight even over the sound of the helicopter rising into the air behind us.

I lowered her, kissing the tip of her nose, and she sandwiched my face between her hands. "Hi, sweet girl."

"Appa!"

Curling my arms around her, I pulled her against my shoulder for a hug. She grabbed onto my shirt, happily kicking her legs.

"You can't ask for a better welcome home than that," Nathan said, slapping my back before walking over to stand beside Sloan.

"No, you can't," I agreed as tears dripped down my cheeks. I kissed her face again. "I've missed you, Iliana."

"Appa," she said, scrunching her nose against my cheek.

"She's trying to give you a kiss. That's her latest thing," Sloan said.

Everything hard and manly in me turned to mush. "I love it so much."

I hadn't seen Sloan since the battle at Echo-5, many years ago for me in Eden's time. She wore a dark floral sundress cut shorter in the front to show off her tanned legs. Her chocolate-brown hair was wavy with golden tones catching the sunlight.

She smiled. "Welcome home, Appa."

I reached for her. "Come here." I pulled her against my side and pressed a kiss to her temple. "God, I've missed you guys."

Sloan clutched the front of my shirt. "We've missed you too."

Chimera and Adrianne were standing in the doorway. Chimera pointed at me. "You promised, Parish. No more tears."

I laughed and shook my head. "I'm not even sorry. How'd you get here so fast?"

"Az asked me to leave early with them this morning so we could surprise you."

I looked around for my father. He'd been there when we got off the plane. Just off the porch, he was holding Fury. Her face was away from us, but I could tell from the rattle of her shoulders, she was crying.

My heart broke.

"How is she?" Sloan asked, concerned.

I shrugged. "How do you think?"

"Hated to hear what happened to her dad," Nathan said.

"You knew?"

He nodded. "Az told me, but he didn't tell the others. He knew she wouldn't want to deal with it. He sent Enzo in a with a crew to clean it up."

"You're both OK, though?" Adrianne asked.

"Yeah. She's got a few cuts and scrapes, but all my wounds healed." I looked down at my daughter. "I'm perfect now. Thank you all for this."

"Come on," Adrianne said, opening the door into the living room wide. "Let's give Fury and Az some privacy."

I followed everyone inside.

"What happened?" Nathan asked.

"I think Flint had an aneurysm. He was gone before the helicopter hit the ground." I took off my sword and satchel, then sat down with Iliana on the sofa. "Which is all the reasons Azrael warns me not to fly."

Sloan and Nathan sat down beside me. "You can't blame yourself, Warren. Aneurysms don't just pop up. It's not your fault."

I nodded, wishing I could believe her.

"I wish I could help her." Sloan's face fell. She knew how hard it was to lose a parent.

"Never thought I'd hear you say that," Nathan said.

"Fury has some sharp edges, but she's not all bad. She helped me a lot." Sloan looked up at me. "If there's anything I can do, will you let me know?"

"Of course."

"Will this change your plans?" Nathan asked.

"I have no idea. It won't stop her from going, and I really don't want her to fly alone, but Az is right. It's too dangerous. And now I don't have a passport or anything."

"I can get you a new one, but it'll take a couple of days, and I have to be in New Hope to do it," Chimera said.

"Thanks. I'll talk to Az later." I turned Iliana around on my lap to face me. "Right now, I want to soak all this in." I bounced my knees, making her giggle.

"How old is she?" Chimera asked from the love seat.

"She just turned one last week," Sloan answered.

Nathan started laughing. "Sloan, show Warren the video of her birthday party."

"Which video?" she asked.

"The birthday crown."

"That's on Dad's phone, remember?"

"Damn. That's so funny."

"I've got a picture," Adrianne said, standing up and walking to the kitchen.

Nathan leaned forward to look around Sloan. "Adrianne bought Iliana this silver-and-pink jeweled crown for her birthday party."

"Iliana hated it," Sloan said.

I grinned. "Wonder where she gets that?"

Sloan raised her hand.

"Every time Adrianne would put it on her head, Illy would scowl," Nathan said, making a mean face. "Like she'd be chatty and giggling one second, and then Adrianne would put the crown on her, and boom. Angry baby."

Adrianne walked over and showed me the screen of her phone. On it was a picture of Iliana wearing the crown with a death glare on her face. "Just like her mama," Adrianne said.

"That's hysterical."

"Did Nathan tell you she's standing now?" Sloan asked.

"No. Really?"

"Yeah. Put her down on the floor," she said.

I slid off the sofa onto the rug, and Nathan pushed the coffee table out of the way.

"Sit her down, and let her pull up with your hands," Sloan said.

Adrianne held out her phone. "Everyone smile for the video."

I waved Iliana's hand toward the camera. "You have to send me that, OK?"

"Of course."

I put Iliana in the middle of the rug, but before I let her pull up using my hands, she frowned and crawled back to my lap. Everyone "awed," including me.

After hugging her again, I pointed to the floor. "Can you show Appa how you stand up?"

Her head fell to the side with a look of confusion.

"Stand up?"

Her lips puckered. *"Pelu nil."*

My mouth fell open. "You little smarty."

"Did she just say stand up?" Chimera asked.

"Yep."

"Warren told me on the way here that Iliana called out to him in the spirit world yesterday," Nathan told Sloan.

"Really?" Sloan asked.

"Yeah," I said.

She touched my arm. "She kept saying your name over and over. That must have been why."

"It was the best sound in the world."

"She says *mama* now, so I totally get it." Sloan got up. "Come here, Illy."

Iliana shook her head, making everyone laugh.

"Come here. Show Appa how you can stand up." She picked Iliana up and put her down on the floor again. I held out my hands, and Iliana crawled toward them. Then she grasped my fingers and pulled herself up to standing.

We all clapped and cheered.

"Babe, where's your phone?" Nathan asked Sloan.

"Check the crack in the couch cushions," Sloan said.

A second later, Nathan started chuckling. "Warren, put her down again, but this time, don't help her."

"Don't help her?"

"No."

I put Iliana on the floor between me and her mother.

"Stand up, Illy," Nathan said.

She frowned.

Chimera crossed her arms. "She's wondering what's wrong with you all."

"Probably," I said. "Iliana, *pelu nil.*"

She flopped forward onto her hands and knees, then pushed up onto her feet. But then she was stuck with her butt straight up in the air.

"Watch this." Nathan held up Sloan's phone and "Uptown Funk" flooded the living room.

Iliana's bottom started to bounce while she was on all fours like some sort of baby yoga-slash-Jazzercize.

We all laughed.

She finally toppled over onto her side and rolled onto her back. I snatched her up and looked back at Nathan. "Parenting is just one giant experiment to make you laugh, isn't it?"

He was almost in tears. "Pretty much."

I kissed her cheek. *"Appa umai alis."*

"Me Appa," she said, patting my cheeks.

The back door opened, and Fury and Azrael walked in. Her face was red, and her eyes were puffy. She sniffed and wiped her nose on the back of her hand. "What's so funny in here?"

It felt a little wrong to be so happy.

"Warren, put Iliana down again," Nathan said. "This can brighten anyone's day."

Maybe he was right. I put Iliana back on the floor, and she danced again. Fury smiled as Adrianne handed her a tissue.

When I caught Fury's eye, I patted the seat I'd vacated behind me. She came over and sat down.

Azrael pointed at my sword on the floor. "Want me to put that somewhere safe until you and Fury leave town?"

"Sure. Where will you put it?"

He leaned down and picked up the sword. "Will a half-ton steel-and-high-Z safe do?"

"It certainly will." I lifted Cassiel's bag. "Can you put this in there too?"

"But what if you need your *manpons*, Warren?" Nathan asked.

"Nate, I'd flip you off if I weren't holding my baby," I said.

When Azrael had gone, Adrianne looked around the room. "This is the first time we've all been together in quite a while."

"And the first time in *never* that it hasn't been in some huge crisis," Nathan said.

Adrianne's head tilted. "You're probably right."

"Do you really think it's possible you can come back and stay?" Sloan asked me.

"I'm not getting my hopes up just yet, but it certainly looks like more of a possibility than it did yesterday. This blood stone is revolutionary. If we can get more of it, I'd love to come back permanently."

"Whoa. Whoa. Whoa." Nathan held up his hands. "Have we *really* thought this all the way through?"

I looked back at him and smiled. "Are you worried, Nate?"

"Hell yeah, I'm worried."

Everyone laughed.

"Don't be. I know Sloan is right where she's supposed to

be." I let Iliana clap my hands together. "All I want is a chance to be a father."

"Just as long as we're clear. We"—he waved his hand between himself and Sloan—"will live at Echo-5, and you can live somewhere *waaaay* over there." He flung his hand wide to the right.

I laughed.

"I hear Tryon is lovely," he added.

"You got it, Nate."

Azrael returned and sat in his recliner. "So what's the plan for the rest of the day?"

I wanted to do nothing but sit in the floor and hold my baby, but I knew that wasn't possible. "We have to get to Oregon tomorrow to catch the flight to South Korea with the team. That means I have to see Shannon tonight."

"Shannon Green?" Adrianne asked, surprised.

"Or whatever her last name is now," I said. "Didn't she get married?"

"Yeah. I talked to her husband this morning when I heard you'd be here today," Nathan answered. "He said they'd be home all day and to text him when we're on our way."

"You ready for this?" I asked with a grin.

He sighed and shook his head. "I feel like I'm taking my life into my hands. I considered wearing a cup."

"Nathan," Sloan chided, rolling her eyes.

"Speaking of people taking their lives into their hands..." Nathan pointed at Azrael. "Did you talk to your father about him trying to get himself killed?"

"I wasn't *trying* to get myself killed," Azrael argued.

"You were standing in a bathtub full of water about to drop a hair dryer into it, while my daughter watched," Nathan said.

"We talked about it," I said. "And he won't do it anymore. Right, Az?"

He rolled his eyes. "Right."

Fury cleared her throat behind me. "Sloan, is it true you got your powers back?"

Sloan looked surprised that Fury was speaking directly to her; they'd never gotten along. Or maybe, like me, she was surprised that Fury was speaking *at all*.

Sloan hid her hands in her lap. "It's debatable."

"I saw you do it in Azrael's memory stone," I said.

"Well, something happened in that electrical storm, but no one knows what," she said.

"Can you show us?" I asked.

She hesitated.

"Oh, come on. It's not a gathering of friends without Sloan whipping out the party tricks," Adrianne teased.

"Only if you want to," Nathan said gently to his wife. Then he looked over at me. "I'm afraid we've all worn her out with it the last couple of months."

He probably meant Azrael.

"Only if you want to," I repeated.

Sloan slowly raised her hands, palms facing each other. Then she pressed her eyes closed. A second later, a bright white light sizzled to life, crackling in the space between her hands.

Azrael was mesmerized. Like a starving man watching the Food Network. Iliana squealed, kicking her feet.

"Try to summon someone," Fury said to Sloan.

Part of Fury's gift was to see how angels used their powers. If Sloan was, indeed, tapping into her old summoning power, Fury would be able to see it.

Sloan's light fizzled out. "Summon who?"

Fury shrugged. "I dunno. Anyone. It doesn't matter as long as they're human. Summon Chimera."

"Huh?" Chimera asked.

"No, she's not completely human," Azrael said. "Summon Fury."

Sloan chewed on the side of her bottom lip. I wondered if

she was nervous she'd fail. Or if she was still afraid of Fury. It was probably a combination of both. Nevertheless, she closed her eyes, and her brow pinched with concentration.

I scooted to the side so I could watch.

Fury's eyes seemed to trace a path between them. "I see it. It's faint, but the power's there."

"I knew it." Azrael clapped his hands together.

Nathan pointed at him. "Don't get any ideas there, sparky."

Azrael cracked a slight smile.

"Do you think it's something she can improve?" I asked Fury.

Fury lifted her shoulders. "We've seen her improve in the past."

That was probably the closest Fury had ever come to paying Sloan a compliment, even an indirect one.

"What if it's harmful for Iliana?" Sloan asked.

"The Father was there," Azrael said. "If it was going to be an issue, he would have put a stop to it when it happened."

Sloan looked at me for confirmation.

"I think he's right." I looked down at Iliana. She was watching her momma, mesmerized. "She clearly loves it."

Sloan was quiet for a moment. "I don't want to get everyone's hopes up to just be a disappointment."

Nathan and I replied almost in perfection unison, "You could never be a disappointment." At the same time Fury said, "She has a point."

Everyone burst out laughing. Even Sloan. "Thank God," she said. "You were being so nice I was beginning to worry you'd been possessed by a demon."

Fury smiled, crossing her boots at the ankles. "You're safe another day, Sloan."

Picking up Iliana, I sat on the couch again by Fury. "Do I still have a go-bag packed at the command center?" she asked.

Azrael answered "yes" and I answered "no" at the same

time. They both looked at me. "Cassiel and I took your bag with us when we went to Italy. She wore your clothes," I said.

Fury scowled, a look she did well.

"Sorry. Desperate times. We were in a rush to save the world, you know."

"I need to go shopping then. Everything I had burned in the crash," she said.

"Me too. We'll go after Shannon's. Nate, can I borrow my car?" I asked.

"It's already here." He pointed out the window. "We decided to store it in Az's barn. It's not really practical with an infant."

I kissed the head of the infant in my lap.

"I heard he's driving a minivan now," Fury said, looking across me at Nathan.

I grinned. "Seriously?"

He sat back in his seat. "Hey, don't judge me. Babies have a lot of shit." He pointed at her. "Just wait. It'll be your turn soon enough."

She smirked. "Over my dead body."

"A minivan?" I asked him.

He pointed at Sloan. "She drives it. I still have my truck."

I shook my head, then looked at Fury. "We'll take my car to Shannon's, then swing by the store on our way back."

"Sounds like a plan. You ready to go now?" she asked.

I looked down at Iliana. "No."

"We'll still be here when you get back," Sloan said from the floor.

"We'd planned to pick up something to grill for dinner and invite a few of the SF-12 guys over, but I'm not sure if that's still a good idea." Adrianne's eyes flashed toward Fury behind me.

I looked back at her. "What do you think?"

"You guys can do whatever you want. I'm fine."

Her refusal to meet my eyes indicated otherwise, but I

nodded. "I think grilling out sounds great." With a heavy sigh, I looked at Iliana. "Guess I gotta go to work, little girl."

"No," she said perfectly.

I laughed. "No?"

"No."

I kissed her head. "I'll be back."

Sloan got up and took her from me. Nathan stood and kissed them both goodbye.

"Az, you coming?" I asked.

"No. I won't be of any use at Shannon's. Just let me know what you think when you see the child. If it's truly an angel, we'll need to take precautions."

"OK."

"Chimera, why don't you go with them?" Azrael said. "If you and Warren both go all the way to Flat Rock, leaving Iliana here wearing the necklace, we should know if it really protects her or not."

Chimera stood. "Sure."

"Where are the keys to the car?" Nathan asked Azrael.

He got up and walked to the kitchen as I started toward the front door. A dark spot on the wall drew my attention. I stopped.

The wall was scorched black around an electrical outlet near the door. When I looked back at Azrael returning from the kitchen, guilt was etched across his face.

"Did you do this too?" I asked.

"It was a faulty cell phone charger," he lied as he handed me my old key ring.

"Really?"

He slowly shook his head.

I jabbed my finger into his breastbone. "No more."

"I promise." He stepped around us and opened the front door. "Call me when you're on your way back."

"We're planning to eat around seven," Adrianne said. "Any special requests?"

I smiled back at Sloan. "Just that my family's here."

"We're not going anywhere," she said. "Illy, tell Appa bye-bye."

Instead, she blew me a kiss.

CHAPTER ELEVEN

"*O*h no. No, no, no, no, no."

Shannon Green—or whatever her last name was now—tried to slam her front door. Nathan McNamara slid his boot in the doorway to stop it.

A baby wailed somewhere in the house.

"Shannon, you knew we were coming," he said.

"The hell I did."

To be fair, it was clear she *didn't* know we were coming. I'd never seen Shannon be anything less than camera ready. Perfect hair. Flawless makeup. Clothes straight off a runway.

Even piss-ass drunk that one time in San Antonio, she'd still looked better than she did right now.

The blonde hair she usually kept meticulously sculpted was lopsided and matted underneath like it hadn't seen a brush *ever*. Her face was *au naturale* with dark heavy bags under her eyes. And her clothes...hell, both shoulders of her holey sweatshirt were covered in baby puke.

Inside, the crying waned to a whimper.

Shannon's entire body relaxed. "Thank God he's finally stopped."

"He cries a lot?" I asked.

That was when her tired eyes fell on me. "Warren? Good lord, aren't you supposed to be dead?"

I held up both hands and wiggled my fingers. "Surprise."

She tried to push the door closed again.

Nathan flattened his palm against it. "I talked to Reese and told him we were stopping by today."

"He did, he did." A tall black guy walked up the hallway behind her. "Hey, Nate. Good to see you, man." He stretched out his hand as he moved between his wife and the door.

Nathan shook it. "Hey, Reese."

"Sorry for the confusion. I knew if I warned her, she'd freak out."

Shannon put her fists on her hips and turned toward him. "Are you serious?"

Reese put his hands on her shoulders. "You know what the doctor said. Our son is different. Nate warned us this might happen. We need to hear them out."

Shannon's gaping mouth snapped closed.

"Come on in." Reese pulled the door open all the way. He saw Fury and Chimera standing behind me. "You brought friends."

"Hopefully, we can get this over with in one trip." Nathan walked inside first. "Reese, this is my daughter's biological father, Warren Parish."

Reese offered me his hand. "Tyrell Reese. I've heard a lot about you lately."

I wanted to say I knew absolutely nothing about him or how he wound up married to Nathan's ex-girlfriend, but I didn't. I shook his hand as I walked inside. Then I gestured toward Fury. "This is my..."

I had no idea how to introduce her.

Shannon beat me to it. "This is Warren's ex-girlfriend. Her name is *Angry*."

Nathan couldn't stifle a laugh. He clamped his hand over his mouth.

"My name is Fury," Fury corrected her.

"Same thing," Shannon hissed.

I grinned. "And this is our friend, Chimera."

"That's a cool name," Reese said.

Shannon rolled her eyes. "I doubt it's real."

"She's pleasant, isn't she?" Chimera asked.

Nathan looked around the floor. "Where's that demonic ankle biter of yours?"

Shannon's nostrils flared. "Baby Dog is at my mother's until we can handle both the dog and the baby."

Reese leaned toward Nathan. "Which will honestly be *never*."

"That dog is evil," Nathan muttered.

Reese nodded. "Like Gargamel-level evil."

"More like Abaddon-level evil."

"Who?" Reese looked understandably confused.

Nathan's eyes widened. "Never mind. Where's the baby?"

I chuckled. Fury sighed and shook her head.

"Why do you want to see the baby?" Shannon demanded. "What's going on?"

Nathan lowered his voice. "We just want to see him. Nobody will even touch him without your permission. I promise." He sounded like a hostage negotiator.

"He's in the living room, and he's finally calmed down." Reese led us down the hall. "The kid has done nothing but cry since he was born three days ago."

"Not surprising," Fury said not-so-quietly behind me.

"Why?" Nathan asked.

"Jett cried nonstop for the first few days. The baby's going through withdrawal."

"Withdrawal?" Shannon spun around so fast Nathan nearly ran over her. "Who do you think I am, lady?"

I looked back over my shoulder and frowned at Fury.

Fury took a step back. "I *really* meant no offense."

"But you think I'm a drug addict? A drunk?" Shannon was teetering on hysterics.

Fury looked at me for help? To defuse the situation? I wasn't sure. I was tempted to leave her out on her limb. I'd reminded her in the car: Shannon didn't know how very real angels were—or that her newborn son was one.

"No one thinks you're an addict or a drunk. But we do agree with the doctors. Your son's different," I said gently.

Tears brimmed in Shannon's eyes. Reese curled his arm around her shoulders. "Babe, it'll be OK." He kissed the side of her head. "Trust me."

Good thing he was so confident. Even if their son was an angel, there was no way to tell if he was a good spirit or an evil one.

"Come on," Reese said, steering Shannon toward the living room.

The living room looked almost as disheveled as Shannon. A bassinet was crammed between the coffee table and love seat. A bouncy seat was on its side near the TV. And a diaper bag lay open on the sofa, its contents strewn across the cushions and spilling over onto the carpet.

"It's been a rough time for you, hasn't it?" I asked, genuinely sympathetic.

"Shut up, Warren," Shannon snapped.

Her husband caught my eye and mouthed the word "sorry."

"It's OK." I didn't have to ask where the baby was. I could feel his presence in the bassinet. I walked over and looked down into it.

The baby boy was wide awake, his dark eyes searching as far as his tiny neck would stretch. His gaze locked on me, and he smiled and kicked his feet.

I spoke to him telepathically. *"Can you hear me?"*

The baby didn't even blink.

We'd determined when Fury's son was born, that angels in infancy can recognize the inaudible voices of other angels in their choir. Jett was an Angel of Protection, we were almost 100 percent certain, because it seemed he could "hear" Reuel.

This kid couldn't "hear" me, but it was clear from the smile on his face, he knew I was like him. Maybe he was just thankful for the break in the migraine.

"What do you call him?" I asked.

"Reginald Nicolas Green-Reese the Fourth," Shannon answered with a sniffle.

My brow crumpled with confusion.

Nathan looked as perplexed as I felt. "Reginald Nicolas Green-Reese the *Fourth*?"

"Reginald Nicolas Green is a family name," Shannon explained.

"*Her* family's name," Reese clarified if there was any question.

Shannon began counting on her fingers. "My grandfather was Reginald Nicolas Green the First, my dad was Reginald Nicolas Green Junior, and my brother is Reginald Nicolas Green the Third. It only made sense that I have the Fourth."

Made sense. Sure.

Chimera leaned toward Nathan's ear. "She knows that's not the way it works, right?"

Nathan didn't move his lips when he replied, "I don't think so."

I just grinned and looked down at the baby again.

"Don't get me started. I only agreed if we could call him Nico. The rest wasn't worth the battle," Reese said.

"Nico. I like it," I said.

Reese moved the coffee table out of the way, then came over and stood beside me. "Unbelievable. I think that's the first time he's smiled."

Shannon rushed over, pushing me aside. "What? Smiling?" Her excitement faded quickly. "He's not smiling."

"He *was*," Reese said, stressing the past-tenseness of it.

With a loud whine, Shannon's knees buckled, and Reese caught her around the waist. "My baby doesn't love me!"

Fury swore, and Chimera rolled her eyes.

"She's so tired," he said with an apologetic smile as he dragged her to the sofa. "Shannon, baby, he does love you..."

I tuned him out and turned toward my friends. Fury had approached the bassinet and was now leaning over it. "Mind if I hold him?" she asked his parents.

I was so shocked I could've fallen onto the floor.

"Go ahead," Reese said, still crouched in front of his wife and holding both of her hands. "But if he starts screaming, don't take it personally. He's been better today, finally, but it's pretty nonstop."

Fury carefully lifted the tiny baby out of the bed and cradled him carefully in her arms. "He won't scream. Warren's here."

Reginald Nicolas Green-Reese IV reached his hand up toward Fury's tan cheek. She bent her head to meet his fingers, and she smiled.

Holy hell. Watching her with him was mesmerizing. Like she'd suddenly morphed into someone else altogether. Something Azrael had said once upon a time floated to mind. *"Parenthood changes people, son. Never discount that."*

She carried him to the love seat and sat down, making cooing noises at him.

"You seeing this or am I hallucinating?" Nathan asked quietly beside me.

"If you're hallucinating, so am I."

"I know I don't know her too well, but this is weird, isn't it?" Chimera asked.

"Oh yeah," Nate and I said together.

"Baby Nico is an angel, but I don't know what kind," I said. "He's not an Angel of Death."

Perhaps I didn't speak softly enough because the conversation on the sofa ended abruptly. When I looked past Nate, Shannon and Reese were staring at us with wide, fearful eyes.

"What did you say?" Shannon asked.

Shit.

"Oh boy," Nathan said with a chuckle.

Shannon got up, and Reese stepped out of her way. She came over and dug her fingernails into my arm. "Did you just say my baby is an Angel of Death?"

My head tilted. "Technically I said he's *not* an Angel of Death."

"Oh no!" She pointed a red fingernail at the tip of my nose. "Sloan tried to feed me this angel nonsense before. It didn't work then, and it won't work now."

I pushed her finger away from my face. "It isn't nonsense, and if you know what's good for you and your son, you'll listen to me."

"You might want to sit back down," Nathan said, taking her arm gently. He guided her backward toward Reese again. Together, they sat on the sofa.

"I want them gone," Shannon said to Reese.

"Let's hear them out," he replied gently. Reese looked at me. "Please have a seat."

I walked to the kitchen—where the sink was piled high with dishes—and picked up a dining chair. I carried it back to the living room, put it facing the worried couple, and sat down.

"Warren, you're scaring me," Shannon admitted.

"I don't mean to scare you. And I'm sorry this is all very hard to understand. I promise you, everything Sloan told you, and everything I'm about to tell you, is true."

"He's right. I can vouch for him," Nathan said.

"Like your word means *anything* at all to me, Nathan McNa-mara," Shannon fired back at her ex-boyfriend.

"Fair enough. But Reese, you trust me, don't you?" Nathan asked.

"With my life," Reese said.

"How do you two know each other?" Fury asked behind me.

"We were on the police force together in Raleigh for several years before he moved here," Reese answered.

"And you married his ex-girlfriend? Geez, this group is like a living episode of *Wife Swap*." Fury's tone was full of derision.

"Moving on." I shook my head. "Bottom line is, we need you to keep an open mind if you want what's best for Nico."

"Start explaining," Reese said skeptically.

I leaned forward and balanced my elbows on my knees, clasping my hands together. "Shannon, do you remember when you went with me and Sloan and Nathan to San Antonio?"

"Of course. You guys stumbled onto that sex-trafficking business and busted it up."

"Yes, but we didn't exactly stumble onto it. I mean, we weren't out looking for it, but the woman who ran it was Sloan's biological mother."

Her face twisted with confusion. "What? But she was our age."

"I know. Her body didn't age normally because she was an Angel of Life."

"Here we go," Shannon said, rolling her eyes as she flopped back against the sofa.

"Do you remember the conversation we had at that Irish bar when Sloan was asking you about angels?"

"No."

That wasn't surprising. Shannon was shitfaced that night.

"You told us you'd known about angels all your life," I said.

"So?"

"You told *us* about them. You believed in them before we

ever did."

She scowled.

"You were right. Angels are real. As real as you are."

She opened her mouth to object, but Nathan spoke first. "Come on. You were preaching at us that night about how they're real. What did your church teach you?"

She huffed. "The Bible says to be nice to strangers because you might be entertaining angels."

"Correct. I didn't know it then, but..." I took a deep breath. "Shannon, I'm the Archangel of Death."

Silence. Dead silence.

Shannon and Reese both seemed frozen. I looked at Nate, who was standing beside me. His eyes were wide, so was his smile, waiting for Shannon's reaction.

After a moment of staring, Shannon burst out laughing. Hysterical laughter. "Oh wow, did Sloan put you up to this? Did Adrianne?" She fanned her eyes.

We all waited for her to finish.

Nathan cupped his hand around his mouth. "Do the light-ball thing," he said in a loud whisper.

"This isn't a joke. What Sloan told you was the truth," I said instead.

Reese rubbed his hands down his face, pulling his mouth into a deep frown. "What does this have to do with our son?"

I cleared my throat. "Your son is an angel as well."

Shannon's giggles finally faded. And her face was suddenly caught somewhere between hilarity and terror. "You're insane! All of you! Completely crazy!" She stood and marched past me. I turned and watched her rip the baby from Fury's arms. "Get out! Get out of my house now!"

I stood. "We really need to talk about this."

"Shannon, you're going to scare the baby," Reese added, approaching her cautiously.

Tears streamed down Shannon's cheeks. "This is crazy talk! I want you all out of my house right now."

Reese turned toward me. "Maybe you should go."

I nodded.

Nathan stepped between us. "But that baby will start screaming again once Warren leaves town. He's having migraines for which there is no medical cure. Mark my words. You'll want to call us."

Reese didn't look convinced, but he nodded.

I looked over at Fury and Chimera. "Let's go."

Shannon stayed behind in the living room with the baby as the three of us walked to the front door with Reese. "I'm really sorry," he said to me. "She's just been—"

I held up a hand to stop him. "No apologies necessary. It's a lot to take in for anyone. Just know I'm telling you the truth, and we can make the next eighteen years of your life much easier if you'll let us."

He looked like he wanted to ask us to stay, but just then, his wife called his name.

"Nathan knows how to reach me," I said.

He nodded, and we walked back out into the bright sunshine. The door closed behind us.

"That went well," Fury said with a smile as we walked back to my car.

I used the key fob to unlock the doors. "It went as well as we expected it to."

"What will you do now?" Nathan asked. "Get Reuel to come meet the kid?"

"Probably not. It won't do us much good to know the kid's lineage yet. Certainly not worth the added stress." Before getting in the car, I stopped and looked across the hood at him. "Have you heard from Sloan?"

He pulled out his cell phone. "Yeah." He read the screen. "Iliana's fine. No migraine symptoms at all."

I let my face drop back toward the sky. "Yes!"

"Did you doubt me?" Chimera asked behind Nathan.

I pulled open my door. "Hey, when you've had as shitty luck in life as I have, you begin to doubt everything."

Fury put her hand on the small of my back. "I'm really happy for you."

"I'm really happy for myself," I said, moving aside to let her get in first.

Inside, through the walls and the distance, I heard the baby cry. Everyone else must have heard it too because they all stopped and looked back at the house.

"You're still here. Think he's got a migraine already?" Nathan asked.

Fury angled to get in the back behind my driver's seat. "The kid's probably freaking out because his mother's batshit crazy."

I tried not to laugh, but failed.

As I pushed my seat back into place, the front door swung open again. Reese was standing in the doorway with his hand up. "Wait!"

"That didn't take long," Chimera said inside the car.

Reese came out onto the porch. "He's crying again. Please wait."

Chimera and I were still too close for the kid's migraine to have returned so quickly. Fury was probably right; Shannon had probably scared the shit out of him. Whatever the reason, I was glad for the invitation back inside.

I pulled the seat lever again to let Fury get back out. Then I started toward the house.

Reese was shaking his head. "I can't take any more of the screaming...from either of them. I want to hear what you have to say."

"All right." I said, and we followed him back inside. Shannon was bouncing Nico in her arms. He was still crying. So was she. I held out my hands. "May I?"

Shannon pulled him away from me.

"Give him the baby, Shannon. Please," Reese begged.

Poor guy. He looked like his ears might start bleeding.

Shannon hesitated again and looked at my outstretched hands. Finally, she huffed, and passed me the baby.

Nico instantly hushed as I laid him against my chest. He was so tiny. Barely bigger than my hands.

"How do you do that?" Shannon asked with a whimper.

"He cries because of the absence of the power of the spirit world. Fury was correct when she said it was a form of withdrawal. Has he had seizures?" I asked.

Her head jerked. "How did you know that?"

"Because Sloan and I have both had them before with the migraines," I said.

"Warren had one this morning," Fury added.

"Iliana's had them too," Nathan said.

Shannon's face whipped toward him. "Iliana is an angel?"

He nodded. "Remember the record-breaking rainstorms last year? It rains when Iliana cries."

"Really?" Chimera asked.

"Oh yeah. Monsoon," Nathan said.

She smiled. "That's awesome."

Shannon pressed her fingertips against her temples and walked back to the couch. "This is too much."

I eased the baby onto his back, cradling him against my forearm. He was smiling again. "I didn't believe it when I first found out either. I meant it when I said you believed in angels before we ever did."

"Maybe I don't believe in them as much as I thought I did," Shannon admitted.

I smiled. That may have been the most genuine thing I'd ever heard her say. "As my father says, that doesn't make it any less true."

"Your father?" Reese asked.

"His name's Azrael."

"His name is Damon Claymore," Fury corrected me from where she was leaning in the living-room doorway.

"Yeah. You're right."

"Damon Claymore? The guy Adrianne is having the baby with?" Shannon asked.

I nodded.

"He's your father?" she asked.

I nodded again.

"But you look like brothers!"

Reese looked at her. "He already told you they don't age the same as us."

"Azrael, or Damon, will age normally now," I said. "He's no longer an angel. His job passed to me."

"An Angel of Death?" Reese asked.

"Yes."

Reese blew out a sigh that puffed out his cheeks. "But Nico isn't an Angel of Death?"

"I don't think so."

"So you're telling us he's like Sloan?" Shannon asked. "An Angel of...what did you say? Of Life?"

"He could be, but there are seven choirs of angels in Eden—"

"What's Eden?" Shannon asked.

"Heaven," Nathan and Fury answered together.

"Correct, but we call it Eden," I said. "Nico could have the powers of any one of the choirs in Heaven."

"What is Iliana?" Shannon's voice had lost its cynical edge.

"Iliana is both Angel of Life and Death because of Sloan and Warren." Nathan smiled with pride. "She's the most powerful angel that's ever existed."

"Does she have a weird blood type?" Reese asked.

"Yes. Rh-null. All angels have it. Did Nico have a blood test?" I asked.

Reese and Shannon were looking at each other. "Yes," Reese

said. "We took him back in after we brought him home from the hospital because he wouldn't stop crying. The doctors freaked out about it. Said that blood type is really rare."

"They call it golden blood," Nathan said.

"Is it dangerous?" Shannon asked.

Fury laughed. "Not for your kid. He's immortal."

There was an odd squeak. I was pretty sure it was from Shannon's throat.

"Immortal?" she asked.

"He's existed from the beginning of time. They aren't easy to kill," Fury said.

"Hold up. From the beginning of time?" Reese asked.

"She's right," I said. "New angels are exceedingly rare. I guess there have only been three since creation."

"Four," Fury said.

We all looked at her.

"My sister."

"Correct. Four new angels that we know of," I said.

"Five," Nathan said. He pointed at me. "You."

"Shit. You're right." I turned back to Shannon and Reese, who looked thoroughly bewildered. "I was born part-angel, part-human."

Nathan jumped in. "But then he was shot to death back in—"

"Will you two shut up?" Fury asked. "Information overload. Bottom line, new angels usually aren't created."

"Yes. But angels from Eden can choose to be born on Earth into human bodies. That's what my father did several millennia ago. It makes them incredibly powerful," I said.

Shannon's face wilted. "So my baby isn't my baby?"

I grimaced. "Well..."

"He will have your DNA," Chimera said.

"Both of them?" Nathan asked.

Chimera shook her head. "Only the mother's."

Reese rubbed both hands down his face.

Chimera continued. "Other than that, the only difference right now is he has an angelic spirit instead of a human one."

"That, and he's lived for millions of years," Nathan mumbled.

I looked over at him. "Not helping."

Nathan folded his arms. "Helping isn't why I came today. I'm here for the show."

I probably would have laughed had the threat of more tears not been so very real in the room. After a second of resetting my composure, I returned my attention to the worried couple. "Think of it this way. You've been given a huge honor. Out of all the families in this world"—I lifted the baby slightly—"one supreme being chose you."

That seemed to comfort Shannon, even if only a little. I stood and carried the baby over to her. His eyes were open, and when she took him, he was smiling.

"Let's say we believe you." Reese took a deep breath. "How do we raise an angel?"

"Nate, wanna take this one?" I asked.

Nathan thought for a moment. "I'm probably the last person to ask for parenting advice. Any day I put Illy to bed with all ten fingers and toes still intact, I consider a win."

Shannon turned to face her husband and flung her hand toward Nate. "If he can do it, anyone can."

"She has a valid point," Nathan said out of the corner of his mouth.

"Fury, Chimera, do you have anything more helpful to add?" I asked. "Fury, you said Jett is pretty normal."

Fury straightened in the door. "He is. Once the migraines pass—"

"They go away?" Reese asked.

"Yeah. And as long as other angels stay away"—she pointed at me—"he shouldn't have them anymore."

"But the migraines have stopped since Warren has been here," Shannon said, a bit reluctantly.

"And they'll start again whenever I leave town." They would start again for me too, but I really didn't want to think about that now. "If he starts having them again, please let Nathan know."

"Why?" Reese asked.

Nathan and I exchanged a glance. I knew we were thinking the same thing. Migraines could mean *other* angels were present in the area. Unwelcome angels. Dangerous angels.

"We might need to adjust Iliana's and Nico's proximity to each other. Prolonged exposure to other angels can be unhealthy when they're children," Nathan said.

I was impressed. Nathan's reasoning was both evasive and factual. Azrael was rubbing off on him.

"We also have resources to help you guys going forward," he continued. "Information, security, medical personnel...whatever you need."

"Why would we need help?" Reese asked.

Nathan shrugged. "Hopefully, you won't, but as you've probably already learned, medical care, in particular, is tricky when your child is different."

Reese pinched the bridge of his nose and pressed his eyes closed.

Nathan walked over and put his hand on Reese's shoulder. "I know it's a lot to stomach, but I'm here, man."

Reese nodded and smiled up at his old friend.

"He is a cute kid," Chimera said, looking at the baby.

"Yeah, he is." Reese slipped his arm around Shannon's shoulders and kissed the side of her head. For a long, quiet moment, they both stared at their son.

"Warren?" Shannon cut her eyes up at me. They were still sparkling with confused and frightened tears. "Why us?"

For that, I didn't have an answer.

CHAPTER TWELVE

"So when are we going to talk about Adrianne?" Nathan asked on our way back to my father's. We'd stopped at a sporting-goods store to replace the gear and clothes Fury and I had lost in the crash.

I stared straight ahead. "What are you talking about?"

Nathan scowled. "You've always been a shit liar, Warren Parish. You know what I'm talking about."

I rested my wrist across the top of the steering wheel. "What makes you think there's something with Adrianne?"

"Iliana knows that baby is different, and she's starting to get headaches whenever Adrianne leaves. Not quite migraines yet, but definitely headaches."

My heart twisted.

"I've not been around many kids before," Chimera said. "How do you tell when a baby has a headache?"

"She cries a lot, holds her head, and pulls at her ears. Sometimes, she bangs her head on the bars of her crib or on our chests if we're holding her. It's really pitiful."

I gripped the steering wheel. "God, I hate that."

"Me too, so tell me why it's happening."

I laid my head against the headrest and focused on the road ahead. The sharp curves of the mountains. The steep cliffs off the roadside. I wanted to tell him. But I couldn't.

"Warren, I mean it," he said.

"Azrael doesn't want Adrianne to know."

"The baby's an angel."

I just stared ahead.

"Is it the Morning Star?"

My jaw tensed.

"Shit." Nathan sat back in his seat, leaned his elbow on the door, and gripped his forehead. "That's why he's been keeping Adrianne away so much. He knows what it's doing to Iliana."

"Probably so."

"What will he do?"

"Nate, you're gonna have to talk to him."

"Like he's gonna tell me anything."

True.

I looked at Fury in the rearview. She'd had lots more practice at spinning Azrael's schemes than I ever had. "If nothing else, you can trust Azrael will do whatever is necessary to keep your daughter safe," she said.

Nathan closed his eyes. "That doesn't make me feel much better. We're talking about my wife's very best friend. They're practically sisters."

"I know," I said.

"Warren, you'd better get to Nulterra and find more of that God stone. I'm going to need all the help I can get."

Fury leaned forward between the front seats. "Why can't you go to the Father and get more of the blood stone?"

"From what Moloch told us, it doesn't sound like that would be possible," Chimera said. "He limits himself here now so that he won't have the power to cause harm."

"Yeah. I'm sure if that were an option, he would've offered it already," I agreed.

I followed the directions on my GPS app and took a hard right onto the road that led to Azrael's.

At the top of the long and winding road, cars were parked like Tetris pieces near the house. I parked on the side road that went down toward the barn.

The four of us got out, and I clicked the button to open the trunk. I looked around at all the cars while I pulled out my bags. "Man, when Adrianne said we'd have dinner, I didn't realize she'd be throwing a party."

"Really?" Nathan asked. "I expected absolutely nothing less."

Fury grabbed her bags too. "It's so weird seeing Az be so *suburban*."

"I dunno." I closed the trunk, and we started toward the house. "My mom talks about Az like he was the life of the party when they were together."

Her eyes were fixed on the ground. "I don't doubt it. Flint spent a lot time with your parents when he was younger. It's just weird for me because I've only ever known him post-Nadine."

"What was he like when you met him?" Chimera asked.

"Scary. And mean as a snake."

"Really?" Nathan asked.

"Oh yeah. He used to scare the shit out of me and Anya."

It was hard for me to imagine Fury being afraid of anything.

"He can be a dick for sure, but I can't believe he'd scare little kids," I said.

"I don't even know him that well, and I wouldn't think so either," Chimera agreed.

Fury squinted against the setting sun, despite her new, cheap sunglasses. "He didn't do it on purpose. It was who he was. Or, I guess, it was who he had become."

"That was what? Five or six years after I was born, and my mother was taken by the Morning Star?"

"Plenty of time for his soul to turn black." She sighed and shook her head. "Losing what you love most does bad shit to a person."

I thought of Sloan and Iliana and shrugged. "Maybe if you let it."

Fury looked at me.

Before either of us could speak again, Nathan nudged my arm. "Hey, I just got a text from Sloan. She said Iliana's asleep, so we need to be quiet when we go inside."

"That sucks," I said.

"It won't be for long. She'll get her up when the food's ready. Trust me, you don't want to wake that kid before she's ready."

"Like her mom, then?"

He laughed. "Yeah. Lethal with the ability to do something about it."

Inside, all the doors were open, and everyone had gathered in the backyard. The air smelled like fire and charred meat. My stomach rumbled.

I touched Fury's arm, then gestured toward her bag. "Want me to take that?"

She handed it to me. "Thanks. I'll meet you out back."

"Nate, where's Iliana asleep?" I asked.

"Probably Az's room," he said.

I gave him a thumbs-up, then started in the opposite direction toward the hallway. A supernatural energy vibrated through the house, and I smiled knowing my baby girl was close.

I walked into the queen bedroom I'd once shared with Cassiel and dropped my bags and Fury's on the bed. Then I started back out to rejoin the party. As I neared the hallway's exit, the bathroom door swung open right beside me.

Reuel screamed.

I screamed.

Then the massive angel started laughing. I, however, was making sure my heart was still inside my chest. He pulled me into a massive hug, nearly crushing all the bones in my torso, and clapped his heavy hand on my back. *"Akai nun cak vera."*

It was a phrase in our language, Katavukai, similar to "long time no see." Or more closely translated to, "I haven't seen you in an eternity," which it had almost been in Eden years.

"Shh, we're supposed to be quiet," I said, reining in my own laughter.

He clapped a hand over his mouth.

"Akai kirek alis," he said quietly.

"I've missed you too, old friend." I took a step back. "But you know you can speak English now, right?"

He hooked his arm around my neck and grinned. "You know I don't want to, right?"

"When did you get here?" I asked as we walked into the living room.

"About an hour ago," he answered in English. "We saw the helicopter go down, and I spoke to Flint at the Eden Gate. How is she?"

"She's Fury. Stone cold as usual."

"Only on the outside. If Anya is dead, Flint was all she had left in the world."

"She has Jett now," I reminded him.

He shook his head sadly. "True, but still not the same. Where is she?"

"Outside, I think." I crossed my arms. "What are you doing here? You told me you didn't want any part of this."

"I still don't, but I have news."

My brow rose. "About?"

"Jett."

"News for me, or news for Fury?"

"Both."

"Is it good or bad?"

He opened his mouth, but before he could answer, I cut him off. "No, tell me after dinner. I'd like one drama free night on Earth before I leave."

He smiled. "As you wish, but I do need to ask something else unpleasant. I've seen Adrianne. Do you have something to tell me?"

I put my hand on his shoulder. "Later. I promise. Come on. Fury will want to see you." We started toward the back door. "You are coming with us to Nulterra though?"

"If I can't keep her here." He sounded exasperated.

"What changed your mind?"

He looked outside for Fury. "I've kept watch over her all her life. Can't stop now, even if she is being hard skulled."

My eyes narrowed. "Hardheaded?"

"Yes. Hardheaded." Reuel struggled with idioms and metaphors, as words were only interpreted literally through Katavukai. "Still no convincing her not to go?"

I shook my head. "No, but I've tried. So did her dad."

"It's sad about Flint. He was a nice human."

"I hate I didn't get to know him better."

"I'm sure he'd say the same about you."

"Have you seen Iliana and Sloan?"

"Only Sloan. Iliana's been asleep since I got here, but I heard it's safe to meet her. Are you excited?"

"My friend, you have no idea."

The backyard had been transformed into a party pad. Between the helicopter and the house, two folding tables were put end-to-end and covered with blue-and-white checkered tablecloths. Azrael tended the smoking grill, while Adrianne and Chimera set the table. I didn't see Sloan or Nathan anywhere.

Fury was talking to Enzo, Special Operations Director of

SF-12, and Kane, one of SF-12's most senior members. When she spotted Reuel, her lips parted, and she sucked in a shaky breath before running to him.

With a jump, she wrapped her arms around his neck.

He held her in the air for a long time, speaking quietly to her in Katavukai, which she spoke fluently. When he finally set her down, he cupped her face in his hands and used his giant thumbs to swipe away her tears.

She held onto his wrists. *"Alis tai,"* she said with the slightest hitch in her voice.

"Of course I came back," Reuel replied in perfect English.

Fury's head jerked back.

"Surprise," he said. "The Council changed the law. We're allowed to speak English now."

Fury looked at me. "Did you know?"

"I found out last night."

"I won't do it often," he said with a grin.

"Because he's terrible at it," I teased.

Reuel held up his middle finger. "Donkey hole."

"Donkey hole?" Fury asked. "I don't get it."

"Katavukai works like an international cipher for languages. Only it interprets them literally. Idioms and metaphors are lost on this guy," I said.

Fury turned back toward Reuel, her face hopeful. "Are you coming with us to Nulterra?"

"I suppose. If I can't stop you from going, I might as well try to keep you alive." He bent to look at her. "Besides, I promised your dad I would."

"You saw him?"

"Yes. He's well."

She hugged him again. "Thank you, Reuel."

I'd never seen Fury show so much affection to anyone. Not that I was jealous, or anything.

"Warren says you've been searching for angels who might

have been born on Earth." The muscles tensed in Fury's neck. "Any luck?"

He smiled, which was reassuring. "We'll talk about it after dinner."

She blew out a nervous sigh but nodded.

"Oh no! Who called the brute squad?" Nathan said behind us. Reuel and I turned as Nathan and Sloan walked off the porch.

Reuel opened his arms wide. "There's my little buddy."

Laughing, Nathan stepped into his giant arms. Reuel lifted him off the ground and spun around in a circle a few times. When he finally returned Nate's boots to the ground, Nate staggered sideways, and Reuel grabbed his shoulders to steady him.

"I've missed you too, man," Nathan said, his head still a little wobbly.

Chimera walked up beside me. "Hey, Reuel, have you met Chimera?"

He turned, looked, and looked again. Then he took a small step back. "Seramorta."

"Yep." She stuck out her hand. "Nice to meet you, Reuel. I've heard a lot about you."

"You two didn't meet at Echo-5?" Sloan asked.

He shook his head. "I'd definitely remember her. You're the one who brought the necklace?"

"Yes, she is," I said, happily.

Sloan kissed Nathan's cheek. "I'm going to finish helping Adrianne."

"I'll come with you," Nathan said.

"I can too," I offered.

Sloan waved her hand. "You two relax and catch up. It's Warren's last night on Earth for a while. There's not much to do."

"You sure?" Nathan asked.

"Positive," Sloan said with a wink.

Enzo and Kane walked over and joined our group. "Warren, good to see you. How's the back?" Enzo asked.

I twisted at the waist, side to side. "Good as new."

"What happened to your back?" Fury asked.

Enzo's face soured. "Doc and Az had to rip a lodged bullet out of his spine a few months ago. On Az's dining room table. It wasn't pretty."

Fury's sympathetic face was mocking. "Oh, and Warren's such a baby when it comes to bullets."

"Hey now," I said, offended but amused.

Fury nudged Nathan's arm. "When we were in Iraq, Warren took a round that didn't even pierce his vest, and you'd have thought it blew his chest cavity open."

The guys laughed.

I pointed at Fury. "Busted ribs are no joke."

"*Verta,*" Reuel said, nodding his head.

Enzo raised his beer. "Hear, hear."

"And I remember you being pretty sympathetic that day," I said to her.

Her sympathy wasn't the only thing I remembered. That was the first time we kissed, on base inside my sweltering and rank desert hooch. She wasn't even supposed to be there, but Fury had never been one for following rules. *Orders,* sure. But she'd never really considered herself under the jurisdiction of anyone, except for (maybe) my father, and only when she was on his payroll.

"Fury? Sympathetic?" Kane asked. "I'm calling bullshit on that one."

Nathan raised a hand. "Seconded."

"Believe what you want," Fury said with a shrug.

I pointed at her. "It was only because she wanted something."

Everyone laughed again.

Kane shoved my chest. "I'll bet she did, brother."

Shit. I rolled my eyes. "Not what I meant."

"Surrre," Kane teased.

"Are you kidding me?" Fury playfully slapped my chest. "Warren could hardly stand up, much less get anything else up that day."

There were echoes of *"Ohhh!"* and *"Burn!"* around the group. I just laughed and shook my head. Fury caught my eye and winked.

"Somebody get this man a beer to put out those flames," Enzo said, laughing as he slapped my back.

Kane handed me a bottled beer from the ice chest. I thanked him and twisted off the cap. He offered one to Fury, but she shook her head.

"Ribs are done!" Azrael called from the grill.

"Everyone find a seat at the table," Adrianne said, carrying a large bowl out of the house. "There should be plenty of chairs."

Sloan was right behind her, carrying more food. Nathan jogged over to help her.

Azrael carried the meat to the table, then took the spot at the head of the table. Adrianne sat on one side of him, and I sat on the other. Sloan and Nathan sat across from me and Fury. It was weird. Like we'd fallen into some alternate dimension.

Adrianne leaned over and pulled the tin foil off the platter of meat. Reuel's hand shot toward it. She held up a finger. "Reuel, we didn't know you were coming, so you need to start small."

He pulled an entire rack of ribs off the plate.

Adrianne's eyes doubled. "I said small!"

He turned his palms up with sad eyes that said, "This is small."

"It's OK," Azrael said. "Reuel, share those, and if you're still hungry, I have some steaks in the fridge I can throw on the grill."

Reuel turned his sad eyes toward Azrael.

Azrael huffed and pushed back from the table. "Fine. I'll start them now."

Reuel smiled as Azrael walked to the house.

Everyone started filling their plates and passing dishes around the table. Azrael carried a plate out the back door a moment later. "Hey, Sloan, I think somebody's awake in there!" he called to the table.

Sloan started to get up.

"Wait," I said. "Let me."

She smiled. "She's in Azrael and Adrianne's room."

I got up and jogged to the house. Inside, I turned left into the kitchen and walked down a short hallway to the master suite. I heard baby babble in Katavukai when I neared the door. I lingered there for a second, soaking it in.

"Appa?"

She knew I was there.

I pushed open the door and found her standing in the portable crib. "Appa!" My heart nearly burst at the sound. Her arms shot up toward me, but she lost her balance. Eyes wide with panic, she toppled backward.

I gripped her with my power before she hit the mattress, and I pulled her through the air into my arms. She giggled. "Appa."

I kissed her cheek. *"Salak, me anlo."*

I felt someone's presence behind me. "What does that mean?" Sloan asked before I could turn around.

"It means, 'Hello, my love.'" I smiled. "Did you not think I could handle this by myself?"

"No. I knew you could. I just forgot to tell you she'd probably need a new diaper." She reached for what looked like a small rucksack, complete with morale patches on the dresser. The one on the front said, "I'm not small. I'm fun size."

"What is that?"

She put it on the bed and opened it. "The diaper bag Nathan picked out. He's a mess." She reached for Iliana. "Come here. Let's change your diaper."

Sloan laid Iliana on the bed, and I sat down beside her and let her hold my finger. "You're a good mom, Sloan."

"I have a lot of help. I don't know what I'd do without Nathan and Adrianne and Dad."

"How is your dad?"

"He's good. He wanted to be here tonight, but he had a call at the hospital."

"It's so good to see you. I have a million questions," I said.

"Me too. It will be so nice if we don't have to be apart when you get back. No more wondering and waiting for you to return."

I chuckled. "I doubt Nathan would agree."

"Don't let Nathan fool you. I think he misses you more than anyone."

"Will you be all right if I do come back? I don't want to get in the way. I know you guys are happy."

"We'll be more than all right. We want you to be here. Iliana deserves it." She picked the baby up and handed her to me. "You deserve it too."

I stood and put my free arm around her. I kissed the side of her forehead. "Come on. We'd better get back out there before Nathan comes in guns blazing."

Everyone else was eating when we walked back outside. Adrianne looked up as I carried Iliana back to my seat. "We've got a highchair. Azrael, go get it and bring—"

"It's OK," I said, sitting down. "I'd rather hold her, if that's all right."

"Of course it is." Sloan smiled as she took her seat by Nathan.

Someone had piled my plate full of food. I looked at Adrianne, hostess extraordinaire, but before I could thank her, she pointed at Fury. "Wasn't me."

Surprised, I looked at Fury. "Thanks."

"No problem," she said, hiding her mouth with a napkin.

"We were just talking about your meeting with Shannon," Azrael said.

"I was hoping you hadn't already talked to them," Reuel told me.

"Why?"

"I was hoping to go," he said.

Realization hit me. "Did you find out who their child is too?"

"Too?" Fury's volume jumped up. "Do you have news about Jett?"

Damn it. I should've kept my mouth shut.

Reuel put his fork down—which never happens—and scooted his chair back enough that he could turn all the way in his seat toward Fury. He took both her hands. "Yes."

Thank the Father I was immortal because I could feel my blood pressure rising in my veins.

At the head of the table, Azrael's jaw had gone slack. "Is this conversation appropriate for the dinner table?"

"Well, you can't stop it now," Fury said. "What have you found out?"

Azrael and I locked eyes for a second before Iliana lunged toward my plate. I grabbed her around the middle.

"I have good news and bad news. Which would you like to hear first?" Reuel asked.

"Definitely good news today," Fury said.

"Jett is not one of the fallen."

Fury dropped her fork and raised both fists in the air. "Yes!" Then she pounded her fists on the table making Iliana jump in my arms.

I'd never seen Fury so excited. But it made sense. Fury had trained her whole life to battle the fallen. And Jett, it seemed, was the only thing she'd ever truly loved.

She hugged Reuel and squeezed his neck until he coughed. Then she sat back with a satisfied huff. "What's the bad news? I can handle anything after that."

"Yes. What's the bad news?" Azrael said, still worried.

"I believe Jett is Malak or Rogan," Reuel told him.

Azrael's worry shifted to confusion.

"The brothers?" Chimera perked up at the other end of the table. "The ones who worked for the Pentagon?"

"Yes. I believe they were reborn here, and that one of them is Jett," Reuel said.

"Are they bad guys?" Nathan asked.

"No," he said.

Sloan looked as confused as the rest of us. "So why is it bad news?"

"Oh shit." Kane's heavy fist dropped onto the plastic table. "Because he thinks the other is Shannon's baby."

"Yes," Reuel said. "And sooner or later, when they are able, they'll want to find each other again."

Fury cradled her head in her hands, swearing under her breath.

Nathan's jaw went slack. "You're going to have playdates with Shannon."

I laughed. I laughed so hard Fury would have probably punched me had I not been holding Iliana. "Shut up, Warren."

Almost everyone else at the table was laughing too.

"That's the funniest thing I've ever heard," Nathan said.

"I don't know why any of you think it's funny," Az said, pointing down the line at Adrianne, Sloan, and Nathan. "We'll all have to learn to get along with her."

"With Shannon? The hell we will," Adrianne said.

"Will you abandon Sloan?" Azrael asked. "Because if it's

really Malak and Rogan, we can't very well keep them apart once they come of age and know who they are. And the whole reason they'll be here is to protect Iliana."

"What?" Sloan asked, probably a little louder than she intended.

I gestured toward Enzo, Kane, and Chimera. "They'll be like SF-12."

"Yeah." Enzo was smiling. "You know, always being nearby—"

"Always showing up at family dinners," Kane said, flashing an evil grin at Fury.

"Spending the night." Chimera laughed behind her napkin.

Fury looked like she might throw up.

"God, this is going to be fun to watch from a safe distance." I scooped up a spoonful of mashed potatoes. "Can Iliana have some?" I asked Nate because Sloan looked too shocked to make decisions.

"Yeah, she'll eat anything you give her," he said.

Iliana engulfed the end of the spoon.

The animosity between Sloan and Shannon dated back to when they were kids. Adrianne still hated her. And Fury...well, Shannon embodied all the things that appeared to drive Fury nuts about humans: emotions, sentiment, whining.

That was me being very judgy, of course. Fury had obviously never said as much to me, but her disdain had manifested in her body language beside me. Arms crossed. Brow creased. Eyes pinched shut.

"At least we know Jett is one of us," Reuel said. "Look on the shiny side. At one time we worried he was the Morning Star."

Despite Reuel's humorous word blunder, the table fell silent. Those of us who had been laughing either knew, or had increasingly strong suspicions, about Adrianne. Even Enzo and Kane were avoiding eye contact with the opposite end of the table.

I focused on Iliana, feeding her more potatoes.

Thankfully, Adrianne broke the silence before anyone could ask questions. "The *bright* side, Reuel."

"Ah, bright. Yes," he said, nodding his huge head.

Azrael cleared his throat. "Warren, where's your girlfriend?"

"My what?"

"Your girlfriend, Cassiel."

Holy shit. Azrael was derailing the conversation by throwing me under the relationship bus in front of *two* of my exes.

Thanks, Dad.

"Yeah," Adrianne said. "I figured she'd have gone with you to see if Satan had given birth to Satan." Ironic, considering who was really giving birth to Satan.

"First of all, Cassiel isn't my girlfriend—"

"Are you sure?" Azrael asked before I could stumble through whatever I was about to spout off next.

"You guys had a fight, right?" Sloan asked, cutting the kernels off her corn on the cob.

"Oh, it was more than a fight," Azrael said. "Cassiel let the Council manipulate her into betraying him."

Fury looked at me. "But I heard she wasn't aware that the Council leader was dirty and working with the fallen."

Wait. Is this conversation really happening?

I opened my mouth to speak, but Azrael beat me to it.

"Cassiel might not have known, but it doesn't change the facts."

"Yeah, but—" Fury started.

"No buts. Betrayal is betrayal," Azrael said.

Fury picked up *my* beer and drained half of it. My head was still spinning, but hell, at least no one was talking about the Morning Star.

Iliana reached for the spoon again.

Sloan slid her napkin piled with corn across the table. "Here, Illy, want some corn? She can feed herself."

"But she kinda sucks at it," Nathan said.

Sloan slapped his arm.

Iliana picked up a few pieces, then shoved her whole hand into her mouth, dropping most of the corn into my lap.

"See?" Nathan asked.

There was a faint buzz down the table. Enzo pulled out his phone and looked at the screen. "It's done," he announced.

"What's done?" Chimera asked.

No one spoke.

Finally, Fury wiped her mouth with a napkin and put it on her plate. "The cleanup from the wreckage is done." She looked at Enzo. "Right?"

He nodded, putting his phone away.

Sloan's face was somber. "I'm really sorry, Fury."

"We're so glad you're OK," Adrianne added, and I was sure she meant it.

"Thanks to Warren." Fury looked over at me. "He saved my life."

Kane leaned forward and cast a smirk down the table. "How'd that feel for a change?"

Fury's sad face broke into a smile.

I laughed softly. "He's such a jerk."

"Enzo, what will they do with him?" Fury asked.

"Once the coroner is finished in Black Mountain, the team will fly Flint back to New Hope. Probably tomorrow," he said.

Azrael leaned his elbows on the table. "Fury, we can discuss what to do later."

She nodded.

Her eyes were fixed on the checkered tablecloth. Holding Iliana firmly around the middle, I lifted my beer with my free hand. "To Flint," I said.

Everyone raised their glasses or beer bottles. "To Flint," they echoed.

A bright white flash lit up the darkening sky. Everyone

looked up as a high-pitched whistle grew louder and louder, like a slow screaming bottle rocket aimed at the Earth.

Enzo and Kane drew their concealed guns, pointing them at the sky.

"What is that?" Adrianne asked.

Reuel and I stood. "An angel."

CHAPTER THIRTEEN

"*N*athan take the baby inside." I passed her to him over the table.

She cried out, sending a streak of lightning across the sky. Still, Nathan and Sloan ran for the house.

"Go with them," Azrael told Adrianne.

Adrianne was holding her belly. "I can't run!"

He pulled her protectively behind him.

"Where's your sword?" Fury grabbed my arm.

"In Azrael's safe."

She swore. It was too late to get it.

My eyes were fixed on the burning orb in the sky as it neared us. "If we were in danger, Reuel would know."

He nodded his confirmation and spoke to us all in English. One finger was pressed to his ear. "He's right. I'm waiting on identification now from the auranos."

"I thought no angel could warp into Asheville," Adrianne said.

"They can't, but they can breach outside Earth's atmosphere and fly here," Reuel said. "But no one who intended us harm would be stupid enough to do that with the guardians watching."

He was right, but no angel I knew would ever employ such a dramatic entrance unless it was an extreme emergency. This wasn't good news on the way.

"I swear if that thing doesn't say 'hark' or 'fear not' I'm gonna start shooting," Kane said, his Glock ready to fire.

"They're from Eden," Reuel said.

"Is it Cassiel?" I asked.

"We're getting ready to find out," Azrael said.

Chimera was shielding her eyes. "It's so bright."

"We're gonna hear about this on the news. I can see the headlines now. 'Unidentified Flying Object Spotted over Arden," Adrianne said.

The orb slowed as it neared us. As it approached, I could begin to make out legs, arms, hair, breasts...

"Hello, Warren, Reuel." The smooth voice was female, with a flawless American accent. Proof that whoever it was had spent a great deal of time on Earth, like Azrael or Cassiel.

The angel's dark eyes amidst all the white light locked on Adrianne as she peeked around Azrael's shoulder. Reaching back, he shielded her with his arm.

"Oh. Hello, Azrael. I didn't *even* see you there." It wasn't a greeting as much as an insult. Because he was now mortal, Azrael's presence to any angel wouldn't have registered as quickly.

But her tone—and the way she cut her eyes—suggested something more. Something deeply resentful. Like someone passed over for a promotion. Or a long-lost relative cut out of a will.

The angel settled on the ground near the house, and the ethereal light consuming her faded. I took in the full, bizarre, sight of her. She was tall, my height, at least. She had a thin frame and dark skin. She was dressed like a local in jeans and a casual top, both made on Earth.

That's where the normality ended. Soot streaked her face. Her shirt was singed. And her dark curly hair stood nearly vertical.

It was smoking...

"Theta?" Fury ran around Azrael, grabbed the woman by the arm, and turned her to the side. Then Fury patted the smoking spot on the back of the woman's head.

I leaned toward Reuel. "Theta, the Archangel of Prophecy?"

He nodded.

"Wow." It was impressive because there were only seven of us in existence, and I'd met all of them except this one.

Theta turned and embraced Fury. "Oh, Allison, I'm so sorry for your loss."

Fury pulled away. "Theta, what happened to you? Are you OK?"

"Do I look OK?"

Fury shook her head.

"I tried to come in dark, to keep from being seen, but without the light, I nearly burned up coming through the atmosphere."

To be honest, I knew my wings of light had protective qualities, but I never would have thought that without them I might burn flying to Earth. Good thing to know. I'd hate for *that* story to get around in Eden.

Theta pushed her tousled hair off her forehead and looked at me. "It's a pleasure to finally meet you, Warren."

Without giving me a chance to respond, Azrael stepped between us, his fists clenched at his sides. "Theta, why are you here?"

Theta smiled, sort of. "It's nice to see you again too, Azrael."

"You're not welcome here." The angry muscle was working in his jaw.

"My business isn't with you."

"You're on my property. I'm sure that it is."

Her bright-red painted lips spread into a thin smile. "My, my. Settled into domestic life, have we? I'll bet if you lived closer to civilization, you'd be shouting at kids to get off your lawn."

Azrael's anger didn't fade. "Why have you come? To stir up trouble, no doubt."

"I came to speak to the Archangel of Death. That's no longer *you*," she hissed.

He started to lunge for her, but I held him back.

Theta's eyes narrowed as she cut them toward Adrianne. "Maybe I should introduce myself to your other son instead."

It was a threat. A dangerous one. Azrael's spine went rigid, and he fell back a step.

"Why are you here?" I spoke more calmly than my father had.

"I have a message for you." Theta looked at Fury. "Actually, an urgent message for both of you."

"A prophecy?" I asked, the skepticism apparent in my voice.

"For you, yes."

I frowned.

I'd never had a good experience with prophecy. I'd once seen a vision of Sloan dying in front of me. All this time later, it still haunted my dreams. I could remember not only what I saw, but exactly how I felt losing her.

Azrael, too, had always warned against prophets, as he believed they bent the truth to suit their own agendas. It was obvious by his sneer, his feelings hadn't changed.

However, because we were about to fly blind through the literal gates of Hell, I knew we could use all the help we could get. "All right."

"Absolutely not," Azrael said.

My face whipped toward him.

"You really want to do this here?" Theta asked him.

My face whipped toward her.

"I don't *want* to do this at all. I *want* you to leave."

My face whipped toward him. It was like Wimbledon. Without the rackets, nets, and tennis skirts.

"She's not leaving," I said, my voice stern. "I should hear what she has to say."

Azrael's scowl strengthened. "She *lies*."

"I. Do. Not," she said, punctuating every word with offense.

Then she launched into a mumbling rant in Katavukai. Something about the past, and things being unexplainable. I heard the word *infallible* twice but couldn't make out who or what she was talking about. If she was anything like most angels I knew, she was probably referencing herself. The angels of Eden were a lofty bunch.

Azrael's glare was so heated, I watched for Theta's hair to start smoking again. There was history there. I just couldn't remember what it was. As I took my seat, I racked my memory —and Azrael's—for information on Theta.

It's interesting how memories work. Details obscure with time. Words fade. But the feelings of moments often survive the erosion with time. And I could recall Azrael's *feelings* toward Theta with ease.

Resentment.

Whatever she'd done or said—or, likely, prophesied—had pissed him the hell off.

"Please," Theta told me. "I mean no harm."

I nodded. "OK."

She looked toward the house. "Where's the child? I know she's here."

I looked at Reuel. "Is this safe?"

"Theta's harmless, and she's an Archangel. She'd make a powerful ally," he replied in Katavukai.

"Enzo, can you tell Sloan and Nathan it's safe to bring Iliana back outside?" I asked.

Azrael's teeth were grinding.

With a nod, Enzo holstered his weapon and walked to the house.

A moment later, Nathan walked outside carrying my sword. Sloan carried Iliana behind him. He came over and handed me the sword and then its scabbard. "What's happening out here? Who's the Bride of Frankenstein?"

Theta's eyes were fixed on Iliana.

I took the sword and sheathed it before handing it to Reuel. Nathan returned to Sloan and Iliana.

"This is Theta, the Archangel of Prophecy," I said.

"Oh boy. You guys never bring us great news," Nathan said, pulling out a chair for his wife.

Azrael pushed past her. "Don't worry. She rarely brings reliable news at all."

"I have news for you too, Azrael," she said.

There was a hiccup in his movement back to his seat, but otherwise, he didn't respond. He sat down with a huff, picked up his fork, and skewered his pile of potatoes like she wasn't even there.

All of us were watching him.

"You don't even want to know what she has to say?" Adrianne asked.

"No."

Adrianne looked dumbfounded. "The last prophecy about Sloan was right. What if Theta's news is about the baby?"

I was sure that was what Azrael was afraid of. Theta had the power to rip the shroud of secrecy off the details of Adrianne's pregnancy. Azrael had found out about it through Sandalphon, another Angel of Prophecy. So it was highly possible Theta knew as well.

"It's about your powers as an Angel of Death," Theta said.

Azrael looked up.

"Of course." Adrianne rolled her eyes. "*Now* he's interested."

He shook his head. "I am absolutely not interested."

"OK," Sloan said with a chuckle as she fed Iliana more potatoes.

Theta walked around the table toward Sloan and Iliana, and I immediately reached for my sword. Reuel held it out of my reach. "She won't hurt them," he said, pushing my hand away.

Theta held out her hands. "May I hold her?"

"No," Azrael, Nathan, and I all said in unison.

Theta took a step back. "Why not? I hear the stone protects her."

"It might protect her from you making her sick or crazy, but I don't want to risk you filling her head with your nonsense," Azrael said.

"Oh my god." Sloan sat up straight. "Angels don't ever shake hands. That's why!"

"Correct. Too many of them use their powers for evil, even when they aren't fallen," Azrael said.

Sloan was still smiling. "I've wondered that for years."

I walked to the end of the table and carried over a vacant chair. Fury and I moved ours back, and I placed the empty chair with ours. "Theta, have a seat."

"Thank you, Warren. You must have inherited your manners from your mother."

Nathan pushed his empty plate back a few inches and balanced his elbows on the table. He looked at Theta but pointed at Az. "Why the bad blood between you two?"

Theta still hadn't added any food to her plate. She stared at it. "Because I foretold the death of the Morning Star, and it didn't come to pass."

"The Thousand Year Prophecy," I mumbled, more to myself than anyone else as a faint memory resurfaced.

"You've heard of it." Theta looked at me.

My head tilted. "Not exactly."

"You saw it in Azrael's blood stone?" Fury asked.

"A long time ago. I don't remember much beyond the name." Or anything, if I was being honest. "I don't think I've ever heard anything about it in Eden, either."

"You wouldn't. The angels would like to forget it," she said solemnly.

"Why?" Sloan asked, feeding a tiny piece of rib meat to Iliana.

"Because it means they're fallible." Fury's answer caught everyone off guard.

I looked at her. "How do you know of it?"

"She told me," Fury said. "It's the reason she warned me about going to Azrael with the vision of my sister. She said he'd never believe it. She was right."

"He believes it now." My voice was loud and aimed right at my father. He was still doing his best to pretend he was ignoring the conversation.

"What was the Thousand Year Prophecy?" Chimera asked.

"It was a spoken word about—"

"It was a joke," Azrael said, cutting Theta off.

"It was not a joke," she insisted.

"Can you tell us what it was?" I asked, speaking over both of them.

Theta put her hands in her lap. "I'd rather not."

"Of course you wouldn't," Azrael said.

Theta closed her eyes and spoke in Katavukai. I translated for all the English speakers at the table. "I saw the great sword come down from Eden...having the key to the bottomless pit. And he laid hold of the dragon...when a thousand years had expired...the devil that deceived them...was cast into his lake of fire...and tormented day and night for ever and ever."

"I'm guessing the thousand years has come and gone," Kane said, farther down the table.

"Yes. The Morning Star was supposed to have been cast into

the pit after a thousand years, and that expired"—Theta cleared her throat—"quite a long time ago."

I thought again about Theta's absence from Eden. I'd *never* seen her there. Had rarely even heard her name mentioned. I wondered if perhaps this colossal mistake was the reason.

"I remember something about this," Enzo said. He pointed at Azrael. "This is what brought you to Earth a bazillion years ago."

Azrael didn't answer, so Theta did. "Yes. He was the first Archangel who wasn't fallen to spend a considerable amount of time here."

It wasn't common for angels to spend much time outside Eden. Even I, with all that I loved on Earth, found it hard to leave or stay away for long. My responsibilities as the Archangel of Death kept me busy in Reclusion, and by nature, Eden made me not *want* to leave. Infinite happiness, constant peace...why would I?

All creatures—angels and humans alike—crave Eden, as it is the life source of all things. Humans just aren't born knowing it. Angels, the ones born on Earth, don't know it either until they come of age. Or so I'd been told.

"I came here chasing a lie," Azrael said, still not looking up.

"It wasn't a lie." The emotion in Theta's voice was clear. Her tone teetered on tears, very uncommon for an angel—much less an Archangel.

She looked at me, her eyes begging for my acceptance of her word. "The Thousand Year Prophecy is the *only* prophecy in history that has been altered or changed."

"I believe you," I said.

She relaxed.

At the end of the table, Azrael was shaking his head.

"So do I," Fury agreed.

Theta's face sobered, and her eyes locked on mine. "The

fact that the Thousand Year Prophecy is the only one to be altered is the reason you need to listen to what I have to say."

"You think your vision for us will help?" Fury asked her.

"No. I'm hoping my vision will stop you."

"Stop us?" Fury straightened.

"If you go"—Theta was still staring at me—"Fury will not come back from Nulterra alive, and I fear *you* will be the reason."

The words dropped like a boulder onto the table. Everyone flinched. No one spoke a long time.

"What did you see?" Fury asked.

Theta shook her head. "Warren can be the only one to tell you as the vision was his. I will show him if he wishes."

Fury grabbed my forearm. "Don't do it, Warren. It will only make you—"

"I'll do it." The words were hard to get out.

Across the table, terror was etched across Sloan's face. If anyone knew how afraid I was to dabble in prophecy again, it was her. She also knew how equally afraid I'd be to ignore it.

When Sloan's death was foretold, had I not had weeks to decide that my absence would be the only thing that might give her a chance to live, I'd never have been able to save her.

"It's going to make you want to change our plans," Fury argued.

I looked at her. "Maybe. Or maybe I figure out a way to change the future. I could even go to Cassiel for help—"

"Cassiel won't be able to help you," Theta said. "While spoken prophecy might be open to interpretation, visions can't be changed by anyone here or in Eden. They aren't subject to choice."

"Which is why Theta is here." Azrael sat back, crossing his arms over his chest, looking even more angry, if that was possible. "You have a plan, don't you?"

Theta hesitated.

"Well?" I asked.

She nodded slightly. "Eden won't be able to help you, but the fallen might. The Morning Star has been the only one able to alter a prophecy."

"Ha!" Azrael threw both hands into the air. "You want him to work with the Morning Star. That's hilarious."

Theta leaned toward him. "You and I both know that's not even possible." She slid her dark eyes toward Adrianne. "Am I right?"

Adrianne stopped chewing. "What?"

Without another word, Theta looked back at my father, her eyes conveying a silent challenge. She knew Adrianne carried the Morning Star, and if he didn't hear her out, she might let it slip for all to hear.

After a moment, his stony expression softened. "Then what do you propose?"

"Moloch," she said.

Azrael laughed loudly. "Newsflash, Theta. Moloch is dead. I killed him myself."

She straightened with surprise. "Dead?"

"He is?" Nathan asked.

Reuel nudged my arm. *"Verta?"*

I nodded. "Yesterday."

"Yes, and good riddance. One less demon to worry about," Azrael said.

Theta looked at Reuel. "Did you know?"

"Nan."

"You wouldn't know." Azrael's voice was even louder. He stood from the table so fast his chair fell over. "Because I built a damn good vault! Maybe everyone should think about that the next time I say I'm handling something!"

He stormed toward the house.

Adrianne got up and followed him.

"Well, I guess my efforts here are futile," Theta said.

"Without Moloch, I don't know that we'd ever determine how to change anything."

I lay my napkin across my plate and stood, then walked to her. "Show me anyway."

"No." Fury grabbed my arm.

I pulled away from her.

"Warren," Sloan said, worry in her eyes.

"I need to do this. The Morning Star isn't the only one who changed a prophecy. I was able to keep Sloan alive by leaving." I knelt in front of Theta and bowed my head. "Shall we get it over with?"

Without pause, Theta grabbed my hand.

My hearing was the first sense to flash to the future. Sweet laughter filled my ears.

The scent of jasmine came next, and when my eyes opened, sunlight burned my retinas. In the sky, there was one sun—not two, as in Eden. I was on Earth.

A woman called my name. I started up a hill. Her back was to me, crouched, looking at something on the ground.

My eyes followed the direction of her finger. Two large flat stones were set in the ground.

Markers.

Graves.

From the ground, death called out to me like an old friend.

On the face of the first marker, words had been roughly etched into the rock. They were hard to make out. Chipped and faded on the weathered stone.

MCGRATH
Allison "Fury"
1985-2015

As I *prelived* the moment, it wasn't the inscription or even the implication of the inscription that bothered me. I was horrified by how I *felt*.

There were other graves too, but this was the only one that mattered.

Sloan called to me. When I turned, I saw her through a halo of sunbursts. Her hand was outstretched, beckoning me to join her. And all that mattered in that moment, all that mattered was her.

All that had *ever* mattered was her.

Suddenly nauseated, I ripped my hand from Theta's and the vision swirled away. I was back on the mountaintop. One knee on the grass. I eased down onto my hip, then cradled my head in my hands.

"Warren?" Fury crouched beside me and curled her arm around my back. "Are you OK?"

No. No, I wasn't.

When Theta had said Fury would die in Nulterra and I would be the reason, I'd thought—worst case scenario—that I might unintentionally cause her death. As I had Flint's.

But I was *glad* in the vision. No sadness. No remorse. In fact, all my feelings were the opposite, to a sickening degree.

Fury lay dead in the ground, and I was laughing.

CHAPTER FOURTEEN

he party died after that.

I couldn't bring myself to speak of what I saw. Not to Fury. Not to Sloan. Not even to Theta, who'd seen it too. There had to be some explanation. I just couldn't figure out what it was.

Holding Iliana made me feel better, and after finishing her dinner and cup of milk, she'd fallen back to sleep.

Nathan and Sloan lingered longer than the SF-12 guys, it was finally time for them to go. They said their goodbyes to everyone else before Chimera and I walked them out.

I carried Iliana through the house and to the front porch. "Sorry the evening took such a nosedive back there. I didn't mean to ruin the party."

Sloan touched my arm. "You could never ruin the party. I'm just thankful we got to see you." She tugged on the front of Iliana's dress. "I'm glad Illy got to see you."

I kissed the side of Iliana's head. "Me too. And it's thanks to Chimera."

Chimera pointed at me. "You know our deal, Archangel."

"No tears, I know." I smiled instead. "What's your plan?"

"I'll follow them back to Echo-5. Once Iliana's safely inside, Nathan can bring me the stone. Then I'll crash at the command center tonight before driving back to New Hope tomorrow."

I bounced Iliana on my arm. "You'll never know how much this means to me."

"You're probably right. I don't foresee babies in my future." She pulled her keys from her bag. "But good luck finding your own stone in Nulterra. I'm sure if anybody can do it, it's you."

"Thanks."

"When I get back tomorrow, I'll get working on your new passport and IDs."

"Can you change the name?" I asked.

Nathan crossed his arms. "And what's wrong with *Angelo Suave*," he said with a fake accent from I had no idea where.

I pointed at him. "Because everyone says it just like that."

He chuckled.

"I'll see what I can do. I'll wait for you guys in my car. Take your time." She waved as she walked off the porch.

Nathan looked at Sloan. "I'll go get the car and give you a minute to say goodbye."

She smiled. "Thank you."

Nathan offered me his hand. I took it, and he pulled me in for a hug, sandwiching Iliana between us. "Be careful, man."

"I will. Take care of my girls," I said.

"Always." He held onto my shoulder. "Can I give you some advice?"

I nodded.

He jerked his chin toward the house. "Whatever you saw back there...trust your gut. Things turned out all right before."

I grinned. "For you. You got the girl."

"Hell yeah I did," he said with a wink. "Seriously though, you've got this, Warren. Don't let the oracle freak you out too much."

"Thanks, Nathan."

When he stepped away, he pointed at my face, then wagged his finger between me and Sloan. "Keep an appropriate distance from my wife, or I'll send you to Hell to stay there."

I laughed and gave him a thumbs-up.

When he was gone, I looked down at Sloan. "Thanks for bringing her tonight. I'm sure it wasn't an easy decision, not knowing if it would work or not."

"It was definitely an easy decision. I'm glad we all got to see you."

"And again, I'm sorry about the—"

"Stop. No more apologies."

I nodded.

When she pulled her hand back, her face fell. "Warren, what are you going to do?"

I thought of Theta's vision. "I don't know." Which was the absolute truth. I felt sick and confused again just thinking about it. I took a deep breath and looked at Sloan seriously. "But I am sure this trip is necessary. Besides rescuing Fury's sister, it's the best shot we've got at securing the future for Iliana."

"How?"

"Most of the fallen stay in Nulterra. They only have two ways in or out: the gate and the spirit line. The angels control the spirit line. Once I seal the Nulterra Gate for good, Samael will block their access to the spirit line, and we'll all be able to sleep better at night."

"What about the Morning Star?"

I gulped, then faked a reassuring smile. "He's just one demon. And for all we know, maybe he's in Nulterra too."

Her brow pinched. "You don't believe that. I can see it in your eyes."

The corner of my mouth tipped up. She still knew me better than anyone. I put my free hand on her shoulder. "I can't let the unknown stop me from doing all I can to keep Iliana safe."

"Please be careful."

"I'm always careful." I lowered my voice. "I'm also immortal, don't forget."

She was clearly not amused. "This is different. This is Nulterra." Fear pooled in the form of tears along the lower shelf of her chocolate eyes.

I cupped her jaw with my right hand. "I'll be back before you know it."

Her mouth smiled, but her worried eyes obviously didn't get the signal.

"And who knows? Maybe I'll find the stone, and we can all be together again. Wouldn't Nathan *love* that?"

The tension finally broke, and she laughed. "Can I ask you something?" she asked.

"Always."

"Are you happy?"

Interesting question.

I bounced Iliana on my arm. "Right now? Without a doubt."

She touched Iliana's back. "I mean, besides right now. All that talk about Cassiel earlier. It sounds like she really hurt you."

"A lot of that conversation was Az being dramatic." I couldn't tell her *why*, but that was the truth. "Cassiel messed up, and it took a long time, but I forgave her. Still, there isn't a future for us, if that's what you're wondering. We want very different things."

"Well...I want you to hear me say this."

My brow lifted.

"I want you to be happy, Warren."

I knew what she meant, but I smiled and looked at Iliana. "I am, and I'll have all I ever need if I can find that stone."

"I know you will. You're a good father."

Those words meant more to me than she would ever know. "Thank you. It feels like I can only do so much for her."

"You've done the hardest things of all. And someday, she will thank you for it."

I laid my head against Iliana's and took a deep breath. "I just hope she understands."

"I know she will."

"Before you go, I have something else to tell you," I said.

Sloan's eyes widened in question.

"Your mother…"

With those two words, tears welled in Sloan's eyes again.

I took her hand. "She asks about you and Iliana every time I see her."

"Is she…" Emotion choked her. "Is she OK?"

"Better than OK. She's happy and healthy. No more cancer, no more pain."

Sloan's chin quivered.

"And she misses you, but she wouldn't choose to come back here even if she could."

"She wouldn't?" Sloan sounded a little hurt.

I shook my head and smiled gently. "No. Your mom understands now how short life here really is and that someday you'll be together again."

With a sniff, she nodded.

"But right now, you belong here with Iliana. And with Nathan." I dramatically rolled my eyes.

She giggled.

I bent so we were eye level. "Keep practicing your powers. I believe in you, Sloan."

"I promise. And I'll try working with Iliana to get her to talk to you more."

My heart swelled. "I'd love that."

Behind her, headlights flashed coming up the driveway.

I smiled and released her. "That's either Nathan saying it's time to go, or for me to stop touching you so much."

She chuckled and rubbed her fingertips beneath her eyes, wiping away some smeared mascara. "Probably both."

"Probably." I looked past her. "Is that the new mom-mobile?"

She laughed and covered her face. "When he brought that thing home, I felt like I aged ten years in a day."

"I'll bet, but motherhood really does look good on you."

Her cheeks flushed. "Thanks." She touched Iliana's cheek. "I'll give you two a minute. Bring her to the van when you're ready."

"Thank you."

When she stepped away, I sat down on the top step of the porch and laid Iliana on my lap. I admired her sleeping face in the moonlight and spoke silently to her in Katavukai.

"Iliana, Daddy has to go away for a little while, but I'm going to try really hard to make this the last time I have to say see you later. I will miss you every second of every day until I come back. And I will always come back." I leaned over and kissed her cheek. *"I love you, Iliana."*

She didn't wake, but when I touched her hand, her fingers closed around mine. Tears dripped down my cheeks as I scooped her up into my arms and carried her to the van.

Sloan helped me buckle her into the car seat, then hugged me one last time. "Let us know as soon as you're back on this side of the spirit line."

I sniffed. "I promise you'll be the first person I call."

"Take care, Warren," Nathan said as she got in the van.

I waved.

They both waved back.

And then they were gone.

Inside the house, Adrianne was making up the couch. "Is everyone else still outside?" I asked, knowing business for the night wasn't finished.

"Yeah, but I'm exhausted. Getting pregnant ended my night-owl days, so I'm going to bed." She stuffed a pillow into a white pillowcase.

"Thank you for everything, Adrianne. This was a great night," I said.

"Right up until all the angel drama, sure," she said with a chuckle.

"I'm really sorry about that."

She waved her hand. "Don't be. I feel bad your evening was ruined. I'd hoped to give you one last peaceful night before you go."

"I do appreciate it."

"I'm really glad you got to spend some time with Iliana."

"Me too. You have no idea."

She put her hands on both sides of her belly. "Oh, but I do."

And just like that, I felt sick again.

"Good." When she finished straightening what appeared to be a handmade quilt, she sat down on the couch and patted the seat beside her. "Can we talk for a second?"

I suddenly wanted to run from the house. What if she started asking questions I couldn't answer? What if she suspected the truth? What if—?

"Warren?"

I took a deep breath and sat down.

"I need your help."

"With what?"

She touched her temples. "Your dad..." Her voice was laced with exasperation.

"I know. Nathan told me about the electrical experiments." I mentally crossed my fingers that Azrael's desperation was the trigger of the conversation.

"It's not just that. I mean, he's going to burn the house down, but that's not all."

Uh oh. "What else is wrong?"

She looked around to be sure we were alone, then clenched my forearm. "He's driving me *crazy*."

My whole body sighed with relief. I smiled and patted her hand. "I'm sure he's nervous about the baby. My mind was a wreck when Sloan was pregnant."

"Oh no. It's more than that."

Yep. I know.

"He hovers all the time. Wants to know where I am, who I'm with, who I've been talking to." She released my arm and raked her nails back through her long auburn hair. "It's like he's suddenly become my psycho jealous baby daddy."

"I really don't think that's it." I knew it wasn't, but there was no way I could tell Adrianne the truth. "He's worried. And with good reason. Think about all we've been through. All *he's* been through."

She looked mildly guilty.

"I'm sure things will be different after the baby is born," I said.

Truer words had never been spoken. *Everything* would be different after the Morning Star was reborn. I just had no idea how different.

"But I will talk to him," I said.

As if on cue, the back door opened, and my father walked inside. Adrianne and I both stood. "What's going on in here?" he asked.

Adrianne shot me a wide-eyed glare as if to say, *"See?"* Then she smiled at him. "We were just chatting after I finished making his bed. I wanted to say a proper goodbye in case he's gone before I wake up tomorrow." She turned and pulled me into a hug.

The supernatural energy swirling inside her made me dizzy. "I'll see you again soon," I said.

"Please be careful and know we love you," she said over my shoulder.

"I love you guys too."

The baby kicked against my midsection, and I shuddered.

"Will you be OK sleeping on the couch?" she asked.

"Positive."

"He doesn't sleep much anyway, remember?" my father said.

"I know. Runs in the family." She leaned over and gave him a solid kiss on the lips. "Do you think you'll be up late?"

"Not too late, and I'll be quiet when I come to bed." He kissed her once more. "Goodnight."

"Goodnight, Adrianne," I said.

When she was gone, Azrael turned back to me. "What were you two talking about before I walked in?"

"About you acting like a crazy man," I said.

His shoulders slumped. "I know I'm hovering and being overly protective, but—"

I held up a hand to stop him. "You don't need to explain yourself to me. I get it."

"What's your plan tomorrow?"

"I'll talk to Fury tonight, but since Reuel is with us, I'll leave North Carolina and warp to the island, or at least warp to Oregon and meet up with them. I don't want to risk that much time in the air again."

"Now you see how I feel."

"You're right. I do."

"I'll take you to Tennessee in the morning, to a secure location where you won't have to worry about being seen. Or heard."

Because warping was *loud*.

"Sounds good."

"What time is that flight out?" he asked.

"Fury said eight."

He frowned. "That's early."

I laughed and shook my head.

"What?"

"You're such a human now."

"Oh, shut up. We'll leave here at six and take them to the airport."

"Six? Will that give them enough time to get through security?"

"It's Asheville, Warren. Not O'Hare. Then you and I can leave from there."

"Sounds good. By the way, I never said thanks for sending your new toy to come get us today." I lifted an eyebrow.

"The assault helicopter?"

"Yes. What the hell is that all about?"

"It's just a precaution."

"For what? The apocalypse?"

He stared at me.

I groaned.

The back door opened again. This time it was Reuel, mid-yawn.

"You going to bed?" Azrael asked.

"Yeah. Too tired to keep fighting with that girl."

"You're still trying to talk Fury out of going?" I asked.

"Warren, we can't let her go. Especially after what Theta told you."

The thought of the vision sent a chill down my spine. I swallowed hard. "I know. No one wishes more than me that we could talk her out of it, but I don't think it will change her mind."

"There has to be a way."

"Well, you keep thinking on it, buddy. I'm open to suggestions."

He sighed. "She's so *hardheaded*."

I gave him a thumbs-up, and the tension finally faded from his worried face.

"No matter what happens, I'm glad you're coming with us, Reuel. I've missed having you around."

"I've missed you too. It's not the same working alone."

"Agreed. Do you have a passport with you?"

"Of course."

"Good, I want you to fly with Fury tomorrow. I'll meet up with you at the Claymore base in Oregon."

"OK. What time will we leave?" Reuel asked.

"Early. By six at the latest," Azrael said.

Reuel's brow crumpled. "Is that early now?"

I chuckled.

"Go to bed," Azrael said, shaking his head.

"Gladly. I haven't slept in weeks." Reuel shook both our hands. *"Bonirav."*

"Goodnight," Azrael and I said together.

When he was gone, Azrael lowered his voice. "Does he know?"

"He suspects. Anyone from my world who sees Adrianne will," I said, barely above a whisper.

He looked out the window. "Theta knows."

"She must, but she hasn't told anyone."

"Maybe that's in an attempt to prove her innocence. We'll see." Azrael jerked his thumb toward the door. "You going back out there?"

"Yeah. I need to see if Theta has anything else for me."

"What did you see?" he asked.

"Fury was dead, and I was happy about it."

His head snapped back. "That's ridiculous."

"It's what I saw."

"Warren, listen to me." He took a step closer. "Theta has an agenda. She always does. When she told us I would be the one to cast the Morning Star into the great pit, I set out for Earth to find him."

I lifted an eyebrow. "What made you think *you* were the great sword? You don't have a sword."

He touched his chest. "Damon *Claymore*. My name is, literally, Damon Sword."

"Sword?" I put my hands on my hips. "I always thought you were Damon '*Explosive Ordinance*,'" I said, using air quotes.

"No. Those came later. *Much* later. A claymore is a Highlander's two-handed sword." Az stacked both fists over his head.

I pointed at my own face. "Like *my* sword?"

"No. Not like *your sword*." He was mimicking me.

"So which came first?" I crossed my arms. "The name or the prophecy?"

He frowned.

Laughing incredulously, I shook my head. "You really are the picture definition of a narcissist."

"I'm confident, Warren. There's a difference." He blinked. "What was I saying?"

"That you were supposed to be the savior of the universe."

"Oh right. I came to Earth looking for the Morning Star based on Theta's word. As you know, the prophecy never came to pass, but guess what *did* happen?"

"You fell in love with two amazing women and had a pretty decent son and a beautiful granddaughter?"

His brow crumpled. "Don't make me sound like an ass."

I lowered my voice and leaned toward him. "You do a fine job of that all on your own. Besides, I'm tired of everyone telling me the world would be better off had I—and Iliana—not been born."

"I've never said that."

"Not directly to my face, maybe."

For once, my father didn't argue. Probably because he knew

I was right. The overwhelming opinion on Earth and in Eden was the universe would be safer without us in it. Iliana's power was too great. Too unpredictable. And potentially, too dangerous.

"I'm not talking about you or Iliana."

"Then what are you talking about?"

"While I was away from Eden, Theta had the ear of the Father. And when I returned, a failure by most accounts, the Angels of Death had lost Celestine to the prophets, and we were banished to Reclusion."

Biting down on the insides of my lips, I considered the accusation. "You think Theta sent you on a wild goose chase to Earth to steal your office? Seriously?"

"Have you been to Celestine?"

Celestine was a bit like the Swiss Alps of Eden, if the Alps were lush and green with lakes made of diamond water.

"Of course."

"Then you know the energy it draws from the auranos. Angels are more powerful in Celestine. Quite the opposite of the dreary pit of Reclusion."

I couldn't argue that Reclusion was a dump by comparison. The current seat of the Death choir was a fraction-of-a-fraction the size, encapsulated in black obsidian, and silent. *Dead* silent. The only sounds were generally the wails of dying souls as I destroyed them.

It was pretty miserable, which was primarily the reason few of us, myself included, spent much time there. Following Azrael's lead, many of the angels took residence on Earth, though none so permanently as he. But none of us actually lived in Reclusion, whereas almost all the prophets resided in Celestine.

"Did the Father give a reason for the relocation?"

Azrael's head tilted. "Does he ever?"

Good point.

"Theta said a vision revealed the prophets should be in Celestine because there will be a time of great unrest on the Earth and the people will need as much insight as can be afforded to them." The muscle in his jaw tensed. "Sounds pretty convenient to me."

"So you really don't buy into prophecy anymore?"

"I've just seen too many times how fallible and manipulative it can be."

"Are you even going to hear what she has to say about your powers?"

For a moment, he looked conflicted. Not something I was used to sensing around him. Finally, he shook his head. "No. I've lived enough of my life in pursuit of someone else's dream. I need to focus on doing what I have to do to protect those I love. I suggest you do the same."

"You're going to bed then?"

His eyes flashed toward the back door one more time. "Yes." He glanced at his watch. "We have an early day tomorrow."

"Six," I said with a grin.

He chuckled. "Yes. Six."

I held out my hand. "Goodnight, Az. Thanks for the welcome back tonight."

He shook my hand, then pulled me into a hug. "It's good to have you here. I've missed you." It was good to know he meant it.

When he was gone to his room, I rejoined Fury and Theta outside. They were standing on the patio. "Is it just us, then?" Theta asked.

I closed the door to the house. "Yes. Everyone's gone or in bed."

"Azrael didn't want to hear what I have to say?" Theta's eyes stared past me.

I shook my head.

"I guess I'm not surprised."

"He believes you lured him to Earth to—"

"Steal Celestine from him? I'm well aware." She rolled her eyes. "It isn't true."

Of course she'd say that, no matter what the facts were.

"Can you tell me about Azrael's powers?" I asked.

"You know I can't."

"What about Sloan's?" Fury asked. "Do you know anything about how or why she got them back?"

"I do not." Theta turned toward me again. "But I am sure we can expect impressive things from your daughter."

I smiled. "I already knew that."

"What will you do now?" Fury asked her.

Theta looked toward the sky. "It is time for me to return to Eden. I've been gone long enough, and I may be of more use to you there than if I was here."

"You think it will help us if you're in Eden?" I asked skeptically.

"My gift is already swirling around this journey of yours. If I'm nearer the auranos, I may be able to guide you."

"How long has it been since you've been home?" Fury asked.

"Hundreds of years on Earth. Tens of thousands of years in Eden."

Now that I'd been there, I couldn't imagine being away from Eden for so long. It was true what I'd told Sloan. No one would wish to come back to Earth. Even me, if it weren't for Iliana. But a lifetime with her was a blink compared to how long Theta had stayed away.

It bolstered my faith in her, honestly. She'd sacrificed quite a bit to still stand so firmly on her belief in her gift.

Theta touched Fury's cheek. "Best of luck to you both."

"Luck?" I asked, smiling. "Is that what we're doing now?"

Theta didn't laugh. "I fear that's all that might help you now, Warren. In Nulterra, you'll be beyond all our reach."

I gulped.

She looked at Fury again and lowered her voice. "Remember what I told you."

Fury gave a slight nod.

Then Theta launched into the night sky.

Fury and I walked inside together, and I locked the door behind us. "What did Theta say to you?"

"What?"

"Before she left, she said remember what I told you. What did she tell you?"

Guilt flashed across Fury's face. "It's not important."

I doubted that.

"Are you still coming with me?" Fury turned her arm over, and touched the symbol etched inside her wrist with her fingers.

"You know I am. Theta's vision freaks me out, but it's just another item on the list of the many things I'm certain will try to kill you."

"What was it?"

I leaned toward her and lowered my voice. "It's not important."

She had the faintest hint of a smile.

"I'm not flying with you, however. Now that Reuel is here, he's a much safer option."

Her eyes darted away.

"Are you all right?" I touched her arm, and she pulled it away.

"I'm tired. I'm going to bed."

As she turned, I grabbed her hand. "Fury." It was like I could feel the pain pulsing within her. When she met my eyes, hers brimmed with tears.

Her jaw tensed. "I'm fine."

My head tilted toward the couch. "I'll be here if you need me."

She looked down at our hands, then her fingers curved slightly around mine. "Thank you," she whispered.

I squeezed, then released her. "Goodnight."

"Goodnight, Warren."

When she was gone, I went to the half-bath and changed into the gym shorts and white T-shirt I'd bought. Then I brushed my teeth before returning to the couch.

Lying there in the dark, I called out to the spirit world. "Iliana?"

No response.

She was probably still asleep. And if not, the power probably didn't work inside Echo-5. Still, I tried one more time before giving up.

Laying there in the quiet, I let the darkness I'd barely been keeping at bay seep into my mind. Flint was dead, and no matter what anyone could tell me, I knew he wouldn't be—at least not yet—had I not been on the helicopter.

And Fury. Even before Theta's vision, the cuffs had already burned her. *Twice.* I was leading her to Nulterra to die, and I knew it.

God, I needed to shut my brain off.

I looked around me, then reached for the remote control on the end table behind my head. I turned on the television, digital escapism with the push of a power button.

American Dad was on. It had been about a century in Eden time since I'd watched it. I turned the volume almost all the way down and settled into my pillow.

My eyelids had just started to fall when my ears heard the unmistakable sound of a door latch sliding.

A moment later, Fury crept by the back of the couch.

"Can't sleep?" I asked quietly.

She stumbled sideways, gasping and grabbing her chest. "Holy shit. I thought you were asleep!"

"Sorry." I tried, and failed, to suppress a grin. I raised my watch and pressed the night-glow button. It was almost 1 a.m. Maybe my eyelids had been a little more than heavy, because I'd been on the couch for over an hour.

Fury walked to the kitchen. I heard a few cabinets open and softly close, then the tap turned on. She returned a few moments later with a glass of water.

I dropped my feet off the end of the couch. "Wanna watch cartoons with me?"

She looked at me, then down the hall, then back at me. After a second of deliberating, she walked around the sofa and sat down on the far end. I moved my socked feet onto her lap, and she immediately shot me a glare.

I smiled but didn't remove them. And she didn't make me. She just sipped her water and looked at the TV.

Family Guy was on.

I lifted the remote off my chest and tapped her shoulder with it.

She shook her head. "I know you love this show."

I had loved it when life was simpler. When life was *life* at all.

"I'm going back to bed in a minute anyway," she said.

The light from the TV flashed on her face, and I noticed her eyes were swollen again. She'd been crying in her room.

My mother had been killed in front of me when I was still part-human. And even though those old feelings had been replaced with new happy ones of her in Eden, they stirred now for Fury.

After another sip of water, she put the glass on the end table and scooted her lower half closer under my legs. Then she leaned against the armrest, using her forearm as a pillow.

I slid my arm down beside my thigh until my fingertips

graced the top of her foot. I slowly released a wave of subtle energy between us.

Sloan had called it my voodoo power to put her to sleep. It was really a tiny bit of Eden that every spirit thirsted for. Nothing soothed a weary soul quite as well, and even as an Angel of Death, it was a healing quality all angels carried to Earth.

Fury yawned. "I know what you're doing."

"Do you want me to stop?"

Her eyes were barely open. "No."

And soon, she was fast asleep.

CHAPTER FIFTEEN

The doorbell rang at 5:17 a.m.

My eyes popped open. An angel was at the door.

Fury bolted upright as Azrael walked into the living room. He paused, looked at us—me on one end, her on the other—and smiled. *Great.*

"Who's here?" I asked, pushing myself up.

Azrael opened the front door.

The angel on the other side spun around, ripping off his (presumably) designer sunglasses. "I'm back!" Ionis walked inside. "Miss me?"

"Not really." Azrael closed the door behind him.

The messenger looked like a sherbet cone in a lime green button up with two-sizes-too-small pink shorts. His hair was spikier than usual. Whiter too, if that was possible.

"Oh, great. Ionis is here," Fury grumbled, flopping back down onto the couch.

"Good morning, *Angry*," he said, cupping his hands around his mouth.

Fury groaned.

"You heard about that?" I slowly stood and stretched my arms over my head.

"We *all* heard about that."

"How?"

"Somebody told."

"Who?" I was alarmed.

Ionis raised his hand. "Guilty."

"You were at Shannon's yesterday?"

"Close. I followed you."

I looked at my father for an explanation.

Azrael walked to the coffee pot in the kitchen. "The messengers and the Angels of Ministry don't have the same effect on other angels the way more powerful choirs do. So I've had Ionis keep tabs on the area. If there's a problem, he can communicate with the whole of Eden if necessary."

Not a bad idea, I guess. But still surprising, considering how much Ionis irritated my father.

Fury walked past me. "I'm going to take a shower."

"Need some help?" Ionis asked.

She shoved him sideways as she walked by.

He laughed. "Always good to see you, Fury."

Ionis and I walked to the kitchen. "What are you doing here so early?"

"Azrael had me bring a load of gear from the command center. Ugly stuff, all camouflage and black."

"I made him a list of everything you might need for your trip that was probably destroyed in the crash. Rucksacks, CamelBaks, the works."

"When do you leave?" Ionis asked me.

"Six."

He covered his mouth. "Oh, I hate goodbyes."

"Good to know." Azrael slapped him on the back. "You're going with them."

Ionis gasped. "What?"

"You heard me."

"Oh no. Oh *hell* no. I'm not going to Nulterra," Ionis protested with a hand on his chest.

"You've sworn your service to me. You don't have to go into Nulterra, but you will go there and be my eyes and ears for what's happening."

Ionis's shoulders sagged. "But it's hot."

"Good thing angels can't melt then," Azrael said, pouring three mugs full of coffee.

"You really think it's necessary?" I asked.

"You said you were having trouble communicating with the natives on the island, so I'm giving you a translator."

"Sorry. He has a point," I said to Ionis.

He crossed his arms. "But I don't have a—"

"Why do you think I had you grab four of everything?" Azrael asked. "You'll have everything you need."

Ionis's mouth opened, but no sound came out. Which was rare.

Azrael handed him a mug.

"But I don't have any clothes." He held up a foot clad in some sort of bedazzled sandal. "And I have no shoes for the jungle."

"I'm sure you and Warren can find plenty of time for shopping." Azrael raised his cup to his mouth. "You love Manila."

"Azrael," Ionis whined.

"You can watch from the auranos once they've crossed over, but I need someone who can get a quick word to Eden if there's trouble."

Ionis's shoulders dropped and his head fell back. He started to say something else, but Azrael shook his head. "Discussion is over."

"Fine." Ionis huffed and walked to the table.

Azrael smiled at me. "How'd you sleep last night, Warren?"

I shook my head. "Don't even go there."

"Why? Where's he going?" Ionis asked.

"Warren and Fury were on the couch together when I got up to make breakfast this morning."

"Ooo," Ionis said.

"We weren't even touching. Nothing happened."

"OK."

"I mean it, Az."

He held up a hand and chuckled. "I said OK."

At six, we dropped off Fury and Reuel at the airport. We'd repacked all our rucksacks, and it was decided I'd take the blood-stone cuffs with me.

At the curbside for departing flights, Azrael and I got out to say goodbye. He hugged Fury. "Please take care of yourself, and don't do anything stupid."

"Do I ever do anything stupid?" she asked, pulling back to look at him.

"Before this weekend, I would have said no. Now?" He nodded his head. "Absolutely."

Behind them, Reuel was nodding too.

Fury held up her middle finger and laughed.

My father pulled her in for another hug. "Seriously, we need you to come back whole."

"You forget, I'm tougher than I look."

He looked at her face. "I never doubted that for a second."

Azrael moved to release her, but she grabbed his arm "Flint would want to be cremated. Nothing elaborate. No wasted expense."

He smiled gently. "I'll take care of it. We'll have a memorial when you get back."

"He wouldn't want that either."

"A small gathering in remembrance then. I would like to have one," Azrael said.

"Why?" she asked. "You, of all people, know he's not there."

He leveled his gaze with her. "It's not for him, Allison."

She looked at the ground but didn't argue. Then she hugged him again before he walked away. "Thanks, Az."

"Thank me when you get back." Azrael shook Reuel's hands next. "I feel better knowing you'll be there. Take care, old friend."

Reuel pumped his fist. *"Cak vira."* There was no word in Katavukai for "goodbye," so "see you later" was our standard farewell.

We stood there as they walked to the sliding glass doors. My eyes followed Fury.

"She'll take Flint's death harder than she'll let on. Keep an eye on her," he said.

"Like it'll do any good."

"Her father died, Warren. I know the two of you have a rocky history, but afford her a little more patience than usual. She needs it."

When we left the airport, Azrael drove me and Ionis two hours out of the state of North Carolina, through Knoxville, and north off the I-40 interstate.

He took a sharp right off the main highway onto an unmarked dirt road.

"Where are we going?" Ionis asked from the middle seat of the transport van.

"Somewhere safe. You'll see."

We drove several miles through the woods until we finally reached pavement again. Then the road dead-ended at a tall chain-link fence with barbed wire coiled across the top. A Humvee was parked just outside it with a .50 Cal mounted on top. The gunner aimed right at us.

Other humans were present in the area, watching us from places even I couldn't immediately see.

"It's Jurassic Park," Ionis whispered, wide-eyed, as he leaned between our front seats.

"Even better. It's the Secret City." Azrael got out as a heavily armed man in a Claymore shirt walked out of the guard post on the other side.

A simple white sign was posted at the walkthrough gate.

NO TRESPASSING
Y-12 SECURITY COMPLEX
US DEPARTMENT OF ENERGY

I should have known.

"What's the Secret City?" Ionis asked.

"Seriously?"

"Warren, I gossip for a living. I don't care what Azrael and his lackeys cook up down here on Earth."

"This one isn't Azrael's doing. This is Oak Ridge. Birthplace of the atomic bomb."

I'd known for a while that Claymore Worldwide Security had an installation outside Y-12, but this was the first time I'd ever seen it with my own eyes. It was pretty impressive to think my father had been so close to something I'd only read about in textbooks.

But I guess that would be true for a *lot* of things in history.

After exchanging a few words, Azrael returned to the driver's seat, and the guard walked back to the small building. The massive, mounted machine gun turned away from us, and the gate slowly slid open.

"You are quite the man of mystery, aren't you?" I said, eyeing my father from the passenger's seat.

He smiled but didn't look at me. "This was the second Claymore base ever, built back in 1943."

"Where was the first?" Ionis asked.

"Chicago," Azrael and I answered together.

That one, I'd never forget.

Chicago. The city where I was born. The city I never hoped to be in again. Too many memories. 99.9 percent of them bad.

"Chicago was where the first controlled nuclear reaction was created. Claymore was originally formed to protect humans from themselves," Azrael said.

Ionis laughed in the backseat. "I remember that. You told the Council that man had started playing God, and none of them were smart enough to have that much power."

I grinned. "Sounds like Az."

"It was true then. It's still true today." Azrael drove to the top of a plateau and turned left. "But this place was my first baby. Even today, it has one of the most sophisticated underground fallout bunkers ever designed."

"More sophisticated than the one you're building for Iliana at Wolf Gap?" I asked.

He shook his head. "No, but this is the test site for everything that's happening there."

"How close is it to being completed?" I asked.

"Maybe two more years."

"I hope we'll never need it."

"Me too, son. Me too."

It wasn't much farther before the trees thinned to open grass. The clearing had a three-story brick building, a portable trailer marked "Office," and an aluminum airplane hangar.

Outside the hangar was a parking lot full of black Humvees like the one we'd seen at the entrance. In the distance, across another narrow patch of woods, was a water tower and the tops of two dormant smokestacks.

The facility appeared to be small, about the same size as Wolf Gap, and it was old, judging from the age on the bricks of the tallest structure. But if I knew anything, it was to not be deceived by the modest exterior.

Somewhere a door would lead to a hidden metropolis.

He parked by the brick building, and the three of us unloaded. "Do you have everything you need?" Azrael asked.

"Probably not, but how the hell do you prepare for this trip?" I strapped my sword across my back, put on my heavy rucksack, and grabbed the blood-stone case off the back floorboard. "We've got first-aid supplies, MREs, and three liters of water each."

"You and Ionis and Reuel should conserve yours for Fury. I'd be leery of the water sources down there, if there are any. What about a gas mask?"

"I brought two from the command center," Ionis said, struggling to get his backpack on.

I looked at the airplane hangar. "Do you have any skydiving harnesses and goggles around here? Might come in handy if we get into another situation where I have to fly us out of somewhere."

"Don't want Fury to have to hang on cowgirl style?" he asked with a grin.

"I'm sure she'd appreciate it."

"Let's go see." He led the way to the hangar.

Inside, a man in mechanic's coveralls walked over to us, wiping his hands on a dirty rag. "Can I help you?" He was eyeing us suspiciously, mostly staring at Ionis dressed like a cupcake and carrying a military bag bigger than he was.

Azrael looked around the large room. It had a small jet and a Cessna. "What's your name?"

"Dave."

"Hi, Dave. Do we have any skydiving equipment?"

The man's face crumpled with confusion. "Excuse me?"

"Skydiving equipment. Harness, goggles. That sort of thing."

The man just stared at us.

"Dave?" Azrael snapped his fingers.

"I'm sorry, sir. Who are you?"

"He owns this place," Ionis said, teetering backward with the weight of the rucksack. I grabbed its top strap to steady him.

"Excuse me?" Dave asked.

Azrael reached into his back pocket and pulled out his wallet. Then he held his Claymore badge in front of the guy's face.

The man looked at the ID, then back at Az with wide eyes. "Seriously?"

"Yes, Dave. And I need skydiving equipment if you'd like to keep your job."

Dave moved like someone had set his shoes on fire. "Do you need a tandem harness or a solo?"

"Tandem," I said.

"Just one?"

I nodded.

Dave entered a closet on the side of the room. A moment later, he returned with a harness, a pair of goggles, and a parachute bag. "No need for the parachute," I said, accepting the harness and the goggles.

Dave's confusion returned.

"Suicide mission," Ionis announced.

Azrael elbowed him in the stomach.

"Well, it is," Ionis croaked out.

"Thank you, Dave," Azrael said.

I put the rucksack down and shoved the items into it.

"Need anything else?" Azrael asked.

"Probably, but I won't remember until Manila what it is." I offered Dave my hand, and he shook. "Appreciate it, man."

"Don't mention it." He still looked a little mesmerized.

"You ready to do this?" Azrael asked, walking back to the hangar door.

"Do what exactly?" Ionis looked nervous as we walked outside. "I thought we were accessing the spirit line from here."

"You are." Azrael headed toward the brick building. "But you don't want to freak out Dave, do you?"

He smiled over his shoulder before opening the building's side door. He held it for us as we went inside. The bottom floor looked like the common room of an old college dorm. "Is this a residence building?" I asked as we followed him down the hallway.

"It used to be. Since the activity of the base has decreased, we don't really need as many overnight personnel here. The ones we do have stay underground. It's much nicer." He opened another heavy door that led to a stairwell. "They are currently renovating upstairs to turn this building into offices, hence the portable office trailer outside."

We followed Azrael two floors down. Then he used a retina scanner to open what looked like a solid wall. A loud buzzer made Ionis jump, and the wall slid away to allow us inside.

I admired its size as we walked in. The walls and the door were at least four feet thick.

"That's a sixteen-thousand-pound door," Azrael said as it closed behind us. On the wall hung a massive metal sign. It had a swastika and a drawing of Hitler beside the words, *Loose lips sink ships!* scrawled in cartoonish script.

"Is that thing real?" I asked.

"We salvaged it from a junk pile after the war." He pointed to an open doorway on our right. "Decontamination shower and biohazard incinerator are through there." We didn't stop to look as we neared a heavy door like the first.

The next door opened up to a lobby, where a woman was waiting to greet us. She was tall, dressed like Fury, and armed better than a GI Joe. "Damon Claymore, in the flesh."

"Hello, Gisele." He looked back at me. "This is Gisele

Palmer, head of Claymore, Oak Ridge. Gisele, this is my brother, Warren, and our associate Ionis."

She shook my hand. "I see the resemblance. What can I do for you, Mr. Claymore?"

"We were never here, Gisele. As always, no questions."

"You've got it, sir. I sent everyone to the command room, so as long as you stay clear of there, no one will see you come or go."

"Thank you. We'll chat on my way out. I want to hear how the renovation project is going."

"Roger that, sir."

Azrael led us down a long hallway with oak doors. I peeked inside the ones that were open. There was a rec room with a big screen and two pool tables, a large kitchen and chow hall, and a first-aid station.

"How big is this place?" I asked.

"Twelve thousand square feet, give or take. The one at Wolf Gap will be six-thousand feet bigger than this."

He led us through a door to another stairwell at the end of the hall. We went down another floor to a hallway of residences. "These are the apartments."

He pushed open one of the doors so we could see inside. It looked like the living room of my first apartment at Camp Pendleton.

At the end of that hall, he punched in a code to open what looked to be the final door. "This is the one reserved for me or any VIP guests we might have."

I wouldn't call it luxurious, but out of all of Azrael's hidey-holes I'd visited, this one was the nicest. "Through here," he said, opening another heavy metal door.

He flipped on the light in the bare concrete room. The only decoration was a single quote, in what looked like Sanskrit, painted on the wall.

"That's creepy as shit, Azrael," Ionis said, staring up at it.

"What is it?" I asked, unable to read the language.

"It's the line from the Hindu scripture, the Bhagavad Gita, that Robert Oppenheimer quoted when they successfully tested the first atomic bomb."

"It's grammatically incorrect," Ionis whispered.

"You guys are absolutely no help."

Azrael apparently wasn't aware that I still didn't know what it said because he moved the conversation along. "You can breach from inside here. It won't be heard aboveground."

Ionis rolled his eyes. "We could have breached from the woods, but whatever."

"Ionis, do you remember the safe spot to breach to at Claymore West?" Azrael asked.

Ionis nodded.

Azrael turned back to me, an odd mix of worry and resolve on his face. "Have you thought of anything else you need?"

I shook my head. I had my sword, my gear, and the cuffs—which, for a second, I was tempted to leave behind. "I think we're good. Any other words of wisdom before I go?"

"I wish I did, but you're about to do something even I have never done."

"What if I fail?"

He put both hands on my shoulders. "What if you succeed?"

Azrael reached under his shirt and pulled out a gold necklace. It was his blood stone, containing all his memories of the supernatural world. "But take this, and revisit all my memories during our time of negotiating the deal with the Morning Star. Something might be helpful." He took it off and offered it to me.

"Now?"

"No." He put the necklace in my palm and closed my fingers around it. "Take it with you. I want to see what it's like down there."

I hesitated.

"It will be fine. I've done without it for a few weeks before, and my memory has been just fine."

"OK." I put on the necklace and dropped it beneath my collar.

My father opened his arms, and I gladly stepped into them. "Be careful, and come back quickly."

"I'll do my best."

He squeezed me tight. "I love you, son."

"I love you too, Dad."

Over his shoulder, the words on the wall triggered a memory in the blood stone.

"Now I am become Death, the destroyer of worlds."

CHAPTER SIXTEEN

*a*side from Ionis's constant whining, the next two days were completely uneventful. Fury and Reuel made it to Oregon with no issue, and in the times Ionis and I had to wait for them, he shopped while I scoured the memories of the blood stone.

The four of us met up at the airport in Manila around lunch on Thursday. Even Fury's and Reuel's checked bags arrived on time—a miracle all by itself.

"Now what?" Ionis asked, throwing his rucksack onto the ground beside the baggage carousel.

"Unav." Reuel pointed toward a sign advertising a restaurant.

"We'll eat soon, but I'd like to try to secure a charter to the island before we get too far from the airport." I looked around for an information desk.

"Now we're going to fly?" Ionis asked.

"It will be short, and I fear warping this close to the gate might set off some supernatural warnings that we might be here."

"Flint had planned to rent a helicopter through a company

called Helifleet Aviation. They might do charter flights," Fury suggested.

"Do you have a number?" I asked.

"No, but I can google it." She pulled out her phone. After several taps, she held the phone to her ear. "Hello?" She caught my eye and pointed toward the outside door before starting toward it.

"Go with her," I said to Reuel.

Reuel followed Fury outside. As they neared the door, I noticed an information desk. "Ionis, I'll be right back."

"Sure. Leave the little guy to defend all our possessions in the world. Great idea," he said with a smirk.

"Good point." I picked up my sword's case and carried it with me. When I neared the desk, the eyes of the small man behind it widened in question.

I waved. "Hi."

"Hello," he said. "May I help you?"

"I hope so. I need to charter a helicopter to one of the islands. Can you recommend a company?"

"I will be happy to. One moment please." He began to flip through what looked like a Rolodex on his desk. After a second, he stopped and pulled one from the file. "This company is very good. Where are you going?"

I accepted the card. "La Isla del Fuego."

"Oh. I'm sorry, sir. A charter flight to la Isla del Fuego is impossible."

"Impossible?"

"Yes. The airspace around the island is closed. Too many planes and helicopters go down there."

"Go down, like crash?"

"Yes. Crash."

"Why?"

He lifted his shoulders. "I'm afraid no one will fly you there."

"Well, shit."

"Sorry."

I dismissed the apology with my hand. "Not your fault."
Beyond the desk, Fury and Reuel came back in. "Any luck?"

She shook her head. "They said helicopters can't be taken to
the island."

I jerked my thumb toward the help-desk guy. "He said the
same thing." I turned back toward him. "How about a boat?"

"That would be possible, but it would be a long journey.
There is a plane that flies into Dumaguete—"

"No more planes." I didn't want to risk checking the sword,
but that did give me an idea. "Thank you for your help."

The man bowed his head slightly.

Fury and Reuel followed me back to Ionis. "What if *we* fly?"
I said, quietly.

"You just said you didn't want to fly," Fury said.

"I don't want to fly in a plane."

Reuel's head tilted like he was considering it.

"What do you think? Could we wait till sundown and go?" I
asked.

"You mean fly like...?" Ionis began to flap his arms.

"Sure. Why not?"

Ionis put his hands on his hips. "Because I don't want to."
Ionis enunciated every word. "It's a thousand degrees outside."

Fury looked intrigued. "It will be cooler when the sun goes
down, and much cooler at a higher altitude."

"What about all her stuff?" Ionis gestured to the bags on
the floor.

I looked at Reuel. "Can you manage the bags if I carry Fury?
We picked up a harness in Oak Ridge."

He nodded. "Now about that food..."

The sun set in Manila at 6:13 p.m. In the six hours we waited
for the sun to make its descent, we ate Filipino food for lunch,
Thai food for Reuel's afternoon snack, and seafood for dinner.

The dinner joint had a view of the harbor, so we stayed there until the sun went down.

I was holding Azrael's blood stone in my hand, lost in his memories once more as I looked out over the bay.

"What is it with you and that thing?" Fury asked, plucking a piece of pineapple out of the remains of her fruity drink. "You've been treating it like a security blanket since we got to Oregon."

I dropped it beneath my shirt again. "I keep rewatching Azrael's memories. The trials where they learned about Nulterra, the Battle of Antioch, the day they connected the spirit line to Nulterra. I've rewatched almost everything from the past millennium. Hell, I even watched Robert Oppenheimer speak about the atomic bomb."

"Sounds like you've been thorough. Learn anything new?" she asked.

"Not really, but the Nulterra stuff is much more interesting after what Moloch told us about Ket Nhila," I said.

"The Bad Lands?" Ionis asked, translating the language. "So glad I don't have to go."

"Nulterra is designed to trap souls there and keep them in anguish for as long as possible. It makes sense that trapping them would be easier if the Bad Lands are an illusion that's familiar." I looked at Fury. "And Moloch said the Bad Lands would depend on you."

"What does that mean?" she asked.

"I think it means we need to start preparing for your worst nightmares."

"Meh," Ionis said, nudging her shoulder. "Fury's not afraid of anything."

I hadn't thought so either. I waited for a while to see if she'd fess up to any fears. She didn't.

"When will it be safe for us to go?" she finally asked, dodging the unspoken question altogether.

The sun was casting a golden hue over the waves. "Soon. The last thing we need is to make national headlines in the Philippines." I raised my hand to flag down our waitress.

"Yes?" she asked when she reached us.

I pointed out across the bay to where a peninsula free of buildings jutted into the ocean. "Can you tell me what that place is?"

She looked in the direction of my finger and squinted. "Far out there where the mountains are?"

"Yes."

"Mount Palay. The Palay National Park."

"Can we drive there?"

"Yes, sir. It will take about an hour."

"Thank you, Thania." I pulled out my wallet. "How much do we owe you?"

She left when I'd paid our bill.

"What are you thinking?" Fury asked.

I tucked my change back into my wallet. "I'm thinking we should catch a taxi out to that beach. If it's a national park, it should be deserted this time of night. We can fly to the island from there."

"It's weird that the airspace is closed around the island," she said.

I picked up the last shrimp on my plate. "The guy at the airport told me lots of planes and helicopters crashed there."

"Sounds like the Bermuda Triangle," she said.

"Bizarre for sure." I popped the shrimp into my mouth, then washed it down with the last of my beer. I sat back in my seat and took a deep breath. "If I eat anymore, you'll have to use me as a raft to float to the island."

"Where will we stay tonight?" Ionis asked. "Or has anybody thought that far ahead yet? I vote for somewhere with air conditioning."

Fury turned on her phone's screen. "I've been looking at this place called the Lazi Beach Treehouses." She turned it around so I could see it. "Looks like they have one treehouse available tonight that sleeps four."

I scrolled through the pictures on the website. It was a two-story structure with a thatch roof. On the ground level was a shared bathroom with an outdoor shower concealed by bamboo. Upstairs were two bedrooms that led out onto a shared deck. One bedroom had twin bunkbeds. The other had a king.

My brain immediately went to the sleeping arrangements.

"May I see?" Ionis asked.

I handed him the phone. "Looks good to me. Where is it in relation to the gate?"

"A two-hour walk maybe," she answered.

"Two hours?" Ionis made a gagging sound. Then his head jerked back while perusing through the pictures. "Fifty dollars a night for the whole thing? I might have to move to the Philippines." He turned the phone around. "Does it come with the girl in the bikini?"

I rolled my eyes. "Fury, can you book it online?"

"I think so. Let me check." She took the phone back from Ionis.

Across the table, Reuel was finishing his banana dessert. "You about ready to go, big guy?"

He shook his head.

"We can't put it off forever, Reuel." Ionis swiped a finger full of whipped cream off Reuel's plate. "My ass wants to go home."

With a huff, Reuel shoveled the rest of the pudding into his mouth.

"Done," Fury said, putting the phone down. "And I let them know we might be arriving late. How long do you think it will take to get there?"

On my phone, I opened an app Azrael had told me about to calculate distance as the crow flies—or in our case, as the *angel* flies. "Looks like it's about four hundred and seventeen miles to the island. If we travel at a hundred and twenty miles per hour—"

"Why so slow?" Ionis asked.

"Because Fury's a human."

"Oh, I forgot. You're not like most humans," he said.

Fury smiled. "I'll take that as a compliment."

"It should take us about three-and-a-half hours in the air." I looked at my watch. "So elevenish, roughly."

"I'm going to have to fly with my legs wrapped around you for three-and-a-half hours?" Fury asked.

I grinned. "You want to get there, don't you?"

"Well, yeah, but my thighs aren't made of steel, Warren."

That wasn't what I remembered.

"I'm kidding. I have a tandem harness in my bag. You won't have to hold on at all."

"Thank God." She stood and put on her rucksack. "Well, what are we waiting for?"

I got up. "Let's go."

———

An hour later, our taxi driver dropped us off at a beach club that had been closed for hours. Not a soul was in sight. Still, I sent my powers out into the night. Nothing.

"Reuel, you getting any signs of life out here?" I asked, trusting his ability to sense the living more than mine.

He turned in a slow 360-degree turn. Then he shook his head. *"Nanta."*

"All right." I still didn't like our position so close to the road. Someone would be stopping by at some point to check for after-hours trespassers, like us. "Let's make it fast though."

I dropped my stuff onto the sand. Taking out my sword, I strapped it to my back. Then I pulled the military-grade harnesses from the bag and tossed one to Fury with a pair of clear goggles.

Fury put on her harness, then strapped her rucksack on over her chest, fastening its waistband strap behind her back. "Will this be too much for you?" she asked me.

"Nah." I held up my own rucksack. "Reuel, can you carry this?"

He nodded, and I tossed it to him. His back was so large that his own backpack didn't impede his wings, and he was able to wear mine on his chest. Then he picked up Fury's gun case and the case holding the cuffs.

"You're not going to hold those for three-and-a-half hours, are you?" Ionis asked, putting his bag on backward as well.

Fury reached into the middle pocket of her bag and pulled out two bungee cords. "Here." She tossed them to him.

He bungeed the cases to either side of my rucksack.

Fury pointed at him. "Are those things secure?"

He tested the tension on one of the cords, then gave her a thumbs-up.

I finished securing my harness. "We ready to do this?"

Fury came over and stood directly in front of me, and I hooked my harness to hers. She tied her ponytail into a knot behind her neck, so her hair wouldn't smack me in the face all the way to the island. "How will you know where you're going?" she asked.

I tapped my temple. "Built-in GPS."

She smirked. "Sure."

I looked over at Ionis, who was double-knotting his shoes. Beside him, Reuel looked like a giant tortoise with two shells. "Ready?" I asked.

All three of us stretched our wings, and white light illuminated the beach. "We need to fly dark," I said, dimming my own wings.

They did the same, and the three of us lifted into the air.

I hadn't done much flying on Earth, but it was wildly different than flying in Eden. The wind on my face was cold, and my eyes watered wildly until they completely dried out. I regretted not bringing goggles for myself.

And while Eden got dark when its two suns went down, it was never completely impossible to see. Earth was a different story. Out over the water, far away from land, we were all but flying blind.

Still, there was something therapeutic about sailing through the air. The freedom. The rush. Even the chill in the air to remind you you're alive.

Even Fury had relaxed in her harness and was letting her arms settle on the rushing wind. I bent so my mouth was close to her ear. "You doing all right?"

She reached up and grabbed my forearm. "Better than all right. This is amazing."

I smiled. "Want to get a little closer?"

She nodded.

I brightened my wings just enough to see the surface of the ocean, then I dipped down far enough so Fury could trail her fingers over the water.

Through the wind and sea spray, I heard her laugh.

Then I heard something else...the crackle of static in my ear. My heart swelled. *"Iliana?"* I asked silently.

"Warren, it's Samael." Samael was the Angel of Death who guarded the spirit line and the Eden Gate."

"What's up, Samael?"

"I thought you were headed to la Isla del Fuego?"

"I am."

"Then why are you flying toward Vietnam?"

Shit.

I pulled my arms in and pressed the night-glow button on my watch. We were headed due east.

"You a little distracted out there?" he asked with a chuckle.

"Shut up, Samael." I took a hard left, nearly doubling back to where we'd come from.

Reuel and Ionis slowed as Fury and I passed them. Ionis held his hands up in question. Reuel just laughed and shook his head. Fury angled her face toward me. "What are we doing?" she shouted.

"Getting back on course!"

I felt her laugh against me. "What about that internal GPS of yours?"

I thought about making some excuse, but I couldn't think of one more plausible than the blood was rushing away from my brain the more she squirmed against me. So I kept my mouth shut.

"You're back on course now. I'll keep watch in case you start wandering again," Samael said in my head.

"Thanks," I grumbled.

I began counting islands. We would pass over four major ones before la Isla del Fuego would be in sight. But I recognized the island as soon as we were over Negros. In the distance, I could see a glowing purple haze.

I tapped Fury on the shoulder, then pointed it out.

"That's it?" she shouted.

"I'd bet my life on it." I looked back at Reuel and Ionis, who was looking exhausted, and made an exaggerated pointing motion up ahead.

With the end in sight, I picked up speed. Fury grabbed onto my arm again, and I wrapped my other arm around her stomach. "You OK?" I shouted.

She nodded, angling her face again so I could see her smile.

I bent my wings into the wind, sailing even faster. When we were over the island, I slowed as we reached its center. The eerie purple glow grew brighter as we approached, but the sky was too dark to see our reflection in the salt mirror.

"Can we get closer?" Fury asked.

I descended toward the gate, then stopped and hovered far above it. Reuel and Ionis stopped on either side of me.

"Nulterra," Reuel said, his voice filled with awe.

"I expected it to be more sinister and spooky," Ionis said.

Maneuvering my arms around Fury, I blasted the circle with my power to try and open it. The "no" sign burned bright neon purple against the dark landscape. It lit up all our faces.

Ionis laughed and nodded his head. "OK. That's impressive."

"Shh," I said. "We don't want to disturb the locals. They aren't exactly friendly."

"Then maybe you should kill the lights," Ionis said.

The lights were already beginning to fade.

"I almost want to try to get in tonight," Fury said.

My arm was still around her waist. "I know it's hard to wait, but we could all use a good night's sleep."

"Amen," Ionis said. "Have I told you how much I hate flying?"

"Only about a thousand times." Fury looked back at me. "I'm ready if you are."

We flew south to the southern tip of the island, an area called Lazi. I cruised past what appeared to be a man-made beach and a small resort. Fury tugged on my arm, and I bent so I could hear her. "It was past this place. I saw this resort on the map."

"How much farther?" I asked in her ear.

"Half a mile, maybe."

I slowed as we approached a dim light on the shoreline. "Is that it?"

Her head bent. "I think so." A second later, she nodded more definitely. "Yes. See how it's built in a semicircle?"

I scouted the shore for the most inconspicuous area. Then I set down on a rocky beach shrouded in darkness about two hundred yards past our destination. The only light was the distant gleam of the stars.

"Anybody know where we are?" Ionis asked.

I jerked my thumb over my shoulder. "The place where we're staying tonight is just back there."

"Hallelujah." He pushed his rucksack off his shoulders and let it fall to the ground with a heavy thud. "I hope they have a masseuse on staff."

I unhooked Fury's harness from mine, and she immediately loosened the straps across her chest. "How was your first flight?" I asked.

She pulled her arms from the harness and pushed it off her hips. "Who said it was my first flight?"

Disappointment hit me like a kick to the balls, but I refused to show it. "Oh yeah?"

"He took me once when I was younger." She looked at Reuel. Then her jaw immediately dropped with shock.

When I looked over, I immediately saw why.

The case containing the blood stone was gone.

CHAPTER SEVENTEEN

The walk to the resort was tense after tears and gnashing of teeth. Reuel didn't even try to pretend it was an accident. He told her he hoped the case was at the bottom of the South China Sea, and he meant it.

Us three angels waited outside with what remained of our luggage while Fury checked in with our hosts. "Why'd you do it?" I asked him.

He stared straight ahead. "You know why."

"Yeah, I do." I looked up at the stars. "But while I understand the *why*, you shouldn't have done it. It was her choice."

Guilt flashed across his face. "If it keeps her here, I'm not sorry."

I sighed. "I know you're not. But you'd better hope we can still get in without taking her inside. Or she might kill you with my sword in your sleep."

Fury returned with the keys. "We're in treehouse three." Before reaching us, she turned and walked toward the treehouses.

Ionis sighed and shook his head. "It's going to be a long journey to Hell."

The three of us followed her, and when we reached tree-house number three, she started up the wooden staircase on the left. I went up the staircase on the right and met her at the top.

"The bathroom is the door downstairs," she announced loud enough for us all to hear. Then she used a key to open the left-side door. "This is the room with a king bed. The other must be the room with the bunks." She tossed me the other key, and I stuck it in the second door.

"Where is everyone sleeping?" I asked.

"I don't care, as long as I don't have to talk to Reuel."

Her words made me cringe for him.

"I'll sleep with you, Fury," Ionis announced proudly, taking a few steps toward her.

She stopped him with a hand to his chest. "I changed my mind. I do care. Warren?" Fury went into the bedroom on the left.

When I passed Ionis, he winked. "You're welcome."

Heat immediately rushed to my cheeks, and I followed her inside.

The room was little more than four walls and a bed. A box AC unit jutted out of the wall beside the window, and each side of the bed had a nightstand with a lamp. Aside from a couple of throw pillows on the white bed and a wall mirror, the only decoration was a dreamcatcher hung over the headboard.

I carried my stuff to the corner and dropped it. Fury did the same on the opposite side of the room. She let out a frustrated groan and folded her arms across the top of her head.

I took off my sword and leaned it in the corner. "Do you want to talk about it?"

"No." With a deep exhale, she bent and picked up her ruck-sack before carrying it over the bed. She ripped it open and pulled out her toiletries bag. "I'm going downstairs to get ready for bed. What time do you want to head out in the morning? The owner said they serve breakfast here from seven to eleven."

"Let's eat breakfast at seven and leave after. God knows we might not get a decent meal again for a while." Or *ever*, I added silently.

She pulled a couple of pieces of clothes from the bag and walked out the front door. I walked out on the deck and over to the next room. The door was open, and Reuel sat on the lower bunk bed, hunched *way* over, with his eyes fixed on the floor.

I sat down beside him and put my hand on his shoulder. "She'll forgive you, eventually."

He replied in Katavukai. "I don't like it when she's mad at me."

"I understand all too well, my friend." I tried to straighten and smacked my upper spine against the top bunk frame. "On another note, how the hell will you sleep here?"

He smiled just a little bit. "Snug as an insect in the carpet."

I laughed and rubbed my hand down my face.

"It's 'snug as a bug in a rug,' you big doof," Ionis said, looking down from the top bed.

I stood. "Breakfast at seven in the morning. We'll leave right after."

"Have fun tonight, Warren," Ionis said, hanging upside down off the bed with a smile.

I pointed at him. "Don't you start."

He chuckled as I walked out of the room.

Fury returned a little while later, her long dark hair wet from the shower. She wore a black ribbed tank top and plaid boxer shorts. It was hard not to stare. "There's no hair dryer, but there is hot water if you want a shower."

Hot water wasn't what I needed. A cold shower, however, might be a necessity. "Thanks." I started toward the door with my change of clothes and toothbrush.

"What side of the bed do you want?"

I shrugged. "It doesn't matter."

"You can have the side by the AC. I know you sometimes get hot at night."

"I appreciate it." And I did. I was also surprised by it. Fury wasn't known for being thoughtful. "I'll be back in a few."

When I returned to the treehouse, I heard Fury talking inside our room. Her voice was small and high-pitched. I slowed my pace so I could listen. "Hi, sweet baby. Mommy misses you. Are you being a good boy?"

Baby Jett was making gurgling noises.

"How'd he sleep last night?" she asked in her normal voice.

"Seven hours." John's reply was curt and emotionless. "Tell Mommy goodbye, Jett."

"But I just—"

Silence. John had hung up on her.

I wanted to choke him. I climbed the last few stairs and walked into our room. She was still staring at her phone, and she quickly put it on the nightstand when she saw me.

"Everything all right?"

She nodded, turning her face away from me.

I carried my stuff back to my rucksack in the corner, putting my dirty clothes away and leaving my toiletries out for in the morning. When I turned to the bed, Fury's back was to me, and she was wiping off her cheeks.

I gritted my teeth. "You wanna talk about it?"

She sniffed. "Talk about what?"

"Nothing."

"The AC doesn't work," she said, pointing at it.

"Wanna sleep with the door open? I can pull the mosquito net over it so we can listen to the waves."

"Sure."

I pushed the front door open and pulled the mosquito netting across it, securing it with the Velcro edging. Then I returned to the bed and switched off my bedside lamp.

After laying there for a while, staring at the plain ceiling, I pressed my finger to my ear and silently called out for Iliana.

Nothing.

My heart sank.

Then I focused on the sound of the waves crashing against the beach and prayed it would lull me to sleep.

But beside me, Fury was crying. It was so quiet no one but an angel would be able to hear it. My protective side considered curling into her back and wrapping her in my arms. My logical side said to keep my distance.

After a moment, she slipped out of bed, padded across the room, and slowly pulled the netting away from the door. *Krrrrchh...* I watched her step out into the moonlight and disappear from my view.

When she didn't return, I got up and went to the door. She was sitting at the top of the steps with her face buried in her knees. I pulled the netting back and walked out to join her.

She looked up, and her eyes were wet with tears. I sat down on the step beside her.

She swiped her fingers under her eyes. "Must be post-pregnancy hormones."

I nodded.

"Sorry if I'm keeping you awake."

"You know I don't really sleep much anyway." I folded my arms on top of my knees and looked over at her. "You OK?"

She sniffed. "Of course."

Shaking my head, I stared out toward the ocean. "It's understandable to not be OK. God, Fury, after the week you had, if anyone has the right to fall apart, it's you."

"I don't fall apart." She pulled up the hem of her tank top to dry her eyes, as her fingers weren't able to keep up with the job.

I looked at her and lifted an eyebrow.

She laughed a little. "I swear I haven't been the same since Jett was born." She fanned her face with her hand. "It's like I can't shut the feelings off. I'm angry. I'm sad. I feel guilty. I'm worried."

"Why are you worried?"

"I'm worried about not finding Anya. I'm worried we'll find her, and it will be too late. I'm worried we won't be able to get in through the gate at all. Now I'm worried you'll have to go alone."

"You know I'd rather go alone, right? I'd rather not risk anything happening to you."

She stared ahead a moment. "Do you know why I'm so hell-bent on going with you?"

"Because you want to be the one to save your sister?"

"No. I don't care who saves Anya as long as she gets out of there. I know you're fully capable of doing that."

"Then why?"

She took a deep breath and held it. "Because what if something happens? What if Anya *is* dead? Or what if Anya is being controlled by Abaddon? How will you ever get out of there without my key?"

Her words slowly sank in.

"I'd never be able to live with myself if something happens to you when I had the power to stop it."

I put my arm around her shoulders. She leaned in and buried her face in the crook of my neck. I kissed the top of her head. "That may be the sweetest thing you've ever said to me."

"It's the pregnancy hormones," she whimpered, her voice muffled against my skin.

I chuckled and kissed her head again. I rested my cheek against her hair. "What can I do?"

She curled her fingers into my T-shirt. "Help me get the cuffs back?"

I'd secretly been relieved when the blood-stone cuffs had been lost, but the warmth of her plea on my skin was about to make me desperate to find them. Closing my eyes, I felt the pressure of her knuckles against my chest and the tickle of her eyelashes on my neck.

"I don't know how," I admitted.

She sank in my arms.

"But..."

She looked up, her eyes filled with hope.

I pushed her hair behind her ear and stared at her perfect pink lips. "I'll go to Eden. If there's a way to get them back, Cassiel will know how."

Fury put both arms around my neck and squeezed. I encircled her waist and held her against me. Her fingers trailed up through the back of my hair, then she turned her face and pressed a light kiss just beneath my ear. Electricity shot through my extremities. I shuddered and smiled.

She pulled back and rested her forehead against mine. "Thank you, Warren."

I let out a slow sigh. "Anything for you, Fury."

CHAPTER EIGHTEEN

I took nothing except my watch, my sword, and the clothes on my back when I set out toward the beach. Back to the spot where we'd landed only hours earlier. Fury and I agreed she'd only tell Reuel and Ionis if/when they heard me breach, and that I would be back by 6 a.m. at the latest.

With a thunderous boom, I crossed into the spirit world and navigated the spirit line back to the Eden Gate. Samael saw me coming and met me on the moonstone steps.

"This is unexpected," he said, his dark robes trailing behind him.

"I'm not here for long." I unfastened my watch and held it toward him. "I just set this to the time on the island, and set an alarm for 5:45 a.m. I need you to call out to me when it goes off. I can't afford to lose track of time while I'm here."

He took the watch. "Why are you here?"

"I need to see Cassiel. Know where I might find her?" We started up the steps toward the massive gate.

"I would assume she's in the Onyx Tower. She hasn't left Eden as far as I know."

I squeezed his shoulder. "Thank you, brother."

"While you're here..."

"Yeah?"

"There's something you should see."

"What is it?"

"Follow me."

I followed Samael up and across the steps toward the door to Reclusion—my chamber, where wicked souls go to die. Sitting in front of the door was Flint.

I stopped. "He's been here the whole time?" A few days on Earth was a long time in Eden.

"The whole time. He begged me to send him to Nulterra. I refused and told him he had to wait here for you."

"I'll take care of it." *Or I'll try to*, I added silently, knowing Flint was just as *hardskulled* as Fury. I cautiously approached him. "Flint, what are you doing here?"

He stood when he saw me. "Warren! Is she with you?" His eyes frantically searched the steps.

I put my hands on his shoulders. "Fury is safe on Earth. Why haven't you gone inside the gate?"

"She's safe?"

"Yes. She's chilling in a tiki hut right now." I looked past him to Samael. "Why does he care so much? Humans are usually pretty oblivious to memories of Earth when they get here."

Samael pointed to his own eyes. "Older ones with the gift are different."

"Did you rescue Anya?" Flint asked.

"Not yet. We're going to the Nulterra Gate tomorrow."

He grabbed my forearms. "Send me down there."

"What? No."

"I can run recon for you. Scout the area before you arrive."

"I don't think you understand how this works. If you're sent to Nulterra, it will be in chains. Not as a scout."

"So send me in chains," he pleaded.

"You know I can't do that."

"But I need to help my daughters."

I shook him gently. "Then let me go back and tell Fury that you are happy and safe in Eden."

His eyes drifted toward the gate.

"Come with me," I said. "I'll escort you through myself."

Flint took a step back. "Not until I know Fury is safe. I know the gate will make me forget."

I sighed and put my hands on my hips. "So you're going to sit outside my office for however long this journey takes?"

"If I have to."

"Suit yourself then." I turned back toward Samael. "Don't let him talk you into sending him."

Samael shook his head. "Of course not."

I started toward the gate again.

"Warren!" Flint called. "Tell her I love her."

"I will."

At the entrance, I stopped and patted my pockets to make sure they were empty. The gate would destroy anything born of Earth. Then I turned and gave Samael and Flint a thumbs-up before walking inside.

Euphoria engulfed my spirit, and I breathed in the scent of Eden—honeysuckle and sea salt. The two Eden suns warmed my face, and a cool breeze floated off the Eternal Sea.

It felt like I'd been gone a million years, and if I wasn't careful, I'd stay for a million more.

My T-shirt, basketball shorts, and sneakers had melted away. They were replaced with the softest jeans throughout eternity, a button-up black shirt made from the night sky, and cushioned boots that fit like I wasn't wearing them at all.

I started through the Idalia Marketplace, holding my breath so as not to get distracted by the manna carts or the fresh gazenberry-juice presses or the taco truck, which happened to be my favorite.

Pausing only briefly to return a few hellos, I exited the market and turned up the hill toward the Onyx Tower. I took the black stone steps two at a time until I passed the marble columns and reached for the heavy double doors.

Inside, the Principality Council courtroom was empty, so I jogged along the side corridor until I reached the winding staircase that wound up through the Tower. Cassiel's home was on the nineteenth floor, so I stood in the open center of the staircase and flew straight up.

I knocked on her door. "Cassiel?"

A few seconds later, the door opened. Cassiel stood on the other side in a long emerald gown with her golden hair flowing over her shoulders. When our eyes met, she rushed out and embraced me. "Warren!" When she finally stepped back, she searched my face. "What are you doing here?"

"I need your help."

"Come inside." She led me by the hand into her apartment.

I'd been there before, but it never failed to impress me. White walls, alabaster floors, and one whole wall made of glass—or probably crystal—with a spectacular view of Eden.

The place was filled with contraband she'd smuggled in her bag from Earth. The floor-to-ceiling shelves were lined with books. Her ice box was covered in tourist magnets. And on the counter was a crystal vase filled with Earth's seashells.

Remembering what Azrael had told me made me smile.

"What's going on?" she asked, sitting down on the velvety white sofa, still holding my hand. "Did you go to Nulterra?"

I sat down beside her. "Tomorrow, hopefully. But I have learned a lot more about it."

"Tell me everything."

There was no time for everything, but I gave her a quick recap. "Azrael killed Moloch before he could tell us more."

"That's a shame."

"For us maybe, but for you? Congratulations." I took both her hands. "You deserve it."

"Thanks. It's a lot of responsibility, but I'm settling in."

I shrugged. "You've been running the Council a long time anyway. You'll be great."

Her cheeks blushed. "I'm going to try."

"What can you tell me about an angel named Torman?" I asked.

"Torman? Wow. I haven't heard that name in a long time. He's an Angel of Knowledge. He was cast out with the Morning Star and the rest of his followers. Why?"

"I met his daughter on Earth. A Seramorta named Chimera. She had a stone given to her by Torman. It protects her from the side effects of being around angels."

"I've never heard of such a stone."

"Me either. Moloch said it was a blood stone called sanctonite, made from the blood of the Father."

Her laugh was incredulous. "That isn't possible."

"That's what Azrael said. Moloch told us that the Father's blood is what powers Nulterra. Az killed him over it."

"Why not ask the Father yourself?"

"Can I? Is he here?"

"I think he's been in Zion since you left. That's what I've heard anyway."

"Thank you, Cassiel."

"I'm glad I could help. Was that all you needed?"

"No. Actually, none of that is why I'm here. We've run into a problem."

"What happened?"

"Reuel threw the blood-stone cuffs Fury was going to use to cross into Nulterra into the ocean."

"I heard about that. I assumed you'd let her open the gate and go on without her."

I shook my head. "I promised her I'd come and try to find a way to recover the blood stone."

Her eyes searched mine. Deeply. Intrusively. "Oh." Angels of Knowledge could extract information with a touch.

I pulled my hand away, guilt flooding my heart.

"Do you love her, Warren?"

I looked away. My feelings for Fury were complicated, and I wasn't ready to admit to them, or have them gleaned involuntarily through a glance. "That has nothing to do with this. Can you help me? I really don't have much time."

Cassiel put her hands in her lap and stared at the wall.

"Please, Cassiel."

She got up and walked to the window. "The only Angels of Life powerful enough to summon blood stone are the Morning Star, which is why he has so much of it, and Metatron and Ariel. Neither of them will return to Earth to help you."

"You don't think Ariel will help me? Even to rescue a human soul lost to Nulterra?"

"The remaining Angels of Life haven't left the Throne Room since the war with Abaddon and Kasyade. They still believe your daughter is too much a risk to the spirit line."

I almost couldn't blame them. If the spirit line were severed, any angels on Earth would be stuck there. Permanently.

"But Ariel is powerful enough to find it?"

"Yes."

"Will you come with me to talk to her? You're much better at persuasion than I am."

She still wouldn't look at me. "I should probably stay here."

"Cassiel." I stood and walked up behind her, gently taking hold of her upper arms. "Don't shut me out."

"It's better this way. Your life is on Earth. You've never made that a secret."

"You're right." I leaned my head against hers, inhaling the

sweet scent of honey on her hair. "But I don't want to hurt you."

She shook her head. "You haven't." She took a deep breath and straightened. "Go to the Throne Room. Find Ariel. That's the only way to get the blood stone back."

I squeezed her arms. "Thank you." Then I released her and walked toward the door.

"Warren?"

I stopped with my hand on the doorknob and turned around.

"Remember to let us know when you descend through the gate. We'll all be anxious to hear of your success."

"I will. Goodbye, Cassiel."

"Goodbye."

The fastest and most distraction-free route to the Throne Room was through the air. I flew past the *Avronesh,* the home of the messengers, over the bay, and up the hillside toward Zion.

Zion was nothing short of a palace with a large open square, spectacular gardens, and a throne room fit for the Almighty.

It was the Father's official residence, though I'd never actually seen him there. Most of his time, he spent on Earth. And when he was in Eden, he could usually be found at the manna carts in the marketplace or visiting in someone's home.

Zion just wasn't his style, but it was used for the official business of Eden, celebrations (which were frequent), and prayer. The Throne Room was the only place where humans could communicate with their loved ones on Earth.

Humans rarely used it, however. They spent their days so caught up in the magic of Eden that the lives of their loved ones passed quickly. And before they knew it, they were reunited in the blissful everafter.

But occasionally, the messengers would send word to the Angels of Life, that a loved one needed help. Help even an angel was unable to give. In those cases, the departed could send messages of comfort or wisdom back to Earth. It was usually reserved for the most dire of cases.

Once, while I was in the Throne Room, a human sent word to her daughter who was clinging to life support. The messenger carried back a memory stone with the mother's words recorded inside it, "Let go, Diane." My angels brought Diane to Eden the very same day.

Maybe I could convince Flint to wait for word on Fury there. I needed to tell him on my way out.

I landed in the square outside the Throne Room, next to the crystal water fountain. Crystal water was rare. The only place in the universe it could be acquired was right here in the home of the Angels of Life. Which was probably why Zion became party-central of Eden. At about a bazillion proof, crystal water made moonshine look like apple juice.

Music was coming from the Throne Room, so I jogged up the marble steps and across the landing.

"Warren?" A woman's voice made me slide to a stop.

Ariel, the Archangel of Life was coming down the outdoor corridor. She had no human body, like most angels who stayed primarily in Eden. Though her form was solely made of light and energy, she resembled a woman. Small with long, flowing silvery hair.

I clasped my hands together. "Just who I was looking for."

"I heard you were coming."

"Cassiel?"

She nodded, then walked—or maybe floated—toward the double doors. "Come inside."

One of the heavy bronze doors opened, and music flooded the square. I expected there to be a party in the overwhelmingly grand hall. There wasn't. Just a lone human on the platform, playing an assortment of instruments seemingly all by himself—Ed Sheeran-style.

We stood there a moment and listened to the eclectic sound. Not quite jazz. Not quite pop. "Who is he?" I asked.

"I have no idea," she said, a bit of wonder in her ethereal voice. She gestured toward the pews.

I sat down on one row. She sat down in front of me and turned around.

I took a second to take in the impressive room. It was massive, though I expected it still took a bit of magic to get all the citizens of Eden inside at once. And all the sections of rows of pews faced the platform. Behind our music-entranced performer were the thrones.

The center for the Father.

Two on the right for Sandalphon and Metatron.

And one on the left—at the Father's right hand—for my daughter. It had once been the seat of the Morning Star. Someday, it would be hers.

Ariel waved her hand, and an invisible shield went up around us to diminish the sound of the music. "How may I help you, Warren?"

"Return to Earth with me."

"Ha! How *else* may I help you?"

"I'm serious."

"So am I."

"We've lost the blood stone that will help Fury and me break into Nulterra. We need to rescue Anya McGrath."

"I'm aware of what you're doing."

"Then why won't you help us?"

"Because it's dangerous." She folded her hands on the seat back of her pew. "Too dangerous for Fury."

"Too dangerous for you, you mean," I said, standing. "I don't know why I even bothered to come here. The Angels of Life are nothing but cowards."

With a flash, she was in the air, hovering inches above me. "Now, see here—"

I pointed at her. "No, *you* see here. I haven't forgotten that Sloan nearly died because you and your angels were too scared to do your job."

"Your child posed a threat to our entire existence. You and your summoner wife started that. Not us."

Shaking my head, I walked toward the door.

"Don't turn your back on me, *human*."

That was it. I spun on my heel and aimed my finger at her shimmering face. "Ariel, war is coming. And when it does, let the chronicles of history show that when the angels who sit closest to the throne had their choice to fight for the sanctity of Eden, *you* chose to take a knee."

When I turned to storm out, I saw him.

The Father was sitting in the very last row.

His presence didn't stop Ariel. She slammed the Throne Room door as she left. I ducked my head and walked to the back of the cathedral.

"Hello, Warren." The Father looked the same as he had on Earth. Old. Pudgy. And with a birthmark that looked like South America stamped on his nearly bald head. He slid over to make room for me beside him.

I grimaced as I sat down. "Did you hear all that?"

"I hear lots of things," he said with a smile. "Aren't you supposed to be somewhere else?"

"Yes."

"So why are you here?"

I turned toward him on the bench. "I need to ask you something."

"OK."

"Did you give your blood to the Morning Star to create Nulterra?"

His face didn't change expression. "I did."

"And you never told anyone?"

He shook his head.

"Why?"

"Why did I give it to him? Or why did I keep it secret?"

I shrugged. "Both?"

"The simple answer is I needed to protect the people I made him capable of hurting."

"But why not kill him? Actually, why didn't you just kill him after the First Angel War?"

He was thoughtful a moment. "You're a military man. Let me ask you this. If a leader strikes down every follower who turns against him, then why do any of his other followers remain?"

"Fear."

"Exactly. What a lonely existence that would be. For the leader and for the people."

"Yeah, I guess."

"And as for why I didn't destroy him in Antioch..." He sighed. "You're a father. I'm sure you already know the answer to that."

I thought of my bond with Iliana. The only thing I'd ever created. "I guess I do."

"And I told no one for a very simple reason. It wasn't time. Time is the most powerful force of all."

"Well, I hope it's time now because I told Cassiel."

"I know. I also told Rogan and Malak before I sent them to Earth."

"You sent them?"

"Of course I did. With two guardians on the ground and the ones watching from the auranos, Iliana will be safe. They can also teach her when she's older."

"Thank you."

He put his hands in his lap. "But none of those questions are what you really want to ask me, are they?"

I sank back in the pew and stared up at the elaborate ceiling. "Why not send someone more capable than me to do this? I have no business going on some rescue mission to Nulterra. I've already gotten one person killed. I'm a nobody. I'm a human."

"Who else should I send?" He crossed his arm and tapped is lips with his index finger. "I wonder...well, Ariel's out. Right? How about Cassiel? No. She can barely stand Earth. Maybe a prophet. No, they always stay clear of a battle—"

"All right. I see what you're getting at. I'm the only one available."

"No, Warren." He turned toward me and locked his eyes with mine. "You're the only one able."

Well.

I stared straight ahead at the stage.

"Hey, Ben!" The Father cupped his hands around his mouth. "Play 'Eye of the Tiger!'"

I laughed, really hard.

He nudged my arm. "Go. Will you do me a favor?"

"Of course."

"Don't hold back when you get there. If you can, I want you to burn the whole realm down."

"How?"

"If it's possible, you already have everything you need."

"Yes, sir."

"Thank you. Warren, I'm sorry for all this trip is costing you, but you'll have plenty of time with your daughter when you get back."

That was all the encouragement I needed. I stood and stepped out into the aisle. "What are you doing here anyway? You don't like Zion."

"It's the easiest place to receive news from Earth except for the auranos." A thin smile spread on his face. "And I'm not crazy about heights."

I laughed again. "Goodbye, Father."

"See you soon."

The only other angel who could help with the missing blood stone was Metatron, and he was a day's journey away in the Fiery. A trip that would be wasted because he wouldn't go to Earth anyway. At least Metatron had a good reason; he was trapped in the body of a nearly four-hundred-year-old man.

I flew across the Eternal Sea and circled the cliff where my mother's house overlooked the beach. She'd be home now. Probably cooking something amazing.

From the air, I could see my own house near the beach. I wondered if Alice was there, waiting with my dog, Skittles, for my return.

As much as I wanted to stop in for a visit, I needed to get back to Earth. The longer I stayed in Eden, the harder it would be to leave. Against everything in my spirit, I turned east and headed back for the gate.

"Well done. You have plenty of time," Samael said, glancing at my watch as I walked back outside.

"Really?"

Nodding, he unfastened my watch and handed it to me. "It's only been a few minutes on Earth. Was your visit productive?"

"Yes and no. The one angel who could help me won't."

"Help you with what?"

"Recover some lost blood stone." I put the watch on my left wrist.

He grimaced. "I'm afraid Ariel and Metatron would be your only options. I suspect neither of them were keen to help."

"You guessed correctly." I looked around. "Where's Flint?"

He pointed behind me. Flint was greeting newcomers to the gate. I chuckled. "At least he's staying busy."

"I'm thinking of keeping him here permanently."

"I hate to ruin your plans, but will you take him to Zion? The Father's in the Throne Room. I thought maybe they could wait for news together."

"I can do that. When do you leave for Nulterra?"

I glanced at my watch. "In a few hours."

"Warren, you're back," Flint said coming toward us.

"Yes, but I'm leaving again. Your daughter is waiting for me back on the island."

His face fell.

"Cheer up. It looks like she'll be staying on Earth, after all. Her plans seem to have fallen through."

He raised both fists in victory. "Praise the Father."

I jerked my thumb toward the Eden Gate. "Speaking of, the Father is waiting in Zion for news. I'm sure he'd be happy for you to join him. Samael will show you the way."

"But once I go in, I'll forget, won't I?"

"Only the bad stuff," I said.

He thought for a second. "Then I think I'll stay here until I know for sure that you're back safe."

I looked at Samael. "Why does no one believe I'm immortal?"

Samael chuckled.

"Do what you like." I offered my hand to Flint. "I'll send word when we're at the gate tomorrow."

"And as soon as you get back?" Flint asked.

"Yes, sir."

He pulled me into a hug. "Good luck, son."

"Thanks."

Then I released him and crossed back into the mortal world.

It was still dark on the island. I walked up the beach and followed the path to our tree house. When I reached the top floor, I saw through the mosquito netting that Fury was asleep.

Reuel looked out his door. Of course, he'd heard my arrival. I held a finger over my lips, and he nodded and disappeared back inside.

I tried to sneak inside, but the sound of the ripping Velcro made Fury stir. She rolled onto her back as I approached the bed. "Well?" she asked, rubbing her eyes.

"I'm afraid I don't have good news." I kicked off my shoes.

Fury propped up on her elbows. "Cassiel wasn't able to help?"

"Cassiel was helpful." I unbuttoned my shirt. "But I'm afraid getting the blood stone back will be impossible."

She flopped back onto her pillow as I grabbed my last pair of athletic shorts from my bag. I slipped out of my jeans and pulled them on while she stared at the ceiling.

I finally pulled the sheet back on my side of the bed. "I'm sorry," I said, laying down beside her.

She draped her arm across her forehead and stared at the ceiling. "I'm sure you tried."

"I did. I swear." I rolled onto my side and propped my head up on my elbow. "I may have even inadvertently started a war with the Angels of Life."

"Don't do that. We might need them on our side."

I sighed. "You have no idea. The Father doesn't want me to just seal Nulterra. He wants me to destroy it."

"How?"

"I have no idea."

"He's not very helpful, is he?"

"Cassiel told me recently that omniscience can be a curse. That sometimes knowing too much can cause us to not act at all. I think that's the Father's sweet spot of operation. Tell us just enough to get us moving, then trust us not to screw everything up." I took a deep breath, letting my eyes drop to the mattress between us. "But I'll be honest, this whole thing has me worried."

"Warren?"

I met her eyes again.

"Thank you."

"I really didn't do anything. I was actually a total failure."

"Never." She reached over and took my hand that was resting across my waist. For a loaded second, she stared at our fingers meshed together. "If things go sideways tomorrow—"

"Shh," I said, shaking my head. "Let's not even talk like that."

She nodded, but it was clear, she was fighting back all her emotions again. Then before she let the tears fall, she rolled onto her side away from me, pulling my arm around her. I laid my head beside hers on the pillow, and before long, we were both asleep.

CHAPTER NINETEEN

rip. Drip. Drip.
Drops of water thumped my forehead in rhythm. I reached across Fury's side of the bed.

She was gone.

But I heard movement in the room, so I rolled toward the sound and opened my eyes in time to see Fury pull on her sports bra. Her back was toward me. *Damn it.*

"Why am I wet?" I used the edge of the sheet to dry my face.

"It stormed last night," she said, sticking her arms through a gray tank top. "Rained really hard. Didn't you hear it?"

"I didn't hear a thing. I slept like the *dead*."

She was smirking when she turned around. "Cute."

"You didn't sleep?"

"I rarely do."

"Since when?"

"Since always."

"That is *not* true. You used to pass the hell out." I grinned and rolled onto my back. "But maybe I had something to do with that."

She laughed and threw her nightshirt at me.

I caught it and held it against my chest. "So when did you become an insomniac?"

She was folding her cotton shorts. "When my sister was taken."

"Really?"

She nodded, not looking at me.

I propped up on both elbows. "I'll get her back, Fury."

When she looked up, I didn't miss the way her eyes snagged on my abs. "I know you will."

I sat up and swung my legs off the bed. "What time is it?"

"Just after six thirty. Are you going to shower?"

Before standing, I adjusted the *bothered* anatomy beneath my shorts. "Nah. I went to Eden last night. The Gate cleans better than any shower." I stood and stretched my arms. My left elbow ached from keeping it straight under her pillow.

"Really?"

I picked up my bag and dropped it on the bed. "Yeah. Everything burns up."

"Even your clothes?"

"Everything. Why? You thinking about me naked?" I reached into my bag for a shirt.

"You're in rare form this morning," she said, stuffing her clothes into her bag.

I pulled out a black tank top. "I'm sorry. I haven't been around that much estrogen in a *while*."

"Really?" She took her hairbrush out of the side pocket. "I thought you and that angel, Cassiel, were a thing."

I thought about how sad Cassiel looked the night before as I pulled the shirt over my head. "We almost were, but then it was over before it ever really got started."

"Because of the whole betrayal thing?" She stood in front of the mirror and brushed her long silky hair.

"Yeah, but I'm pretty much over that."

She stopped brushing. "You are?"

I nodded. "But on top of all that, we want different things. She has no interest in living on Earth ever."

"And you do?" she asked, surprised.

"I'd rather be in Eden, but I want to be here with Iliana as much as possible." I turned my back to her, dropped my shorts, and stuck my right leg through a clean pair of underwear.

"Warren, I need to tell you some—whoa! Oh my god!"

Glancing over my shoulder, I saw Fury whirl back around with her hand over her eyes. I chuckled.

"Geez, warn me next time!"

I pulled my shorts over my butt, then picked up my tactical khaki cargos. "You have a mirror."

"But I wasn't looking!"

Obviously. "Sorry."

"Sure you are."

"What's the big deal? You're the one who said it's not like there's anything down there you haven't seen before."

"I was joking."

"But you have seen what's down there."

"That was different."

"Was it though?" I buttoned my pants and turned around. "We weren't dating then. We aren't dating now. You're hot. You're cold. I'm frustrated. I'm confused. Feels exactly the same to me."

She was braiding her hair. "Are we getting into that again?"

"It's been a while. Why not?"

In the mirror, I saw her roll her eyes.

"Why did you leave me, Fury?"

Boom. There it was. The question was out. Dropped on our treehouse like a bomb. And it surprised me every bit as much as it surprised her.

Her hands stopped twisting the strands of hair. "You know why."

I shook my head. "I really, *really* don't. I don't believe for one second that you just had to take a job in Somalia with your sister."

"Because you were a job, Warren." She slowly turned around. "Because you were a job."

I stood there in stunned silence. While this wasn't exactly *news*, it was still shocking to hear her admit it aloud. Hurtful too.

"Wow. That's great." I slammed my clothes back into my bag with so much force I nearly ripped the zipper. "I'm so glad to know I was nothing but a paycheck."

Clenching her hands into fists, she let her braid unravel. "But you weren't, and that was the problem!"

My backpack fell over. "What?"

"My assignment was to bring you into Claymore, help you get through training, then take you to Somalia. But I walked into a conversation I was never supposed to hear. Enzo telling Azrael they needed to move you soon because someone named Sloan had just received a big job promotion in North Carolina."

"You didn't know about Sloan?"

"I had never heard her name until that day. When I asked Azrael, he told me of the Morning Star's plot to get the two of you together. That you were destined to breed some superangel called the Vitamorte.

"Then he said I was doing such an impeccable job at keeping you entertained that he was beginning to feel like Sloan was no longer a threat." She sank down on the corner of the bed. "I was his hired whore, and I was too stupid to know it."

I walked closer. "But you started flirting with me the day we met."

"I flirt with *everybody*. The majority of men in our line of work are morons who think with their dicks. There's no better weapon on a battlefield for a woman."

"Well, that's true." I sat down beside her.

"All of it's true. Then a few days later, you dropped the *L* word, and I freaked."

"Why didn't you tell me?"

"Because at that time, the entire Claymore billion-dollar corporation centered around one purpose—you and Sloan. If I had told you, Azrael would have killed me. Literally, killed me."

As much as I hated to agree, that was probably true.

"I told Azrael I would quit if I wasn't reassigned. So he sent me to Somalia with Anya instead of with you."

I put my hands in my lap as the dots of information finally connected. "And my unit relieved yours in Somalia."

"I was there the day you showed up."

"Really?"

She nodded.

"I had no idea."

"I know."

"Knock, knock, bitches!" Ionis called, sauntering into our room wearing white shorts, an orange shirt, and a white blazer with the sleeves rolled to his elbows. His sunglasses were perched on his white head, and I'm pretty sure he was wearing lipstick.

Fury groaned. "What are you wearing? You look like the third rejected member of Wham!"

"This, my dear, is a LULUS exclusive." He did a full turn. At least he was wearing the walking shoes I'd bought him.

"What do you want, Ionis?" I asked.

He tapped the glittery watch around his wrist. "Just keeping to your schedule, my good sir. It's breakfast time."

"We're running a little behind," I said.

"You? You're always up with the birds."

"I had a late night."

"Ooo, I'll bet you did, you dog." He covered his mouth with his hands.

"He went to Eden, you idiot." Fury got up, signaling the end to our conversation. She walked back to the mirror and began to braid her hair again. This time, much faster.

"Eden?" he asked with a gasp. "And you didn't take me?"

I stood and returned to my backpack. "I was on a tight schedule."

"Doing what?"

"Never mind. Where's Reuel?"

Reuel stepped into the doorway. *"Ven ta."*

"You ready to go eat?" I asked him.

He smiled for the first time since we'd landed on the island.

I strapped on my sword and picked up my backpack. "Everybody take your stuff. We'll leave as soon as we eat."

By eight thirty, we'd made it through the village of Tigbawan. With the added weight of our packs, and with Ionis in tow, it would take us three more hours to reach the Nulterra Gate. The sun was already beating down, and all four of us were sucking on the straws of our CamelBaks as we walked along the muddy side of the narrow road.

"Don't forget, we need to conserve water," I said over my shoulder. "I'd rather not depend on Nulterra for any necessities if we can help it."

Fury was walking beside me about twenty yards ahead of Ionis and Reuel. "You can use mine to refill yours when we get there since I won't be needing it."

My heart sank. "I want to say I'm sorry you won't be going with us, but I'm really not."

"That's fair. I'd probably slow you guys down anyway."

"Not a chance."

She looked up at me and smiled.

"You should really make peace with Reuel before we part ways. If something happens down there —"

"You said we weren't going to talk like that, remember?" she asked.

"Right."

"I'll talk to him. I guess I was pretty mean last night."

"We are all kind of used to it by now."

She jabbed me in the ribs with her elbow, and I laughed.

"Stop!" Ionis yelled.

We both turned around.

He was standing in the middle of the path, looking down at his shoes. "We need to return to the village immediately. These fourth-century roads are ruining my new shoes."

"They didn't have pavement in the fourth century," Fury replied. She turned back around. "Why did Azrael send him with us?"

"He's probably hoping we'll take Ionis to Nulterra and leave him there," I said.

"Probably. It's not a bad idea, actually."

"Can we at least find some water so I can wash off the mud?" He called to us.

"Only if we start making up some time," I said. "So you'd better hurry up."

We walked for another forty-five minutes and started seeing signs for Cambugahay Falls. Then we reached a trailhead with a giant red welcome sign and scooters parked along the road. "Warren! Can we stop?" Ionis called.

I looked at my watch and sighed. "Fury, what do you think?"

"They probably have public access to drinking water," she answered with a shrug.

"We'll stop, but make it quick!" I called back as Fury and I turned off the main road.

I followed her down the uneven path, and I caught a flash of turquoise through the trees. "Fury, look at the water."

She stepped to the side and pulled the gnarly vines apart.

"Wow. That's gorg—" Her foot slipped on the mud, and she went down hard on her thigh.

I grabbed her with my power before she slid off the bank. Thank the Father she was laughing. "You all right?"

"Oh god," she whined, rolling to the side. The back of her shirt, her entire left ass cheek, and her whole leg were covered in thick brown mud.

I offered her my hand, and she took it, leaving mud prints around my thumb. "Couldn't let Ionis be dirty alone, huh?"

"Ugh. It's cold and sticky." She took a few steps and stopped, her face melting with disgust. "It's up my shorts."

I laughed and walked past her. "Come on."

The base of the trail opened to one of the most beautiful scenes I'd seen outside Eden. The large lagoon, with water every bit as blue as the Eternal Sea, lay at the base of a semi-circle waterfall. A boy swung out over the water on a rope swing and squealed as he splashed down.

"I'll put my winter home right there," Ionis said, pointing at the other shore as they caught up with us. "What are you losers waiting for?" He walked past us toward the water, his massive backpack bouncing up and down on his shoulders.

Fury looked up at Reuel. "You can swim?"

He smiled, probably because she was talking to him again. "No swim. Sink."

The three of us laughed. Fury shielded her eyes from the sun cutting through the rainforest trees. "Is that more falls at the top?"

"Looks like it," I said.

"Let's go up there. I don't see as many people."

I lifted an eyebrow. "You're going to climb that embankment?" I let my eyes fall to her muddy half.

"It's not like I can get any dirtier, right?"

"Right. Lead the way."

Thankfully, no one fell on the way up to the top set of falls

—or the *middle* set of falls as we discovered when we reached them. A third set was above those, and it created a small pool before the edge of the big falls. And she was right. There were zero people other than us. We piled our bags on the driest bit of rocks we could find.

Fury had never been one for modesty, so I shouldn't have been surprised when she kicked off her hiking boots and stripped down to her low-cut sports bra and boy shorts. But after our conversation that morning, the sight of her so scantily clad stirred a hunger I'd kept beaten down since her sudden reemergence back into my life.

For a quick second, I allowed my eyes to skim the delicious length of her body. Fury had always been sexy. Tight body. Full breasts. Dangerously seductive eyes. But now...

She was all that and more. Smooth curves had replaced her sharp edges. Made her touchable. Inviting. Supple and soft. Her breasts jiggled playfully, and a few silvery lines streaked what were once hard, sculpted abs. It was all I could do to restrain my fingers from tracing them.

Good god.

I forced my eyes away before things got embarrassing.

On her ribcage was something I hadn't seen before. A tattoo. Words in black script, but I was too far away to read them.

She carried her shorts and tank top to the water's edge and knelt down to wash them against a submerged rock. "It's warm."

"Aren't waterfalls usually ice cold?" I asked.

"They are in North America," she said. "Are you getting in?"

"Don't want to swim in my shorts."

"So take them off." She wrung the water out of her tank top and draped it around her neck. "I saw your underwear this morning. They'll dry fast."

Reuel looked at me with wide eyes.

"It's not what you think." I took a step backward. "I'll keep Reuel company."

She dunked her shorts under the water, then scrubbed them against the rock. "You are about to visit Hell, Warren. Live a little. Besides, where else will you find water like this?"

"Eden."

"Oh." She smiled and dunked her shorts again. After a few more rounds of dunk, scrub, and repeat, she looked at her shorts with defeat. "It's like supernatural mud. They're ruined."

I looked at Reuel. "Could it be supernatural mud?"

He lifted both his shoulders.

Fury tossed the shorts at my feet, then walked over and spread her tank top on top of her rucksack.

"Uh, Fury." I patted my own backside. "You missed a spot." Her leg was still covered in sludge.

"Don't worry. I've got this under control." She started up the rocks to the riverbank. Then she carefully waded across the top of the waterfall. On the other side was a boulder and a rope swing.

"How deep is the water?" I called up to her.

She grabbed the rope. "You sound like such a grandpa. It's deep enough if there's a rope."

I shook my head. "Reuel, can we take turns carrying her to Nulterra?"

He grunted.

Fury toted the rope back onto the bank behind her, then jumped. She sailed over the water and let go. Her head completely disappeared below the surface, then bobbed back up. She was laughing. "That was amazing!" She dipped her head backward to smooth her hair away from her face.

I let out the breath I didn't realize I was holding.

"Come on, Warren. You'll love it. Trust me!" she yelled.

Reuel shoved me sideways.

"Oh, what the hell." I unlaced my boots and stripped down to my black boxer briefs.

Someone at the lagoon below let out a whistle. I turned and saw Ionis with a mocking smile, fanning his face. I shot him the bird, then scaled the bank up to the top of the falls.

The water was warm as I navigated through the current to the boulder on the other side. Fury was still treading water below.

I peered down at the water as I grabbed the rope. "You sure it's deep enough?"

"Bwooock, bwock, bwock, bwooock," she teased.

Less motivated by Fury's taunts, and more so by the fact that the swimmers down below had spotted me in my underwear, I swung out and let go. Opening my eyes underwater, it was crystal clear. I could see Fury's perfect legs within reach, so I grabbed her knee.

When I broke the surface, she splashed my face. Laughing, I splashed her back.

She turned back toward the shore and cupped her hands around her mouth. "Your turn, Reuel!"

He shook his head.

"It's not too deep!" I called back over the noise of the falls. "Look! I'm standing!" Granted, I was dancing rock to rock on my tiptoes, but still.

He shook his head harder.

"Come on! All will be forgiven if you jump in this water."

"Ooo, manipulation." I clicked my tongue. "That's dirty."

"I promise," she added.

Reuel scowled. But then he stood.

Fury slapped my shoulder. "It worked!"

With an angry huff, the angel pulled off his T-shirt. Then he dropped his shorts displaying shockingly bright green boxers. Fury swam toward me. "Is that Bigfoot on his underwear?"

I chuckled. "I think so."

Reuel started up the bank, and Fury grabbed my arm. "Oh my god. His ass says 'Sascrotch.'"

She was right. The word "Sascrotch" was scrawled across his ass in giant white letters. I laughed out loud. Correctly sensing he was the *butt* of our joke, Reuel covered his backside with his hands the rest of the way to the top.

"I love that guy," I said, watching him cross the falls.

When he reached the boulder, I realized how tiny the rope —and the tree that held it—looked by comparison. "Maybe you should just jump!" I called up to him.

"Smart," Fury said. "He would snap that tree like a toothpick."

Reuel looked over the edge. Then he shook his head and took a few steps back. Fury and I both started cheering for him, chanting as we slapped the water. "Sascrotch! Sascrotch! Sascrotch!"

He broke into a run and leapt off the edge, curling his legs up into a cannonball. When he crashed through the water, the tsunami knocked Fury back into me and sent a wall of water over us both. As the wave toppled her over me, I grabbed her around the waist to keep her from being thrown into the shallows.

Obviously dazed by the water and coughing violently, she hooked an arm around my neck and ran her free hand down her face.

"Are you OK?" I asked when I could talk.

She laughed and coughed again. "That was the best near-drowning experience I've ever had."

I held onto her, letting our bodies slide against each other with the current. And she didn't immediately let go. When she did, she swam toward Reuel, who was now easily standing in the pool. She jumped into his arms. "You did it!"

He pushed her back to arm's length. "All is forgiven?"

"A promise is a promise. I'm sorry I got so angry with you."
She sighed. "I know you were just trying to protect me."

He pulled her in for a tight hug and kissed the top of her
head.

I waded out to them. "Nice shorts, Sascrotch."

With a laugh, he skimmed his giant arm over the water,
dousing us both again. When the water war ceased, I saw Ionis
standing on the shore with his hands on his hips. "What is this?
Angels *playing?*"

Reuel and I exchanged a mischievous grin, then both turned
and grabbed him with our power.

"Oh no!" he squealed. "Warren, Reuel, don't you dare!"

His white shoes once again dragged through the mud as we
pulled him toward the water. He strained and strained but it
was no use. "My jacket!" he wailed as he tumbled off a particularly tall rock into the current.

Once Ionis went under, Reuel gave me a high-five.

Ionis stood, his white-blond spikes now flat and mascara
dribbling down his cheeks. "You both deserve Hell."

Reuel splashed him again.

It was a much-needed break from the tiring and stressful week
we'd all had. Even Ionis enjoyed himself, despite what he'd have us
all believe. Fury looked downright *refreshed.* And as we hiked back
out to the road, I realized I'd never heard her laugh so much.

"So are we not going to talk about Reuel's underpants?"
Ionis asked a few minutes down the road toward Nulterra.

"Avarkai doro," Reuel said with a curious smile.

Ionis looked up at him, surprised. "A gift from whom, might
I ask?"

Reuel shook his head.

"Yeah, Reuel. Who do you know on Earth buying you underwear?" I asked.

Fury stared straight ahead. "I bet I know."

"Who?" Ionis asked.

Reuel growled at her.

"You know the owner of that bakery in Asheville that he and Nathan like so much?" she asked, grinning.

My face whipped toward him. "Shut up. Are you serious?"

He didn't respond.

"Damn," I said with a laugh. "What's her name?"

Ionis tapped his fingers on his lips. "Something very Game of Thrones-ish."

"Brienne. That's right. Wow." I shook my head in awe. "I'm impressed. How long has that been going on?"

"En nan," Reuel said, his eyes fixed on the ground.

"You are lying. *Something* is going on if the girl is buying you underwear," I said.

"He means he doesn't get to see her because he can't be that close to Iliana." Smiling, Fury looked across me at Reuel. "But they are quite friendly whenever he pops into town."

I slapped him on the back. "So I guess I'm not the only one whose love life got screwed up in Asheville, huh? Sorry about that."

Reuel shrugged his hulking shoulders, and we walked on.

All signs of civilization began to fade away. Roadside houses dwindled to none. The road turned to dirt. And cars passing by became so infrequent, I began to wonder if it was shut down up ahead.

We turned a corner, and my suspicions were confirmed. In the distance, yellow barricades blocked the road with what I suspected were "No Trespassing" signs written in the native language.

"Anybody else getting a real Stephen King vibe?" Ionis asked as we neared it.

Fury slowed to walk beside me. "Pretty sure that's our inner compass telling us we're in the right place."

Ionis gave a nervous whimper. "This is such a bad idea."

"Come on." I quickened my pace, taking the lead. "Let's get it over with."

After another mile, the rainforest closed in around us. The winding road narrowed until only a faint path remained through the twisted palms and thick foliage. We trudged through the undergrowth as water dripped from the trees above, plunking our heads in almost a constant rhythm. The air was hot and thick and laced with a euphonic menagerie of sound.

Birds whistling through the high canopy.

Frogs croaking and squeaking.

Insects buzzing around my ears.

"Fury, did you put on bug repellent?"

"Yes, Dad."

I took out my sword when the vegetation began to overtake the path. "Watch out for snakes," I said over my shoulder as I sliced through a massive fern blocking our way.

"How much farther?" Ionis whined behind Fury.

"He's great training for having a toddler," Fury said.

"Or a hemorrhoid." Light glistened through the trees up ahead, and dread bubbled like hot black tar in my stomach. "We're almost there."

When we stepped out into the bright sunlight, we were almost at the salt-mirror's edge. Fury stopped beside me. "This is it?"

"This is it." I took off my rucksack and dropped it on the ground. The others did the same—and Ionis added a melody of profanities.

I pulled out my cell phone and dialed my father. He answered on the first ring. "I was beginning to get worried," he said without a greeting.

"We're here. Had a long hike in this morning, and cell service is hit or miss."

"So this is it?"

"This is it."

"Take care of yourself."

"You taught me well, Dad."

There was a pause on the other end of the line, which was Azrael's equivalent of getting emotional. After a second, he cleared his throat. "Let me know as soon as you're back."

"I will."

Then he ended the call without a goodbye.

I put the phone away, then pressed my finger to my ear. I called out to Samael. "Samael, it's Warren. Can you let everyone know we made it to the gate?"

"Cassiel's already here with me, waiting for word. Good luck down there."

"Thanks. If you don't hear from me again, assume we made it inside."

"Roger that."

I laughed.

"What is it?" Fury asked.

I pointed to my ear. "Samael just said 'Roger that.'"

Reuel shook his head.

"That's funny," Fury said, walking toward the circle. "It's so blue."

"It's a mirror." I pointed up. "It's reflecting the sky."

"Really?"

I offered her my hand. "Come on."

She took it and followed me as I walked out on it.

"Eshta!" Reuel shouted, reaching to snatch Fury back.

But it was too late. Her boot settled on the circle, and the Earth gave a thunderous shake. The entire circle shifted under us.

I grabbed her and launched high into the air. The rumbling

stopped and the glowing purple gas dissipated. I blew out a sigh of relief and swore.

Her back was against my chest, and both my arms were locked around her. I felt her laugh against me. "I guess we don't have to wonder how to open it."

"Shit. You think?" My heart was thumping in my ears, and I rested my forehead against the back of her head. "I'm sorry. I completely forgot you were the key."

"I'm safe. Relax." She patted my arm, then pointed at the ground. "Look! I see us."

I tilted forward. As the ripples on the salt water calmed, our reflection became clear. I tightened my arms and took a deep breath, realizing fully how thankful I was that she was safe and that she was *not* going with us.

"It's so huge. And it's a perfect circle." Her eyes scanned the island. Then she jerked. "Warren, what's that?"

I looked in the direction she was facing. On a large rock, at the far edge of the circle, something shiny reflected the sunlight...

The blood-stone case.

CHAPTER TWENTY

"You asked *Ariel* for help?" Ionis asked, dumbfounded. Fury had opened the case. It was a bit water-logged, but all the pieces were there. Reuel looked far from relieved, and I completely understood.

"Yeah. She refused, but I guess she changed her mind." I grimaced. "I did give her a lot of shit about it."

"That's impressive. She hated coming to Earth even before Iliana's presence threatened to unravel our existence." Ionis grinned. "Did you ask her to be *part of our world?*"

Fury rolled her eyes.

"Or did you just ask her to go *under the sea* and get them?" Ionis snickered.

"You are an idiot," Reuel said in perfect English.

Fury carefully picked up one of the cuffs, but my hand shot out to stop her. "Wait. Why don't we try to open the gate and let me inspect the situation first?"

"So you can leave me here?" she asked.

I took her hand and turned her arm face up. "How would I do that? You have the key, remember?"

She blinked, then pressed her lips closed.

"I'm just thinking since this is a door from Earth, it might not go directly through the spirit line."

"You think it might have an entrance hall?" she asked.

"It's worth finding out before you strap those torture devices on you. If we can cut down the time you actually have to wear them in this realm, it might save your life."

Shaking his head, Reuel walked away. Fury's eyes followed him. "I'll be right back." She put the cuff back into the case and jogged to catch up with him.

Ionis was rocking back and forth on his heels. "What shall we do while we wait? Sing Disney songs?"

"No," I said, watching Fury. She was holding onto Reuel's hand while he looked at the ground. I tried not to listen, but it was impossible...until Ionis started whistling a tune I recognized from *The Little Mermaid*. My eyes slid toward him.

"What?" He spread his arms in question. "I love that movie."

I chuckled and shook my head.

After a moment, Fury and Reuel walked back toward us. She was hanging on his arm, and his eyes were red and wet.

"Everybody OK?" I asked.

She looked up at him. "Yeah. We're all right."

With a sigh, Reuel nodded.

"Shall we try this, then?" I walked toward the edge of the circle. "I'll go to the center while Fury touches the edge. Reuel, you can pull her back if necessary."

He grunted.

Fury knelt on the ground by the edge while I walked a few feet out onto the mirror. Reuel knelt and took hold of her upper arm.

"All right. We ready?" I asked.

Fury extended her hand. "Ready."

"Go ahead." I watched my reflection in the mirror.

Her touch rippled the surface like she'd smacked water

instead of dipped her fingers into it. The ground rumbled again, and purple mist rose all around me. The whole circle turned slowly to the right. "You good?" I called to her.

"Yeah. The whole thing is moving...and sinking, I think!"

I looked over. Her hand on the surface had dropped a few inches, and a definite rim was showing around the edge where it had been flush with the grass before. I had to turn to keep my eyes on her. The whole thing slowly spun like a disk, sinking deeper into the ground. Six or seven inches down, the turning stopped like it hit a wall.

Behind me was another loud thud, then another, and another... I turned and walked toward a definite hole in the surface. Like a pie piece had fallen into a hole. The noise continued as more pie pieces fell around the perimeter.

Kerthunk. Kerthunk. Kerthunk.

"What do you see?" Fury shouted.

I looked into the hole. "Stairs!" One by one they were dropping down and sliding into shallow slots along the perimeter wall. "It's like a spiral staircase!" I started down the first few wide steps, waiting to feel the shift of a spirit line. There was none.

As stairs appeared, I took them, winding around the circle and descending farther and farther into the cavity. Another violent shift nearly knocked me over as the stair underneath my feet catapulted me out of the hole as it sprang back to the surface.

Good thing I could fly.

I steadied myself in the air just above Fury and Reuel, where he had obviously tackled her back onto the grass. She was panting under his heavy arm.

"Whoa!" Ionis started clapping. "That was like you were shot out of a cannon!"

"What happened?" I asked, still stunned.

Before she could answer, I saw why. Half of the staircase had formed, and when the piece under Fury's hand dropped out, she could no longer touch the circle. The stair I was on was the last one that had dropped, and the first one to spring back into place. I'd probably almost killed them when the stair shot me up to the sky.

I landed beside them on the grass and pulled Fury up. "Thanks," she said, trying to catch her breath. "I had no idea it would close up so fast."

"I almost took your heads off, didn't I?"

"Yeah." She looked across the circle. "But I think I know how to prevent it now."

Reuel and I followed her around the perimeter to where the first step had dropped down. Ionis hurried to catch up with us. "Wait for me!"

When she stopped, she pointed at the mirror near our feet. "We stand on it together until the staircase is complete. Then you can check it out while I wait up here with Reuel."

I looked at Reuel. He shrugged.

She offered me her hand. "Hang on to me in case this goes wrong."

My chest tightened, but I wrapped my hand around hers. Then we both stepped onto the circle again. Her hand clenched as the ground shook again. Then it sank down and the steps started dropping a few feet ahead of us.

"What was it like down there?" she asked.

"I was still very much on this planet."

"What do you mean?"

"I expect that crossing into Nulterra will be similar to walking through the Eden Gate. It's almost like walking through a wall of energy. You can't see it, but you can sure as hell feel it."

"What does it feel like?"

Just the thought made me smile. "Amazing. Like an orgasm for your whole body."

She belted out a laugh.

I shrugged. "It's true. And you know that peaceful, relaxed feeling afterward?"

She nodded.

"It lasts as long as you're there."

"Wow. That's one way to sell it." Her cheeks had the slightest pink tinge. "Tell me more about Eden."

I thought for a moment. It was hard to sum up Eden in a conversation. "It's the most beautiful place I've ever seen. Everything's clean and bright. Oh, it's bright because we have two suns."

"Two? Is it daylight all the time?"

"No. They're pretty close together, so two sunsets and two sunrises one right after the other. I don't even know how to describe the colors that paint the sky."

"I can't even imagine."

I looked around the circle. Half of it had dropped out of view. "And Eden has all the things you love...except for guns."

She smiled. "What do you know about the things I love?"

"I know you love mountains and waterfalls. You love perfectly ripe fruit, and anything made into a noodle. You only prefer summer over fall because of how much you love fireflies, and your favorite band is Shinedown."

Her mouth was gaping by the time I finished.

I snapped my fingers. "Oh, and your favorite scent is honeysuckle, which you'll really love about Eden. It smells like honeysuckle and sea salt."

"How do you know all that about me?" she asked, still wide-eyed.

"I pay attention."

"*Eden vacan pen kek,*" Reuel argued.

"Eden doesn't smell like cake." Ionis shook his head. "You're both wrong. Eden smells like fresh cotton and linen, like new American money."

"Whatever, Ionis." The dropping steps were nearing us. I pulled Fury back onto the top step. "It's almost finished."

She was still staring at me.

"What?"

She turned her eyes toward the horizon. "I just can't believe you remember that much."

"I can't really either, to be honest." My head tilted. *Maybe I knew more about Fury than I thought.*

The last step fell all the way down to the bottom of the glowing purple hole. I tightened my grip on her as we both peered over. "I wonder if this is why they call it the pit."

"It's certainly an appropriate word," she said.

Because each step had anchored itself into the wall, there was an open hole right down the center, allowing us a view of the floor below. "It's so bright down there," Fury said.

She was right. Unlike a man-made hole, this one had almost more light at the bottom than at the top. Like a giant spotlight was shining onto the bottom off the stairs.

"Eden's Gate is pretty bright too," Ionis said.

"He's right. I guess it's time to find out where the light is coming from." I held Fury's hand toward Reuel. When he took it, I started down the staircase.

As I descended, I touched my ear and tried calling out to Iliana. "Iliana, can you hear me?"

Nothing.

Despite the separation of the mirror, the steps were still wet and glassy, though some of the water had been displaced. The entire structure, I realized, was made of salt, or some otherworldly compound of it.

As the walls and steps glowed, and the purple smoke they emitted twisted and curled around me, I thought of the day with Cassiel when I'd tasted the substance. Perhaps that wasn't one of my better ideas.

Halfway down, I looked back up. "Everything OK up there?"

Reuel held up a thumb.

"You look like you are headed to a rave!" With a wild smile, Ionis cupped his hands around his mouth. "Don't do drugs, Warren!"

Shaking my head, I continued on until I reached the bottom. On the last step, I peered down a tunnel into a bright purple light. The tunnel created the spotlight we'd seen from above.

I looked up again. "There's a tunnel!" I shouted. "Stay there until I come back!"

"Be careful!" Fury called down.

I pulled my sword from its scabbard and started down the corridor. Its walls were different from the steps, darker and more reflective. It was tall enough for me to walk with plenty of room overhead and on each side.

Abaddon, the Destroyer, came to mind. He had made Reuel look small, so this hallway had been built to accommodate demons his size. The thought made me shudder.

There was a slight hissing sound, a crackling and tinkling all around me like the slow shattering of thin glass. Looking closer at the walls, I saw tiny crystals growing on the surface. "Osmium," I whispered.

Before I had the opportunity to forget, I jogged back to the bottom step and looked up. "Fury! You'll need your mask on before you come down here. Actually, you should put it on now just to be safe!"

"Do you want me to come down?" she yelled back.

"Not yet! I'll be back soon!"

"OK!"

I started down the tunnel again. It wound through the earth like a snake. Around the final bend, the tunnel ended in a massive cathedral...or an ossuary.

A cathedral decorated with human bones.

Purple light glowed through the eyes of the skulls, thousands of them, that adorned the walls and high arched ceilings. In the center of the room, an elaborate chandelier made of intricately strung bones hung over pews made of osmium. Osmium, I was now certain, had created the elaborate trappings of this chapel of death.

The deadly pews faced an altar, which had legs made of femur bones and a tabletop that was covered with an old dirty linen cloth. Fifteen feet behind the altar, on a pedestal made of skulls, was a throne carved out of glittering osmium. It was crowned with an elaborate bone mosaic, that spelled out a single Katavukian phrase:

Mit akis magnus anlo, Akai aut uruva me teva.

Or in English, "On his greatest love, I will build my church."

In a word, the whole place was wondrous.

And wicked.

I cautiously walked down the aisle between the two sets of pews. On the first row on my right, a flash of pink caught my eye. A doll with pink-yarn hair lay facedown on the seat. I picked it up and looked at its worn and dirty face. A chill ran down my spine, and I shoved the doll into the deep side pocket on my thigh.

When I reached the altar and could see beyond it, I realized the bright purple light was being emitted from another staircase down through the floor, just in front of the throne.

Without even touching it, I knew...

This was where blinded souls had been led to die.

This was the new spirit line.

The gate to Nulterra.

CHAPTER TWENTY-ONE

*a*gain, the thought occurred to me that I could go into Nulterra without Fury. But I was reminded that *she* had the key, not me, and she'd follow me anyway. I reluctantly returned to the steps and looked up.

She was now sitting at the top with her boots crossed over the steps in front of her.

"Hey!" I yelled.

She flinched, startled, and looked down. She wore a gas mask like I'd asked, but she removed it to reply. "We were about to come look for you! What took you so long?"

I looked at my watch. I'd been gone less than ten minutes. I shook my head. "A little patience would be nice! I was exploring the gate to Hell, you know?"

"You found it?" Her hands were clasped beneath her chin.

"Yes! Tell Ionis to grab our gear. It's safe to come down without the cuffs on!"

She jumped up.

"Fury!"

She looked back at me.

"Keep the gas mask on. The chamber down here is filled with osmium!"

She pulled the mask back over her face.

While I waited, I sat on the bottom steps and let my mind stir on all the things that could go wrong.

We'd verified everything we could about osmium through Chimera and Google, but what if Moloch lied? What if there were other effects we didn't know about? What if it wasn't osmium at all and only something that looked and behaved like it, but was really much more deadly? What if the cuffs didn't work? What if the *new* spirit line burned everything away including human flesh—

Gunshots jarred me from my thoughts.

I jumped to my feet and flew straight up the center hole of the staircase. When I shot up above the surface, I saw what looked like the same militia who'd threatened me and Cassiel. All their guns were now pointed at me.

Fury was still standing on the top step, and all three of my companions had their arms raised over their heads. Thankfully, none of them appeared to have been shot.

Ionis was clearly trying to negotiate, as he was the only one who could communicate with them. It wasn't working. One of the men fired a shot off at me. I dodged sideways.

"What are they saying, Ionis?" I called.

"Something about payment. A young girl was killed. Did you do that?"

"Seriously?" I asked him.

"You *are* the Angel of Death."

The man shouted louder.

"He wants to know about payment," Ionis translated.

"Do you know what he's talking about?"

"Do I look like an Angel of Knowledge?" he shouted up at me.

But Cassiel, an Angel of Knowledge, hadn't known what

they were talking about either. The deal these people had made was not with the angels. It was with the devil.

"Ionis, find out who died and what payment. Reuel, take Fury halfway down the stairs and wait for me!" She was the only one of us who could be mortally wounded by a gunshot, so I wanted her out of the line of fire.

Before the gunmen could retake aim, they ran down the stairs.

Ionis started talking as calmly as possible. He took a few steps forward, and they opened fire.

"Shit," I muttered, diving toward the ground.

When I landed in front of Ionis, they fired their AK-47s at me. Not many bullets hit, but a few rounds tore through my chest. One struck my thigh, dangerously close to parts I'd rather not have to heal. I stormed forward through the spray. One younger man dropped his gun and ran. The others kept firing.

I stopped in front of the man who appeared to be the leader and pressed my palm against the end of his barrel. He fired, and the bullet shot straight through my hand and lodged in my shoulder. I watched his startled face through the bloody hole until it closed completely. The bullet squeezed back out of my skin and tumbled over my shirt to the ground.

The man fell to his knees, dropping the rifle in front of him. He was begging. That much was obvious. Several other members of the group dispersed.

I knelt down in front of the leader and beckoned Ionis forward. The man was sobbing hysterically. I put my hand on top of his head. "Shh. It's OK. I won't hurt you."

"I got shot!" I looked back as Ionis neared me. A deep red stain had blossomed on the breast of his blazer. "I've been on Earth for a thousand years in complete peace. I'm with you for a couple of days, and I get shot!"

"Ionis, tell this man I'm not going to hurt him," I said.

"But he hurt me!"

I glared.

Ionis spoke to the man in what sounded to me like English. That was the way the messengers worked on Earth. They could be understood by all, no matter the language. "Relax. No one here is going to hurt you. We want to help you."

The man looked up.

"Tell him we didn't come from the hole." I pointed back to it. "We're trying to close the hole forever."

"What if he doesn't want the hole—"

"Ionis," I scolded.

Ionis told him what I'd said.

The man replied, this time no longer screaming. Ionis translated. "He said they will give you anything you want if you will close it."

"Ask him again what happened here. Find out why he is afraid of us."

When Ionis asked him, the man launched into a tearful rant. "He says the other men came out of the hole and took his daughter. Her brother saw a shining man lead her into the hole. She never returned."

"How long ago?" I asked.

Ionis asked, then translated. "Nine months, three days, and a few hours."

My heart ached for the man. "I'd bet anything that shining man was Moloch." I swore.

"You think so?"

"Yeah. He'd possessed the body we saw him in when he was with the prime minister of Malab.

"He says there are old stories about the stairs leading to a church with a high priest who could heal. They would take their sick and dying loved ones there, along with a prisoner or someone they didn't like. The priest would trade a life for a life and heal the loved one in exchange for the prisoner. Sometimes they would trade people to the priest for money or food.

"The people thought they were just stories to scare children and make them behave. Then his daughter went into the hole and didn't come back. He says he doesn't want payment. He just wants his daughter back." Ionis's whole body deflated. "That's sad."

"The healing priest. That would be the Morning Star." I remembered what I'd found down in the cave. I pulled out the doll. The man let out a painful wail. I looked at Ionis. "Guess I don't need to ask if it belonged to her or not."

"You found that down there?" Ionis asked.

"Yeah." I stood. "Ask him what her name is."

He did, and the man answered through his cries. "Hannah."

"Tell him I'll find out what happened to Hannah."

Ionis told him, and the man looked up with tears streaming down his face and said in shaky English, "Thank you, sir."

Leaning down, I put my hand on his shoulder. We locked eyes. Man to man. Father to father. Chances were high there was nothing I could do to save the man's daughter, but I was sure as hell going to get retribution on his behalf.

I walked back to the hole. "Fury! Reuel! It's safe to come up." Then I returned to where our gear had been dropped during the holdup. "Ionis, stay here until the gate seals up behind us. Call Azrael and tell him we are gone. Then you're free to leave."

Ionis was still watching the man holding the doll. "Maybe I'll hang around here a little while. In case you need something."

"You're not going soft on me, are you?" I asked, unzipping a pocket on Ionis's backpack.

He put his hands on his hips. "Maybe I like the weather here. Did you ever think of that?"

"Whatever you say." I pulled the hydration bladder out of

his pack and unscrewed the lid. "But I'm sending Fury down with what's left of your water."

She walked across the grass with Reuel and took off her mask. "Everything OK up here?"

"No. The demons took that man's daughter. That's why they were shooting at us."

"I'd shoot at us too. Why'd they take her?" she asked.

I poured Ionis's water into Fury's hydration tank. "My guess would be to replace the power they lost when they let the three human souls loose last year."

Fury's tank was full, with water left over. I handed it to her. "Finish drinking this. I don't want to waste any."

She took it and guzzled the rest of the water straight from the reservoir. When she finished, she tossed it to Ionis. "Are we ready?"

I stood and put on my rucksack. "Let's do this."

As I started back to the mirror, I heard static crackling in my ear. I froze. "Iliana?"

More static.

"Illy, can you hear me?"

"Appa!"

My face rose toward the sky. Then I smiled and whispered to whoever might be listening, "Thank you."

———

Fury carried the blood-stone case down the stairs. If she'd had handcuffs, she'd have probably chained herself to it.

When we reached the bottom, she stayed on the stairs until Reuel and I were off. The second both her feet were on the osmium with us, the staircase behind us shifted. Immediately, the steps began to close back up to the surface.

We stood there and watched as each step snapping into place sent a gunshot-loud sound ricocheting around the chamber. The hair on the back of my neck stood on end, and even though I'd never had a problem with enclosed spaces, it was hard to not feel a little trapped.

When the whole thing closed, there was nothing but a solid translucent disc above us. The sunlight was barely visible through it.

"Anyone else feel a little like the tomb door just slammed shut?" Fury asked, over-enunciating through her gas mask.

"Think this is a tomb?" I turned back toward the hallway. "Just wait."

We started toward the demons' sanctuary. Behind me, the sound of Fury inhaling and exhaling through the gas mask was almost comforting as the osmium crystals crackled all around us.

"What's that noise?" Fury asked.

I pointed to the walls. "That's the osmium Moloch told us about. See how crystals are forming on the surface?"

"At least he didn't lie to us about that," she said. "Moloch was a brilliant deceiver though. We can't forget that."

She was right. Next to the Father and the Morning Star, Moloch had probably been the smartest being in existence. And, even if he had been trying to save his own skin, he in no way had our best interest at heart. I *had* to remember to judge everything he told us with those facts at the forefront of my mind.

I stepped into the cathedral.

"Holy shit," Fury said, her muffled voice filled with awe. Behind the window of her gas mask, her mouth was gaping as she looked at the soaring ceiling and the elaborate throne.

Reuel's face looked the same when he emerged from the tunnel.

"It's like the catacombs of Paris," Fury said.

"Yeah, on LSD."

"Satan's throne," she mumbled almost to herself as she

walked toward it. She read the words above it out loud in Katavukai. "That's a direct shot at the Father himself, isn't it?"

"Yeah," I said. "Everyone knows there's nothing the Father loves more than humans. It's what started the first great angel war to begin with."

She put her hands on her hips as she looked around. "This is twisted."

"You can say that again." I looked at Reuel. "Doesn't it remind you of the Throne Room?"

He nodded, but his wide eyes were everywhere except on me.

I walked down the center aisle, and they followed me. "Fury, be careful. A lot of stuff down here is made of osmium. It really is designed to kill anyone who comes here, hence all the decorations."

"Ai alis eriva patuk?" Reuel asked Fury.

She tapped the glass of her face mask. "Still secure. Don't worry."

I pointed to the pew on the right. "I found a doll belonging to the daughter of the guy who shot at us right there."

"That's sick," Fury said. "Where's the gate?"

I tilted my head toward the front of the room. "There are steps leading down just beyond the altar."

The three of us walked around the osmium table and dropped our heavy bags on the floor. We peered down into the hole. Only the first few steps were visible. The rest were obscured by Nulterra's magic before they disappeared completely.

Just to be safe, I stretched my arm in front of Fury. "That's it?" she asked.

"Pretty sure. I didn't go down it yet to see what's on the other side though," I replied.

"No time like the present." Fury put the blood-stone case on the altar and opened it.

I pushed the lid closed. "I'll go first. Then you. Then Reuel."

"OK."

When I looked at Reuel, he was reluctant.

Something occurred to me. There would be no way Reuel could help Fury into the cuffs. Once she started screaming, it would be over. I wasn't so sure I'd be able to handle it myself, but I knew I'd have more success than he would. "On second thought, Reuel should go first. Then I'll help Fury into the blood stone and send her through."

The suggestion seemed to relieve him. His shoulders relaxed, and he walked over to Fury. He cradled her face in his giant hands, and in Katavukai, he begged her one last time not to go.

She gripped his wrists. "Thank you for loving me so much." She put her arms around his neck and hugged him. "Let us know, if you can, what's on the other side."

He nodded, but tears sparkled in his eyes. When he stepped away from her, he offered me his hand, just like a human. I smiled and pumped his fist, then pulled him in to wrap my arm around his shoulders. "She'll be fine," I whispered—maybe even lied—in his ear.

He stepped back and picked up his rucksack. When he had it on, he turned toward the throne. I reached for Fury's hand as he stepped down onto the first step.

"You OK?" I asked.

He held up a thumb as he took another step. He descended another and another until he completely vanished.

"Reuel?" she called out.

Silence.

I pressed my finger to my ear. "Samael?"

More silence.

"Nothing. We're completely dark down here."

Fury was still staring at the hole. I squeezed her hand.

She didn't squeeze back. The hissing breaths through her mask were much quicker now.

"What's the matter?"

She was quiet for a beat, and her hand trembled in mine just enough for me to notice. "I'm afraid, Warren."

"You don't have to do this." I turned her toward me.

She looked down at our hands. "Yes, I do."

"Look at me."

Her eyes finally met mine. She was terrified.

"Reuel and I will be fine down there. You can wait here. It's OK."

"We can't hear through the gate. I won't know if you need me to let you out." She took a deep, shaky breath, then nodded her head. "I can do this."

"Of course you can." I bent to look her square in the eyes. "Fury, you can do anything."

"Warren?"

My brow lifted.

"I'm sorry for hurting you. That was never my intention."

"Don't." I shook my head. "Don't turn this into a goodbye."

"It's not." Her arms circled around my neck. "It's just long overdue."

I held her for a moment and closed my eyes, whispering a silent prayer I knew no one could hear.

She turned toward the altar and opened the case again. This time, as much I wanted to, I didn't stop her. She pulled out a wrist cuff and pressed the latch on the side. It sprang open. "I'm going to open all three cuffs, so we can get them on as fast as possible."

"I'd like to say that's a good idea, but *none* of this is a good idea."

She opened the other wrist cuff. "The sooner we get it done, the sooner it will be over." Last, she clicked the button on the neck ring—the one I truly worried might kill her.

I picked up my heavy rucksack and slipped my arms through the straps. She did the same, pulling her ponytail out from under it when it sank onto her shoulders.

Then she held her injured wrist to her mouth and grasped the edge of the bandage with her teeth and fingers. It ripped open, and she winced as the air hit her raw skin.

I grimaced. "Is it bad?"

"No," she lied.

On top of the altar, Fury arranged the two smaller cuffs and hovered her wrists above them. "Let's try to get this done in as few movements as possible. I'll lower my hands, and you close both cuffs around them. Then do my neck."

I groaned and readied my hands.

"On the count of three," she said, her breathing erratic through her gas mask. "One...two...three."

She lowered her hands, and I snapped both cuffs closed around her wrists. Her screams echoed around the chamber as her knees gave way, and she slumped across the altar. I grabbed the collar and yanked her head up by her ponytail. I forced my hands to close the collar over the scar tissue around her throat.

She choked on a scream.

Then went limp.

And dead silent.

I grabbed her by her arm and rucksack and dragged her down the steps.

CHAPTER TWENTY-TWO

*W*e were both naked when we came out on the other side. I'd had to grab her around the middle when her rucksack vaporized halfway down the stairs. In that way, the spirit line that brought us to Nulterra was much like the gateway into Eden.

I should have anticipated that.

Carefully, I lay Fury on the ground next to...*Fury?* I flinched. *Wait...what?*

There were *two* Furys.

Reaching over her, I realized the second was her reflection. "A mirror?" A flash of blue caught the light in front of me? Behind me? It was Reuel, covering Fury's body with one of his giant shirts.

I quickly checked her vitals. Her heart rate was strong. Her breathing too. The gas mask was gone, but looking around, I saw no visible osmium. Heard no crackling either. The bedrock must have been far beneath the—*shit*—beneath the mirrored floor we stood on.

"What is this place, a funhouse?" I asked.

"Not my kind of fun." Reuel dropped to his knees beside me.

I touched his face to be certain he was real.

He swatted my hand away.

"Sorry. This place is messing with my brain."

"I think that's the idea." He looked down at Fury again. "She's not waking up."

"She will." I hoped.

In nothing but my Eden-made black boots and scabbard, I walked back to where a few of my things were strewn down the lower half of the staircase. All that survived was the stuff made in Eden: some of my clothes and Cassiel's bag.

I took off my boots and scabbard and got dressed quickly in the jeans and T-shirt. "I should've thought about losing everything through the gate. That was stupid of me."

"You couldn't know. None of us could."

I looked up at the staircase. It was much bigger on this side, with at least ten stone steps after a high, glowing archway. At the top of the arch was a glowing purple stone. Sanctonite. It was identical to Chimera's, except a hundred times the size.

The stone powered the gate. That much was evident.

Zipping my pants, I climbed the steps for a closer look. If I stretched, I could touch it, but I didn't for concern of the consequences. I tried to rise into the air, but it seemed my wings were weighted down by some supernatural force. "We're grounded."

Reuel was checking Fury's wrists and throats.

"How's her neck looking?" I asked, walking back down and picking up my boots.

"The skin is red, and underneath the blood stone seems to be oozing blood and water."

My head jerked up as I put my boots back on. "A lot of blood?"

"Not a lot. It's more clear than red."

I realized his English sounded different. "What language are you speaking?"

"Katavukai."

"Damn. This place is a *lot* like Eden." In Eden, there was no such thing as a language barrier.

"Will she be all right?" he asked.

"I think so. Her vital signs are strong, but we need to find water for her soon. And clothes."

"And food." He touched his stomach. "I'm starving."

I took in our surroundings. A twisted funhouse indeed. This place was a thing of nightmares. Angled mirrors bounced my reflection in every direction. And it was dark. The only light was the purple glow from the spirit line. I spread my wings, letting their light illuminate the room.

Blinding light shined in every direction. I shielded my eyes and dimmed my wings. "Well, that won't work." I conjured a ball of fire into my hand instead.

Reuel clapped.

Making fire wasn't something just any angel could do. I'd been working at it for years in Eden.

The fire helped, but it also cranked up the creepy factor times a thousand. Now I had a hundred floating heads around the room. Or maybe it was a hallway. I wasn't sure which. There was nothing but mirrors any way I looked.

On the ground, Fury moaned in pain. I extinguished my flame and dropped back down by her side next to Reuel.

"Fury?" I asked gently.

Her entire body began to tremble. She was regaining consciousness, and she was in pain. Tears streamed back in her hair and her chin quivered.

I leaned toward her. "Fury, can you hear me?"

Her hand slowly rose, shaking violently. I took it and looked at her wrist. It wasn't sizzling or smoking like it had the last time. Her breaths became jagged, and she rolled toward us, pulling her knees into her chest. "Oh god," she groaned.

"Breath, Allison," Reuel said, adjusting his shirt around her to keep her covered. "Try to breathe."

I brushed her sweaty hair off her forehead. "The worst is over. You're through the gate. We're in Nulterra, and you're alive."

She sobbed, unable to catch her breath. "It...it hurts."

Unsure of what else to do, I kissed her knuckles. I thought of Cassiel's bag, but she'd been clear: *"Don't open the bag unless it's a life-or-death situation."* This, thankfully, wasn't life or death—I was mostly certain.

Death was kind of my specialty, and I didn't sense that Fury was near it. But I wasn't sure I could convince her of that as she writhed in pain. I stroked her hair again. "We need to get moving because we're completely out of water. Remember what Dr. Rothwell said about dehydration. Want me to carry you?"

She shook her head.

"I will," I said.

"N-no." Her lower jaw was still quivering. She pulled on my hand to try to sit up and winced from the pain. I helped her up to sitting, and she crumpled forward against my chest, swearing into my shirt.

I rubbed her back. "I'm sorry."

"It's m-my st-stupid fault."

I couldn't argue.

"Wh-where are my c-clothes?"

"Burned up, I'm afraid. Reuel covered you with one of his shirts from Eden. Think you can stand?"

"W-will you help m-me?"

"Always."

I curled my arm around her back and pulled her up as I stood. Her knees wobbled, and I held her until she was steady. The blue shirt she was now holding over her chest looked like a bedsheet over her. "Reuel, can you hand me that black shirt?" I nodded to where my other clothes were in a heap on the floor.

He picked it up and carried it over.

"This might fit a little better," I said, offering it to her.

When she reached a shaky hand up to take it, blood and water oozed down her arm. We didn't even have anything to clean around the cuffs with.

"Turn around," she said.

"Can you manage?" I asked.

"You t-trying to see m-me naked?"

I smiled. "I already have."

"T-turn around."

I released her and made sure she was steady before turning around with Reuel. I even closed my eyes to prevent seeing one of her many reflections around the room. My sensitive ears heard Reuel's shirt land on the floor, and I swallowed. Hard.

"How's it coming?" I asked after moment.

She didn't answer right away. Then she let out a frustrated sigh. "I c-can't manage the b-buttons."

"Want some help?"

"Please."

When I turned, she was holding my short-sleeved black shirt closed around her. Watery blood drizzled from her neck down her cleavage. My hands started at the top button, and I refused to let my eyes drift down the slit at the top. But it was hard.

"I c-can't stop sh-shaking," she said with a shiver.

I buttoned the second button. "It's probably adrenaline. And your blood pressure might be out of whack."

"She needs water," Reuel said.

"That too." I moved to the third button. "How's the pain?"

"S-starting to go n-numb."

"That's probably a blessing. We need to keep an eye out for signs of infection." I buttoned the fourth button.

She looked around as much as she could without moving her neck. "It's a m-mirror maze?"

"Looks like it."

"I hate m-mirror mazes."

"Me too." My fingers worked the last button. "Hold on." I went and picked up my extra pair of socks. Then I knelt down in front of her. "They'll be too big, but it's better than being barefoot." She held onto my head as I slipped the socks over her feet.

"Th-thank you."

I stood and smiled, letting my eyes drift down the length of her. "You look a little *Risky Business,* but it will do until we can find something more your size. Think you can walk?"

She nodded, then winced as the skin around her neck pulled against the collar.

I put my sword on my back and draped Cassiel's bag across my chest. Glancing at my wrist for the time, I realized my watch was gone. "Shit. I loved that watch."

"Why d-didn't your man purse b-burn up?" Fury asked.

"It's a *satchel.*" I frowned. "And it didn't burn up because it's from Eden, just like our clothes."

"What's in it?" Reuel asked, offering Fury his arm.

"No idea. For emergencies only Cassiel said." We started walking forward? Maybe? I couldn't really tell. "She told me it could get her kicked out of Eden."

Reuel's head pulled back. "What could it be?"

I turned my palms up just as I walked into an angled mirror. I swore and rubbed the spot where my forehead had bounced off it.

"You all r-right?" Fury asked, her teeth still chattering.

"I'm fine." I put my hand on her forehead. The adrenaline should've left her system already. She didn't feel feverish. "Are you cold?"

"Fr-freezing."

I looked at Reuel. "Are you?"

He shook his head. "Maybe it's the burns."

"Maybe it's this p-place. Why is it so d-dark?"

"Oh." I opened my hand, calling fire into my palm again. It sparked to life and lit up the mirrors around us.

Fury smiled, impressed.

I started walking again, using the fire and my sword to navigate the path ahead. Movement caught my eye to the left. "Did anybody see that?"

"S-see what?" Fury asked.

I continued creeping forward. "Not sure."

In one of the mirrors, I saw Reuel's face whip to the right.

"What was it?" I asked.

"I don't know." Reuel and Fury were right on my heels.

A sliver of ghostly white appeared along the edge of the mirrors. I stopped walking so suddenly Reuel caught my shoulder to keep from running me over.

"What is it?" he asked.

I pointed with my sword. It was low, knee-height from the ground. About five inches tall and an inch wide with a black fringe going down the left side.

Fury grabbed the back of my shirt with her free hand as the sliver of white slowly widened. Two eyes, tilted sideways, appeared. They blinked.

"Warren." Fury's fist twisted my shirt.

I moved the flame closer to the face. One of the small eyes flared green.

It was a child, peeking around one of the mirrors.

He ducked out of view, and I said the F-word. "Creepy demon kids are the worst. Let's get the hell out of here."

I quickened our pace, and after every few turns, the boy ran past one of the mirrors. Like it was a game. A game I knew in my bones we were probably going to lose.

We walked for what felt like eternity, until finally, a shimmer of something purple flickered in the mirrors. I turned right and headed for it. The purple light grew brighter...brighter...

"Damn it," I said, letting my flame extinguish.

Fury's teeth were chattering louder. "It's the-the s-s-steps again."

I turned in a slow circle. "Reuel, what if we destroy the mirrors?"

"Want me to try?"

"Yeah." I reached for Fury and pulled her against my chest, wrapping my arms tight around her. Partly to protect her from shattering glass. Partly to try to stop her shaking. Her body was ice cold. "God, you're freezing." I laid my head against hers.

"I already t-told you th-that," she said, shivering violently against me.

Beside me, Reuel opened and closed his fists a few times. Then he rubbed his palms together. Taking a deep breath, his hands shot forward, releasing a wave of energy so powerful that it rippled the air.

Looking over my shoulder as far as I could without turning Fury toward the imminent blast, I watched the mirrors wobble. They twisted and turned and bent backward as the force pushed them down. But they did not shatter.

Then as violently as they were pushed back, they catapulted upright volleying all the energy right back at us. Reuel turned, shielding us from the blast. Still, it blew us all forward, and we narrowly missed crashing through the steps.

When I rolled off Fury, she was crying again and holding one of her wrists.

"Are you all right?" I asked, concerned.

She covered her face with her arms and cursed over and over.

"I'm sorry," Reuel said.

"Not your fault. Geez, it was my idea. Didn't expect that to happen." My eyes drifted toward the stairs. "Fury, maybe it's a sign for you to stay here. Reuel can take you back, and I can go on—"

"No." She rolled onto her side and forced herself up. "I'm fine." She sniffed back tears. "L-let's go." When she moved to get up, her arm gave out, and I caught her before she landed on her face.

I stood, pulling her to her feet again. While she held onto me to steady herself, I looked at her arms. The right one was dripping blood. I turned it toward the light from the steps for a clearer look.

"The cuff t-twisted when we fell."

I tried tearing off the hem of my T-shirt to make a sling. I failed. "Damn indestructible fabric," I muttered. "Can you hold it elevated? We need to slow the bleeding."

Reuel picked up his blue shirt off the ground, twisted it into a thick rope, and tied it around her shoulders, so it didn't rub her neck. She bent her arm and he tightened the shirt, trapping her forearm against her chest.

"Th-thank you." Her teeth still rattled so hard I worried they might crack.

Reuel curled his arm around her back.

I shined the flame toward the mirrors again. "Shall we try this again?"

"We're right behind you," Reuel said.

This time, I dragged my sword along the right wall of mirrors, hoping if we could stay oriented, we'd have easier time getting out. The tip of the metal scraping the glass bounced a faint, shrill *screech* around the room.

Keeping contact with the mirror led us in a different direction—I was pretty sure, anyway. We rounded one corner, then another, then another.

"Warren, s-stop," Fury said.

I stopped walking, but the sound continued. No. It was a

different sound altogether. A piercing *chirp*. Or *chirps*. Millions of them. "What the—"

A heavy hand slammed into my shoulder, buckling my knees. I whirled around. Reuel shrugged. "It was a spider."

"No. It was a c-cricket." Fury's eyes were frantically searching the floor. Another cricket jumped onto my white shirt, and I brushed it away. She screamed, wildly flailing her arms, when one jumped in her face.

Before I could find it amusing, crickets swarmed us. Leaping onto our clothes. Flying into our hair. Reuel inhaled one, doubling him over coughing. The majority of the bugs were concentrated on Fury. Creeping, crawling, covering so much of her bare skin, she almost disappeared into the darkness.

I put my sword back into its scabbard and grabbed her shoulders. "Fury!"

The whites of her eyes flashed in the dark.

"Are you afraid of crickets?"

She couldn't even respond.

"Close your eyes."

Her eyes snapped shut.

I lit a fire in both my palms, then cupped my hands together and lowered them toward the ground. As I blew gently at the base of the flames, bright golden embers showered the ground around her feet. The bugs began to scatter. Reuel brushed countless crickets off her face, her body and her legs. He was pulling them out of her hair when I finished exterminating on the ground.

He cupped her face in his big hands. "It's over. Open your eyes."

She didn't.

"Trust me," he said.

Finally, her terrified eyes fluttered open.

"It's over," he said again.

I passed the flame to my left palm, holding it near her face.

Her lips had a bluish tinge, and they were beginning to crack. "This place is subjective, remember? You're the only human here. It's projecting your fears."

With a blink, her eyes changed from afraid to surprised.

"Fury, what else are you afraid of?"

"I d-don't know."

She wasn't lying. I suspected Fury kept her fears so buried even she didn't know what they were.

"Why are you so cold?" I asked, knowing if we didn't fix that soon, hypothermia would become a real problem.

Her shoulders rose.

"Come on. Let's keep moving." Dragging the sword across the glass once more, we walked. With another turn, we started down a long, straight hallway. "This is definitely new. We haven't been here before." I took it as a good sign.

Far beyond the reach of my firelight, something moved. I gulped and slowed my steps. As we neared, the light bounced off two eyes. One of them was bright green. The boy was small. Maybe two or three years old. He had colorless skin and black hair...*jet*-black hair.

I stopped and reached back for Fury. My fingers couldn't find her. When I glanced over my shoulder, she'd taken a step back, even from Reuel. She was shaking her head.

"Come on. You have to face him." I held out my hand. She only looked at it. "Is it Jett?"

She visibly swallowed.

"Fury, Jett is a baby. He's safe at home with John." I stretched my hand farther. "You have to face him so we can pass."

She inched forward and took my hand.

"Mommy?" The boy's hollow voice sent a ripple of fear down my spine. "Mommy?"

"He's not real," I reminded her, or myself, I wasn't sure.

Fury knelt down a few feet from him. "Jett?"

He shook his small head.

"Malak?" Reuel asked.

The boy shook his head again.

"Rogan?" Fury asked.

The boy's eyes narrowed to evil slits. He shook his head a third time, smiling. Baring pointed teeth dripping with black blood.

Fury sucked in a brave breath and reached for him. I raised my sword. But she didn't flinch as he ran into her arms...and vanished.

She fell back onto the ground. I knelt beside her. "You all right?"

Her head nodded, but she was anything but all right.

I pulled her ponytail off her shoulder, as it was getting matted in the blood oozing from her throat. "He's not evil, Fury. You don't need to worry."

"Don't you worry about Iliana?" she asked.

Truthfully, I didn't. "No. I know how she's being raised. And I know you'll be a good mother to him."

"How?"

"Because you care too much not to be."

Her eyes sobered. "What if he's part of the fallen?"

I looked at Reuel behind us.

"He isn't," he said, confidently. "I'm sure of it."

"See?" I put my arm around her back. "You ready to keep moving?"

She nodded, and I pulled her to her feet.

Back along the side of the room, I continued to drag my sword across the right-side mirrors. It seemed we walked for miles. Hours, for sure. But, thankfully, we encountered nothing else sinister in the twisted maze.

Not that Fury would care any longer. Her pace was slowing, and her breaths were dry and ragged. Funny thing about fear, it can't exist without attention. Without a heart that cares enough to race. Fury was fading. Fast.

I stopped and offered Reuel my sword. "Wanna switch places for a bit?"

He hesitated, and I realized why. Fury wasn't well; I'd only make her worse.

I nodded.

"We have to get out of here soon," he said.

"I know."

Fury stumbled.

Without asking, he scooped her up in his big arms. She didn't argue, which was the most alarming sign of all. After a few more turns, the room brightened slightly. I looked back at Reuel, and Fury was fast asleep.

I stopped again. "She's afraid of the dark."

Reuel gazed down at her peaceful face. Her lips were still blue, but against Reuel, the shaking had stopped a little. I wondered if part of it was fear. "She's so strong."

She drew in a shallow breath.

"We need to hurry, Warren."

Navigating the maze was both easier and harder with the light. Harder because now even our reflections had reflections, and each mirror looked like its own fractaled hallway. But it was easier because we no longer needed the fire, and I could clearly see which mirror's we'd already passed because my sword had etched a crooked line in the glass.

I turned to the right. *My sword etched the glass.*

"Reuel, move back."

Reuel backed up as far as he could. I gripped the sword's hilt with both hands and swung it as hard as I could at my face.

The mirror shattered in a million pieces.

Reuel howled with joy. I raised the sword over my head in victory before driving it through the next mirror. The room slowly darkened again. I stopped.

"What's happening?" Fury asked, her voice weak and small.

Reuel kissed her forehead. "Go back to sleep. Warren's getting us out of here."

"I knew he would," she mumbled and snugged her face into his chest.

I continued crashing through the walls until I saw light—bright *yellow* light, not purple—and the end of the mirrored tunnel. "Holy shit, we made it," I said, slamming the sword's blade against another one.

Together, Reuel and I jogged toward the exit, and when we reached it, we both stopped. Wide-eyed and worried.

"Where are we?" he asked.

"Ket Nhila." I felt sick. "The Bad Lands."

CHAPTER TWENTY-THREE

"Fury," I said, jostling her face. "Fury, wake up."

She'd been jerking and moaning in her sleep, likely delirious from dehydration. Her lips were dry and cracked, her eyes were shadowed and sunken, and her skin was taut and ashy. We'd piled every blanket we could find on top of her, and thankfully, color was starting to creep back into her cheeks.

"It's probably better if she's asleep." Reuel nudged my arm. "Just do it."

"You do it."

He held up his hand. "My fingers are like sausages, and I don't know how."

"*I* don't know how."

"You know more than me."

I closed my eyes. "This. *This* is my hell."

"*Bwooock, bwock, bwock.*"

"You're picking up bad habits from her," I said, pointing at his face.

He grinned and pushed the IV pole toward me. "Tick tock. She's dying, Warren."

"You're such an asshole." I pulled the rolling stool over to her bedside. Then I stretched out her arm on the bed. Luckily, her veins were dark blue beneath her skin. I put on a pair of surgical gloves, then ripped open the IV start kit and pulled out the tourniquet.

"How'd you learn this?" Reuel asked as I wrapped the blue band around her upper arm.

"Claymore made us take a class in combat medicine. We had to be able to start an IV to pass." I swabbed the inside of her elbow with an alcohol wipe.

"Is that the class where you passed out?" he asked.

I looked up and frowned. "Did my father tell you that?"

He smiled.

"I didn't pass out. I got a little light headed. That's not the same thing."

"He said you fell off your chair."

I huffed. "Will you shut up and let me do this?"

His lips pressed together.

I picked up the smallest needle I could find in the drawer and tore open its plastic wrap. I found the vein with my finger-tip, then bent over her arm. I took a deep breath and moved the needle close to her skin. My hand was shaking, and stars speckled my vision, so I stopped and shook out my hand.

"You can do this," Reuel said.

I rolled my eyes. "Now you're going to be supportive?"

"I could go back to mocking you."

"Be quiet." I bent over her arm again and slid the needle into it. I missed the vein. "Shit." I pulled it out and pressed my finger against her skin. "She's so dehydrated, I'm not sure I can do it." I took a few deep breaths and punctured the skin again. Blood filled the catheter. I let out a massive exhale. "It's in."

Reuel clapped. "I knew you could do it."

"No, you didn't."

He chuckled. "No, I didn't."

I held the catheter in place and pulled the needle out. I tossed the needle onto the counter—no need for sterile practices here—and grabbed the IV line I'd already hooked up to the bag. I hooked the tube to the catheter spilling a minimal amount of her blood in the process. Then I sat back, let my face tilt toward the ceiling, and blew out the breath I'd been holding.

Reuel slapped me on the shoulder. "Nice job, Nurse Warren."

"No thanks to you." I shook my head and stood up, stretching my arms over my head. Then I checked to make sure the fluids were dripping into the line.

"Some luck winding up here," he said, looking around the triage room. It was just as I'd remembered it.

"It's interesting we wound up here." I wasn't sure how I felt about Fury's personal hell being the place we first met. "But fortunate, too, I guess."

"This is a military base, yes?"

"Yeah. A small one."

"Is there a dining room?" His smile was hopeful.

I pointed out the window. "The chow hall is the light gray building. Not sure how stocked it will be, but we did have IV and saline, so..." I shrugged.

"I'll bring back whatever I can find."

"I'll be here," I said, opening one of the cabinets. After searching all the cabinets in the room, I started on the supply closet.

Bingo.

A camouflage bag was on the top shelf. I pulled it down and carried it back to the gurney beside Fury's. Inside was exactly what I'd hoped for: penicillin and morphine. I had no idea how any of this was possible, and I didn't really care. I kissed the bottle of liquid penicillin and tucked it back into the bag.

"Warren?" Fury reached out from under the blankets.

I moved the bag off my lap and closed the space between the beds with one long stride. Grabbing her hand, I eased down onto the edge of her mattress. "Hey, how are you feeling?"

"Head hurts," she said, her eyes still closed.

"I imagine so." I ran my knuckles down her cheek. "You've had a hell of a day."

She had to force her eyes open, as they seemed to have dried shut. The light made her squint, so I shielded her face with my hand. "Where are we?"

"It appears your psyche is very afraid of the base in Iraq."

She looked around the room. "We're in Baghdad?" Her voice sounded like her throat was coated with gravel.

"Some version of it. Only parts of the base seem to exist though. The parts where I was." I pointed to the floor. "I was treated for my broken ribs in this room, but I don't remember you being here for that."

"I came here first when I was looking for you."

I wanted to ask why *this* was hell for her, but she'd had a rough day already. Her eyes drifted toward the IV bag. "Medical supplies?"

"Yep." I proudly tapped my chest. "Guess who inserted your IV? You're welcome."

She smiled, but it obviously hurt her lips. "Thank you."

"Are you warmer now?"

"Much."

"Think we can sit you up and get some of the blood cleaned off? I'd like to see if I can check out those burns?"

"Yeah." She moved to get up.

I held my hand on her chest. "Relax. The bed moves." I stood and used the lever at the back to tilt the bed up. Then I carefully folded the blankets down to her waist. The blood had crusted in dried drizzles down her neck. Her hands were stained red.

I walked to the supply closet, where I'd seen some towels.

Then I took one to the sink and turned on the faucet. Nothing came out. "Well, it probably wouldn't be safe anyway. God knows it wasn't when I was here." I returned to her bedside and carefully picked up her arm. "How does it feel?"

"It hurts, but not as bad as I thought it would."

"I'm sure it burned through the nerves." The edges around the blood stone were bright red. "I wish we could take these off even just to clean it." I sniffed her wrist. "But if it starts to smell rank, it might be a sign of infection. I found some penicillin if it does. Morphine too, if you want it."

"No. I need to keep my head clear." Her bottom lip was bleeding.

I opened the medical bag on the other bed and found a plastic packet of Vaseline. I tore it open with my teeth, then spread some on her lips.

"Thank you," she said.

The door opened and Reuel walked in with an armload of water bottles.

"Get out," I said, walking around the bed to help him.

He looked surprised and turned toward the door. "Really?"

"Sorry. I forgot you don't do figures of speech." I took a few of the bottles off the top. "Where'd you find these?"

"I haven't made it inside the chow hall yet. I saw these piled on a pallet outside and thought you might want them."

"Yes," Fury said, then coughed.

I carried some to her, laid my haul on the other bed, and twisted off a bottle cap. "Small sips," I said as I handed it to her.

Not listening, she guzzled a quarter of the bottle. Then she looked at the label. "This is a US brand. How did it get here?"

"I have no idea." I opened a bottle for myself. "I just hope it's not poisoned."

"I don't even care," she said, tilting it up to her lips again.

Reuel put the rest of the bottles on the counter. "I'm going to check the chow hall now."

I drained half my water. "Don't eat it all before you get back here."

"No promises."

When he was gone, I carried one of the bottles to the sink and soaked a towel. Then I returned to Fury and held it up. "May I?"

She offered her arm. "Go ahead. Be gentle."

I sat down beside her again, carefully stretching her arm across my thigh. I gently cleaned her hand first. Thin blood had streamed all the way down to her fingertips.

"Thanks for getting us out of there. I know you saved my life."

I grinned. "I've one upped you now. You officially owe me."

She chuckled, then coughed. "Don't make me laugh," she wheezed.

"Sip your water."

"How did you do it? How'd you find the way out?"

"You don't remember?"

"I was totally out of it."

"The sword broke the mirrors." I turned her palm over and pressed the wet towel to it to soften some of the blood. "I smashed our way out."

"Nicely done."

"Thanks."

"How's the headache?"

"A little better." She sipped the water again. "I wonder why we're here."

I'd been wondering the same thing since we'd arrived. "I'm trying not to take it personally." I was failing too, but I kept it to myself.

"Because this was our beginning," she said.

I nodded and focused on wiping her palm clean. "Do you regret meeting me?"

Silence hung between us for long enough to make me squirm on the bed. She drank more water, then hugged the bottle to her chest. "Yes."

My fingers stopped working.

"But it's not why you think."

I took her water and put it in her other hand. "Why then?"

"Maybe if I'd never helped recruit you to Claymore, none of this would have ever happened."

I smirked. "You really don't think Azrael would have found another way?"

"He could have found another way that didn't involve me. Or Anya."

"What does Anya have to do with it?" I folded the towel around her hand, rubbing gently.

She laid her head back against the pillow and stared at the ceiling. "He never would have taken her if he didn't think I could get to you."

I straightened. "What?"

"Abaddon knew you and I had been together. He came to me in Somalia when I was there with Anya and tried to convince me to get you to help the fallen. When I refused..." Emotion choked her.

I put the towel down on her lap and held her hand. "Abaddon took Anya?"

Her eyelids blinked a few times, but no tears came. She was still too dehydrated.

"Why didn't you tell Azrael?"

"I did, but I couldn't tell him everything, so he didn't believe that Anya could still be alive."

"What couldn't you tell him?"

She opened her mouth to speak. Then closed it, pulling her hand from mine to cover her face.

"Hey," I touched her arm. "It's OK. You don't have to tell me. Not now. Not ever, if you don't want to."

She relaxed a little.

"Can I finish cleaning you up?" I asked.

When she removed her hand from her eyes, they were bright red. Like she desperately wanted to cry, but couldn't.

"Drink some more water." I looked up at her IV bag. It was still over half full.

With a shaky hand, she tilted the water up to her mouth again.

I reached for the top button on my shirt she was still wearing. "Can I undo a couple of buttons?"

She nodded slightly, laying back against her pillow again.

My fingers worked the top button, then the second, as my brain spun on what could be so terrible that it would drive the toughest woman I'd ever met to tears. I laid the towel on her chest for a moment, then gently began to clean the streaks away. Blood had spilled down her neck, over her collarbones, and into the crevice hidden beneath the Eden-fabric of my shirt.

When I moved the towel lower, the third button fell open. The dizzying inner curves of her perfect breasts drew my eyes and my hand. I grazed the towel over the right swell, then sucked in a sharp breath.

She could do that later herself. This was no time for distraction.

Her eyes locked with mine as I closed the button again. "I'm tired."

I nodded. "Rest. We'll stay here tonight and leave early in the morning."

"Where will we go?"

"Our teams were searching for a hostage the last time we were here."

"You think she might be in Tuz Sehir?" she asked.

I shrugged. "It's my only guess. This is your nightmare, after all."

Fury was asleep again by the time Reuel returned with food. Bags of chips, packs of crackers, and granola bars were the bulk of what he'd found. I tore open a bag of Cheetos like my life depended on it.

"What was it like out there?" I asked, popping a cheese curl into my mouth.

"There was nothing beyond the chow hall, but the buildings and main roads that way"—he pointed toward the door —"seemed to all be intact. There isn't much if you wander off the main road."

"If this illusion is somehow built on what she experienced here, then the stuff that exists must be along the route Fury used to visit me here."

"Perhaps you're right."

I stood and picked up my sword. "I'll check the hooches and see if I can find her something to wear. There weren't any females in my unit, but there were a few men on the smaller side." I thought of Earp and Chavez, in particular. Two of my buddies from our tour here.

"You think stuff will still be there?"

"Most everything in here looks exactly as it did the time Fury was here, but who knows? You'll stay with her?"

"Of course." He sat down on the other gurney and tore open a granola bar.

I picked up my sword. "I'll be back."

Camp Victory had an eerie hue, more green than gold with the setting sun. Beside what was once a busy street, I stopped and looked up. The "sun" was sinking in the east instead of the west. It was weird enough to send a chill straight to my bones.

I listened carefully for any other signs of life. Nothing. But Iraq still smelled the same, like gasoline, sweat, and death. Somehow, it was oddly comforting.

A Humvee was parked in front of the hospital. I tried my wings again. Nothing. So I walked over to it and checked for keys. They were dangling from the ignition. I threw my sword into the passenger's seat and got inside.

The engine fired right up, and it had a full tank of gas. Had that ever happened before?

I drove to my old "neighborhood" between the hospital and the front gate. It was a small trailer park, a collection of "hooches" grouped in clusters of three or four behind concrete barrier walls. But the road was populated with buildings as far up ahead as I could see.

Perhaps it would lead me to whereever Fury had stayed during her time here. I drove through the base, then beyond the gate. There were a few side roads lined with buildings, but none with as much detail as the main one in front of me. I followed it all the way to a gated compound. A Claymore compound, like others I'd stayed in during my time with them overseas.

The gate was open, and I drove through it to the inside courtyard. The pre-fab barracks would be built in a large square around a common building at the center.

High-ranking females, there never were many, were typically given solo rooms along the east side. I drove there, parked, and started checking rooms.

In room three, pictures of me, taken with a long-range camera, were taped to the wall. "This must be it," I said to no one, stepping inside.

The twin bed was neatly made up with a standard-issue black comforter and white sheets. She'd had a private bathroom and a large wardrobe closet. I pulled open the door. Inside, Fury's clothes hung neatly on hangers.

Jackpot.

On top of the wardrobe was a backpack. I pulled it down and started stuffing clothes and a pair of boots into it. Then I went to the bathroom and grabbed her toothbrush, toothpaste, and a box of tampons, just in case.

In her room, I paused to study the recon work she'd done on me. There were pictures of my face from every angle, and handwritten details about the movements of my unit. Handwritten by Azrael. I hadn't known it then, but he'd been present during my entire stay in Iraq and Afghanistan.

Beside the bed, on the small nightstand, were two books. One of the Harry Potter books, which was a shock to my psyche, and a book called *On Bullshit* by Harry G. Frankfurt, a professor at Princeton. Interesting choice, but understandable given whom she worked for.

I should check Azrael's room.

Fifteen minutes and a hundred doors later, I found it. A nondescript room with nothing in it but a change of clothes (which I stuffed into the bag for myself) and a small safe bolted inside the wardrobe.

I tapped in the combination, my mother's birthdate. He used it for everything.

Inside the box was the blood-stone necklace. The *same* necklace I was wearing. Thinking it might have been an illusion, I picked it up. It wasn't.

Wherever my father had been during this snapshot of Fury's reality, he hadn't been wearing the blood stone. Whatever he was doing, he didn't want a record of it. I clenched the second stone in my hand.

Interesting.

I dropped the necklace in my pocket and walked out of the room. Before I left, I stopped by the supply cage and grabbed some extra toothbrushes, deodorant, and a few fresh pairs of socks. Then I drove back to the hospital on base.

It was almost dark by the time I arrived. And a dark night it would be. There were zero lights. Not in the sky or on the ground. No stars. No moon. And no electricity.

Fury was still asleep, but not so peacefully. Her eyelids fluttered, and her fists were clenched on top of the blankets. But her color had definitely improved, and her lips looked less like roadmaps than when I'd left. Almost the entire bag of saline had dripped through her IV.

Reuel was sitting on the second gurney in a pile of snack wrappers. "Any luck?" he said around a mouthful of food.

"Yeah. I found *her* stuff where they were staying when we were here before." I put the bag on the foot of his bed. "I found Azrael's room too." I pulled out the necklace. "How much do you know about this?"

He shrugged. "Not much. Why aren't you wearing it?"

I pulled the other blood stone out from under my shirt. "I am."

"There are two?"

"It's the same one." I held up the necklace in my hand. "This one was locked in the safe in Azrael's room. Why do you think that is?"

"Probably because Azrael didn't want a record of what he was up to. Your dad has more secrets than anyone I've ever known. You should already know that."

The problem was, I did. But what had he done that I didn't know about? I twirled the stone around my hand. "You know, I have very little memories of his time on Earth after I was born. I'll bet he only wore the stone a handful of times."

"Once Azrael no longer had the threat of losing Eden, he made some questionable decisions. I believe he genuinely thought they were for the best, but I doubt he would want to be reminded of them."

"Like what?"

Reuel gestured toward Fury.

I studied her exhausted, peaceful face. "Do you think she really didn't know her job was to get in my bed?"

"I *know* she didn't."

Fury's shot up straight in the bed. I got up and went to her bed, covering her hand with my own. "It's OK. You were having a nightmare."

It took a few blinks for the disorientation to clear from her eyes. "How long have I been asleep?"

I looked at my bare wrist again. "Damn it. I don't know."

"An hour, I'd guess," Reuel answered.

I squeezed her fingers. "I have some good news."

"You found Anya?" She looked around the room.

I grimaced. "Not that good."

"Oh."

"I found some clothes and shoes that are actually yours." I released her hand and pointed to the backpack. "Your room is completely intact over at the Claymore compound."

"Really?" She pushed herself up in the bed, wincing as she put pressure on her arms against the mattress.

"Yeah. I even got your toothbrush."

"Thanks, Warren."

"No problem. How are you feeling?"

"Like I have to go to the bathroom."

"That's a good sign." I glanced up at the bag on her IV pole again. It was empty. "I don't think I want to unhook you just yet though. Another bag of—"

"I'll be fine. I'll drink plenty of water."

Scowling, I put my hands on my hips.

"We're finally here. I want to get moving to find my sister."

"Not tonight." I walked around to the other side of her bed. "Rest tonight and we'll go in the morning."

"But I—"

"No buts." I picked up the IV line. "If you want to argue, I'll leave you tethered to this pole."

"All right. Tomorrow." She'd given up pretty easily considering she could've yanked the catheter out herself had she really wanted to. "Are we staying here or at the Claymore compound?"

"Wherever you would be most comfortable."

"Was there real food at the Claymore compound? Azrael tends to feed his humans stuff fit for rabbits and birds," Reuel said.

I chuckled as I pulled on another pair of rubber gloves. "We should probably stay here then. The beds in our hooches are about the same as the Claymore beds anyway." I sat down on the rolling stool again.

"Do they sleep more than one person?" Reuel asked.

"Not in the specific spot where we were, and I don't think I saw any barracks between here and the gate either. If you think we should stay together, maybe we should go back to Claymore." I unhooked the IV line from her catheter.

"If we are going to sleep on those god-awful bunks at the compound, we might as well not even sleep at all," Fury said. "The hooches are fine with me."

Reuel looked worried.

"You and I can keep a lookout. We don't need to sleep," I said, gently removing the tape around Fury's IV. The sight of the catheter moving beneath her skin made my stomach wobble.

Reuel tapped his chest. "I'll keep a lookout. I am the guardian here, after all."

"Suit yourself." It didn't really matter. I knew I wouldn't be getting much sleep anyway, if any at all. "Reuel, hand me a cotton ball and a Band-Aid from the medical kit."

Fury was watching my hands carefully. "You're not too bad at this. If things don't work out in Eden, maybe medicine could be your backup career."

"Right." I put pressure on her arm with the cotton ball, then slid the catheter out of her vein. I covered the puncture wound with the bandage. "If you only knew how hard I had to fight through this not to black out."

She smiled and rubbed the bend of her arm. "I appreciate you suffering on my behalf."

I slid back from the bed on the rolling stool. "How far does that appreciation go back then?" I asked with a teasing grin.

"Ooo," Reuel said.

Fury held up her middle finger, and all three of us laughed.

We loaded her into the Humvee and drove to the tiny trailer that had been my home for a miserable seven months. Even then there was no running water or air conditioning. Now there was no electricity either.

Reuel stood on the porch between the hooches with his wings illuminated so we could see.

"Fury, you can take Burch's room. He was probably the cleanest of any of us." I opened the door next to mine, hoping it would be intact even if she'd never been inside it. It was.

I held the door as she walked in. Sergeant Brayden Burch had kept a tidy room, and a tidy life for that matter. His bed was made. There were no dirty clothes on the floor or dirty magazines stashed under the mattress. A photo of his wife and kids was on his nightstand. I put a few bottles of water beside it.

On the bookcase was a small LED lantern he'd bought for reading. I picked it up, and it turned on without a hitch.

"So batteries work," she said, shaking her head as I gave it to her. "So weird."

"It's better than nothing." I looked around the room. "Honestly, I expected Hell to be worse. This isn't too bad."

Fury didn't comment.

"You good?" I asked.

She held the lantern in her hand. "Yeah. Thanks to you."

I gently grasped the front of my shirt she was still wearing and pulled her to me. Wrapping my arms around her, I pressed a kiss against her hair. "I'm glad you're OK." Then I released her and walked to the door.

"Warren?"

I looked back.

She shook her head. "Nothing. Never mind."

I waited in case she might change her mind. She didn't.

"Try to get some rest. I'll be next door if you need me." I walked out, closing the door behind me.

"Is she all right?" Reuel asked.

"I think so."

He looked up at the black sky. "If you'll be up for a while, I think I'll scout the area."

I reached in my pocket and handed him the keys. "Be careful. I'll keep my door open."

With a nod, he walked off the deck.

I pulled open the door to my old hooch, and the familiarity of the place smacked me in the face along with the rank odor. I grabbed the small metal trashcan at the foot of my bed and put it at base of the door to hold it open. Even more than Fury needed my protection, the room needed the air. *Good god.*

The place wasn't *always* a filthy mess, but the day of this particular memory for Fury, I wasn't physically up to cleaning. She'd visited the morning after I'd taken a round to my side body armor and had wound up with several busted ribs. There were still painkillers by my bed, and gear and rancid clothes piled in the corner. I gathered the clothes, toted them outside, and tossed them over the concrete walls that surrounded our trailers.

Back inside, I searched my rucksack for the headlamp I knew was buried in it somewhere. When I found it, I switched it on and tied it around the light bulb in the center of the ceiling. It wasn't much, but I didn't need to use my wings.

I kicked off my boots, took off my sword and Cassiel's bag, and laid down on the bed, bending my arm behind my head. The memories of that day so long ago replayed in my mind with vivid clarity. The blinding pain in my side. The shock of Fury at my door. The pressure of her lips on mine. "Damn," I said, shaking my head.

"Warren?"

I popped up on my elbows. Some protector I was; I hadn't even noticed Fury step into my doorway. "Hey. Everything all right?"

"I'm kind of afraid to fall asleep. The nightmares..."

"They looked pretty intense earlier."

"They're awful." Emotion choked her words. "To be honest, I don't think I can do this alone."

"You don't have to." I moved my legs toward the side wall. "Come in, if you can stand it."

She walked into the room and stood beneath the dim light overhead. She still wore my shirt, and she was barefoot. "It smells like something died in here."

"Yeah, I know. Want to sit down?"

She hugged her arms. "I need to talk to you."

"Do you have to talk standing up?"

She didn't move.

"OK." I pushed myself up and leaned against the back wall. "Talk."

Fury took a few deep, shaky breaths. "Abaddon said he'd trade your daughter for my sister."

"What?"

"When I refused to help Abaddon, he took my sister and said the only way I'd get her back is if I cooperated."

"I thought he took Anya so he wouldn't be tied to Earth anymore and could use the spirit line again."

"I'm sure that was part of the reason, and that's what Azrael assumed. I never corrected him because I couldn't without telling him everything."

"Why couldn't you tell him?"

"If I had, I would have become a liability. And if he'd had me killed or locked up, there would be no one to save Anya."

"Maybe in the beginning, but not now. You might have been a total bitch to Sloan, but you certainly proved your allegiance to her. To *us*." I crossed my arms. "Why would you be afraid to tell me the truth?"

Fury was visibly trembling again. "Because I was going to try."

CHAPTER TWENTY-FOUR

"You what?"

Fury was wringing her hands. "I agreed to help Abaddon take Sloan and Iliana."

Her words went up like a wall between us.

Fury took a step toward me, but I put up a hand to stop her. "Please let me explain," she begged.

I ignored her. "My god. That's how Chimera knew you wanted to find Sloan. You were searching for her through the Claymore servers."

"Yes, but—"

"And when Chimera sent you the video of Sloan on the news, you sent it to me, knowing I would seek her out."

"Yes—"

"Then you waited until I was happy. Getting married, about to be a father...And you were going to turn my whole world over to the demons."

"No!" she cried.

"No?"

She took another step toward me. "No. I was sorry as soon

as I heard Sloan was pregnant. Before even. I couldn't believe what I had done."

"Sure you were sorry." I shot off the bed, ready to throw her out my front door.

She grabbed hold of my shirt. "I swear I was. I even told Abaddon I couldn't do it, and he almost killed me. He probably would have if he'd been able. That's how I knew somehow his powers no longer worked around me.

"He gave me one hell of a beating though. You can ask Azrael. He visited me in the hospital."

I remembered the blood stone in the pocket on my thigh. I'd never seen a memory of Fury being in the hospital, but knowing my father, that probably didn't mean a whole lot.

"I came back to Claymore when I found out Sloan had the power to kill angels. I thought maybe I could undo some of the damage I knew I'd caused if I could help train her to kill Abaddon and the Morning Star."

I blinked. She *had* trained Sloan to use Iliana's power to kill demons while she was pregnant.

"And I knew she'd be safer from Abaddon if I was around. My presence affected his powers."

"Why should I believe you?" I asked.

"Because you know I could have let the demons take Sloan in Chicago, but I didn't."

That much was true. She'd been our sniper in the cemetery in Chicago when we were first attacked by the Morning Star and his demons.

"Warren, I made a mistake—I made a million mistakes—but everything I did was only because..." Her voice cracked. "I'd rather die than let anything happen to you." When her hand touched the collar around her throat, I realized she was quoting me.

That had been *my* thought when I'd worn the blood stone

she was wearing now. She could see and feel that memory of mine.

My heart shattered, and all the hurt from all my moments with Fury bled out. "You threw me away, and then you used the first woman who ever loved me to—"

"Not the first." Tears erupted from her eyes. "I loved you, Warren."

I gripped my forehead for fear it might explode. "I can't do this."

"Please believe me," she cried.

"Just go." I couldn't even look at her. I pointed past her toward the door. "Get out of my room."

She left, and I stood there frozen, staring at the spot on the floor she'd vacated. I couldn't believe it. I couldn't believe after everything she'd put me through there could possibly be any more.

The door to Burch's hooch slammed, and through the walls, I heard her crying. I sank onto the edge of my bed, slumping forward to cradle my spinning skull in my hands.

Another thought occurred to me. We were in Hell. And Hell was subjective, meant to torture and break humans.

Fury was broken.

And this was her worst nightmare. The place where she met me was the one place in all the universe that could torture her the most.

Shit.

I was making it all come true.

But she deserves it.

I sat upright. Where had that thought come from? Not from me, certainly. I shook my head to clear it and felt a buzz overhead.

She betrayed you.

Reaching behind my feet, I grabbed my sword and eased it from its sheath.

She doesn't love you. No one does.

I picked up my feet, spun the sword forward underneath them, then stood and drove the blade straight up over my head. With a piercing shriek, the demon hovering above me erupted in a shower of sparks.

Next door, Fury's door flew open, and she ran into my room again. "What happened?"

I jerked the sword free from the ceiling tile. "A ministry demon. It must have slipped into the room when we were fighting." I raked my hand through my hair. "I think this place is affecting me more than I thought."

She looked up at the hole in the ceiling. "Do you think there are more?"

"Yes." I leaned the sword against the wall. "But not close."

"OK." She turned to leave again.

"Fury."

She stopped and looked at me. Her face was red. Her eyes swollen.

"Why did you do it?"

"Abaddon said if I wouldn't help him, then you and Anya were worthless. He said he'd kill you both if I didn't."

My head dropped under the pressure of my racing mind. She'd only agreed because Abaddon had threatened me.

"I'm sorry I didn't tell you the truth. I was afraid, and then Theta warned me the other night not to tell you."

"Why?"

"She guessed what had happened between us. She knew what I'd done, and she worried..." Fury's dry voice cracked.

"That it might be the reason I would take pleasure in your death?"

Fury lifted her shoulders.

I crossed my arms. My jaw shifted, and my eyes glazed as they stared past her. She took that as her signal to leave. Her bare feet turned on the dirty old floor.

With a long step, I closed the space between us and pushed the trashcan outside with my boot. Then, standing at her back, I reached over her shoulder and pressed my hand against the closing door. "You did it for me?"

She didn't respond, but her shoulders shook with silent sobs.

"Turn around."

She stiffened.

I pulled her hair back off her shoulder. "Fury, turn around."

Slowly, she turned and looked up at me, fear now in her mismatched eyes. Fear that she'd gone too far. Fear that I'd never forgive her. Fear that I would dismiss her again.

"Did you mean it?"

"Yes. I tried to—"

"No. Did you really love me?"

Her lower lip trembled. "Warren, I love you still."

My stomach clenched, every emotion known to man and angel surging inside me. My heart thumped so hard, I wondered if she could hear it.

"Please say something," she whispered.

I swallowed to wet my dry throat.

"Warren, please."

My eyes fell to her chest. "Take off my shirt."

Her lips parted, and she took a shallow breath. Then, with trembling hands, her fingers worked the top button. I took a step forward, backing her against the door. My right hand twisted the lock on the handle before flattening on the door beside her head.

Pinned between my arms, she freed all the buttons, then pulled the fabric back off her shoulders. The shirt dropped behind her, sliding over her arms, and over the wrist cuffs before finally falling to the floor.

My breath stopped dead in my throat as I took in the sight of her standing naked before me.

Unwilling and unable to stop myself, I let my right hand glide down the side of her neck. My fingers traced the curve of her collarbone, down the center of her chest, to her taut stomach. Every inch of her tightened at my touch.

Her hands curled around the hem of my shirt and pushed it up. When she had it around my chest, I reached behind my shoulder blades, grasped a handful of the fabric, and yanked it over my head. Her fingers found my belt next, then the button and zipper of my jeans.

My hand returned to her waist, pulling her against my body as she freed me from the denim. Then I slid my palm over her ass and down the back of her thigh until my hand curled behind her knee. I pulled her leg up over my hip and buried myself inside her.

And right then, nothing else mattered.

Not the past.

Not the future.

Not the hell that surrounded us.

"Fury," I breathed.

Her hand tangled in my hair as she rocked into me. "Call me Allison."

I took her to my bed after that. The same bed where, during my time in the desert, I'd dreamed for months of what I wanted to do to her. I did everything and more.

Much more.

As always, the sex was mind-blowing. Hot, toe-curling, and desperately raw. It was the only part of "us" that had never been shrouded in mystery. And our bodies picked up right where our relationship had ended, reflexively knowing where to touch, where to taste, and when to absolutely unleash.

But one thing was wildly different. The knowledge that Fury loved me. That she'd always loved me.

All my life on Earth, people had feared me. Or, at least, they feared the death they could sense inside me.

But not Fury.

Never Fury.

Despite everything I was created to be, everything that made me inherently rejectable—Fury loved me.

In the tiny twin bed, she'd fallen asleep with her head on my chest. I held her naked body against mine until the sun came up. We'd *never* done that before.

There was a light knock at the door.

"Allison," I said softly, stroking her arm with my fingertips.

"Hmm?"

"It's morning."

She stretched her arm up my chest and curled it around my head on the pillow. "Mmm-hmm."

I dragged my fingers down her ribs and over the curve of her hip. "How did you sleep?"

"There's a puddle of drool on your chest, Warren. How do you think I slept?"

I smiled. "Any nightmares?"

"Not one."

I kissed her forehead. "Good. You need water." Reaching to the nightstand, I grabbed a bottle. Then I twisted the cap off behind her back.

She sat up on her elbow, pressing it into the pillow beside my head, and I gave her the bottle. When she turned it up to her lips, I noticed the redness beneath the blood-stone collar had spread. I did a side crunch to get a better look.

"What?" she asked.

"I think it's getting infected." There were a few red streaks down her throat. "You need penicillin."

She grinned. "You gonna give me a shot?"

"Hey, I did an IV successfully."

"How bad did you want to pass out?" She took another drink.

"You have no room to talk, Miss Fear of Crickets."

She laughed, sputtering water onto my chest.

"Seriously, why crickets? They're harmless."

She put the water back on the nightstand. "Because one minute they're over there chilling on a blade of grass, and the next, they're in your mouth."

"Swallowed a lot of crickets, have you?"

"It only took one," she said, smiling down at me.

My fingers slipped into her hair and behind her head. I pulled her lips back to mine. Then I broke the kiss on a moan. "We have to get out of this bed, or I won't ever leave."

Lying beside me, Fury traced the thick lines of the black tattoo across my chest. "Anya is close. I can feel her." She moved her leg across mine, then sat up, straddling my hips. Her long silky black hair cascaded over her shoulders. "We're going to find her today."

I gripped her thighs as my eyes fell to her breasts. "This is not the way to make that happen."

Biting her lower lip, she rocked forward, making stars twinkle in the corners of my eyes. "But it really is perfect, isn't it?"

"Perfect," I whispered, digging my fingertips in as I let my eyes roll back.

Her warm hands touched my sides. "What will happen when we get back?"

"Well, if you go back to John after this, I might have to kill him." My hands slid up to her hips.

"It's been over with me and John for a while. Jett was the only reason we were still together, and now..." Her shoulders lifted.

"Fury, I still can't be around Jett."

"You can be if you get one of those stones."

"That's a big if."

She sat back. Her face went slack. "Unless you plan on picking up your life with Sloan."

"God no. I'd never even try. She's married to Nathan now, and that's how it's supposed to be. But, Fury, there's still no guarantee I'll get one of those stones. I don't want to start making plans around such a huge maybe."

"Then how about we make plans on a *regardless* scenario? Even if we don't get a stone, I'll wait for you. Jett will come of age around—"

"No. I won't let you do that. It will be years before Jett's old enough to not be affected by me. You can't put your life on hold that long. I wouldn't let Sloan do it, and I won't let you either."

"Sloan had another option. I don't want anyone else but you. I never have."

"Could've fooled me when you showed up that day with John."

"I wanted to make you jealous."

"It worked." I looked up at the ceiling. "I was pissed."

"I couldn't take it anymore. Watching you with her. So happy. So in love. I know it was my own fault—"

"Yeah, it was."

She nodded. "That didn't make it hurt any less."

"But you stayed with John for over a year."

"We found out I was pregnant." She shrugged. "And for a long time, I really thought the baby was his."

"When did you know?"

"Third trimester, I guess. There was just too much power for the baby to be human. But by then, John was so excited, I couldn't bring myself to tell him. I kept putting it off." Her face fell. "And, selfishly, I didn't want to do it alone."

"You owe him an apology."

"I know I do. I'll talk to him when we get home."

"Whatever happens, I don't want you to get back together with him."

"I won't be with anyone but you."

I pulled on her hips. "Allison, I'm serious. You can't wait for me. Make a life with someone else, just not John."

"Aside from the obvious, what do you have against John?"

"A man who loves you won't grab you the way he did."

"I kind of deserved it."

"You never deserve a man putting his hands on you in anger. I meant what I told him. I'll kill him if he ever does it again."

She rocked forward again, making me completely forget what I was saying. I moaned as her hands slid up my chest. Then she bent and kissed me, her knees tightening against my sides. I pushed my hips up into her as my hands slid over her ass.

There was another knock at the door, louder this time. "Warren, we have a problem out here." It was Reuel.

With a heavy sigh, my whole body deflated. *A problem?* "Coming!" I patted the side of Fury's thigh. "We'd better get up before he breaks down the door."

Leaning onto her right knee, she dismounted and sat on the edge of the bed. The black script across her ribcage snagged my attention again. I graced my fingers across it, and she flinched away from me with a laugh.

"Ticklish?" I asked, surprised.

"A little."

"You never had a tattoo before. What does it say?"

She raised her arm so I could read the words, *You don't need wings to fly*.

"I like it. What's it mean?"

"I got it when Anya was taken. It was one of the last things she said to me before Abaddon showed up that day."

"Why?"

She took a deep breath. "It was a dark time for me. After

everything that had happened with you, I was feeling pretty shitty about myself."

"You had a self-confidence crisis?" I asked in disbelief.

"It wasn't the first time. Anya was the only one who ever noticed. She always knew it was hard for me that she was born an angel while I was born human, and we were both stuck in this world where neither of us quite belonged.

"The day Abaddon took her, she was giving *me* a pep talk. And that's what she said. *You don't need wings to fly.*"

I rubbed her bare back. "I love it."

Then she stood as I desperately tried to think of anything else besides how good it felt to be with her. The sight of her made it impossible. "God, you're beautiful."

She smiled over her shoulder before walking to the door to pick up my shirt she'd discarded the night before. I sat up, and she tossed me my underwear and pants. It was a struggle to get them on, but I finished stuffing myself into them just as she opened the door.

Reuel was standing just outside. His worried look was alarming. Still shirtless, I followed Fury out the door. "What's wrong?" I asked him.

Outside, the stench of rotten eggs filled my nose. The sky was gone, replaced with an eerie orange light I'd mistaken for the sun.

"Go look outside the barriers." Reuel pointed off the porch.

Barefoot, I descended the stairs with Reuel and Fury right behind me. I walked around the concrete walls that protected the trailers and gasped.

Everything—the whole base—was gone.

Our trailers, along with the Humvee sitting right outside, were now a lone fort at the top of a mountain. Beneath us, the Bad Lands were exposed, a smoky wasteland of knotty dead trees and massive stones...God, I hoped they weren't made of osmium.

Fury walked past me to the edge. "What the hell?"

Those words had never been so literal before.

I grasped the back of my shirt she was wearing. "You're making me nervous." It was a *long* way down.

"Ket Nhila," Reuel said.

"Is that the tower?" Fury asked, a surge of hope in her voice.

In the distance, the wasteland ended in cliffs that dropped into a fiery magenta lake. A large stone bridge arched over to an island with a dark city surrounding a fortress. The city was small, but even from our great distance, I could see dim lights on the buildings. In its center was a tower that soared into the hazy orange atmosphere.

"I think so."

"Anya," she whispered.

I pulled her against me and kissed the side of her head.

"But I don't understand," Fury said. "What happened to Baghdad?"

Reuel turned toward us and awkwardly lifted an eyebrow. "Sounded to me like you conquered your fear last night."

I bit down on the insides of my mouth to pin down a smile, and Fury covered her face with her hand.

He shook his big head as he looked toward the tower. "I waited in the vehicle for a while, but when I finally came back here, everything was still as we'd left it last night."

"So when did all this happen?" Fury asked.

"When you fell asleep," I answered.

Reuel nodded. "That's what I thought too."

I looked back at the trailers, the only things left intact. "I'm glad it didn't take the bed out from under us."

"Me too. But I suggest we don't stick around long. Now that it's so obvious that it isn't real, I don't trust it," Reuel said.

"Yeah. Let's get changed and pack up our gear." My head jerked upright. "Shit." I took the steps two at a time.

"What's the matter?" Fury asked, coming after me.

I threw open the door to Burch's trailer, stretching my wings for all the light I could get. Fury's rucksack was on the floor. I picked it up and dumped its contents on the bed. Then I began to frantically search the floor.

Fury was behind me. "You're freaking me out. What is it?"

I dragged my fingers through my hair, nearly tearing my hair from my scalp. "The medical kit. I left it at the hospital." I slowly turned toward her and Reuel now standing in the doorway. "The penicillin is in the bag."

Fury looked slightly relieved. "It's OK. We'll find Anya and get back home. Then I can have the burns treated properly. I'll even go to a burn center. It will be fine."

"Let me see." Reuel turned her around and inspected her neck. When she tilted her chin up for him, she winced. Then he locked eyes with me. "We should hurry." He saw it too. The redness, the swelling, the oozing flesh around the collar.

Ten minutes later, we were all dressed and had packed as much as we could into the two rucksacks I'd found. Reuel and I carried them out of the trailers. I handed Fury one of the remaining bottles of water. "Keep sipping on this as much as possible."

She nodded and fell in line between me and Reuel as we walked off the porch steps and around the barrier. Even the Humvee was now gone.

I stopped walking and clotheslined Fury as she tried to pass me.

"What is it?" she asked.

I stared down at the base of the mountain. "Demons."

CHAPTER TWENTY-FIVE

"Well, well, well. Boys, I think we've caught ourselves an Archangel." The demon, a giant red-headed guardian like Reuel, couldn't seem to tear his eyes from me as we descended the mountain. He carried a sword like mine, but bigger, on his hip. And around his neck was a purple sanctonite stone.

Our wings still wouldn't work, controlled by some kind of magic. There were six angels waiting for us: a messenger, four guardians, and an Angel of Ministry.

"Hello, Reuel," the guardian with the red hair said.

"Etred." Reuel's direct glare was dangerous.

The demon Etred spotted Fury. "Who do we have here?"

Reuel moved Fury behind him. I stayed by her side.

"We don't want to fight," Reuel said as we reached the bottom.

Etred laughed. "Then you have come to the wrong place, my old friend. Unless you've come to join the dark side."

One of the smaller demons, the messenger, walked in a wide circle around us.

The Angel of Ministry, a rare one in human form, was a

hunched-back white woman. She inched toward Fury. "This one is human." She sniffed the air. "And she is dying."

The word made my stomach turn. I wasn't helping keep her alive. The events of our previous night might have been her death sentence.

One of the other guardians crouched down. She was also a white woman but far less like Old Mother Hubbard than the Angel of the Ministry. The guardian sprang into the air and landed with a powerful thud between Fury and Reuel. "I know this one," she hissed, grabbing Fury's wrist, the one with the key.

Reuel spun and grabbed the demon by her curly black hair. He snapped her arm that was holding Fury, then whipped her over his head and slammed her into the dry cracked dirt, creating a massive crater. The whole ground shook beneath our feet.

The other demons laughed and clapped their hands. "Still got it, I see," Etred said.

Reuel was panting, snarling through clenched teeth.

The messenger, who I was carefully watching creep behind us, darted suddenly back to his group. He said something in Etred's ear, then cowered behind him. I felt the weight of my sword at my back and realized he'd seen it.

He was also afraid of it.

"Relax, Reuel." Etred put his hand on his own sword. "We don't want to fight either if we can help it, but we have to take you back to the Tower."

"We need to go there anyway," Fury whispered.

I pulled the sword from its scabbard, and all eyes followed the blade. "Lead the way."

"I don't feel so good." Fury grabbed onto my arm as we neared the wasteland's cliffs.

Reuel slowed to walk beside us.

"What's the matter?" I asked.

"My eyes. They won't stop watering. Now they're starting to burn."

"Look at me." When she did, I saw her eyes were bloodshot and wet. "Try to keep them closed. Reuel, you take her."

He held her hand and wrapped his arm around her waist. Knowing my presence wasn't helping, I hung back to give them as much space as possible.

The demons started down a stone staircase at the edge of the cliff. The bridge was about fifty feet down. The lake beneath it was filled with what looked like fiery molten lava, churning and sloshing against the cliffs. It had a purple glow, and it smelled like rotten eggs.

This was what Hell was supposed to look like.

As we neared the bridge, I heard a faint haunting sound. The hiss and crackle of deadly osmium. I double-stepped to catch up with Fury and Reuel, and when I did, I pulled the front of Fury's tank top up over her nose.

Unfortunately, she was panting from the walk. She barely opened her eyes. "Moloch...he said...there wasn't any more... osmium inside."

"Moloch lied. Surprise, surprise. Keep your eyes closed and your breathing shallow."

The bridge had no walls or handrails, but it was wide enough for four or five of us to walk side-by-side. It was at least a quarter-mile across to the city. I prayed Fury could make it that far.

In 2005, with a stroke of shitty luck—surprise, surprise—I wound up in New Orleans working body recovery after Hurricane Katrina. The French Quarter was closed. Debris and water sloshed through Bourbon Street. And looters smashed windows and set shit on fire.

Still, a handful of bars were running on weak generators and pumping out screwdrivers served in paper cups.

That was the city at the base of Hell's fortress. Without all the water. And in this wicked city, my friends and I were freaks, drawing curious stares from the demons—and human souls—who loitered along the streets.

Whispers followed us as we passed.

"The Archangel of Death."

"Reuel."

"Azrael."

And several derogatory remarks flew by about Fury. Miraculously, the three of us didn't retaliate. Not that Fury could have. The coughing had begun while we were still on the bridge, and now, her wheezing was so loud I could hear her lungs twenty paces behind her.

Fortunately, the farther we got away from the bridge, and the higher we climbed up the city hill, all signs of osmium began to disappear.

But I feared it was too late.

The soul of a human male flung himself at my feet. "Kill me," he begged, grasping for my legs. "Please, dear God, kill me!"

A symbol glittered in the center of his chest. It was a roman cross with two *S*'s mirroring each other. It was my mark. The symbol of the Archangel of Death. But the man's face was unknown to me, meaning he'd been here so long my father was the one to kill him.

I shook him free from my leg and stepped over him, much to the amusement of the voyeurs of death watching nearby.

Etred and his demons started up a steep stone staircase

toward the palace. Purple light emanated from the entrance hall at the top. There was another sanctonite stone inside. I could feel it.

Fury stumbled on the stairs, and Reuel caught her around the waist. "Are you OK?" I asked, catching up with them.

She nodded, but her face looked clammy and gray. We'd been walking for hours, and it was clear, the exertion was taking its toll.

I put the back of my hand against her cheek. She was burning up. "Drink some water." Pulling a bottle from the side pocket on my rucksack, I untwisted the cap and handed it to her. Her shaky hands held it to her lips, dribbling water down her chin.

So far, the demons hadn't confiscated anything from us. They also hadn't spoken again, at least not since Reuel's refusal to answer Etred's questions about why we were in Nulterra.

I glanced back to the wasteland we'd trekked through. The trailers were gone, and the entire mountaintop had vanished. Without the illusions, I could see a faint purple light over the horizon.

The gate.

It was comforting to know at least its general direction. I searched the land for anything else I could use to map our surroundings. A tall spire of one of the buildings in the city seemed to point right at it from this vantage point. I made a mental note of it.

"Are you coming, Archangel?" Etred called down. The group had reached the top landing without me.

"Just taking in the view. Impressive place you've got here," I said, joining them.

"It's no Eden, but it's ours." He turned toward the high arched entrance. "Welcome to Vykaria."

I looked at Reuel.

Arai meant throne.

Vykara meant the Destroyer.

As in Abaddon, the Destroyer. If we were going to find Anya, this would be the place.

The doorway led into a massive entrance hall. On the floor was a map, of what I assumed was Nulterra. We weren't able to stop and linger as the demons started up another staircase to the right.

In the center of the room, high in the ceiling, a bright orb glowed. The sanctonite stone was several feet across, shining down on a cylindrical pillar beneath it. The pillar was covered in capsules. Capsules holding human souls.

The capsules seemed to be rotating around the cylinder, gradually moving down to where they disappeared beneath the floor.

I didn't have to ask what I was seeing. This was the place souls were destroyed. Near the top, a tiny figure floated inside a capsule. Children were never sent to Nulterra. That was Hannah, the little girl from the village.

Anger raged inside me, but I knew I needed more information before taking action. Before ending this evil practice forever. Before burning Nulterra and all its demons down.

Up ahead of me, Fury stopped walking, her bright-red eyes fixed on the cylinder. "Can you see them?" I asked when I was close enough.

She looked like she was about to cry as she nodded her head. Her shaky finger pointed toward Hannah. "Is that..." Fury's barely there voice sounded like it had been rubbed down with sandpaper.

"Yeah, that's her."

Fury doubled over, coughing again.

"Reuel, help her?" I asked as I backed away.

He scooped her up in his arms, carrying her up the steps.

The Angel of Ministry waited on the top platform. "She doesn't have long now, does she?"

"We need an Angel of Life to help her," Reuel said.

"There are no Angels of Life here." The old woman's eyes narrowed. "And we wouldn't help her anyway. In fact, she's much more useful to us dead."

Reuel backhanded her with so much force she flew sideways off the landing and crashed to the bottom. Two of the guardians lunged for Reuel and Fury, but I stepped in front of them, holding my sword up to block their attack.

They cowered back.

Etred held up his hands. "Come now. Let's all take a deep breath." His eyes were fixed on my sword. "If we can avoid any further delays and violence, I'd like to show you to a room where you can tend to your friend."

I gave a slight nod.

Etred took a few steps backward cautiously, before turning and continuing down a hallway filled with prison cells. Prison cells that held demons. All of them were watching through the bars on their doors.

Another guardian watched over the hallway.

"Irek," Etred said, nodding toward the last cell door at the end of the hall. The guardian placed his palm on the door, and it swung open.

Something told me, my powers or Reuel's wouldn't be able to do the same.

"Wait here. Someone will come and get you shortly," Etred said.

I didn't budge. "I want to see whoever's in charge here."

"You will, you will." Etred gestured toward the room. "Please, you're our guest. May I take your sword?"

My fist tightened around it. "You can try."

I'd be in trouble if he did. He was over seven feet, and easily outweighed me by a hundred pounds. Again, he backed away. "Make yourself at home. Someone will come get you shortly." He walked away.

The guardian didn't even close our cell door when we walked inside. "This is weird. Something is very wrong here," I said.

Reuel set Fury down on a bench along the wall. "Would you rather they disarm and shackle us?"

"It would make more sense." I laid the blade of my sword across my hand. "That guy was carrying a helkrymite sword just like mine. Bigger, even. But mine was making him nervous. Did you see that?"

"I did." He helped Fury lay down on her back. "Warren, this isn't good."

I put the sword in its scabbard and knelt by Fury's head. Her cheeks were flushed, and she was sweating. I pushed her hair off her forehead. "How are you feeling?"

She shook her head and started to cry. Then she started to cough violently until she rolled sideways, and I had to keep her from falling onto the stone floor.

"What can I do?" I asked.

"My eyes."

I pulled a bottle of water out of my bag and unscrewed the cap. "Reuel, you do this. I need to back away."

He took my place on the floor and poured the water slowly over Fury's eyes. "Fury, you need to blink. Let the water wash it out."

She screamed out when she tried. Then she started coughing again.

"It's no use!" someone called from outside.

I looked out our cell door and saw an Angel of Knowledge through the cell door facing ours. He was locked behind his. "What do you know about it?" I asked.

"It's osmium tetroxide poisoning. She's drowning from the fluid in her capillaries leaking into her lungs."

"How do we fix it?"

"At this stage? You don't. By this point, it's probably starting to destroy her kidneys as well. She's a goner."

"How long does she have?"

He shrugged. "A few hours maybe. Is that a helkrymite sword?"

"Maybe."

"You're Warren, Azrael's son. You're the new Archangel, aren't you?"

"How do you know who I am?"

"Everyone knows who you are."

Heavy footsteps echoed down the hallway. I looked out and saw Etred returning with more fallen guardians. I hurried back into the cell. "He's coming back. Is she strong enough to move?"

Reuel shook his head, but Fury reached up for me. "Help me," she said between coughs.

I pulled her up to sitting. Balancing her elbows on her knees for support, she coughed until I feared she might pass out. Then she spat blood on the floor between her boots.

"Maybe you should stay here with Reuel."

"My sister is close. She might even be in one of the cells. I have to find her."

Etred entered the room. "All right, Archangel. Your audience has been granted."

I bent and pulled Fury up. Then Reuel took her from me, and they followed me out of the room with Etred. I looked at the demon in the other cell as we passed. He waved. "Good luck."

Etred and the other two guardians led us to a long open hall filled with fallen angels. It had large columns forming hallways down each side, and in the middle was an open floor, like the feasting hall of Zion.

Except here, instead of a banquet table in the center of the room, a platform with three more pillories faced an elevated throne.

This wasn't a place of celebration. It was a courtroom. A sentencing hall. And on the judgment seat was a woman wearing blood stone...

Who looked a hell of a lot like Fury.

CHAPTER TWENTY-SIX

*F*ury crumpled to her knees when she saw Anya on the Nulterra throne. Reuel had to hold her upright.

Up until that moment, I'd never as much as seen a picture of Fury's twin, but there was no denying the women were sisters. Same black hair. Same tan skin. Same dangerous curves.

The only way to tell them apart? Anya's eyes were both solid black. Because of her spirit, I was sure she could recognize other angels, but Anya didn't have the power to see all that Fury could.

Anya slowly stood. She wore a sleeveless skin-tight black bodysuit made of something that looked like rubber. She had blood-stone cuffs around her wrists, biceps, and throat. Dangling around her neck was a purple stone—the Father's sanctonite.

"My sister," she said, hatefully.

All the demons in the room were watching us. Whispering. Waiting.

Fury was crying and shaking in Reuel's arms. "No," she whimpered.

Anya looked at me. She wore thick eyeliner and dark lipstick. "Nice to see you again, Warren. How's the baby?"

My jaw tightened. "What have you done, Anya?"

She spread her arms. "What have I done?" Her smile was wicked as she let energy surge in her hands. "What have I *not* done?"

Everyone besides us in the great hall cheered. Looking around, it was an odd mix of angels. The majority were guardians, not surprising since this was Abaddon's palace. There were messengers, Angels of Ministry, and a few prophets, but the rest of the choirs were glaringly absent.

Not surprisingly, there were no Angels of Death. But, Azrael excluded, none of my angels had ever fallen.

What was shocking was the lack of Angels of Life and Angels of Knowledge. After all, the Morning Star—an angel with both those gifts—had created the place.

Anya continued her rallying cry. "I have conquered the Neverworld, united the fallen, and have freed us from the Morning Star!"

The demons cheered again.

"Freed from the Morning Star?" I asked, confused.

She looked at me and smiled. "Of course. The Thousand Year Prophecy wasn't meant for us. We *all* weren't sentenced to die. So when the Morning Star's plan to destroy the spirit line failed, condemning him to his fate, we secured his place on Earth for his final days." She turned back toward the crowd. "And we will live happily ever after right here!"

Applause and cheers echoed around the hall again.

I didn't understand. "What do you mean, you secured his place?"

"An angel can be born to any human of age with a womb. The Morning Star planned to be born to Torman's daughter, but I presented the option of Azrael's human instead. After all, what better place for the Morning Star to grow up than with the Daughter of Zion, the exact target he intended to kill?

"At that time, Azrael was still in Eden, welcomed back into the arms of the Father. Little did the Morning Star know that we'd learned of Azrael's plans to return."

"How?" Reuel asked, behind me. "Who told you?"

"Oh, Guardian, the only thing that travels faster through the spirit line than spirits is information."

The other demons laughed.

"Only days before Azrael's return to Earth, the Morning Star implanted himself into Adrianne. At the very least, I assumed Azrael would imprison him. But now that his son possesses a helkrymite sword"—her eyes flashed to the sword on my hip—"I'm sure the plan is to destroy the Morning Star once and for all!"

As the room exploded in thunderous praise again, Fury erupted into another coughing fit.

Anya slowly descended the steps between us. "And here I have what I've always wanted most." She twisted a button on the front of my shirt. "An Angel of Death. Join me, Warren."

I smacked her hand away. "You're as crazy as your father."

Her eyes flared red. "I am my father," she hissed.

I took a step back. She'd said it was good to see me again. But I had never met Anya. I'd only met the Destroyer.

"Join me, Warren," she said. "I'll teach you about true immortality."

"The blood stone." My eyes fell to the cuff around her throat. "When Abaddon was destroyed, Anya was wearing the blood stone."

"He's not as dumb as he looks," Anya said, smiling.

Abaddon had somehow trapped himself inside Fury's sister.

She? He? took a step toward me again, this time holding out the stone necklace. "I can also give you what you want most in all the worlds."

My eyes fell to the stone.

"Warren!" Reuel yelled.

I spun and saw that his shirt and arms were covered in blood. Something inside Fury's chest had clearly ruptured. As he cradled her in his arms on the floor, I could feel death creeping over her like a shadow.

"What justice is this?" Anya cackled like a madwoman and climbed the steps back to her throne. She sat down and watched. "My sister's soul is about to join us!"

I knelt beside them, putting the sword under my knees in case anyone tried to take it. I pulled Cassiel's bag around me, opened the flap, and then slid open the zipper. A piercing *screech* echoed around the room, jarring the demons, and sending them cowering behind each other.

Inside the bag was a small glass vial. I pulled it out. Etched into the cork stopper was the word *Drink*. I unplugged it and tilted it up to Fury's bloody lips.

I looked at Reuel.

He nodded and pulled Fury's mouth open.

I poured the few ounces of liquid down her throat.

All the demons were watching. Everyone was silent. Anya leaned forward on her throne.

Then with a violent gasp, Fury bolted upright in Reuel's arms, and a reverberation like a bullet breaking the sound barrier, sent a shockwave of energy around the room. The windows shattered as the echo shook the fortress.

Fury was panting.

I sniffed the bottle, then recoiled from the powerful smell. My eyes watered. "Crystal water."

Reuel snatched the bottle from my fingers and smelled it. I bent toward Fury and grabbed her face. "Are you OK?"

She flexed her fingers and held up her hand like it was the first time she'd ever seen it. Upon closer inspection, it almost appeared to be glowing. "I'm better than OK. I'm great. What did you do?"

"Cassiel. She sent crystal water, the life water of Eden. I had no idea. She sneaked it in my man purse." I lifted the bag.

Another loud *pop*, like the sound of thick ice cracking underfoot, shook the palace.

Anya bolted off her throne, running to a window. "What have you done?"

I really had no idea. "Oh boy."

"Guards! Take them back to their cell!" she screamed.

I snatched up my sword before the nearby guardians got their hands on me. A group of them forced the three of us back down the hallway to our cell. This time, they slammed the door.

Even though I knew it wouldn't work, I tried to use my power to open it. The door glowed purple but did not open.

Fury used a bottle of water to clean her bloody face. I walked over and put my hand to her wet cheek. "The fever's gone." I looked at her wrists. "The burns too, it seems. How are the lungs?"

She took a deep breath in. "I feel great."

Grabbing the back of her head, I rested my forehead against hers. "Thank God."

"Gratal Cassiel," Reuel corrected.

"Yes. Thank Cassiel."

"I feel..." Fury's bright eyes darted back and forth as she searched for the word. "Like Wonder Woman. We need to get some more of that stuff."

"Not possible," I said. "The use of crystal water is absolutely forbidden outside of Eden. Cassiel will be in a lot of trouble for this."

"What the hell happened out there?" Fury asked.

"Well, you almost died. The crystal water brought you back." I pointed out the door. "And that woman out there is *not* your sister, Anya."

"What?"

"I'm not sure how, but it seems Abaddon has taken up residence in your sister's body through the blood stone. She was wearing it the day Sloan killed him."

"I knew she'd never join the fallen. How do we get him out of her?" Fury asked, panicked.

"I have no idea."

"They really did send the most inept of the inept down here, didn't they?" the demon in the cell across from us said.

I ran to the door. "Who are you?"

"A prisoner. Same as you, apparently."

Fury joined me at the door. "What do you mean he's inept? What does he not know?"

"He obviously doesn't know that he is the most powerful angel down here." The demon laughed. "Why do you think no one's been brave enough to take that sword away?"

I raised the sword and looked at it.

"Send your power through it, you idiot."

I gripped the hilt with both hands and held it out in front of me. Then I conjured all my killing power into it, and the sword burst into a white and purple flame. I'm pretty sure Reuel, Fury, and myself all said "whoa" at the same time.

"You're welcome," the demon said. "Now let them try to stop you."

"What is it?" I asked, admiring the blazing blade.

"The most powerful forces in all of the realms. The Father's. And yours."

Reuel joined us at the door. "Nicely done."

"Hello, Reuel," the demon said.

Reuel didn't smile. "Torman."

"Torman?" I asked. "We know your daughter."

"You know Chimera?" He gripped the bars on his door.

"Yes. She helped us get here," I said.

"Where is she?"

My eyes narrowed. This was still a demon, no matter if he was being helpful or not. A commotion outside helped me dodge his question.

"What's happening?" I asked.

"It seems whatever you did in the great hall has pierced the darkness veil around us."

"The darkness veil?" Fury asked.

"It's whatever keeps this place hidden from Eden," Reuel said. "We've never been able to see in or even see the gate. Not from the auranos. Not from Eden. Not from Earth."

"He's right," the demon across from us said.

"What does that mean?" Fury asked him.

"It means things are about to get really interesting," Torman said.

I hoped it meant that Eden could see that little girl's soul on the demon's wheel of destruction. That way, I'd have less explaining to do when I got back.

"Why are you in prison?" Reuel asked.

"Because I'm an Angel of Knowledge. Anyone Abaddon thought might be a threat was imprisoned when he was strong enough to reclaim the throne."

"Why are you a threat?" Fury asked.

"When Moloch's plot with the Council was exposed, Abaddon knew he'd been betrayed. He ordered the arrest of all Angels of Knowledge and Life. Even I, one of the chief members of his inner circle. Many of us have already been executed."

"I'd like to say I feel bad for you, but I don't," I said.

"How did you get here if your daughter is on Earth?" Fury asked.

"The Gate. Once Mihan joined the fallen, we began using it again some. Not enough to draw attention, of course."

When the Nulterra Gate was sealed, two angels had been

given keys. Abaddon and Mihan. One angel of the fallen. One of Eden. Only, Mihan had joined the dark side.

"Torman, I'm willing to make you a deal," I said. "The Father wants me to destroy Nulterra. If you help me do that, then I will set you free and allow you a chance at survival."

"Can you even free yourself?" the demon asked, skeptically.

"I guess we're about to find out." I checked the hallway through the window to see if it was clear. Then I sent my killing power through the sword again.

Swinging with all my might, I slammed the blade into the cell door's lock. It exploded in a million tiny shards. Everyone, including me, stared at the door in stunned silence.

"All right. You've got a deal," Torman said. "Get me the hell out of here."

I carefully checked that the hallway was clear before crossing it. There seemed to be turmoil in the great hall, and fortunately, it seemed, we'd been forgotten about. I swung the sword at the lock on Torman's door. It too shattered all over the hall.

I pulled it open, and he held up his hands. They were chained together, and his feet were shackled to the wall. With a few more powerful swings, I freed him from his restraints. "Start talking. Fast."

"Come with me." He rushed out of his cell, his clothes torn and soiled with blood. We followed him down the hallway away from the room. Other demons hissed and begged from their cells. We ignored them.

At the end of the hall, Torman checked around the corner. A few guardians armed with swords raced by, and he shoved us all backward against the wall. We waited for them to pass. Then he checked the outer hallway again. "Let's go."

He turned left, away from the way we'd come in. A roar from a crowd at the entrance hall echoed around the chamber. "What's happening back there?" Fury asked as we ran.

"If the veil is breaking apart, the demons will try to flee Nulterra. They'll storm the palace because the only way out is through the spirit line. Its entrance is this way!"

The four of us ran to the end of the hall.

"Hey! Where do you think you're going?" someone yelled behind us.

I glanced back and saw Etred chasing us.

"Go!" Reuel said. "I'll deal with him."

"He has a sword," I said.

"Go!"

With a powerful roar, Reuel charged Etred head-on as Fury and I continued with Torman. He took a hard right through a closed door into a room with a long glass wall that looked outside.

I jogged to it and looked out. Above the palace, light fissured through the orange like electric spiderwebs. Huge chunks broke apart, falling into the burning sea around us, and leaving black holes into the darkness above the Neverworld.

We were on the back side of the palace, opposite the side Etred and the demons had brought us in through.

Demons flooded the courtyard, climbed the walls, and ran toward the lower gates.

Beyond the castle wall, a bridge like the one we'd crossed into the city stretched across the fiery lava. On this one, human souls trudged in a single-file line toward the palace as demons fled past them.

"If you want to bring Nulterra down, you have to destroy the three sanctonite stones," Torman said, joining us at the window after locking the door behind us.

"The Father's blood stone?"

"Yes."

"What does it do exactly?" Fury asked.

"The main stone in the center hall powers the cylinder. When the souls in the capsules are destroyed, the cylinder harnesses the energy and deposits it into Nulterra's core. If the core stops receiving energy, everything crumbles."

"Will it crumble on top of us?" Fury asked.

"The places farthest from the power of the stones will crumble first. It should give us time to get out."

"Where are the other two stones?" I asked.

"One powers the gate to Earth, and the other powers the gate to Eden and the spirit line. To destroy Nulterra, you'll have to destroy all three."

He pointed out the window. "Do you see the bridge? At the end of it is the gate to Eden."

"Those demons are trying to use it to escape?" I asked.

"And they will. While they can't go to Eden, they can take the spirit line anywhere else. I would destroy that stone first, then the stone over the pit, and finally, the last stone on our way out."

There was a heavy pounding on the door. *"Nakai!"*

"It's Reuel." I ran back to the door and opened it.

Blood was splattered across his face, and he was panting.

"Are you all right?"

He smiled.

"Etred's dead?"

He held up Etred's sword and his scabbard.

"Nice work." I locked the door behind him. Then I filled him in as we rejoined Torman and Fury at the window.

"Once we destroy the last stone, what will happen to the demons left here?" I asked.

"They'll be consumed by the pit."

"How do we free my sister?" Fury asked.

"I'm sorry. I don't know how that's possible without killing her."

Fury's whole body wilted.

"Abaddon's spirit is locked within the blood stone, which is connected with Anya's bloodstream. To free her from him, you'll have to destroy the blood stone, but if you do that inside Nulterra, she won't survive without it."

"Even though Anya is an angel?" Fury asked.

"Her body was made to be mortal. Physically, she's very much a human. Her spirit would survive, but she'd have to go to Eden before she could even think of returning to Earth in any form."

I looked at Fury. "That's a better option than leaving her here to die with Abaddon."

She looked at Reuel with tears in her eyes. He pulled her into his arms and kissed the top of her head. "He's right."

"I need you to be strong, Allison." I took hold of her arm and ran my hand over the symbol of the Nulterra key. "I'll need you to get me out of here."

Her back straightened, and she grasped my arm. "I promise, I'll get you out."

I kissed her, then turned back to Torman. "How do I get a soul out of one of these capsules at the pit?"

His head pulled back. "Why would you want to?"

"Because there's an innocent child in there who belongs in Eden. I'm not leaving her behind."

He sighed. "Humans. You're all so sentimental."

The ground shook beneath us. Reuel grabbed Torman by the arm. "Tell him. You're wasting time."

"You'll have to climb it to free her. It's dangerous. If you fall..." His lips closed.

"I fall into the pit." I nodded. "Got it."

"We need to hurry. That rumble was them shutting the front gates. We need to get out the back before they close them too."

In the pandemonium of everyone running inside, we made it

out of the palace without being seen by anyone who knew who we were. Torman led us downstairs and out the back door where the human souls were slowly walking inside as the demons pushed past us, fighting their way toward the bridge.

"There are so many humans," I said to Reuel. "We never send this many down at once."

A huge chunk of the orange sky crumbled and fell, landing like a bombshell about a hundred yards away from us. It blasted apart the rock terrace surrounding the palace.

"If one of those hits us, we're in trouble," I said, looking up in the black sky beyond the veil.

Reuel pushed me forward. "Let's hurry."

We crossed through the palace wall toward the bridge. Frantic demons slammed into us and each other as they raced to escape. A few were knocked into the boiling fire of the pit, their spirits screaming in agony as they were consumed.

"There's too much chaos! This isn't safe!" I shouted over the noise.

"Go! I'll hold the demons back!" Reuel shouted, raising his sword as he spun around to fight.

I grabbed Fury's hand, and we ran toward the bridge. Reuel held the fleeing demons back. When we reached the bridge, I threw my arm across Fury to stop her. "Osmium."

Torman went ahead of us. "She'll be fine, Archangel! For at least twenty-four hours while the crystal water is still in her system." He started out across the bridge first. I was still hesitant.

Fury pulled on my hand. "We've come this far. Let's finish it." She dragged me out onto the bridge.

We weaved through the souls coming toward us. Most of them were crying. Several begged us to help them. Then a man coming toward us stopped me dead on the bridge. Recognition blazed in his eyes as clear as my symbol blazed on his chest.

"Larry Mendez," I whispered.

"Who?" Fury asked, stopping beside me as Torman went on.

"One of the ring leaders of the human trafficking business Sloan and I took down in San Antonio. He was a child rapist. I killed him well over a year ago before I became the Archangel."

Another large chunk of the sky landed in the lake, sending a wave of lava toward us. I grabbed Fury and shuffled backward as the wall of fire washed over the bridge. As it spilled back out to the pit, it took the soul of Larry Mendez with it.

"Warren! Hurry!" Torman shouted.

The lava hardened on the osmium, and Fury and I ran across it. Torman was stopped near the end of the bridge. I could see another archway on a stone staircase up ahead. A sanctonite stone gleamed above it.

"What are you waiting for?" I started past them, but Torman grabbed my shirt.

"Stop!"

"What?" I asked.

He pointed to the ground beyond the bridge. There were three-inch holes covering the surface. "Those are helkrymite spikes. If an angel not of Nulterra sets foot on it..." He dragged his finger across his throat. "It's meant to keep Eden out."

So Moloch hadn't lied about everything.

"How do we get across it?" I asked.

"We don't. Even I have been stripped of my right to pass. The only one who can do it is the girl." He turned to Fury. "You'll have to take the sword and destroy the stone."

Fury looked terrified.

I gripped her chin. "You can do this. I know you can." I held up the sword, letting my power flow through it. When I handed it to her, the flames didn't go out.

Her hand steadied as she took it. She started forward, cautiously watching the ground as she passed over the holes.

When she reached the arch, she stretched the sword over her head, but she wasn't tall enough to reach it.

I held my hands toward Fury, and she flinched as I used my power to lift her. I'd levitated people and objects a thousand times, but this was different.

Everything in me strained against the weight of her small frame against the force of Nulterra. Sweat blistered on my face, and the veins bulged in my neck as I fought to keep her in the air. It was like she weighed a million pounds.

Fury swung the sword at the stone.

Nothing happened.

She swung again.

Nothing.

And again.

Panting, I carefully placed Fury back on the ground and turned to Torman. He was staring slack-jawed at the stone. "I...I don't know why it isn't working. The sword should be powerful enough to break the stone."

A loud buzzer made Fury jump back.

"I know that sound," I said, staring at the stone as it glowed brighter. "It's the alarm we use when we send a soul from Eden."

The archway brightened with energy swirling inside it. Then the light vanished, and a soul stood in its wake.

Flint.

"No!" The sword clanged to the ground as Fury's knees gave way. Flint's ghostly form caught her and held her as she cried. "What are you doing here?"

He pulled back to look at her. "I've come to help." Flint picked up the sword and led her back to us.

"How did you get here?" I asked, my heart heavy with dread over the implications. I had no idea if I could get Flint back out.

"I volunteered." He pressed a stone—a memory stone—into my hand. "Cassiel sent you this."

I turned the stone over in my hands. "You shouldn't have come."

He put his arm around Fury. "Would you leave your little girl stuck down here?"

I stared at him.

"Go on then." He nodded to the stone. "It must be important."

A loud crack through the sky drew all of our attention. We looked up as another chunk dropped from the veil. It crashed right on top of the gate, blasting it apart. I spread my wings to shield us as the sanctonite landed in the rubble.

"The memory stone, Warren. Hurry!" Torman shouted.

I closed my fist around the stone, and an image of Cassiel flashed in front of me. She was watching me in the crystal fountain in Zion. "Warren, we don't have much time. Theta and I have seen inside Nulterra, and she's had a vision in Celestine of how to get you out.

"You have to destroy the sanctonite stones. The sword alone will not work. Remember what I told you about nuclear energy. The explosive material has to first be made unstable. The stones need heat to weaken them. Then the sword can destroy them.

"You must hurry. You're already out of time, but there's one more thing." Cassiel looked worried. "The final stone, the one at the gate to Earth, must be destroyed from the inside. You must get everyone out safely first, or the portal will be closed." She broke then and cried. "I'm so sorry."

The vision faded away. For a moment, I stood there shocked.

"What did she say?" Torman asked, shaking me.

I blinked, then tossed the stone into the lava. I looked at Fury, and my heart broke again. "What did she say?" she asked.

I took a shaky breath. "She said the stones need heat to weaken them." I pulled her behind me. "Everyone stand back."

Aiming my hands at the sanctonite stone on the ground, like a human blowtorch, I blasted it over ten feet away with my fire. The remaining pieces of the veil were incinerated. The crumbled stone of the arch melted into the ground. And the sanctonite stone burned, changing from purple to red, then red to orange, orange to yellow, and finally from yellow to blue.

There was a loud hiss, and a puff of steam or smoke twisted from its center. "Now." I looked at Fury. "Now the sword."

Flint walked with her. Together, they gripped the hilt, raised the sword above their heads, and drove it through the heart of the stone.

Light detonated from the center, exploding in every direction. It knocked Fury and Flint back into the stairs, and the three of us took a knee to avoid being blown into the lake of fire.

The first stone was destroyed.

Everyone but me cheered. My brain was still spinning on what I'd learned in the memory stone. Fury and Flint had embraced. And when they started back toward us, Flint froze, horrified as he stared behind us.

I turned, and saw Anya facing off with Reuel at the other end of the bridge.

CHAPTER TWENTY-SEVEN

Flint was right.

There was nothing I wouldn't do to save my daughter, including sentencing myself to eternal destruction in Hell. So I understood why he was there. I also understood why he crumpled to the ground at the sight of Anya on that bridge.

No one had to tell him that she had joined the dark side. It was obvious from the hatred glaring through her eyes.

I hauled Flint off the ground, and we all walked back across the bridge. Fury tried to explain about Abaddon, but it didn't matter to Flint.

His child was lost.

"What are you trying to do?" Anya asked when we reached Reuel.

"Whatever's necessary to stop you once and for all." I raised my sword, so the tip nearly touched her chin.

Anya laughed. "Do you even know how to use that thing, Warren?"

Flames surged through the blade. Her laughter faded, and she started backing up. We all followed her until we reached the center of the terrace. I pinned her against one of the large hunks of the darkness veil.

"You know, if you destroy the three stones, you'll lose any chance of ever being with your daughter." She gripped the stone around her neck. "If you destroy those, these die as well."

My heart twisted, but I refused to show it. "As long as this place dies with it, I'm OK with that."

She visibly swallowed because she knew I meant it. Anya opened her arms wide, arcing her back so that the tip of my sword was aimed straight at her heart. "What are you waiting for then?"

Flint stepped forward, and Reuel held him back. But it was enough of a distraction for the demon to clap her hands together over her head. A thunderous crack blasted us all backward. Even I slid on my ass halfway across the terrace.

Stunned, I jumped back up, ready to start swinging. With the full force of Abaddon, Anya hit me again, slamming me sideways into the castle wall.

Reuel attacked with his sword, but he was overpowered by the Archangel. She hurled him into the side of the fortress like he was nothing at all.

Out of the corner of my eye, I saw Torman lead Fury and Flint safely behind the gate.

Conjuring all my killing power, I hurled it at Anya. She deflected it with her fist, something I've never seen anyone do before. My left hand shot forward, and I blasted her again, this time with a wall of energy that sent her sailing backward.

When she regained her footing, she dropped to a knee and slammed her fist against the ground. A wide chasm opened between us, and the lake of fire bubbled up over the rocks. Circling it, I charged her again. Her hands sliced through the air, throwing me to the chasm's edge.

Before I could get back up, her foot slammed down into the

center of my chest with all the weight of Abaddon's true size—an angel who dwarfed even Reuel.

I strained but couldn't budge. The rock was crumbling beneath my shoulders, and I could feel the heat burning the back of my scalp.

Then I heard Torman's voice in my head from earlier. *"Send your power through it, you idiot."*

I sent all of my killing power through the sword again, this time tilting the blade up at the demon. The power surged out like a death ray, and Anya barely intercepted it with her hand.

Any other angel would have been dead, but this one only faltered. It was enough to overtake her, and I swept my feet under hers, knocking her to the ground, and pinning her with my knee in her chest.

Then I raised the flaming sword and aimed the sharp edge of the sword at her throat. Fury screamed as the blade connected, and she charged me from behind the gate.

But my blade hadn't severed the demon's throat. The blood-stone collar around her neck exploded in a hissing shower of red sparks.

Fury skidded to a stop.

The bulk of Abaddon's power rose in a black cloud above us as I drove the sword through the cuff around Anya's right wrist. The demon screeched and snarled as I grabbed her other arm.

I raised the sword to sever the final one. Abaddon was fading. So was Anya.

"Wait!" Fury screamed.

She ran to us and dropped to her knees. Flint came over behind her.

Despite both angels being weakened, I was struggling to keep Anya subdued. "Fury, I have to—"

"Just wait." She reached behind her neck, and before I could stop her, she unfastened the clasp of her own collar.

"Stop!" I yelled.

But before I could react, she closed the collar around Anya's neck. Then she grabbed my arm and drove the blade through the wrist cuff.

With Anya gasping and panting under my knee, I grabbed Fury and searched her face. "Are you crazy?"

She put her hands on mine. "I'm OK, Warren! I'm OK!"

I tilted her chin up and inspected the scar tissue around her throat. Then I met her eyes again. "You're OK?"

"I'm OK. I promise."

I pulled her to me. "You're a damn fool, Allison McGrath!"

Laughing through her tears and adrenaline, she shook her head against mine. "I couldn't let her go, Warren. I'm sorry, I couldn't let her—"

I kissed her to shut her up.

Anya slapped my thigh. She was gasping beneath the weight of my knee in her chest. "Can you two lovebirds do that shit later? I can't breathe here."

I eased off a bit of pressure. "Who are you?"

Anya looked at Fury and pointed at me. "Is this guy for real?"

Her eyes were no longer black. They were both bright emerald.

"She's back," Fury said with a smile. She stood and pulled me off her sister. Then she grabbed Anya's hand and pulled her to her feet.

The girls embraced. Both laughing. Both crying.

"Can I get in on that?" Flint asked, approaching them.

Anya did a double take when she saw his soul. "Dad?"

He shrugged. "Can't live forever, I guess."

"Oh, Daddy." Anya pulled him into their hug, and she cried even harder.

Flint palmed the backs of both their heads. "Shh. Don't cry for me, girls. I've got all I ever wanted." Then he pulled back and kissed both of their foreheads.

Reuel limped over and stood beside me.

"You all right?" I asked him.

He shook his head. "Too old for this feces."

I laughed really hard. "Oh god, I can't wait to tell that one to Nathan."

Reuel put his hands up. *"Akai nan pecum English ini melam."*

"It's OK. You don't have to speak English. We'll translate for you."

He pointed at Flint, Anya, and Fury, where they were still embracing each other. *"Aval un tacin."*

"I know. I'm surprised they're able to touch him too. But, then again, souls are tangible in our spirit world. Why shouldn't they be in this one?"

With a grunt, he nodded.

Fury turned toward me and hooked her arm through her sister's. "Anya, this is Warren. Warren, this is my sister, Anya. For real, this time."

Anya offered me her hand. "I've heard a lot about you, Warren."

I smiled as I shook it. "In the last few days, I've heard a lot about you too."

Fury laughed. "We have plenty of time to make up for that in the future."

I remembered Cassiel's words, and my smile faltered.

"I hate to break up this happy reunion, but we have two more stones to destroy," Torman said, joining us. "And I don't know about you, but I'd really like to get out of this place."

With her hands on her hips, Anya looked around. "We're still in Nulterra? How long have I been here?"

Fury grimaced. "Four years."

"Damn! It feels like I just got here."

"You've had Abaddon inside your head. It would affect your memory," Fury said.

"So how old are we now?"

"Thirty."

"Man, I feel like I lost a whole decade. I was robbed of my twenties."

Fury draped her arm around Anya's neck as we walked. "You didn't miss much. Turning thirty sucked."

Flint fell back and walked beside me. "You did it, Warren. You saved my girls."

I looked up at the looming fortress. "Don't thank me yet, Flint. We still have to get out of here alive."

Inside was mayhem. Demons were everywhere. All the riffraff from outside was now inside.

Torman backed us all into a corner near the door we'd come in. "Listen up. This is where things get tricky. We have to get through the castle back to the entrance hall. Abaddon may be dead, but there are plenty of other demons who'd like to see us all thrown into the pit."

"Tell us what to do," I said.

He looked at Anya. "You no longer have Abaddon's spirit, but they don't have to know that. If you play your part correctly, you can command this entire palace." He took a step toward her. "And we need you to command this entire palace."

Anya nodded. "Be the ultimate bitch? I can totally do that."

"Runs in the family, huh?" I asked Fury.

She elbowed me in the ribs.

"I need everyone to be a lot more serious," Torman said.

I bit down on the insides of my lips.

"Abaddon would love nothing more than to have an Angel of Death in his inner circle."

"He tried to recruit me earlier," I said.

"You need to pretend that he succeeded. And you need to

scare the absolute shit out of everyone with that sword. Got it?"

I raised the sword. "Got it."

"Reuel, you need to carry the girl." He looked at Fury. "And you need to pretend to be almost dead."

"What about me?" Flint asked.

"We must get Warren near the containment chamber, so he can rescue the human girl and get close enough to destroy the sanctonite stone." He pointed at Flint. "You and I will be the reason he goes up there."

"You want me to pretend like I'm putting you and Flint in those pods?" I asked.

"That's exactly what I want you to do. It's a big deal around here when demons are brought into the inner circle. Each of them are expected to add fuel to our fires."

A chill rippled my spine.

"Once you start blasting the stone, you'll have to act fast. The demons will react quickly, and it will be challenging to get through them to free the young human girl and get out alive."

"I can help him take Flint up to the chamber," Anya said. "Who are we saving?"

"A child. One who was stolen from her home outside the Nulterra Gate. I refuse to leave her behind."

Anya looked at Fury. "You're right. I like him."

Fury smiled.

"Any questions?" Torman asked.

We all looked around at each other. "Where will you be? Aren't all the Angels of Knowledge supposed to be in prison?"

He took a deep breath. "That will all be part of this ceremony. I'll go with you to the mouth of the pit. You'll be taking my place in the inner circle."

"They would execute you?" Fury asked.

Torman nodded. "They would cast me into the pit." He quickly looked up at me. "Please don't execute me."

"I'll think about it."

"What's our exit strategy? How will we get out?" Anya asked.

"We will have to fight our way out." Torman quickly looked around. "And by *we*, I mean all of you. I'm a thinker, not a fighter."

Typical.

He looked up at me. "That death-torch thing you pulled outside would be handy. Think you can do it again?"

"I'll do my best."

"Are we ready?" he asked.

I took a deep breath. "As ready as we're going to be."

My sword blazing, Anya and I walked side-by-side through the halls of the castle. Flint trudged behind us, faking the same trance-like style we'd seen from the other souls. And Reuel followed him, with Fury looking mostly dead in his arms.

Torman walked in front of my flaming sword, mostly so he could lead the way back to the entrance hall.

The demons scurried out of our way as Anya did a lot of impressive snarling and glaring. When we reached the steps leading up to the mouth of the pit, my throat tightened. Hannah's capsule was about to reach the bottom of the cylinder.

Torman led us up the steps all the way to the top. Anya turned toward the crowd, gestured toward me, then raised her fists in victory. The demons cheered.

I looked down. All the way down. There was a wide gap—wide enough for a grown man to fall—between the cylinder and the floor. The gap was much wider at the bottom than between the platform where I stood and the top of the cylinder. On the other side of the hole, burning lava bubbled and churned.

"Hold out your hand toward the cylinder," Torman muttered, trying not to move his lips.

Anya aimed her hand at the device.

"You have to pull another capsule out of it," Torman said.

"What capsule?" Anya whispered back.

"Focus."

Her fingers tensed, and slowly, a clear membrane began to rise out of the middle.

"Good job," I muttered.

Torman's angry eyes flashed toward me. "Shut up. You're a demon, not a cheerleader."

I bit down on the insides of my lips again.

The capsule fully formed on the side of the cylinder. Torman took a deep breath. He was visibly sweating. "Now put me inside it, but don't forget to get me back out."

I grabbed hold of his arm. When I did, the demons below cheered again. The capsule opened. "Once I'm inside, they'll cheer again. That's your chance to fire the stone. Then destroy it and get me out of there."

"Got it."

Torman grabbed both my arms. "I mean it, Archangel. We had a deal."

"But I'm a demon, not a savior, right?"

His eyes flared. Then he began to fight me for real. I shoved him into the capsule, and it closed over top of him. The demons went wild as Torman fought against his new cell.

I aimed my hands at the massive stone above us, releasing all the firepower I had in me. The cheers below faded to confused whispers, then escalated to shouting and arguing.

Anya tried to calm them, but as the stone changed from purple to red to orange, the demons became enraged. They began to charge the steps. Reuel returned Fury to her feet to get ready to fight.

The stone turned yellow.

Keeping my hands in place, I backed to the edge of the landing. The demons were right behind me.

The stone turned blue.

I took off running, then leapt toward the cylinder and planted my foot upon its rim. I pushed off, catapulting myself up, and I drove the flaming sword into the center of the stone.

Light exploded in every direction, followed by another shockwave that blasted the unsuspecting demons off the steps. The cylinder stopped spinning, right before Hannah's capsule reached the bottom.

I jerked the sword free from the dead stone, dropping back onto the platform beside Anya. But there was no time for celebration. The demons were racing up the stairs again.

Stepping in front of Fury and Reuel, I sent an explosion of death through the sword into the demons. Light fractured through their bodies, splintering like broken glass before blowing them apart.

Demons began to scatter and flee when they saw we wouldn't be stopped. Reuel, Fury, Anya, and Flint followed me as I cleared the path down the stairs. When we reached the bottom, Anya and Reuel battled the few remaining demons.

"Fury!" I yelled, crossing the floor to the cylinder. She ran to catch up with me as I approached the hole in the floor. Even standing on the edge, I was still a good twelve to fifteen feet from the cylinder.

The steam rising from below burned my face.

"Warren, you can't make that jump," Fury said, grabbing onto my arm.

"I have to try."

Her fingers dug into my skin. I turned and kissed her, long and hard. Then I pulled away and smiled. "For luck."

After checking around me for anymore threats, I sheathed my sword on my back. Then I backed all the way to the main door. Taking a deep breath, I stared at my goal ahead. The cylinder had curved groves where I could grab and get a foothold...I just had to get there.

I took off running, and when I reached the edge, I flung myself over the gap. When I opened my eyes—I hadn't even realized I'd closed them—I was clinging to the side of the cylinder beside Hannah's capsule.

Fury screamed with delight on the floor. "I'm not done yet," I said, straining as I lowered myself closer to Hannah.

Inside, the girl's soul was entranced. Her eyes were coated with a white film, and she wasn't moving.

I grabbed my sword and slit open the membrane. I'd just gotten the sword back into the scabbard before the girl began to slip out. I caught her, barely, by the arm.

"Reuel, help!" Fury yelled.

Fortunately for that moment, the girl was small. Which, while it made the task easier, it sickened me even more.

Reuel came to the side of the gap, then he used his power to grab hold of Hannah. He strained as he lifted her safely over the gap, then Fury grabbed her. The two of them fell to the floor.

I looked up. Torman stared down at me from near the top. He banged uselessly on the membrane, his mouth flapping wildly.

"What are you going to do about him?" Reuel asked.

I sighed and started to climb.

"You're going after a demon?" Flint asked.

I strained to reach the next groove. "If I don't keep my word, what makes me any better than the rest of them?"

"Allison McGrath," I heard Flint say with a stern voice, "if you don't cherish that man, I'll haunt you for the rest of your days."

I laughed, and my hand slipped.

My companions below gasped.

Quickly recovering my grip, I continued to climb. But with

the intense heat rising out of the pit, my whole body was beginning to sweat.

I thought of the recruits on the Claymore tower just a few days before. At least they had a safety harness.

God, how much had changed since then.

"Reuel, I need you up top!" I yelled down when I reached the bottom of Torman's capsule.

I climbed past him, every muscle in my body screaming, and when I got to the top, I waited for Reuel to reach the platform. He was still almost twenty feet above us. "I'll slit open the top, then help him climb the rest of the way. Can you grab him when we get closer?"

Reuel held up both thumbs.

Above the capsule, I held on with one hand as I wiped the other on my jeans. Then I grasped the groove with the dry hand and reached for my sword with the other. I slit the top open, and Torman stuck his head out, gasping for air like he needed it to live.

"You came back for me," he said, wild-eyed with astonishment.

"I said I would, didn't I?"

"But I didn't actually believe you."

"Well, that's the difference between you and me." Straining, I hoisted him out of the capsule. "You have to climb. When you're close enough, Reuel can help you the rest of the way."

"I can't do this," he whimpered.

"You have too. I didn't come all this way for nothing, and there's no other way down except through that hole."

Torman looked down.

"Eyes up, Torman. Focus on where you want to go."

"This would be so much easier if we could fly," he said, reaching for the next groove in the cylinder.

"Why can't we fly?" I asked, knowing it was better to keep him distracted...and I *really* wanted to know.

"It's the gravity of the bedrock." All the muscles pulled in his face as he reached for another groove. "It's so dense, it actually keeps us grounded."

"If gravity's that strong, why does nothing else seem to be affected?"

"Who says that's true?" He looked at me, and his foot slipped.

I grabbed the back of his collar and held him against the wall. "OK," I said. "No more talking. Pay attention. We're almost there."

Reuel held onto the rail of the platform with one hand and stretched to grab Torman's arm. Torman tried to reach him but could only graze his fingertips. When Torman reached again, I pushed his shoulder the extra inch.

Reuel grabbed him.

And I lost my grip completely.

CHAPTER TWENTY-EIGHT

They say because it's not as dependent on oxygen, the last part of the brain to die is the same part that stores autobiographical memories. This is why so many people report seeing their lives "flash before their eyes" during near-death experiences.

I couldn't believe I was about to screw this up *twice*.

The first time I died, I dove in front of a spray of bullets to save Nathan McNamara's life. As I lay bleeding to death on the battlefield, all that replayed in my mind was, "I can't believe I'm dying so this motherf***** can have sex with my wife."

Now this?

As I fell to the pit of Hell, all that replayed in my mind was...*I'll bet Gene Simmons can lick his elbow.*

Profound, I know.

Lucky for me, right before I splashed down to my eternal death, an invisible force lassoed my waist. I stopped falling with so much force that it almost snapped my back.

Suspended nearly upside down, I saw Anya with her hands outstretched on the floor below me, and when I looked up, Reuel's hands were extended from the platform above.

Fury leaned over the abyss and grabbed the collar of my shirt, yanking me back to safety. I landed on the floor with a thud.

Laughing like a madman, I rolled onto my back and pulled Fury's head to my chest. "Oh my god, I thought I was a goner." I raised a hand in the air. "Thanks, guys!"

Anya leaned down over me. "Is this how this relationship is going to go? Me saving your ass all the time?"

I was still panting on the floor. "God, I hope not."

When I sat up, Reuel and Torman were coming down the stairs. Torman was clapping. "Nicely done, everyone."

The map on the floor underneath me began to crumble at the edges. I got up, pulling Fury with me toward the door.

"Hannah!" she said, reaching for the soul of the little girl. Hannah's eyes had cleared, and she was more alert. Poor thing was shaking uncontrollably, and Fury pulled her between us.

I put my hand on her head. "Hello, Hannah."

She looked up at me. My heart broke. She couldn't have been more than four or five years old.

"We'll take care of you, OK?"

She nodded and reached for my hand.

"We don't have much time," Torman said, looking over the map. "Nulterra is falling apart."

I nodded as more of the floor crumbled into the pit. "Let's get the hell out of here. Torman, lead the way."

Our group raced down the fortress steps that we'd come in, but the entire city now appeared deserted. When we reached the city wall, I fashioned a mask for Anya out of one my shirts, then she closed her eyes and let Reuel lead her across the osmium bridge.

Mountains in the distance to our right were collapsing. "We have to hurry!" Torman shouted.

I carried Hannah on my back as we ran through the wastelands of Ket Nhila, and when we crested the hill near the glowing purple horizon, everyone stopped dead in their tracks.

The mirror maze.

"Oh no. We'll never make it through that in time," Torman said.

"You're an Angel of Knowledge. You can't beat a mirror maze?" Anya asked.

Torman looked out toward the crumbling landscape. "Not before the edge of this world reaches us."

"Can you smash the way through?" Fury asked me.

"I'm sure as hell going to try." I passed Hannah to Reuel, then ran toward the mirrors with my sword, ready to start swinging.

"Stop!" Fury shouted.

I did. When I turned to look back at her, her eyes were fixed on the ground. She started walking toward me without looking up. "My god, she's done it."

"Who's done what?" I asked as Fury walked past me. Her pace quickened to a jog. "It's Sloan's summoning power. She's leading us out! Follow me."

My face erupted into a smile so huge it hurt my face. Then we all ran, following Fury as she twisted and turned through the maze.

We were all out of breath when we reached the gate back to Earth, even the ones of us who didn't need oxygen to stay alive. In the distance, I could hear the land falling apart.

"Everyone, come here," I said at the bottom of the stone steps.

Torman tried to run past me to the gate, but I stopped him with my sword. "No, no, no. We are all in this together until the end."

He took a step back to the rest of the group.

"Reuel, take Hannah through first. Then Torman will follow. Fury and Anya will go through one at a time after that. Reuel and Torman, you'll have to get the blood-stone cuffs off them as quickly as possible. Understand?"

They both nodded. Torman more reluctantly than Reuel.

"Don't forget, that cathedral on the other side is coated in osmium. Anya, keep your eyes closed and the mask on. There should be an extra gas mask in the rucksack we left there."

Anya held up a thumb.

"Flint will follow Fury, and I will come last. I'll put the sword through the stone as I cross through the gate. Any questions?"

"Nope." Torman started up the steps again, and once more, I stopped him. He huffed.

"Reuel?" I stepped to the side and put my hand on his arm as he passed. "Keep her close until she can be sent into the spirit world."

He nodded.

"And get those cuffs off Fury."

He nodded again.

Then he disappeared through the gate. Torman bolted through after him so fast it made me roll my eyes. "Anya?" I said.

She paused in front of me. "See you on the other side."

When she was gone, I reached for Fury. "Give her just a minute for Reuel to get the collar off her."

She stepped close to me and put her arms around my neck. "We did it," she breathed into my ear.

"Yeah. We sure did." I pulled back and cupped her face in my hands, then I pressed my lips to hers in a long, slow, deep kiss. When I broke it, I rested my forehead against hers. "I love you, Allison."

"Don't." She shook her head. "Don't turn this into a goodbye."

I forced a smile. "I'm not. I don't even have a word for goodbye in my language anymore."

She kissed me once more. "I love you too, Warren," she whispered.

The ground rattled underneath us. I took a step back. "You need to go. Flint will be right behind you."

She wiggled her fingers in a wave. *"Cak vira."*

"See you soon," I echoed with a smile.

Then she disappeared through the archway.

With a deep breath, I conjured my killing power into the sword. I offered it to Flint. "Mind holding this while you wait for Fury to get her cuffs off?"

"Of course." He took hold of the sword and stepped to the side as I blasted the stone above the arch with fire. It turned from purple to red.

I climbed the steps to stand directly beneath it.

For this death experience, I was determined to make my last thoughts count. Iliana's sweet little face was the first thing I thought of. Then her dancing with her butt in the air. And her scrunching her nose against my cheek.

Then I thought of Sloan and how proud I was of her. One more time, she'd saved us all. I wished I could tell her how much I'd always love her.

I even thought of Nathan, and how—aside from the sleeping with my wife part—he was, truly, my very best friend.

And then there was Fury. Unyielding and fearless. Dedicated and strong. The only woman to every truly break me. And the only one to make me whole again.

Maybe Cassiel was right about omniscience. Had the little boy lost in Chicago ever been told how much he'd be loved someday, that he'd someday fly, and would someday save the world, it's not that he wouldn't have acted—he would've never believed it to begin with.

I wished I could tell Cassiel thank you...

The stone turned from red to orange.

"All right, Flint. Your turn. When we get on the other side, I'll take you back to Eden."

"Son, I worked with your father for half a century. Don't you think I can spot a bullshitter when I see one?" Flint walked up the steps beside me.

"What?"

"You. You just lied to my daughter. Now you're lying to me. I saw your face when you held that stone of Cassiel's."

"I don't know what you're talking—"

"She told you someone would have to stay behind, didn't she?"

The stone turned from orange to yellow.

"Flint, you need to go. I'm not sure how much longer the gate will stay open!" Its light had begun to flicker.

"Now you listen to me. All I've wanted my whole life is for those girls to be happy. To have a family. And to be loved. You won't take that away from my Allison. Do you hear me?"

"Flint, you really have to—"

"Warren!"

The ground rumbled under us again.

He aimed the flaming sword at the center of my chest. "You either go back, or I'll kill you as punishment for breaking my daughter's heart. What shall it be?"

"Flint, you can't—"

The stone turned blue.

"Take care of her for me." Then he kicked me in the center of the chest and sent me flying back through the gate.

CHAPTER TWENTY-NINE

The light went out when I stumbled up the stairs. I fell on my hands and knees, then flipped around and scrambled backward in horror.

There was nothing there. Just a dark stone staircase to nowhere. Without the light from the gate, it was pitch black in the demon's cathedral.

Light from Reuel's wings flooded the room.

"Warren?" Fury ran to me. "Warren, where's Flint?"

Shaking my head, I still stared at the hole.

"Warren?" she asked again, kneeling beside me.

I looked around the demon's cathedral. Torman was sitting on the Morning Star's throne. Reuel was behind me, bandaging Anya's neck. And Hannah was skipping down the center aisle.

"He—" I swallowed. "He stayed behind."

Fury drew back. "What?"

"When the stone was unstable, he pushed me through the gate." My words sounded like they belonged to someone else.

"Why would he do that?" Anya, wearing a gas mask, was on her feet now.

"He knew I was lying. He knew one of us would have to stay

behind to destroy the last stone." My body went limp on the cool stone floor, my empty scabbard squashed between shoulder blades.

Fury slowly sank down beside me in a daze. "You meant it. You *were* telling me goodbye."

I nodded, my eyes burning. "He sacrificed himself for me."

"Our dad's gone?" Anya asked.

When I didn't respond, Fury slumped over, burying her face in my chest as she cried.

I threaded my fingers through her hair. "I'm sorry, Fury. I tried to—"

"Don't." She shook her head against my chest. "I know you didn't choose this."

I pulled her down and held her. Anya joined us. Then Reuel.

I wasn't sure how long we stayed there, but at some point, we all sat up and faced the stairs. Nulterra was gone forever, and with it, one of the bravest men I'd ever met.

Anya was sitting diagonal to me around the stairwell. "Do you want some good news?" she asked, her voice muffled through her gas mask.

"I'd love some," I said.

She touched the sanctonite stone around her neck. It was still glowing purple. "I hear you were looking for this."

Fury's head was on my shoulder. "It seems Abaddon lied. Torman said the stones did not lose their power."

I looked back at Torman, who was now sitting on the front osmium pew. "True?"

His expression was smug. "Are you really questioning if Abaddon would lie?"

"Fair enough." I turned back to Anya.

She reached behind her bandaged neck and took it off. Then she dangled it toward me.

"What? I can't...I mean, I couldn't possibly—"

"Seriously? It's only fair payment for rescuing me from Hell." She pressed it against my chest. "Take it."

"Are you sure?"

"I'm positive. Thank you for saving me."

I held up the necklace. "Thank you for this."

Fury looked up at me. "Maybe sometime we can borrow it for Jett."

I realized what she was saying. "Two babies. Only one necklace."

Reuel made a humming noise to my right. Then he leaned to the side and pulled something from his pocket. When he opened his big hand, a second stone sparkled in his palm.

My eyes doubled. "Where did you get that?"

"Etred." He smiled and handed it to me. *"Akai nan enta."*

I laughed. "No. He definitely won't need it anymore. Thank you."

He gestured toward me and Fury. *"Te aval omnes val makil pira eptom."*

And they all lived happily ever after.

I kissed Fury's forehead. "Shall we get out of here?"

She smiled up at me. "Please."

Sunlight on my face never felt so amazing.

The sky was blue. Jungle frogs were singing. And the light rainforest mist sprinkled my face. I breathed in deep letting the sweet jasmine fill my lungs.

We'd made it.

And even though I was technically dead, I'd never felt more alive.

Anya ripped off her gas mask and inhaled fresh air for the first time in four years. She faced the sun, closed her eyes, and smiled.

"What will happen to her now?" Fury asked, taking my hand.

"At some point, I think Anya will be heading to Eden. With Abaddon gone, the mantle of the Archangel should be hers."

"That's as it should be."

Anya lay on the ground, rolled onto her back, and let her arms flop out at her sides.

Fury stretched on her toes and gave me a long, slow kiss. "Thank you, Warren."

I held her hand over my heart. "I'm sorry I couldn't get Flint—"

She pressed her finger over my lips. "No more apologies. Flint made his choice. He'd make it again."

I kissed her finger.

I put my arm around her waist. "Can you still see Sloan's summoning power?"

Fury traced an invisible (to me) line across the ground. "Yep. As clear as if it were drawn in chalk."

"Wonder if she's mastered that all the way to Asheville," I said.

"Impressive if she has." Fury was staring across the gate as it closed. "What do you think he's gonna do?"

My eyes followed her gaze. "Torman?" He was stripping off the top layers of his bloodstained clothes. "Who knows? Who cares?"

"Think he'll stick with the dark side?"

I nodded. "Coming back from it isn't that easy. Azrael's the only one who's managed to pull it off."

"Torman is the reason we got out alive."

"He got himself out alive. We only followed. Don't forget that."

Giggles made me turn my head. Hannah was chasing Reuel, her ethereal hair swishing as she ran.

"What is it?" Fury asked.

I pointed. "Can you see Hannah?"

She looked in Reuel's direction. "Not anymore. I can see Reuel though. He looks like a crazy person."

"Ha. Yeah." I closed my eyes.

"You all right?"

"I just wish I could return her to her family."

"You're returning her to Eden. Ultimately, that's even better."

"You're right. I guess I'd better let Eden know we're back."

She looked over to where Anya was sprawled on the ground. "I think I'll roll around on the grass with my sister."

"God, I wish I had a camera."

"This is completely classified," she said with a smile as she got to her feet. Then she jogged to meet Anya, joining her on the ground.

Turning my back to them, I touched my finger to my ear and called out to the Angels of Death. "Nulterra to Eden, do you copy?"

"Warren, is that you?" Samael sounded like he might jump through the airwaves.

"Yes, sir. Back on the ground on the Island of Fire. I need some help. Can you send someone to escort a soul to Eden?"

No answer.

"Samael?"

Nothing.

I tapped my ear. "Samael?"

A faint whistling sound overhead drew my eyes toward the sky. Like an incoming missile, the sound grew louder and louder until a projectile bent the tops of the trees as it tore through the atmosphere.

Samael landed in front of me so hard his boots—American-made—sank deep into the soil. "Warren." He was breathless and wide-eyed, and for the first time ever, scruff covered his jawline and sweat dotted his brow.

"Hey, man." I looked up again. "Where'd you come from?"

Samael embraced me. Something I don't think he'd ever done before. "You're alive."

It took a second for my stunned arms to close around him. "Yep. I'm alive, and I missed you too." I patted his back. "Everything all right?"

He pulled away and gripped my shoulders. "Everyone thought you were all dead."

Smiling, I shook my head. "So little faith in the human angel."

"Can you blame us?" he asked, bewilderment in his eyes.

"I guess it was Hell, after all." I held out my arms. "But we're back safe. At least most of us are. Flint..."

"He didn't make it out?" Samael asked.

I shook my head. "He stayed behind to save us."

"Cassiel knew someone would have to. She feared it would be you."

"It should've been me."

"No, Warren. This world needs you here."

The urgency in his voice was troubling.

"Why? What's happened?"

Samael's eyes drifted past me. I turned to see what he was looking at. Hannah was chasing Reuel up a hill on the other side of the gate.

"Her name's Hannah," I explained. "The demons kidnapped her. Can you take her to Eden for me? I'm afraid being here will confuse her, and that little girl has been through enough."

"She was in Nulterra?"

"Yeah. So take extra special care of her."

He just stared at me.

"Warren!"

I looked back and saw Reuel standing on top of the hill. He was holding Hannah now, and staring at something beyond my view.

"Alis cak esta!" Reuel yelled.

"Come on," I said to Samael.

Anya and Fury joined us as we walked to meet him. At the top of the hill, I froze when I saw what he'd found.

A gravestone.

Fury's gravestone, chipped around the edges and covered with moss.

I laughed, just like I had in Theta's vision. "Oh my god. They *really* thought you were dead." I knelt down and traced her name with my fingertips.

Fury walked past me and knelt down to pull some vines away from the ground. "There's one for Flint. Is his body buried here?"

I felt the presence of death in the ground. "He is."

"Warren, your marker is here too. And Reuel's." Anya was pulling at the vines. "Hey, here's mine."

"I guess you weren't the only one who thought we wouldn't make it," I said to Samael.

He looked dazed. Like he wanted to speak but couldn't.

I stood. "I guess we'd better get word back to Eden that I've returned. Can you take—" His bewilderment gave me pause. "Samael?"

"Whatever happened down there..." Emotion choked him.

"What is it?" I asked as all the dread that had preceded this mission returned like a tidal wave.

"Warren, the spirit line is gone."

I fell back a step.

"We're completely cut off from Eden."

"Iru?" Reuel asked, panic clear in his voice.

Torman dropped his head back, laughing at the sky. "I hadn't even considered this! You used crystal water."

Fury joined me, and I looked at Samael for an explanation. "It's forbidden to use outside Eden for this reason," he said.

"For what reason?" Fury asked.

"Because, in the same way it destroyed the darkness veil around Nulterra, it destroyed the veil that kept the spirit line blocked from the Morning Star," Torman said. "He created the spirit line, and he has the power to undo it. That's why it's been off-limits to him all these many years."

"Cassiel thought in his new human form, the Morning Star would be too young to breach." Samael's face fell. "She was wrong."

I ran my hand down my face. Everything we'd put all our energy into preventing, we'd caused. *I* had caused.

With her hands on her hips, Fury shook her head and walked back to our graves. As she dropped to her knees in front of her headstone, I wondered if her thoughts were riding a similar wave as mine.

Earth. Iliana. Jett...everyone would be better off if we had died.

"Hang on." Fury bent forward, tracing her fingers over her name. "How did they have these made and installed so fast?"

I looked down at Fury's stone again. "And they're already overgrown."

"Oh wow." Behind us, Torman laughed again. Harder this time, if that was possible. "You didn't know?"

I turned to face him. "Know what?"

"Time doesn't work the same in Nulterra as it does on Earth or in Eden."

"What?"

"The Morning Star created Nulterra after the Thousand Year Prophecy. It was foretold that he would be destroyed after a thousand years, so the Morning Star created a loophole."

Fury stood beside me, her face pale. "What are you saying?"

"The days are much longer in Nulterra than in this realm. It was how he bought himself more time."

"How much longer?" Anya asked.

He shrugged. "Every ten years or so on Earth is only about a day in Nulterra. The time you must have spent in Ket Nhila must have been particularly distorted."

I stopped breathing.

"Warren, we've been gone for almost two days." Fury's voice was hollow and distant in my ears.

"No," Samael said. "You've been gone for over seventeen *years*."

His words sank in as we all stood there in frozen silence.

Fury's eyes flashed toward the ground and widened. They seemed to be following something across the grass and back down the hill.

"Hello?" I heard Sloan's voice behind me.

Then I turned, and I saw her.

I blinked.

No. It wasn't Sloan.

It was Iliana.

THE NEXT BOOK

Book 9 - The Daughter of Zion

Coming 3.31.2020

Join Elicia Hyder's newsletter and get a free book at

www.eliciahyder.com

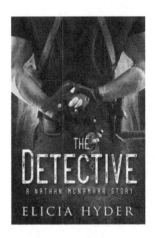

★ Want leaked chapters of new books?
★ Want the first look at a new series I'm rolling out?
★ Want to win some awesome swag and prizes?

Join HYDERNATION, the official fan club of Elicia Hyder, for all that and more!

Join on Facebook

Join on EliciaHyder.com

OFFICIAL MERCHANDISE

Want Nathan's SWAT hoodie?
Want to start your own patch collection?
We've got you covered!

www.eliciahyder.com/shop

ALSO BY ELICIA HYDER

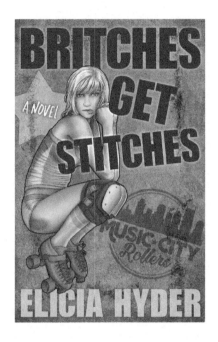

Britches Get Stitches

IN STORES NOW

Made in the USA
Monee, IL
10 March 2020